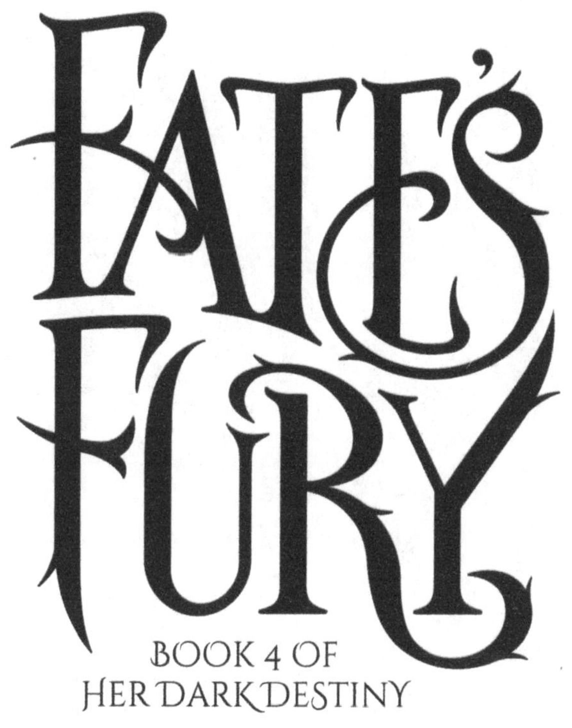

T. RAE MITCHELL

PRAISE FOR HER DARK DESTINY SERIES

"FAN'S OF GAIL CARSON LEVINE AND CASSANDRA CLARE WILL WANT TO ADD T. RAE MITCHELL TO THEIR READING LIST."

~ Readers' Favorite Editorial Review ★★★★★

"THIS FANTASY HITS ALL THE RIGHT SPOTS."

~ Artistic Bent ★★★★★

"EVERYTHING I'VE BEEN MISSING IN THE YOUNG ADULT SCENE."

~ The Passionate Bookworm ★★★★★

"BRILLIANT, WITTY AND FUNNY, A JOY TO READ"

~ Book Traveller ★★★★★

"A HIGHLY ADDICTING SERIES... BE PREPARED TO LET THE REST OF THE WORLD GO BY"

~ Amazon Reviewer ★★★★★

"DELIGHTFULLY ENTERTAINING AS WELL AS INVENTIVE"

~ Award winning author, Kay Gregory ★★★★★

"NOT YOUR TYPICAL YOUNG ADULT NOVEL."

~Top Knot Librarian ★★★★★

"LOVED IT! ACTION UP THE WAZOO! THIS WILL BE ONE I WILL READ AGAIN AND AGAIN"

~Netgalley Reviewer ★★★★★

Original Mix Media Inc.
1685 H Street #1046
Blaine, WA 98230
www.originalmixmedia.com

Ordering Information:
Quantity sales. Special discounts are available on quantity purchases by corporations, associations, and others. For details, contact the publisher at the address above.
Orders by U.S. trade bookstores and wholesalers. Please contact Big Distribution:
Tel: (604) 725-4284 or visit www.originalmixmedia.com.

Printed in the United States of America

Library of Congress Cataloging-in-Publication data
Mitchell, T. Rae.
Fate's Fury / T. Rae Mitchell.
p. cm.—(bk. 1)

Summary: As seventeen-year-old Fate Floyd struggles against the curse of a dark legacy, a reckless quest in pursuit of a fabled black unicorn takes her to Oldwilde's darkest forest with its fierce elves and deadly dryads. When deceitful secrets steeped in vengeance come to light, Fate is forced to confront the blood-soaked sins of past mistakes and ultimately make the painful choice of who lives or dies.

ISBN 978-1-7771472-4-2 (hardcover)
ISBN 978-1-7771472-5-9 (paperback)
ISBN 978-1-7771472-2-8 (ebook)

[1. Supernatural–Fiction. 2. Myths–Fiction. 3. Legends–Fiction.
4. Secret Portal–Fiction. 5. Fairies–Fiction. 6. Druids–Fiction.
7. Magic–Fiction. 8. Sorcery–Fiction. 9. Romance–Fiction] 1. Title.

10 9 8 7 6 5 4 3 2 1

For my dad Larry,
my shining example
of perseverance and
sheer tenacity

Frost Giant Territory
Hinterland Ice-Drifts
Scarbroath Ridge
Duenthorn
Icewall Cliffs
Mount Helgunth
Brynmoor Highlands
Well of Eyes
Mount Alderath
Twisted Bone Forest
Sunder Run
River Torle
BELDERETH
Springs of Almsdeep
Dragon's Bite
Loch Windmere
NORTH ENDLUND
Ridge
Raven's Run
River Torle
Feldoril Forest
Forest
Kildaer Peak
Shoreless Bay
Mystwitch Woods
Moors
Glyndaer
Gloriana Mountains
SOUTH
Shadowless
Swamplands
Morna Valle
River Torle
Feldoril
Shytuckle
Great
ENDLUND
SERPEN EMPIRE
Mount Fargrum
Wanderer's End Bay
Innith Tine
Graven's Tideway
Dreaded Oak Wilds
Eldun Islar
Bloodthirsty Oak
Stormfront Channel
ASGAR
OCEANUS CIATHRA

OLDWILDE
&
ShALAMORAIZE
TRITON'S DEPTHLESS EXPANSE
Elzanar Kingdom
MIRAJARAN
Natreehla Oasis
DESERT
Peadh-Ree Gateway
N
W
E
S
Teeth of Killkush
BIRAKTAR
DUNEBALA
Desert of the Living Sands

I
BENEATH THE SKIN

FATE BOUNDED OUT THE DOOR of her personal suite, thrilled and excited. Finally, some good news. Jessie was awake and talking! Her relief was overwhelming after being forced to accept the loss of her childhood friend to Kaliena's control. Even though the cybernetic suit had been removed safely, the wait for Jessie to wake had been excruciating. The possibility that she could be a mindless, empty shell when she woke had been a constant concern.

But if Jessie was asking for her, that could only mean her friend had recovered fully intact. Fate chewed on her bottom lip, wondering if Jessie remembered the brutal fights they'd had.

Their last fight had been especially vicious. Fate still winced with the memory of Jessie's sharp metal fists smashing the bones in her face. The blow would've killed Fate, or disfigured her for life, had it not been for the regenerative powers Hippolyta's magical girdle granted her. Not that Fate would ever hold any of that against Jessie. Her friend hadn't known what she was doing.

Fate rounded a corner, accidentally bumping into a man who was a solid wall of sinewed muscle. "Watch it," the Serpen knight growled, before shoving her so hard she hit the wall.

Weeks of suppressed rage blazed in Fate's core, a volcanic heat that overrode all sense of reasoning. Twisting around in a flash, she used the wall to propel herself into the air feet first, her boots aimed at his head. She grinned when her heels struck his jaw and knocked the sneer off his jiggling lips. The blow flattened him before her feet hit the ground. Stunned and lying on his back, he stared at the ceiling.

Fate planted her foot over his neck and leaned forward. His forehead beaded with sweat as his dark eyes found hers. She applied more pressure when she caught the same scarlet glint in his eyes she'd seen in Moria, their Serpen Dragon Empress, whose thirst for vengeance had ruined the kingdom of Asgar.

"Watch your manners," Fate told the man. "Remember, you're a guest here. If you can't behave, I'll throw you to the desert."

The red-faced soldier fumed, his mouth tightly closed as he nodded.

Fate ground her heel into his Adam's apple, making him struggle for air before finally lifting her foot. The other Serpen knights quickly cleared a path for her as she resumed her speedy pace down the hall. The crowds thickened at the lower end of the Keep's residential suites, and Fate was forced to dart and weave her way through the populace once again.

Three weeks had passed since the Great Desert War–as many were now referring to it–and she still felt invaded by the thousands of people milling within the walls of the ancient structure. This latest run-in with the Serpen soldier served to magnify the intrusion. But these were the surviving remnants of allied forces. Despite the large numbers, they really only occupied a small percentage of the Keep's available residential suites. If only she'd been able to convince Brune to open a different section, instead of putting them where she and her friends had been living.

Housing them wasn't the most pressing issue though. As each day passed, their unexpected guests were beginning to act as if they owned the place. Such as taking over the sparring arena, which Fate was accustomed to having all to herself. They were also taking liberties by trespassing beyond closed off sections within the colossal rings.

Even more alarming, was the trespass into the vaults on the Keep surface. Fortunately, they couldn't enter most of them. To do that, they needed the Keep Guardian seal, which only she was equipped with, as well as Brune and Jessie after she'd made them her proxies. Any vaults they could walk into were safe from thieves since the treasures inside were either locked or hidden by a riddle to solve. But Brune had found entrances damaged from failed attempts to force their way in.

While the situation troubled Fate, Brune had become absolutely livid. If Fate hadn't signed full guardianship over to Brune, she would be the one feeling the relentless, painful call to protect the Keep at any cost. All the more reason to cut Brune plenty of slack for being extra cranky lately.

At least they had the support of Rudwor and his knights of Beldereth. Fate was grateful for Rudwor's decision to stay longer than planned, assigning his knights as peacekeepers to prevent things from escalating whenever fights broke out. So far the Eldunough soldiers, who were recovering from injuries and the riders who'd been grounded after losing their hawks, appeared to be civilized and respectful. Though they'd remained neutral as to whose side they leaned toward.

The Serpens were causing most of the trouble, bulldozing their way through the halls, cutting in on food lines and hoarding weapons they found in the armories. She wasn't surprised though. When she'd faced their dragon empress in the *Book of Fables*, she'd seen first hand what a warring race they were. But their rude behavior seemed to be contagious, because the Asgar army was growing hostile as well. Having taken the heaviest hit in numbers of soldiers, morale was lowest amongst them. King Tynan's death had only served to leave them directionless and rebellious.

Fate ducked into the infirmary, her step quickening as she moved past bed after bed of critically injured soldiers. When she reached the private rooms at the very back, she slipped through the door and closed it behind her.

Jessie was sitting up in bed talking to Eustace. Her long dark hair hung in smooth waves over her shoulders. She was smiling and animated–a human being again. No longer the killer automaton Kaliena had turned her into.

"I hear someone was asking for me," Fate interrupted.

They both turned to look at her. Jessie's smile widened, crinkling her warm hazel eyes into gleeful crescents. Giddy with excitement, she waved Fate over. "That would be me! How's it going?"

Seeing Jessie's beautiful face was a welcome sight after being hidden behind ensorcelled machinery for so long. Fate ran over to her, arms held wide as she dove in for a hug. "How am I? How are you?" She squeezed Jessie hard, afraid to let go.

Jessie tapped her back lightly. "Finding it hard to breath," she gasped.

Fate let go. "Oh sorry!"

Jessie rubbed her arms. "Whoa, who turned you into Captain Marvel?"

Fate glanced at her father and sighed. "How much time do you have?"

"Loads. Apparently, I'm being held for further tests," Jessie informed her.

"Lucky you." Fate sat on the end of the bed and crossed her legs.

Eustace patted Jessie's hand and stood. "I'll leave you two to catch up."

Fate chuckled. "What? You don't want to hear this all over again?"

"Not so much." Eustace reached around to rub the small of his back with a pained grimace. "Especially since I have a pile of research waiting for me in the library."

"What sort of research?" Fate wasn't aware of any urgent need for cracking the books open. Was he making unnecessary work for himself? She hoped this wasn't the case, because she really didn't like how tired he looked lately.

Eustace seemed caught off guard by her question. He grew stiff and nervous all of a sudden, which made her tense. "Oh, I uh... I've been helping Brune find remembering spells for Gerdie."

Fate frowned. Why would he be nervous about that? Something was off. What was he hiding? Her stomach tightened into a knot of suspicion. She narrowed her eyes on him, watching as he squirmed under her scrutinizing gaze.

Was she looking at her father, whom she loved with all her heart? Or was she looking at Farouk? The demon could be lurking behind any face. After all, Farouk had fooled Azrael by hiding behind his mother's face. And Darcy had never suspected she was sleeping with the demon when he'd pretended to be Mason.

If there was one cringy picture she didn't want in her head, it was that one.

She shook it off, telling herself to stop being paranoid about everyone around her. She'd even begun to worry if Finn was Finn. Every now and then, she sensed the same sort of secretiveness from him as well. This constant underlying fear was wreaking havoc with her sanity.

Jessie waved her hand in front of Fate's eyes. "Hey, where'd you go?"

Fate blinked. "Oh, I was thinking about something I need to do." She glanced at Eustace, who was about to make his escape. "You should have Sithias help with the research."

Eustace froze in the doorway without turning around.

"He's practically been living in the library since he got back," Fate continued. "Come to think of it, I haven't seen him in the last few days. I really need to find out what's up with him. It's weird for him to be so antisocial."

"Will do," Eustace replied, offering a limp smile as he glanced back at them.

"Is it me, or does your dad seem a little on edge?" Jessie asked, after he left.

Fate stared at the empty doorway. "He's definitely not himself." She didn't voice all of her thoughts. "I think something's bothering him."

"You going to talk to him about it?"

Fate nodded. "Yup."

"Good, but first things first. I want to know how you powered up." Jessie plumped up her pillows before settling back into them.

"Well, it's probably easier to just show you." Fate lifted her shirt enough for Jessie to see Hippolyta's magical girdle lighting her waistline from within.

Jessie's eyes rounded as she leaned forward to study the girdle's interlocking design. "What exactly am I looking at? Is that a pattern of snakes and eagles?"

"It's a magic corset."

"But it's under your skin!"

"Yeah, it melded into me only a few hours after I put it on."

"Does it come off?"

Fate shook her head, clamping down on a growing desire to remove the girdle. Ironically, the very thing that had given her the superhuman powers she'd wanted so badly had also become her Achilles' heel. How could she have known that whenever Farouk chose to fully reveal himself that her godlike powers would be weakened by his presence?

Jessie's green eyes grew wide. "Whoa, that's some serious business. Are you okay with having it be a permanent fixture, just stuck there under your skin like that?"

Fate let her shirt drop back in place. "I pretty much have to be."

"Do you have other powers besides super strength?"

"I guess you could say I'm invulnerable."

"As in nothing can kill you? Like, if your head gets cut off you'll grow a new one?"

Fate chuckled. "Either that, or I'll be a talking head rolling around on the floor."

"I got one! Maybe your veins will shoot out your neck like long spider legs and creep over the floor feeling around for your body." Jessie laughed at Fate's horrified expression.

"Gross, I'm not The Thing!" Fate shrugged. "I don't know what I am exactly. I'm basically the same, except for this fiery burn in my belly whenever I get angry. It kind of makes me want to go postal on people."

"You always did have a bit of a short fuse."

"Believe me, this is more than a hot temper. I get Hulk angry. It's because the girdle was made by Ares."

"The god of war?"

"Uh huh."

Jessie leaned back against her pillows again, watching Fate with a quizzical frown. "What is it with you and gods of war? Didn't you say that Miranda chick was a goddess of war?

"Who?"

"You know, the one who gave you all those kickass wind and lightning powers."

"*Murauda.*" Fate smiled wryly. "And yes, I seem to have a type when it comes to ancient deities."

"Huh, I wonder why that is?"

Fate hesitated, unsure if she should share what Azrael had told her when they'd been in the Dunebala Desert.

"You know, don't you?" Jessie pressed.

"It's going to sound crazy," Fate warned.

Jessie laughed. "Shooting through a secret portal into a gargantuan storehouse of magical objects and being made a power-hungry sorceress's cyborg bitch sounds like an everyday thing to you? Nothing will ever sound crazy to me anymore."

Fate laughed too, but curiosity cut her laughter short. "Do you remember everything that happened while Kaliena was controlling you?"

The twinkle in Jessie's eyes vanished and she glanced down at her hands.

"Sorry, Jess, if it's too fresh to talk about, I can wait until you're ready."

When Jessie looked up, her eyes were glassy with tears. "Yeah, it's too soon. I'd much rather hear about your stuff."

Fate waved her hand to show it was no big deal. "Right, back to me and why I'm a war god magnet. Are you ready for this?"

Jessie nodded, looking all of a sudden like the little girl Fate had first met in kindergarten. Her heart ached for what her friend must have endured under Kaliena's iron grip.

"From everything I've gathered, humans are too weak to contain the massive energy housed in an instrument of a god, such as this lovely magical girdle, which according to the history books, Ares made as a special gift for his daughter, Hippolyta. The only way for any human to survive wearing, or wielding such an object, is to be a descendant of a god."

Confusion played across Jessie's face. "Are you saying you're a descendant of Ares?"

"I don't know, maybe. There's no way to know for sure."

Jessie stared at her like Fate had suddenly sprouted an extra nose. "That's *huge*! How did you find out?"

Fate pointed at Azrael, who was lying in the bed next to Jessie's. "Him. He told me."

Jessie's mouth fell open as she glanced over at Azrael. "You know him? I've been doing nothing but staring at him since I woke up." She fanned her face. "I cannot get over that long black hair, mocha skin and gorgeous face. He's totally hot! So tell me, who is he?"

"That's Azrael, and... we're married." Fate muttered the last part under her breath.

Jessie laughed cynically. "You wish! Wait a minute. What about Finn? Does he know you've been crushing on this guy enough to wish you're *married* to him?"

Fate stared back. "It's no joke. And yes, Finn knows all about it."

Jessie shook her head in disbelief. Then her gaze settled on the back of Fate's hand, taking in the henna tattoo that was only now beginning to fade. She glanced over at the tattoos on Azrael's neck, exotic markings, which were similar in design to Fate's. "Whoa, what the heck happened while I was away?"

"A lot. Too much, now that I'm looking back on it all," Fate admitted.

"Start from the beginning." Jessie reached for a cup of water and took a sip, her eyes wide with anticipation of what Fate would say next.

"When the portal opened to send the Keep into this world, it didn't land in Oldwilde as planned. Instead, it crashed in the Mirajaran Desert on the continent of Shalamoraize. Picture it like shooting for the British Isles and hitting the Middle East."

Jessie nodded–a hint that she remembered and had been fully aware of the situation. Fate pretended not to notice and continued. "I somehow got thrown even further away and ended up in Dunebala, the Desert of the Living Sands."

"Oh wow, what was that like?"

"Don't even get me started on that awful place. It's enough to say, Dunebala was a miserable, blistering hot, dustbowl full of sand monsters that wanted to eat me. And that's where I met Azrael. Super romantic, let me tell you."

Jessie made a face. "Ew yeah, I suppose you were both sweaty and covered in sand."

"Oh, I was a stinky mess for sure. But Azrael... he was fresh as line-dried laundry, because *he* was taking baths everyday." Fate held up her hand when Jessie started to ask why. "We didn't exactly get along when we first met. I actually kind of hated him in the beginning. Mostly because he enslaved me for having saved my life, but also because he tried to kill me for not being honest, when in actuality, I'd lost my memory. The last thing I remembered, before making my big face plant in Dunebala, was the book signing at the library, so you can imagine how freaked out I was."

"Totally!" Jessie folded her arms and frowned at Azrael with disappointment. "So he's an angel-faced jerk."

"He was at first." Fate glanced at him, her heart softening as she watched the steady rise and fall of his chest. "He wasn't so bad once I got to know him."

Jessie pointed at Fate and gasped. "You like him! Are you in love with him?"

"No!" Fate knew the denial had come way too fast and loud. "I don't *love* him. But I do care about him."

Jessie took another sip of water. "Tell me everything."

There was no getting out of it now. Jessie was like a dog with a bone when there were secrets to share. Fate shifted uncomfortably as she recounted how Azrael had saved her from becoming a desert monster's snack, which resulted in the soul ring around her ankle.

Jessie leaned forward. "Let me see it."

Fate lifted her leg to show the thick brass ring around the ankle of her boot.

"Wow, another magical thingy you can't take off." Jessie shook her head, and then looked at Azrael. "I suppose it could be worse though."

"How do you figure?"

"He could've been an old toothless dude with long dirty fingernails."

"Ew!" Fate screwed up her face.

Jessie fell back into her pillows, laughing.

"It's not funny, Jess. This is serious. As long as I'm wearing the soul ring, Finn and I can't be truly together."

Jessie's playful grin turned to curiosity. "Well how come? Especially when there's no way to know if Azrael will ever wake up?"

"Finn and I can't be *all-the-way* together." Fate's face warmed with embarrassment. "The soul ring burns my skin every time we get any closer than a hug and a kiss, if you know what I mean."

Jessie's mouth fell open. "Are you saying you were actually ready to get horizontal with each other?"

"I've been ready for a long time now." Fate wondered whether to tell Jessie what Finn had told her. That they'd made love before he left for Oldwilde to organize the army that fought Kaliena's undead legions. Of all the memories she'd lost and still eluded her, this one pained her the most. She decided to hold onto this one personal secret and continued on with what she felt most comfortable telling her friend. "I don't remember any of it, but Finn made a pair of hand fasting bracelets for each of us and we declared ourselves married."

"What? No way!" Jessie squealed. "Are you wearing it? Let me see!"

"I don't have mine anymore. It was taken from me when I married Azrael."

Jessie clapped her hand over her mouth. Her eyes were round as marbles when she finally lowered her hand. "Do you realize you're married to two guys? Fate Floyd, that makes *you* a bigamist."

Fire exploded in Fate's belly, burning hot with rage. She closed her eyes and clenched her fists. "Don't say that! It's hard enough for me to wrap my head around being married at all. Let alone to two different guys."

"Sorry," Jessie muttered.

Fate sucked in enough air to cool the anger boiling beneath her skin. "It wouldn't be so bad if I could actually remember Finn giving me the bracelet and the promises we made to each other. You know what's weird? I loved that bracelet, even though I didn't have a single memory of Finn. Yet I knew it had been made with love, because I could *feel* it."

Jessie shifted nervously. After an awkward stretch of silence, she asked, "How'd you lose your memory?"

"Azrael's mother told me I have a memory too painful to live with, which made my soul shatter into lost pieces." When Jessie looked confused, Fate waved it off. "Her words, not mine. Anyway, she said the most damaged part of my soul drifted too far away for her to retrieve. She said it's a form of self-protection, and whatever that traumatic event was must've happened just before the Keep went through the portal."

"Sounds complicated. But at least you got most of your memories back, right?"

"Most of them, I guess." Fate stared into space. "As for what caused the amnesia, I'll probably never know what that was."

"It sounds like Azrael and his mother were a huge help getting you back on track." Jessie glanced over at him again. "Is that when you started to like him?"

Fate resisted the urge to look at Azrael. Seeing him in such a vulnerable state made her sad and stirred feelings she wasn't fully prepared to deal with. Mostly because of how unfair it was to Finn to be indulging in emotions that caused her to feel confused and divided. "Let's just say I eventually grew to respect Azrael after I learned more about him. But I never *ever* fell in love with him." Her chest tightened. "Finn's the only one I love."

"That's good to hear."

Startled by Finn's voice, Fate turned to see him leaning within the doorway sporting a teasing smile; his muscled arms crossed and tousled waves of bronzed-gold hair falling over his emerald green eyes in the most irresistible way.

Heat flooded up Fate's neck, warming her face. "You're not supposed to sneak up on two girls talking. This is sacred space and there's no boys allowed," she admonished him.

Finn nudged his chin at Azrael as he strode all the way into the room.

"What about him? He's a boy."

Fate frowned, despite the smile tugging at the corners of her mouth. "Unconscious boys don't count."

Finn leaned down and kissed the side of Fate's neck. The warm touch of his lips shot delicious tingles down her spine. He stood to face Jessie with his hand lingering on Fate's shoulder. "Hey, Jessie. It's good to see you're back. Fate's been miserable without you."

Jessie wriggled with delight. "I can see why. Nobody else can get brownies out of the food simulator like I can."

Fate nodded. "You know me too well."

Jessie winked. "Always have. Always will."

Fate continued nodding, but what she really wanted to say was that nobody knew her at all. Not Finn. Not Eustace. Not Sithias. And not even Jessie. She was changed. Changed by the power embedded beneath her skin. More so, she was being changed by something else, something nameless that was buried deep down inside. Something she very much wanted to stay buried. But it was rising, pushing to the surface little by little, and that terrified her.

2
PARANOID

FINN DIDN'T STAY LONG to chat with Jessie. It was obvious Fate wanted her best friend all to herself. Not that he minded. He hoped having Jessie back would help Fate relax a bit. He'd thought surely the end of the war would have brought about some measure of relief for her, but instead she'd become increasingly restless, growing more and more uptight with each passing day.

The main question was why? Was she growing suspicious of the huge, terrible lie they'd all been telling her? His guilt weighed heavier each time he perpetuated the lie that Eustace was alive, when it was actually Sithias pretending to be him.

His gut twisted into knots whenever he thought about what the truth would do to Fate. He was convinced finding out would literally destroy her–the very thing that would give Ananke the opening she needed to fully emerge and obliterate Fate's existence. Along with everything else.

Finn increased his pace to a jog, as if to outrun his own thoughts, not really seeing whom he passed in the halls. They were merely insignificant shapes of gray blurring by and all he could see up ahead was a dark future filled with despair.

He entered the library and stopped within the entrance, searching the expansive main floor and its many groupings of tables and chairs. Sithias could usually be found there buried behind a stack of books. Instead, he saw Darcy absorbed in studying a very long scroll spread out over the twelve-foot stretch of table.

He strode over the marble floor, glancing up at the six wraparound terraces ringing the walls of the library, each level filled to the brim with all manner of ancient texts in the form of carved tablets, countless leatherbound grimoires and stack upon stack of scrolls. There was no sign of Sithias in the upper levels.

"Have you seen Sithias around?" he asked Darcy.

She jumped, her charcoal-rimmed blue eyes wide, like she'd been caught red-handed. "Uh... he went to see Jessie as soon as he heard she woke up."

"I was just there to see her, but he wasn't."

Darcy straightened her back and frowned, an expression made all the more severe by eyebrows carefully darkened and plucked into arrogant arcs. "Do I look like his keeper?"

Finn clenched his jaw and took a breath to control his tone. "Never said you were. I just thought since you two are in here together all the time, you might know his whereabouts." He dropped his gaze to the scroll. There were illustrations of flaming chalices, temples and maps, all surrounded by columns of text written in an ancient language he didn't recognize. "What's that?"

Darcy moved to the end of the table and started rolling the scroll rather hastily. "Nothing. Just another dead end." Her voice pitched high, like she was either nervous or angry. It was hard to tell with Darcy. She mostly leaned toward being perpetually grumpy, but Finn had seen enough hysterics from her to know this could be a sign of overwhelm.

"I take it you're no closer to finding a way into Hadean's Kingdom to steal Dantalion's Key?"

Darcy capped the scroll and tucked it under her arm. "Nope, not yet."

Finn sagged into one of the chairs. "Not exactly what I'd hoped to hear."

"We're getting closer. I can feel it."

Finn was about to ask to what degree she was feeling it, when the sound of footsteps and clomping echoed through the library's vast space. He turned to see Brune marching toward them, dressed in full Keep Guardian uniform, her spine straight and blonde hair pulled into a tight bun. Gerdie skipped alongside, her frizzy hair flying loosely around her impish features, happy and content with her clockwork, bunny-eared doggit bouncing in time with each step.

Brune stopped in front of the table, skimming over the titles of the books Darcy had arranged in different stacks. "I don't see *Paracelsus's Book of Memini Spells* here. Did you even bother to look for it?" Speaking only to Darcy, she didn't bother to acknowledge Finn. Brune had never been one for niceties. She was all business.

Darcy's dark eyebrows knitted into a look of Vulcan-style disdain. "It's not in the library, which means it's up to you to figure out if it's in one of the vaults." She grabbed a book set off to one side. "I did manage to locate the *Alphabet of the Magi*, which *you'll* need to decipher Paracelsus's remembering spells."

Brune set her fists on her hips. "Which *I'll* need? I already pinpointed the crucial book. Are you saying you can't accomplish this one last task?"

"Oh, you mean in amongst researching an entrance into a Hell dimension filled with demons, along with devising a plan to break into their precious sanctum of highly prized possessions so we can steal Dantalion's Key out from under their salivating fangs?"

Brune huffed impatiently. "We went over this already. Our first priority is restoring Gerdie's memory. With our best researcher back, you and Sithias will be able to get through this mountain of work faster."

Darcy's fuming gaze shifted to Gerdie, now playing hide-and-seek with the doggit. "Like I said, if you're so anxious to be rid of babysitting your little sister, go find the book yourself."

Brune closed the space between them and pointed at the library entrance. "Do you have any idea what I'm dealing with outside that door?" She didn't wait for an answer. "It's nowhere near as peaceful out there as it is in here. I've got five thousand Serpen knights acting like they own the place, and another fifteen thousand Asgar soldiers joining in. They're all questioning if we're the rightful heirs to the Keep, constantly challenging my position as Keep Guardian and threatening to assume ownership. The only thing holding back a complete hostile takeover, are Rudwor's knights, which only number half of those two armies combined. Add that to the few hundred automatons I've managed to repair and reprogram so far and we're *still* dangerously outnumbered!"

Darcy glanced sheepishly at the floor.

Brune's hardened expression warmed as she glanced at Gerdie and watched her sister playing without a care in the world. After a moment, she returned her attention to Darcy. "Believe me, I'd much rather let my sister enjoy the childhood she was robbed of. But none of us have that luxury. Not with Eustace out of the picture and the possibility of Fate finding out he's dead."

The gut-churning guilt Finn was forever battling returned with Brune's blunt reminder. He wanted to untangle the web of deceit they'd woven more than ever. But it was too late. All they could do now was move forward with the solutions they'd been seeking and hope they carried them out in time.

"If you can tell me which vault that book is in, I can strap on an aeronaut pack and fly down to the surface with Fate and get it for you," Finn offered. His spirits sank even lower with the reminder that he'd lost his ability to fly, along with his superhuman strength and speed. Without the Elder race runes, he was pretty much useless these days.

The tension in Brune's face eased as she nodded in agreement. "I'll get you the coordinates to the vault." That was as close to a thank you as Brune would ever offer.

Finn stood and headed for the tall double doors, then stopped halfway across the long stretch of floor when Sithias entered the library. His golden-brown wings sagged, dragging on the marble surface as the overly large ivory-colored snake slithered over to him.

"Shouldn't you be looking like Eustace right now?" Finn asked.

Sithias wound into a coil and rested his head on the top ring. "Being sssomeone else all the time is exhausting." He let out a weary sigh. "And it doesn't help that I'm buried in research every sssingle minute of the day. All thisss reading and thinking is killing my creativity, therefore, killing me."

"Didn't you say you'd die happy if you could live in this library? Well look around. You got your wish."

"I take it back." Sithias raised his head an inch to look up at the terraces and the vast wealth of knowledge they held. "I've since dissscovered that too much of a good thing is a very bad thing."

Finn shook his head. "You know what I'm going to say."

"Yes, yes, yesss," Sithias hissed. "It's my own fault. I'm the one who decided to pretend to be Eustace... all on my own, without consulting anyone else, as you keep reminding me."

"Serves you right." Brune said as she strode past them with Gerdie and the doggit in tow. She quickly ushered Gerdie through the doors before Sithias could say anything in his defense.

"You'll get through this... somehow," Finn assured him.

Sithias's amber eyes grew watery. "Will I? I'm not so sure anymore. I'm certain Fate is sssuspicious of me. When I was in the infirmary visiting Jessie as Eustace, she was asking all kinds of questions she wouldn't normally ask. I became nervousss and then she started looking at me like she didn't believe a word I was saying. I think she knows I'm not Eustace! I even went back in as myself to see if she acted any different, and she did. I didn't get the twenty questions and that bone-chilling stare. She knows Eustace isn't Eustace."

The muscles in Finn's neck and shoulders tensed into tight painful cords. "No, the fact that you're still standing is proof she doesn't know you've been impersonating her father. Otherwise we'd all be piles of ash."

Sithias quivered violently. Several feathers shook loose from his wings and drifted to the floor. "Oh dear me, I'm utterly petrified. I can't do thisss anymore!"

"You *have* to," Finn insisted. "You have no choice but to carry this charade through to the bitter end."

"The bitter end is what ssscares me!"

Finn closed his eyes, taking a split second to calm his nerves. "You can do this, Sithias. It may be the most challenging performance of your life, but I know you've got this."

Sithias gulped and nodded frantically. "Yesss, I can do this. I can... I can..."

"You can do what?" Fate asked as she strode up behind him.

Sithias shrieked and launched into the air, his wings flapping furiously as he rose into the arched ceiling. Strangely enough, he fit right in with the ancient frescos of mythological creatures, gods and angels painted over the ceiling.

"What's wrong with you?" Fate called out.

Sithias stared down at her in horror. "Nothing!" he squeaked as several feathers loosened from his wings and fluttered to the floor.

Fate dropped her gaze to Finn. "Why's he so jumpy?"

"Uh... sleep deprivation, I suppose." Each lie Finn spoke, no matter how small, added itself like a rock to the quarry of lies he'd already told. He didn't know how much longer he could last before caving under the sheer weight of guilt.

Sithias landed beside them. "Finn's right. I've been burning too many candles all at once."

"You mean burning the candle at both ends," Fate corrected him.

"That too, and I should really get back to doing jussst that." Closing his eyes in concentration, Sithias morphed into what he considered his library persona–a tall, lanky man in his thirties, wearing an argyle sweater vest over a stiff-collared shirt and polka dot bow tie. He lifted a hand to smooth his fine white bangs, neatly parted to one side and held in place with shiny gel. His hand shook so much he dislodged a chunk of hair from its mold.

"If you'll excuse me," he muttered. Pushing his round spectacles up the bridge of his nose, he hurried over to the table to join Darcy.

Fate watched him go with a baffled expression. "He's up to something, and whatever it is, I'm pretty sure it involves my father."

Panic thudded through Finn's veins. "What do you mean?"

"Eustace has been acting weird too. He said he's been researching remembering spells for Gerdie, but I don't buy it."

"Why not?" Finn's heart hammered.

"How long have they been looking for a way to restore Gerdie's memory?" Finn started to answer, but Fate kept talking with her gaze glued to Sithias. "You'd think they would've come up with something by now. And if not, why keep beating that dead horse? I say, it's high time we accept that Gerdie's just going to have to grow up all over again and make new memories.

We're actually doing her a favor by keeping her from remembering the horrors of what Old Mother Grim did to all those poor children. Don't you think?"

"Aye, when you put it that way..."

"Exactly. So given this sound reasoning, I'm starting to think that Eustace and Sithias are researching something else. Something they don't want me to know about." Fate tore her gaze from Sithias and looked at Finn. "What do you think they're up to?"

He gulped dryly. "How would I know?"

Fate stared off in space, chewing on her bottom lip. Concern filled her beautiful brown eyes. Or was it fear?

"What else are you thinking?" he asked, holding his breath as he waited for an answer.

Fate's chin quivered like she might break out in tears, but then she pressed her lips tightly together in a defiant line. After a tense pause, she finally spoke. "Every time someone acts even the slightest bit strange, I get afraid that maybe Farouk's hiding underneath. What if the reason my dad's been twitchy is because it's not actually him?"

Finn began to breathe again and pulled her into his arms. "Eustace isn't Farouk. I know it."

Fate rested her head against his shoulder. "How can you be so sure? He fooled Darcy and Azrael, the only two people who should've known didn't even have a clue. And look where that left them. Azrael might never wake up, and Darcy... Well, Darcy's back to being cranky and annoying as ever, but she was seriously traumatized to find out she'd been snuggling up to Farouk and not Mason."

She leaned back to look up at Finn. "I've even gone so far as to wonder if you're Farouk sometimes."

"Why in the world would you think that?"

Fate stared at him, visibly shaken by her suspicions. "Every once in a while I get the feeling you're keeping secrets from me."

Finn's pulse gunned and his heart pounded. "I've only ever wanted to protect you, Fate. I promise."

"Then you're not holding back on anything I should know?" Confusion formed a frown on her lovely face. "I'm just being paranoid?"

Finn steeled himself as he layered on another lie. "Aye, while it's understandable fear, it's mere paranoia all the same."

Fate let out a deep, heavy sigh. "Okay, I'll try not to–"

"What are you two waiting for?" Darcy yelled to be heard from far across the library. "That *Book of Memini Spells* isn't going to magically arrive on its own. Move it. If Brune finds out I don't have the book *today*, it's my head on the chopping block."

"What's she going on about?" Fate asked.

Finn headed for the doors, pulling Fate along by the hand. "We need to fly to the Keep's surface to fetch the book Brune wants."

"Happy to. I can use the distraction."

They pushed their way through the throng of soldiers in the halls and headed for the sanctuary. Fate waved the Keep Guardian seal embedded within her palm over the panel to unlock the door and they stepped inside.

The huge gaping hole Kaliena had made during the war was filled and solid once more. Repairing the wall had been Brune's first priority, which she'd accomplished by reprogramming the maintenance bots. It had been a long, arduous process to remove the kill directive Kaliena had infused within the machines, but once Brune had flushed a few dozen bots clean, she had them repeat the process for the thousands of other infected maintenance bots. All of which were now assigned to retrieving vaults buried in the dunes that had come dislodged on the Keep's initial crash landing in the desert, as well as reinstalling or repairing any vaults damaged on impact.

Fate quickly entered the book's title into the motherboard. The record came up instantly. "Oh, it looks like the vault's below the subsurface." She sounded as disappointed as Finn felt.

He nodded, knowing he couldn't go with her since he'd had his teleportation device removed. "Guess you'll have to do this one without me then."

"I'll be back in a flash," she promised.

Her smile was almost mischievous as she stepped in close and raised her lips to his. The soft press of her mouth made his blood pump hard and fast. Anxious to feel her body against his, he pulled her by the waist, but his hands swept through air and clapped together. Opening his eyes, he frowned at the glinting cloud of stardust Fate had left behind.

"Vixen," he growled.

Fate wasn't gone for more than a few minutes when the sanctuary door opened to allow Brune, Sithias and Rudwor inside. Brune stopped when she saw Finn. "What are *you* doing in here?" She glanced around. "Alone."

Rudwor crossed his meaty arms over his barreled chest with a wink and a smile. Obviously tickled as to what Finn had to say about being caught in the Keep Guardian's sanctuary without Brune's permission.

Finn gave them both a flat stare. "Waiting for Fate to return with the

Book of Memini Spells you wanted so badly. The vault is below the subsurface, so she teleported down there."

Rudwor strolled over to Finn and gave him a hearty pat on the shoulder. "Don't go feeling like a feckless bump on a log, laddie. You might be as normal as the rest of us mere humans, but don't forget, you're still Beldereth's First Knight, and we need you with your head about you."

"Why, what's going on?" Finn asked.

"We've spotted a fleet of Biraktar ships headed this way. Battle ready."

Finn wasn't following. "We fought with them in the war. They're one of our allies. Why would they attack us?"

"Maybe because we have their prince?" Brune reminded him.

"We've done nothing but care for Azrael."

Brune nodded. "Uh huh, who happens to be unconscious and stricken by a mysterious life-threatening heart condition brought on by a demon who was pretending to be his mother. Try explaining that to them when they get here."

"Aye, I see where you're coming from," Finn agreed. "What's the plan then?"

Brune walked over to the motherboard and read the log Fate had left open. She turned back to the others. "She'll be gone a few hours. Fate has to open a puzzle box before she can access the book. Go ahead, Sithias. Tell him the plan."

Sithias worried his hands together, looking utterly miserable. "Me, sssir, I'm the plan."

3
PRESERVED? LIKE A PICKLE?

FATE STUDIED THE HUGE, dark hardwood box sitting in the otherwise plain vault. It was a perfect square and stood about five-feet-tall. Slowly, she circled the box, counting nine square drawers in rows of three on all four sides. "Terrific," she grumbled. "A puzzle box. I'm going to be here forever."

She scrutinized the ornate brass handles on the drawers. They were all different, most of them a varied collection of intricately detailed mythical beasts. She grabbed the handle of a roaring dragon and shook it to see if the drawer jarred loose, but it stayed firm. A sharp jab in the palm of her hand had her jerking her arm back.

She stared at blood beading from a small bite mark. "What the...?" Fate frowned at the handle. Leaning closer, she gasped when she saw the dragon's fangs stained with her blood. "You bit me!"

The dragon's silent, open-mouthed roar remained fixed, as though it had never moved.

Fate wiped the blood off with her thumb as the puncture marks healed over. "See?" She held her palm up to the brass dragon. "You can't scare me off. I'm like Wolverine. I can do this all day." She let out a sigh. "Except that I have much better things to do," she muttered, thinking of the kiss she'd teased Finn with and wanted to finish as soon as possible.

She closed her eyes, offering up the question of how to unlock the box to the collective knowledge of all the Keep Guardians before her and waited for the answer to come to her as it had so many times before.

The wait seemed longer than usual and wasn't as clear as what she was expecting when the information finally surfaced. From what little she was able to glean, no other guardian had opened this particular puzzle box. But there was a general rule to opening magical objects of this nature, and that was to do it in steps. Meaning, only one specific drawer would open first, which when chosen properly, would then allow the next drawer in order to open, and so forth.

Fate tapped her chin. "Think, think. Which one opens first?" She glared at the dragon handle. "Obviously not *you*. Although... I suppose I could see if your buddies react the same way. At least then I can eliminate a few more of you."

She gripped a handle in the shape of a sea serpent, releasing it when it slithered and cut her hand with its sharp scales. "Ew!" She shuddered as she eyed the rest of the handles. "Only thirty-four more to go."

Taking each side of the box, Fate went through each row of drawers and squeezed every handle. Her trepidation grew as the injuries happened faster than her skin could heal. Half way through with raw, bleeding fingers and palm, she began avoiding the more dangerous looking ones for what should be more benign creatures. But she was wrong, because she was stabbed by a unicorn, pecked by a griffin and clawed by a mermaid.

It wasn't until she came to a hand holding onto a simple doorknob that she wasn't attacked. In fact, the hand opened in a welcoming gesture, shaking her hand, gently and firmly. The hand then resumed its original position and the drawer slid open.

"Eureka!" Fate kneeled down to the floor level drawer to have a look inside. It was empty. "Now what?"

No answer came.

Out of pure frustration, Fate yanked the drawer fully from the box and sent it sliding across the floor. The sound of it hitting the wall echoed within the hollow chamber, loudly and with far more clatter than it should be.

But that was because it wasn't the smashed drawer making all the noise. It was the puzzle box rearranging its order of drawers, each one moving in to fill the empty space she'd made at the bottom corner, slotting them around until the hole was at the very center of the nine slots of drawers.

Fate moved to the next side of the box, looking for a handle that was unlike any of the others, just as the hand had been. Then she spotted a handle in the shape of a key. She pulled at the key and it dislodged, revealing a keyhole behind where it had been anchored. Slotting the key in she turned it, smiling at the sound of the locks inside clicking over.

The drawer slid open and she pulled it all the way out. The puzzle box reordered itself. Once again leaving the hole at the center of the nine slots.

Feeling encouraged, Fate ran to the next side, this time finding a lantern. As soon as she touched it, the lantern lit with a gleaming gold light. The drawer opened and the box immediately slotted the hole at the center.

Fate ran around to the fourth and last side of the puzzle box, searching for another oddball handle. At this point, it was easy to spot and this one was in the form of a flourished anchor. Using her fingers, she went to flick it forward, but it didn't budge. Wrapping her hand firmly around the handle, she pulled, fully expecting the dangling part of the handle to move.

Using both hands, she tugged at the anchor, and still couldn't get it to move. Exasperated, Fate stood back to frown at the handle. "Oh, I get it. You're an anchor and as heavy as a real one." She laughed bitterly. "Well, guess what? I have super strength."

Fate gripped the handle again with both hands, put her foot on the box for extra leverage and pulled with all the strength she could muster. The groan of heavy iron echoed within the chamber as the anchor slowly lifted. The drawer suddenly gave way and fully released. Fate flew backward, hitting the wall hard enough to knock the air from her lungs.

She slumped against the wall, recovering her breath as she watched the drawers shifting to make the hole at the very center. Fate rose to her feet and shuffled over to the puzzle box to peer into the opening at the center, where the *Book of Memini Spells* sat nestled inside the four-way tunnel running within the center of the box.

Fate swiped the book from its resting place. "Gotcha." She turned the leatherbound book over to look at the back. There was nothing remarkable about it. Opening the book, she flipped through the pages, wondering if there was a spell to help retrieve the memories she'd lost as well. Having such a big hole in her memory banks haunted her daily.

She frowned at the foreign language it was written in. "It's all Greek to me," she grumbled, but then smiled nonetheless. She'd accomplished her task and could leave the deciphering to Brune.

Her smile broadened with the thought of returning to Finn to finish that kiss and she was feeling mischievous enough to make a game of it. Squeezing her eyes shut, she visualized the large circular room of the sanctuary and the unused alcove holding stacks of tomes needing to be brought back to the library. Once she had the shadowy alcove clearly pictured in her mind's eye, she triggered the teleportation device.

Fate's awareness sped along the scattered particles of her body jetting through space, lasting only a few short seconds before materializing back into solid form. The dizzying sensation of teleporting lingered a few heartbeats longer as she stood still, waiting for her equilibrium to return.

Smiling wickedly, Fate tiptoed forward to keep from alerting Finn of her return. She'd taken two steps, when she heard Sithias's voice and stopped to listen.

"When the Biraktar fleet arrives, I'll present myself as Azrael to show them he's alive and well. Then I'll tell them to return home without me, because I'm quite happy ssstaying here with my wife."

"Have you lost your mind?" Finn asked. "What happens when they start speaking in their own language?"

"I… w-well," Sithias stammered, "I'll demand they ssspeak in English out of respect for everyone else. They'll have to obey. Azrael's a prince, after all."

"The language barrier isn't a problem," Brune said. "We have transmodulators for that."

There was a long pause, at which point Fate thought it best to join the conversation. But then Finn said something that stopped her cold.

"That's all well and good, but what if they decide to stay instead? How do you plan to be Azrael, Eustace and yourself during that time without Fate becoming even more suspicious than she already is?"

An icy, sick feeling spread through Fate's gut. Why would Sithias be pretending to be Eustace?

"I've done it thisss long, haven't I?" Sithias argued. "I'll have you know I've performed many a one-man show, with as many as twelve different characters in one play. Three is nothing for me."

"No, Finn's right," Brune interjected. "You've barely been able to hold it together with the two you're playing now. I don't see how you can maintain three identities. The decision's made. You have to be firm with the Biraktar fleet and order them to return home immediately."

"Aye, I second that." The shock of hearing Rudwor's voice increased Fate's queasiness. "As it stands, we've got our hands full with the Serpens. The last thing we need is another powerful army thinking they can take possession of the Keep."

Fate's legs turned to stone. She couldn't move a single foot forward. Couldn't speak. Blood pounded in her skull. Her head was swarming with questions, her gut bound in tight, nauseating knots. The *Book of Memini Spells* slipped from her hand and fell to the floor with a loud thud that made her jump. She started shaking.

"Who's there?" Brune shouted. She stormed toward the sound and stopped. "Fate?"

Finn raced over, his pace slowing as he caught sight of Fate standing beneath the eave of the alcove. "Did you just get back?" His voice was faint, as though guilt had stolen his breath.

Fate shook her head as his face blurred behind tears.

Sithias and Rudwor moved in behind Brune as Finn edged closer. "Are you all right, love?" he asked. "You don't look–"

"What's going on here?" Each word Fate spoke cut like shards of glass in her constricted throat. "Why has Sithias been pretending to be my dad?"

Asking the question aloud made her dizzy and physically ill. She grabbed her stomach and dry heaved.

Finn lunged forward to catch her before she fell. He scooped her up in his arms. "You're sick, Fate. I'm taking you to the infirmary."

Fate started to nod but then pushed away from him so forcefully, he nearly dropped her. "Answer me!" She squirmed until she had a leg free from his grasp, and then the other. She staggered backward, searching their faces for the truth. "Where's my dad? I want to see Eustace, right now!"

Sithias inched forward. His amber eyes were huge with sorrow. "You can't, misss. Your father… isn't here anymore."

"Where is he?" Fate's voice pitched into a scream that caused Sithias to cover his ears. Whatever sadness had been in his eyes was swiftly replaced by fear.

Rudwor took several big steps toward the door. "Do something, lad, she looks ready to blow."

Finn reached out for Fate's hand. "Calm down, love."

Fate refused him as rage burned through the nauseating fear. "Somebody tell me where my father is. *NOW*!" Her voice boomed, a shocking, inhuman volume that rattled the sanctuary walls.

Sithias yelped and trembled, his long skinny legs knocking together at the knees.

Finn stepped closer. "Fate, I'll tell you everything, but first you need to–"

"Do not dare to tell me what I need to do." She was breathing hard, filling up with a ferocious, all-consuming power that lived to feast on weaknesses of the soul, lifting her far beyond the insignificance of human cares. The call to surrender completely to this mysterious pulsing force of will was overpowering, and Fate began to give in little by little.

"I'll take you to your father."

Fate glanced at Brune, detached but still affected by a small shred of human interest.

"What the hell are you doing, Brune?" Finn's voice was a low warning growl. "Eustace is *gone*."

Fear and anger erupted from deep within, destroying the seductive pull of power Fate had nearly succumbed to. Her dread of the truth returned full force, but she needed to know. Regardless of how tempting it was to allow the nameless power to swallow her pain.

"There's something I haven't told you all." Brune strode to the door. "Follow me everyone."

Rudwor and Sithias appeared surprised as they trailed after Brune. Finn touched Fate's hand, but she brushed past him, walking fast to catch up, but mostly wanting to leave him behind. She was so angry with him for lying to her she couldn't look at him.

Brune strode down the hall a short ways and unlocked a door Fate had never paid any attention to before. There was nothing special about the room. It was mostly empty, save for a green tarnished copper screen. A warm glow from the other side of the screen cast gold pinpricks of light through the filigree, burnishing the walls with shifting shadows.

Fate swallowed down a rising panic as Brune gestured for her to look behind the screen. Her feet turned heavy as she moved toward whatever dreadful thing waited on the other side. She slowly rounded the corner, seeing a wooden, waist-high pedestal holding a long, rectangular glass case filled with clouds of sparkling gold dust.

Her breath caught in her throat. A body lay within the thick cover of twinkling particles.

Unable to see any distinguishing features, she forced her legs into motion and moved stiffly to the case. The moment she put her hands on the glass, the gold dust cleared away, revealing Eustace's face. Her next inhale was a sharp gasp, which felt like fire filling her chest. His silvered hair was brushed neatly back from his smooth brow and closed eyes. There was no expression on his face, except maybe a peaceful repose that made her next breath a little less painful.

"Is he asleep or–" Fate's voice cracked and broke. She cleared her throat. "Is he in some kind of coma?" Her heart thudded when no one answered.

Finn was the first to say something. "Fate, we wanted to tell you, but there's much you don't know. The magic from Hippolyta's girdle has made you vulnerable to being–"

"What does that have to do with why Eustace is lying in this case?" Fate couldn't control the volume of her voice. She was yelling. "What's all this stuff swimming around him?"

"I don't know what it is... I didn't know he was here." Finn was obviously baffled. "What is this, Brune?" he asked. "What have you done?"

"Eustace's body is being preserved with magic." Brune's tone was calm and matter-of-fact.

Fate's pulse pounded loudly in her ears. "Preserved? Like a pickle? Why would he need to be preserved? That would mean he's..." Nausea combined with a throbbing ache in her chest as her mind went to the only place it could go. Losing all balance, she had to grab hold of the glass case.

Brune nodded grimly. "You have it right. Eustace is dead."

"Wait... What about the elixir of life?" Fate asked. "Why didn't you use it to bring him back? There were vats of the stuff."

"It was all destroyed." Brune seemed ready to say more on the subject, but she glanced away.

All the strength drained from Fate's limbs and her knees buckled out from under her. With her back against the pedestal, she slipped to the floor and stared at the wall. "How? How did this happen?" The last word was a garbled sob.

Finn moved to comfort her, but Brune held up a hand for him to wait. "Farouk did this."

Tears distorted Fate's surroundings as she tried to focus on Brune's face. "Farouk–" A painful sob choked off her voice and she had to swallow the hard lump in her throat before she could finish her sentence. "Killed Eustace?"

"Yes," Brune answered.

Finn started toward Fate again. This time Brune grabbed him by the arm. His features tightened with fury. "This is cruel even for you, Brune. Why would you show her this without preparing her first?"

Brune shook her head. "There's no way to prepare anyone for this kind of news. We should've told her the first time she asked about Eustace. I never agreed to keeping this a secret, but thanks to Sithias, we had no choice in the matter."

Sithias let out a frightened squeak. "I only ever wanted to help." He turned his anxious gaze to Fate. "I couldn't bear to see you in pain, misss."

Fate watched them through a thickening fog of pain, but the shock and confusion were wearing off as she listened. Heat churned within her core, searing from the inside out. Fiery rage coursed along her veins, exploding in her chest, blazing up her neck and into her face. Her breathing came in bursts and her heart filled with hot, bitter betrayal. How could they do this to her? How could she ever trust them again?

Finn's expression turned to one of fright when he looked at Fate. He jerked his arm from Brune's grasp. "Everyone out! Go! Now!"

Sithias and Rudwor hurried toward the door, but Brune didn't move. "No, I'll stay with Fate. It's best *you* leave."

"I'm not leaving her alone with you!" Finn stood rigid, his fists curled like he wanted to punch her. "You're the last person she needs right now. Fate needs *me*."

Hot, scorching air swirled around Fate as she rose to her feet. The indwelling power burned like an inferno, demanding to be unleashed. Burning through the paralyzing grief, it scorched away the anguish of being lied to, especially by the one person she thought would always be truthful with her.

Her heart deadened and it was all Fate could do to hold the power in.

She pointed at the door, where Sithias lingered, his body quaking and amber eyes filled with terror. Her voice was an inhuman roar as she fixed her gaze on Finn. "*Leave now, or I swear, Finn, I won't be able to keep myself from killing you.*"

4
APOCALYPSE AVERTED

BRUNE CLOSED THE DOOR and leaned against it. Sweat stung her eyes and dripped from the tip of her nose. She wiped her forehead while doing her best to breathe evenly, but the air was blistering hot and suffocating. The small chamber was filled with heat waves radiating off Fate's body, suffusing the air with the metallic scent of smelted iron.

Summoning all her courage, Brune turned to meet Fate's piercing gaze. Her niece's auburn hair flew around her face in a wild array of curls blown upward. Veins of fiery light spidered beneath Fate's skin, lighting her face, chest and hands with a preternatural gleam. Her usually warm brown eyes blazed so bright from within, they were almost white.

Fate hadn't yet transformed fully into the terrifying godlike being she had when Eustace was murdered in front of her–the being that had grown golden armor around Fate's body out of nothing and had walked through thick iron walls like they were air. Brune hadn't known why at the time, except to blame Hippolyta's girdle, but it was Ananke who had emerged. She would never forget Ananke's killing rampage and near destruction of Kaliena's undead legions. All without breaking so much as a sweat.

Ananke was close to fully possessing Fate again. Frighteningly close. If Brune didn't act now, there was no telling what horrors would follow.

"There may be a way to bring Eustace back to life." Brune disliked hearing the nervous quell in her own voice. She would need to control her fear if she was going to gain any modicum of control over the situation. A show of weakness in the presence of such a powerful being could be her undoing.

Fate's expression remained cold and impassive. Was it too late? Was she already out of reach?

Brune forced herself to move, hoping she wouldn't be struck down as she strode past Fate to the far corner of the room, where she'd stored the box. Unlike the others, Brune had known this day would come sooner rather than later. She'd prepared a solution she hoped Fate would latch onto, and in turn, strengthen her against Ananke's emergence.

Brune lifted the lid, retrieving the top book from the stack in the box.

She opened it to a page marked with a red ribbon and held the book out for Fate to see. Her arms trembled as she stepped closer. "This is a black unicorn. Its horn is what you will need to resurrect Eustace."

Fate's gaze flicked to the page and her lids widened, as if in recognition.

"Do you know about the unicorn?" Brune asked.

The heat emanating from Fate decreased slightly as she tilted her head and stared at the illustration. Depicted as a rearing steed of pitch black, the unicorn was both beautiful and grotesque. Its strong, lithe muscles were marked by glossy highlights, its cloven hooves fringed with wavy hair. Leathery wings folded against its ribcage, interrupting the sleek lines of its otherwise graceful, equine form. The statuesque head and thick flowing mane could have matched that of *Black Beauty*, save for the white vacant eyes and sharp fangs glimpsed behind its soft muzzle. The long spiraled horn was more like a deadly spear on this creature, as compared to the elegant alicorn of its gentler cousin, the white unicorn.

Fate nodded yes to Brune's question.

Encouraged by the response, Brune's nervousness eased slightly. Though she was puzzled as to how Fate might have any knowledge of a black unicorn. This particular beast was as rare as hen's teeth. "Have you seen this picture before?"

The inner fire lighting Fate's skin waned to a dull glow as she blinked and shook her head. "A dream," she whispered. "It came to me in a dream."

Brune was even more baffled. "How long ago?"

Still staring at the illustration, Fate frowned in concentration. "I think it was... after the war ended."

"What did the unicorn do in the dream?"

"It took me for a ride in the stars."

"Oh." Brune's surprise was mixed with concern. Her research on the black unicorn was limited due to a lack of written texts on the beast and little time to look for more on the subject. While she was relieved Fate's dream hadn't been unpleasant, she wasn't exactly comfortable with Fate having warm, fuzzy feelings for the creature either.

"Can the black unicorn really bring my dad back to life?" Fate stared at Brune, her eyes normal again, lit with hope, rather than Ananke's terrible power. The hot wind streaming off her skin ceased altogether and the room began to cool.

Brune sighed with relief. Apocalypse averted.

"Yes, but hunting the black unicorn will be extremely dangerous," Brune warned.

Fate waved her hand dismissively, a gesture Brune found annoying, because more often than not, it meant her niece was being overly confident. "Phhh, danger shmanger," Fate said. "Like that's ever stopped me. Just tell me what I need to do."

Brune cleared her throat, frowning as Fate grabbed the book from her hands. Flippant Fate was back. But she couldn't complain. Flippant was preferable to furious.

"You see that box?" Brune attempted to direct Fate's attention to its contents. "Please read through everything before you sail off half-cocked to hunt the black unicorn."

Fate wasn't listening, she was reading intently from the bestiary. She looked up from the pages. "It says the black unicorn lives in the Feldoril Forest. Where's that?"

"It's the most ancient forest in Oldwilde. You'll have to study up on the terrain and all the known creatures living there. The forest is full of wild, vicious beasts of magic, many of which have never been recorded. That's how dense and enormous the Feldoril is. Most of the explorers that have gone into the forest were lost and never seen again."

Fate glanced at the glass case and all former impudence dropped away. What was left was untold sorrow thinly veiled with determination. She closed the bestiary, set it down on top of the other books and picked up the box. "I'll read through every page. Thanks, Brune. Thank you for not giving up on Eustace." Tears welled in her eyes. "I'll never forget this."

Surprised by this sudden outpouring of gratitude, Brune swallowed down her own grief. "Your father was a kind, caring man. We all loved him very much."

She opened the door for Fate and found Finn and Sithias standing in the hall. The relief on their faces was evident when they saw Fate had returned to normal.

"How are you feeling, misss?" Sithias asked.

Fate kept walking.

Finn fell in step beside her as Brune lagged behind them. "You had us worried there, love. It's good to see you're–"

"Don't call me that." Fate's voice was sharp and clipped. "I'm not your love. Not anymore. Not after the way you lied to me."

Finn stopped walking, stricken like he'd been punched.

As much as the two lovebirds nauseated Brune, she felt for Finn. The boy was besotted with Fate and she could only guess at his pain.

Fate glared at Sithias. "And you! Pretending to be Eustace and lying straight to my face like that!"

Sithias shrank against the wall as Fate stormed down the hall. "I'm so, so sorry, misss," he called after her. "Please forgive me!"

Brune rushed over to them. "You two! Stay away from Fate before you undo everything I've done to calm her down! She needs time to cool off."

Finn watched Fate leave. "She's never spoken to me like that... so... *final.*"

Brune patted him awkwardly on the shoulder, mostly to keep him from going after Fate. "I've seen how you two are together." She held her eye roll in. "She'll get over it soon enough and you'll be back to grossing us all out again with your endless mushy hugs and kisses."

Sithias made a sad, squeaky sound. "I don't think she'll *ever* forgive *me.*" He sniffed. "I fear I'll never again feel the warmth of her friendship."

Brune squashed her building irritation and patted Sithias on his bony shoulder. "If there's one thing I've learned about Fate, she doesn't hold grudges. I'm proof of that. Remember, I gave her plenty of reasons to hate me, but she eventually got over it all."

Finn nodded. "Aye, she really did hate your guts. There's hope for us yet, Sithias."

Sithias slumped forward and glumly nodded in agreement.

Happy to be done playing nursemaid to their hurt feelings, Brune wiped her hands together like she'd gotten them dusty. "All right, I'll go make sure Fate stays cool and calm long enough for her to become thoroughly convinced I've given her what she needs to resurrect Eustace."

Renewed concern developed on Finn's face. "Wait. What exactly was in that box?"

Brune huffed with impatience. "Books. Nothing but books."

"I hope you don't mean books on necromancy." Sithias's face had gone paler than usual. "That's dark magic, which could very well result in making things much, much worssse. Eustace could come back wrong!"

"Obviously, I of all people know that better than anyone after enduring my zombie debacle." Brune shook her head. "There's another way. It's much more complicated and dangerous, but it shouldn't backfire like necromancy would."

"Shouldn't, or won't?" Finn's voice dipped into a growl.

Brune pressed her lips together to halt a hot-tempered retort. "We've all been at this long enough to know there are no guarantees when it comes to magic. Suffice to say, I've given Fate hope in the face of what would otherwise be unbearable grief. She now has a mission she can focus all her energy into, a purpose unlike any other. As far as I can see, Fate's desire to have her father back alive and well will be more powerful than Ananke's desire to play out her grand plan. All we have to do is keep it that way. So that means you two staying out of Fate's way."

"But you said it was dangerous. I won't have you sacrificing Fate just to save the rest of us. We deserve what we get for lying to her."

"Oh really?"

The muscles in Finn's jaw tightened.

"You fool. We're not the only ones at risk here." Brune laughed sharply as the truth revealed itself in Finn's expression. "Wow, you'd actually allow the entire world–hell, the whole universe–to be destroyed by the mother of all gods, rather than give up your precious Fate."

The narrow hallway fell quiet as Brune and Finn glared at each other. The moment dragged out until Sithias broke the silence with a loud gulp.

"I want to know everything about this so-called mission you've filled Fate's head with," Finn demanded.

"I'll have the list of books sent to your bedchamber by nightfall," Brune conceded. "Sithias can find out what's in them with the help of the librarians. As you know, they can recite everything that's ever been stored in the library."

Finn leaned close to Brune's face. "Brilliant, you do that. And if I find anything suspicious, anything that looks like you're trying to get Fate killed, I'll put a swift end to this diversion you've cooked up for her. Hear me?"

Brune crossed her arms. "Unfortunately, yes. Are we done here? I've got Fate to baby sit and the Biraktar fleet about to arrive in the next few hours." She pointed at Sithias. "Meet me in the sanctuary with your best Azrael face on. I'll be there in an hour."

Sithias drooped like a wilted rose, his long arms limp as floppy leaves. "I'm ssso tired of being other people."

Brune stepped around him. "Look on the bright side. At least you don't have to be Eustace anymore."

"Oh, I feel much better now." The sarcasm in Sithias's tone was unmistakable.

Brune left them both standing in the hall and took the corridor leading to the residential section. The halls were filled with more soldiers than usual, all moving in the same direction. Curious as to where they were going, Brune followed them into the sparring arena. She stopped near the entrance as soldiers streamed past, many of them roughly bumping into her shoulders as they passed by.

The massive arena was already half filled with soldiers.

Alarmed by this unexpected mass gathering, Brune moved forward with the throng, while slowly edging her way to the sidewall in the direction of the armory. Her nerves jittered with urgency, certain she was about to face some sort of rebellion. There'd been too much dissention, especially amongst the Serpens, to think otherwise.

She slipped into the main room of the armory, expecting to find the maintenance bots had replenished the supply of armor and weapons. But the space was again, a mess of leftover pieces of armor strewn about the floor. All the broad swords and sabers were gone. Only a few small, unwanted daggers remained in the detritus.

Brune ran over to the lockers, where the laser guns and rifles were kept under lock and key. The solid metal doors were warped from being pried back and broken off their hinges. Whoever had forced them open had used some serious brute strength. Nothing of any worth was left. It was bad enough that weapons weren't being returned after sparring sessions, this was outright theft and vandalism.

Rage burned in Brune's chest. How dare they!

Pulling her laser gun from its holster, she checked the gauge. It was only half charged. She shook her head. "Lazy. You let yourself get lazy, Brune," she admonished herself.

Breathing deep, she calmed her racing pulse long enough to take stock of what little she was equipped with. Her review was done within a split second. All she had was the teleportation implant, the telegrapher she used to control the maintenance bots, and a half-charged laser gun.

"Lovely. I'm not only outnumbered, I'm outgunned."

Tense and furious, Brune peeked her head out of the armory before heading back into the open arena. The Serpen knights had arranged themselves at the back end and were looking down on the horde filling the sunken arena. A commanding position, which allowed them to face anyone entering the arena as well. Every Serpen was geared up in full armor, solid black with scales, spikes and horned helmets. Each was holding spears or swords unsheathed.

The thousands of soldiers looking up at them comprised the whole of the Asgar army. The majority was dressed in their dead king's royal crimson colors, though several hundred of them sported armor from the Keep–her thieves exposed. She spotted a few dozen Eldunough hawk riders amongst them, which either meant they were supporters, or possibly spectators. What worried her most was the total absence of Rudwor's Beldereth knights. A sure sign this meeting was intended to exclude his powerful peacekeepers.

A booming voice disrupted the din of thousands of voices echoing off the walls of the cavernous space as they congregated. "We have gathered you all here for one purpose. To declare that the Serpen Empire is taking possession of the Keep."

A chill ran through Brune as a cacophony of outrage rose from the ranks below.

A loud, sharp order silenced them, an authoritative shout that came from a high-ranking Asgar officer. "Asgar will not relinquish its rightful claim! This so-called alliance was based on shared ownership. You'd best rethink your choice of words, because you'll not stand a chance of winning against the Beldereth knights without Asgar's might behind you."

The Serpen leader stepped to the very edge of the arena. He was a huge man, bigger than any other in his legion. His face was hidden within the shadows of a black helmet hammered into the shape of a dragon's head. "We don't need Asgar to help us take the Keep."

The officer aimed one of the stolen laser guns at the Serpen leader. "Ready and aim!" he bellowed to his army. At least half of his army raised laser guns and rifles, while the rest nocked arrows in bows and raised swords and battleaxes.

The Serpens responded in a sudden, fluid movement of shields–a solid wall that locked into place with a clamorous ring of iron hitting the granite floor. At the same moment, the Asgar army fired. Arrows ricocheted off the shields harmlessly, while red beams blasted against Serpen crests, burning in, lighting the twisting patterns of snakes with a deep red glow.

The Asgar officer shouted another order. Soldiers on the outer fringe of the sunken arena raced up the ramp but were met with another wall of shields pushing them back down into the hole they'd walked so willingly into just moments before.

In one unified movement, the Serpens threw their huge heavy shields down onto the Asgar soldiers standing directly below and jumped onto shields, crushing the soldiers underneath. The Serpens were immediately on the soldiers crowded in the middle who were still standing. They hacked their way through the stunned Asgar army, regardless of being outnumbered three to one, stepping on the dead as they cleared bloody paths for more Serpen knights to swarm in from the edges of the arena.

Knowing there was nothing she could do to stop the carnage, Brune visualized the sanctuary, triggering her teleportation device. In the flash of a second she was there, racing over to the motherboard, hitting the alarm and declaring an outbreak in the sparring arena.

Her fingers flew over the keys as she activated a hologram of the arena. It was shocking to see how the Serpens snaked through the overcrowded confines, moving like they were of one mind even though they'd split off into separate units. On the other hand, the Asgar soldiers were panicked, each one fighting for his life, no longer working together the way the Serpens were.

The Beldereth knights swept into the arena, splitting off on both sides to surround the sunken arena. The women lined around the edges with arrows aimed and fired all at once. Their arrows hit true, slipping between the tiniest cracks of armor to pierce the jugulars of hundreds of necks. They took down enough Serpen knights to gain majority attention, bringing their insurgence to a swift end.

Their bows were nocked with fresh arrows, aimed at new marks as Rudwor strode in, flanked by his officers. Brune's heart thudded in response to one of them.

The king surveyed the slaughter of at least a thousand fallen Asgar soldiers and the few hundred Serpen knights lying dead amongst them with Beldereth arrows stuck in their necks. One of Rudwor's officers leaned over to speak to him and he nodded. "Congratulations," he announced to both armies. "By your actions today, you have created your own prison. From here on you will remain in this section under lock and key until further judgment."

Rudwor started to leave, then turned back to them. "And unless you want to live with the stink of death in your noses, I advise you to pile the dead by the door for disposal."

A savage uproar ensued from the Serpen knights, many of whom charged up the ramp to chase after Rudwor with swords in hand. But swift, ready arrows picked them off and they dropped dead to the ground.

Brune clicked off the horrible scene and fell into a chair, exhausted and overwhelmed. This was only the beginning of a whole new set of problems.

5
An Unexpected Guest

FATE CLOSED THE DOOR of her bedchamber and set Brune's box down beside one of the over-stuffed chairs in the sitting area. She curled into the opposite chair and hugged a soft throw pillow, wishing she were holding her cat, Oz, instead. His purring had always comforted her, something she desperately needed, like never before.

Anxious determination swirled and fluttered in her chest as she stared at the books. There was hope written on those pages, but the heaviness of grief made her want to crawl into bed and never wake from the merciful oblivion of sleep.

Eustace was dead.

Disbelief pushed against what she'd been told and what she'd seen. Seeing him lying in that glass case blanketed in a cloud of sparkling gold dust had been like a vague dream. She couldn't wrap her mind around it. Not after she'd just talked to Eustace less than an hour ago when she'd gone to see Jessie.

But that had been Sithias *pretending* to be her father.

She was too stunned and sad to hold onto her anger. If anything, she wanted to ask Sithias to walk in as Eustace right now, because then she could delay the sharp knife of sorrow ready to twist in her heart. She wasn't sure she could survive that kind of pain.

Eustace had been in her life from the beginning. How could he be gone? He was her rock. Her strength. Her home. Eustace had always been there, watching over her, even when she'd thought he wasn't.

Like the time she and Jessie had announced they were old enough to go trick-or-treating by themselves. They'd thought they were so grown up running from door to door through the dark of night without parental supervision. They'd been so proud of themselves afterwards. Until the next day when Fate discovered the big sheet printed with the word, "Boo!" on the front–the same ghost costume they'd seen on a tall stranger who'd kept mysteriously appearing around each corner on that wonderful Halloween night.

The memory curved her lips into a wistful smile, but it faded just as quickly.

Eustace had promised he would always be there to protect her. Fate knew he'd certainly done his best to do just that. But how does a parent protect a child against the worst possible agony in the world? Not even Eustace could keep such a promise, because the day comes when every parent dies.

She swallowed down the ragged sob building at the base of her throat and frantically emptied the box of its contents. Two scrolls and three books. She unrolled the first scroll–a map detailing Feldoril Forest and its massive coastline, numerous rivers, lakes and sprawling mountain ranges. From what she could tell, there didn't seem to be a single kingdom or village established in the forest. The second scroll detailed the magnification of a much smaller area called Mornavar Valley.

Setting the scrolls aside, Fate stared at the titles: *Feldoril Bestias Silvam, Feldoril Historia Silvam Primo*, and *Flora et Feldoril Silvam Agri.* She chose *Beasts of Feldoril Forest* and opened it to the marked page of the black unicorn.

Fate studied the inked drawing, tracing a finger along the curve of the unicorn's ebony neck. The same thrill of excitement flushed through her as her dream of the unicorn returned, vivid and strong. She closed her eyes, instantly breathing in the honeyed, musky scent of the galloping unicorn, feeling its muscles bunch beneath her legs. She sighed, surrendering all cares as the unicorn carried her higher and higher, until the brilliant flash of stars, nebulas and shooting comets swirled around them.

They rode into the deepest reaches of the heavens, where there was no light and only darkness. Nothing existed in that black nothingness, except a feeling of peace. She felt it even now. Nothing to fight against. Nothing to fear. Nothing to lose. The unicorn had sensed her yearning, because when its gallop slowed to a trot and then a complete standstill, the temptation to slide off its back and remain in the void had been overpowering.

A hand on Fate's shoulder broke the spell. Disoriented, she glanced up at the round grandmotherly face of her chamber bot, whose pleasant smile remained fixed as she gestured at the door and the urgent banging from the other side.

Fate rushed across the room and opened the door to Brune. Stray blonde locks of hair had come loose from her usual tight bun and her expression was strained. "I was hoping we could handle this on our own, what with you just finding out about Eustace and all, but the king of Biraktar is here, demanding to see his son and his *wife*."

Fate stepped out into the hall and closed the door. "That's fine. There's a lot to cover in those books you gave me. It's not like I'm going to get through them all in the next five minutes."

They were close to reaching the sanctuary, when Fate realized the halls were empty. "Where'd all the annoying crowds go? Is it dinnertime already?"

"Oh, right. You missed all the action earlier. The Serpens announced they were going to take the Keep and not share the spoils with the Asgar army. Fortunately, I was able to call Rudwor's knights in to break it all up before that happened, and now they're being forced into one big sleepover in the arena."

"Nice. I wish I could've seen the Serpens get a good spanking though. They've been getting on my nerves for weeks."

Brune threw her a disgusted frown as she pushed through the door of the sanctuary. "It was a massacre, Fate. Hundreds of them died."

"Oh," Fate muttered. She stopped just inside the threshold when she saw Finn standing next to Azrael, who by some miracle was cured and back to normal. For a half second she was happy to see he'd woken from his mysterious sleep sickness, but then she knew it was another lie and she was furious all over again.

"Uh-uh, we're not doing this anymore." Fate marched across the room. "No more lies. No more pretending to be someone else!"

Azrael's warm complexion paled as his long dark hair turned white, his muscular physique swiftly stretching into the tall, lanky form of Sithias's librarian personage. "The king is waiting for Azrael to make an appearance in the next few moments!" Sithias clasped his hands together in an imploring gesture and held them up to his chin. "You're asking for outright war if they find out we–"

Finn put a hand on Sithias's shoulder to hush him. "You should listen to him, Fate. The king must be assured his son is alive and safe. If we–"

"I can't believe you!" Fate's voice was an angry whisper, but it might as well have been a shout for the way it hit Finn. "How can you be so willing to repeat the same mistake? Don't you realize your weak disguise will get us into unimaginable trouble? At least with me, you only had to deal with one person's hurt and anger versus an entire kingdom reigning down on us."

Sithias's eyebrows shot up in fear. "Well, actually misss, you're scarier because–"

Finn elbowed him in the ribs. "Don't listen to him. He doesn't know what he's talking about." He shot Sithias a warning look, triggering another round of questions for Fate.

She narrowed her eyes on them. "I don't know what's going on here, but I intend to find out after I've dealt with this Biraktar situation."

She strode to the hatch and punched the button. The iris spiraled open with a low metallic groan, revealing an entire fleet of Biraktar airships hovering within the vast circumference of the colossal rings enclosing the Keep.

The flagship floated just outside the hatch and moved closer when they saw her standing inside the open doorway. Fate could easily fly onto the deck of the ship, but thought it best to wait for them to extend a gangplank. She wasn't ready to tip her hand when it came to the various powers she possessed. An element of surprise was often the most effective defense.

A few minutes later, the ship was in position, extending the plank. Fate strode across and stepped down on deck, where several rows of guards stood in a wall of protection. They moved aside in an orderly fashion, making a path for her to walk through to whomever waited on the other side.

She'd expected the king, but it was Azrael's brother, the crown prince, who stood in front of the captain's cabin. Two high ranking soldiers flanked him and he was wearing an expression that was nothing short of hostile. He and Azrael shared the same dark coloring, strong jaw line and high cheekbones, but their eyes couldn't be more different. While Azrael's were as bright and blue as the sky, the crown prince's were of such a deep brown they were nearly black.

"I have come for my brother," he demanded in careful English. "Why is he not with you?"

"He was injured during the war," Fate replied.

His brow furrowed into a forbidding scowl. "Is he dead?"

"He's alive," she was quick to say, "and in the best of care. It's just that he's been in a coma."

"I do not understand this word, coma."

"It means he's in a deep sleep he hasn't been healthy enough to wake from."

"Take me to him," the prince ordered.

"I can do that," Fate agreed, "but it really won't make any difference. He's been comatose for weeks now."

The captain's door opened and a woman stepped out. Terror iced through Fate when she saw her face. It was Azrael's mother, Mahelia. But that was impossible. Farouk killed her and had assumed her identity, just as he had with Mason. Fate had seen him shred Mahelia's skin from his beastly form and discard the husk like garbage.

Pointing at her, Fate edged away. "Get back, that's not Mahelia! That's the demon who killed my father and wounded Azrael!"

The crown prince stared at Fate like she was insane. "What nonsense is this?"

Stepping in beside the crown prince, Mahelia placed a hand on his arm to quiet him. "She speaks of the Hinn and she has every right to be cautious." Her blue gaze moved to Fate as she smiled warmly. "The Hinn came to me on the day of your wedding to my son. We battled, and I lost. The Hinn cast me down into the desert, where I was forced to survive on my wits alone until my depleted powers returned."

Too shocked to speak, Fate could only stare at her. The woman who had forced her into marriage with Azrael using whatever means of fear tactics and emotional manipulation she could. Mahelia stared calmly back, a picture of perfection, strength and beauty in the way she wore her native desert garb so easily, but with the glossy dark hair and polished skin of a queen.

The crown prince appeared truly baffled. "Why would you not speak of this to me, Mahelia? And to my father, your husband!"

"I did not wish to add to the many problems Biraktar was already facing." Her voice was steady and soothing as she spoke to him, almost hypnotic. "We had all too many injured souls to attend to, and a whole city and fleet to rebuild. As you know, I am of the Djinn, and perfectly capable of handling the worst of my kind."

"But you did not," he argued, though with less fury in his tone. "By your own words, you *lost* against the Hinn."

"I lost the last battle, but I will win the next should we meet again." Mahelia ran her hand down his arm like someone petting a dog. The gesture relaxed him more than it should and he stared off into space with a blank look in his eyes.

Mahelia left him standing there and moved toward Fate. "Now then, daughter, I would thank you to escort me to my son."

Unsure if she could believe this was truly Mahelia, and not Farouk, Fate stepped backward. Her heart thundered with distrust. Even if the story was true, and Mahelia really had survived a battle against Farouk, Fate hated her and would never be caught in this woman's sticky web again. "I'm not your daughter," she fumed.

"You married my son. That makes you my daughter."

Fate shook her head. "I don't consider us married anymore."

"Saying it does not make it so, especially in regards to an entire kingdom." Mahelia walked ahead and climbed the steps to the gangplank. When Fate continued to stand there, she turned back. "Are you coming?"

Mahelia told the subdued crown prince and his two officers to wait for her on the ship.

Fate reluctantly led her across the gangplank to the hatch. "Wait here a minute," she told Mahelia. She entered the sanctuary, stopping just inside the threshold. "Prepare yourselves, we have an unexpected guest." But Mahelia didn't wait as instructed and stepped in beside Fate.

Finn grabbed Brune's laser gun from her holster. "Don't come any closer!" he warned Mahelia.

"What's going on?" Brune asked in alarm.

The muscles in Finn's arms tensed as he inched closer with the gun aimed. "That's Farouk!"

Sithias shrieked and ran to the back of the sanctuary.

Fate stepped in front of Mahelia. "The jury's still out on that so don't shoot."

Confusion played across Finn's face, but he didn't lower the gun. "Move aside, Fate. Give me the shot!"

"The story is, she fought Farouk on the day of the wedding." Fate didn't specify anything more about the day she was coerced into marrying Azrael. As furious as she was with Finn for the lies he'd told, she didn't want to rub his face in her marriage to someone else.

Finn winced at the word wedding, a barely noticeable flinch in his eyes only she noticed. Fate glanced at Brune and continued. "Apparently, Farouk kicked her butt and tossed her into the desert with her powers depleted." She rolled her eyes. "Which is why she never showed up until now." She might not be convinced this was the truth, but killing 'Mahelia' while the Biraktar fleet awaited her return was not the wisest choice.

Sitihias inched his way out of the shadows, only to retreat again as Brune moved in beside Finn, her sword unsheathed and stance defensive as she glared at the woman. "I'm with Finn on this. If there's any chance this is Farouk, we deal with this here and now."

She charged and Fate tackled her to the floor to stop an attack that would launch a war. But not before Brune chucked something the size of a grenade at 'Mahelia' and yelled, "*Aperta Captionem Reverti!*"

Fate twisted around in horror, expecting to see 'Mahelia' blow up into gruesome bits but she was unhurt, though trapped inside an octagonal cage of bronze bars. Rising to her feet, Fate noticed the glowing binding sigils engraved all over the crisscrossed bars, quickly recognizing it as the miniature version Brune had been working on months ago.

"Oh, very cool." Fate rose and walked up to the cage with a smug smile. "So this is the expandable cage you made for Farouk. Nice work, Brune."

Brune stood and dusted off her uniform. "Thank you."

'Mahelia' waited serenely inside the cage.

Fate could hardly believe they had Farouk trapped. All the grief and anger she'd been holding in erupted with a burst of heat raging through her core. "You're going to pay for what you did to Eustace and all the others."

Finn handed her the laser gun and backed away. "Go for it."

Fate raised the gun and took aim between 'Mahelia's' blue eyes... so much like Azrael's. Her arm began to shake.

Brune swiped the gun from her hand. "It's not Farouk."

"What? It has to be, the real Mahelia's dead!" Fate looked at Finn to back her up.

"It's true," Finn confirmed, his tone dejected. "We were there when Farouk revealed himself. Mahelia never could've survived what happened. Her skin tore away from his true form. Her body was completely destroyed by Farouk's possession, the same way Mason's was."

Brune sighed impatiently. "Are you two done?" When they didn't answer, she continued. "The incantation for triggering the cage should revert Farouk back to his old, relatively harmless self." She waved a hand toward Mahelia. "Do you see the puny fox-faced monkey we used to know and tolerate?"

"No way." Fate wasn't convinced. "I think we should keep her in there until we're a thousand percent certain it's not Farouk."

"If I were the Hinn, do you think I could do this?" The edges of Mahelia's body smudged into dark misty tendrils. Her form glimmered into transparency and then dissipated entirely into hazy streaks, which sifted through the cage. Within seconds she materialized, whole and solid, outside the cage.

Fate stood ready to fight. "I've seen Farouk vanish into a stinky black fog before. So yeah, I think he could do exactly what you just did there."

Mahelia glanced at the ceiling before lowering her gaze to Fate with a soft sigh. "I meant, do you think he could escape the cage so easily?"

"It's a fair enough question," Brune agreed. "The wards on the cage would've kept Farouk locked up tight." Regardless, she gripped the hilt of her sword as she stared at Mahelia. "What are you?"

Any relief Fate felt was overshadowed by her chagrin at being in Mahelia's presence again. "She's Djinn, and capable of doing serious damage, so we all need to watch our backs around her."

"I'll second that," Finn joined in.

"And I'll third it," Sithias added as he sidled cautiously to the front of the room.

Ignoring the majority vote, Mahelia answered Brune's question. "I am also part human and not a threat, as my daughter would have you believe. I came only to retrieve my son."

"Stop saying I'm your daughter!" Anger boiled inside Fate, shooting plumes of heat to her face. The only person who could call her that was Eustace, and right now, Mahelia was blocking her from making it so her father could return to do just that–call her his daughter.

Mahelia tilted her head with sympathy in her eyes. "I am sorry you feel that way. It grieves me to see you could leave Azrael's side for even a second when he is suffering. In Biraktar, a good wife is expected to sit vigil with her ailing husband, either until he heals, or dies."

Fate laughed bitterly. "Well, we're not in Biraktar, are we?"

The feigned warmth in Mahelia's blue eyes iced over. "Oh but you will be, and soon, daughter. Very soon."

6

MEMORIES TOO FEARSOME TO FACE

"I DON'T THINK US SIDING WITH FATE against Mahelia changed her feelings toward us at all," Sithias whispered to Finn as they lagged behind Brune, Fate and Mahelia on their way to the infirmary. "She's still furiousss."

"Aye, she can hardly look at me." Finn swallowed down the ache in his chest. "I'm beginning to believe she may never forgive us for lying to her like that."

Sithias's pale-blonde brows drew together into sad darts. "She has to. She mussst, because if she doesn't, we'll be miserable for the rest of our lives."

"We deserve to be miserable. How would you feel if everyone you trusted lied about something that important?"

Sithias thought about it. "If they were truly, really sorry for lying, I'd *have* to forgive them. I'd have no other choice."

"But you probably wouldn't come around to it right away, would you? You'd need time before you could start doling out the forgiveness in any great amount." Finn clamped down on the doubt churning in his gut.

"Yesss," Sithias admitted reluctantly. "I might need a year or two, but I'd come around eventually."

Panic moved in. "A year or two? You really think it'll take that long?"

"Oh! No, not for Fate. I meant for me." Sithias smiled sheepishly.

Finn heaved a sigh of defeat and walked into the infirmary.

Fate stood next to Brune on one side of Azrael's bed while Mahelia took the other side.

"Who's she?" Jessie asked in a hushed tone as she wedged in between Fate and Brune.

"Azrael's mother." Fate spoke loud enough for the woman to hear, not caring that her tone dripped with malice.

Mahelia leaned over Azrael, running her hands slowly above his head, chest, solar plexus and then down his legs to his feet. She returned to his chest and bent to listen to his heart. A long black lock loosened from her headdress and fell against her smooth cheekbone. Obvious love and concern showed in her ageless face as she continued her examination, and Finn thought she might even be beautiful if he didn't resent the woman so deeply for how she'd treated Fate.

At last, Mahelia straightened and sat down in a chair. "I can heal Azrael, but I will need to take him back to Biraktar to do that."

"I'm glad to hear he'll be all right." The relief in Fate's tone was undeniable, cutting Finn to the quick. Her eyes suddenly filled with fear. "Wait, Azrael can't be removed from life support. It'll kill him."

Mahelia frowned with distaste at the apparatus and wires–glowing bright with multidimensional magic–strapped to Azrael's arms. "Do not concern yourself. I know what must be done to see my son safely to Biraktar."

Fate and Brune exchanged a doubtful look.

"Leave me alone with him." Mahelia stood, her frown deepening as she glanced at the med bots. "And take these machines with you."

Brune ushered them out through the door, then stopped next to Sithias. "I could use your help with the remembering spell now that I have the book we've been needing."

"Certainly." Sithias turned and left with her.

"Jess, you can come back to my room," Fate offered.

Jessie eyed Azrael longingly. "I probably shouldn't leave. I'm still waiting on my tests." A sharp look from Mahelia wiped the lovestruck expression from Jessie's face.

"On second thought, I think a night of staying up all night eating chocolate will be way more fun than hanging around here," Jessie added hastily.

Fate smiled fondly at her friend, but there was sadness in her eyes at the same time. "Sounds amazing, and exactly what I need right–"

"This will not take long, Fate," Mahelia cut in. "You are best to use the time to pack for a long stay in Biraktar. We will be leaving shortly."

Fate turned with flushed cheeks and fists clenched. "I'm not going with you."

A cold smile formed on Mahelia's lips. "If you say so."

Fate spun sharply and stormed from the room with Jessie chasing after her. Finn left Mahelia to prepare Azrael for transport and hurried after the girls.

"Fate," he called out. "Can I have a word?"

Leaving Jessie to wait for her up ahead, Fate strode back toward him. Finn's pulse raced out of control as he met the icy gaze of his sweet lass. "I hope you know how awful I've been feeling. All the lies I had to tell. You'll never know the toll it's taken on–"

"Just stop, Finn. I can't listen to how bad you feel. Nothing you can say is ever going to make up for what you did. *You* most of all, should've been honest with me." Her voice was flat and her expression blank. "Please... just leave me alone."

Her words alone sliced into him, but the complete absence of emotion in her voice felt like a spike driven into his heart. Finn leaned against the wall, barely able to breathe for the agony in his chest.

He'd lost her.

He slid to the floor, staring at nothing. He'd known the emptiness of being apart from Fate before, but this time was different, because back then he'd felt the love she had for him.

This time there was nothing. Not even hatred, which he would willingly bear because even that was at least a connection. All that was left now was a terrible void, a vast gulf between them he feared they'd never bridge.

Filled with despair, he rose to his feet and walked aimlessly down the hall. He briefly considered going to Rudwor's suite to find company in a night of excessive drinking until he was numb beyond all care. But morning would come, bringing with it a pounding headache and an emotional avalanche that would bury him in darkness–a darkness he wasn't sure he'd ever recover from if he didn't face this breakup with Fate head on.

It was best to stay busy, except there was no place to go really. It wasn't as if he was needed anywhere in particular. He'd been rendered pretty much useless ever since the Orb of Aeternitis had remade him. He couldn't fly anymore, and the Elder race runes Tove had inked onto his skin were gone.

Of course, there'd be no asking her to renew the tattoos either. She hadn't spoken to him since the war ended. Tove blamed him for the loss of Grysla and her brother, Leif.

Finn's breath constricted in his chest as the pain doubled. He too grieved the loss of the wise, compassionate tree troll who'd welcomed him into her small family circle. Leif had never liked Finn and they hadn't been friends, but he felt horrible that Tove's reunion with her brother had been short-lived. Finn hung his head. He never should've involved them in the war.

Another deep regret he would have to live with.

He came to the branch in the hallway and started down the corridor leading to his suite, then stopped. The thought of being alone in his room was more than he could take. Finn took the other hall to the library, where he knew Sithias had gone. It mattered little that he wasn't needed there. Being around people was preferable to dwelling on Fate and whether she would ever forgive him.

Finn pushed through the huge double doors and walked over to where Sithias and Brune had gathered everything they needed for the remembering spell. A pile of dried herbs, corked potions, an obsidian pillar the size of a two-foot statue and a row of wands were spread out across the surface of the huge table.

He spied the large spell book Fate had retrieved a mere hour ago. The sound of that book dropping to the floor, when she'd overheard them conspiring, still rang in his ears, sharp and hollow.

Sithias was grinding some dried leaves with a pestle. "Is thisss enough hawthorn yet?" he asked Brune. He shook his wrist with a pained grimace.

Brune looked at the tiny amount he'd already poured into the large brass bowl and then at the pile of herbs. She leaned over the open pages of the *Book of Memini Spells* and frowned. "Does that look like a bushel to you?"

Sithias huffed. "No..."

"Grind it all and then do the same with that box of berries," Brune ordered.

"*All* of it?" Sithias asked in dismay.

Finn moved in next to him and took the pestle from Sithias's weak grasp. "I'll do it," he offered.

"Why thank you, sir." Sithias raised his chin as he glanced at Brune. "That will free me up to choose the wand I'm going to use for this ssspell."

Brune jerked her head up from the book. "You're not doing the spell. I am."

Sithias grabbed his chest, like he'd been shot in the heart. "Isn't that why you asked for my help?"

"No. I wanted help with the ingredients. I would've asked Darcy to do it, but she's too busy with research." Brune returned her gaze to the pages of the book. "You're free to join her now that Finn's taking care of it."

Sithias squeaked out a cry of outrage. "I'll have you know I'm quite capable of performing this spell."

Brune didn't bother to look up. "In what world?"

Sithias stamped his foot, his long skinny arms flapping at his sides. "Well, I never!"

Two Beldereth knights entered the library. There was a hurried stride in their disciplined march as they crossed the large expanse and stopped at the table. "Rudwor requests your presence in the arena. There are riders of Eldunough who say they were not part of the uprising. He needs to know what you witnessed."

Brune nodded and stood. "You'll finish grinding the herbs?" she asked Finn.

"Aye. Anything else I can do while you're gone?"

"No, that's the last of it. Everything else is in place and ready." She started to leave before turning back to Finn. "Keep an eye on Gerdie until I get back."

"She's here?" Finn glanced around for her.

Brune pointed at the far end of the library, to an archway leading into a small wing housing galleries filled with different collections of statues and artwork. "She's playing with the doggit." She turned and followed the knights, leaving them alone to finish up.

Sithias watched her go with an offended shake of his head. "I cannot believe she doesn't trussst me to do the spell!"

Finn poured the last of the ground herbs in the bowl and reached for the box of berries. They were dried as well, but hard as pebbles, forcing him to put more muscle into it before they finally pulverized into gritty powder. "Don't take it so personally, Sithias. You should know by now what a control freak Brune is."

"Hmmph. She thinks she runs the place!"

"Well, she does actually. Brune's the resident Keep Guardian now. You know that."

"Being a guardian doesn't make her a *wizard*," Sithias muttered. He strolled over to the selection of wands and ran a spindly finger over each one. "Doesn't she know I studied under a sorceress? In fact, I was the lover of a sorceress. I learned things Brune couldn't begin to imagine!"

Finn stopped grinding for a second to look up. "I take it you mean Elsina?" The question was rhetorical and didn't require an answer. "I thought you were her spy, not her apprentice."

Sithias's posture stiffened. "Technically, yesss, but I picked up quite a lot about magic while we were together."

Finn raised a brow. "She taught you how to do spells?"

"Not exactly *taught*. I may have only watched from the sidelines, but I absorbed more knowledge that way than I ever have from reading any of these books in the library."

"Uh huh." Finn went back to grinding with even more force to finish off the berries. Having worked up a light sweat, he wiped his brow and poured the dark purple powder over the crushed sage-green hawthorn leaves. He set aside the pestle and sat down, when he noticed Sithias holding a wand. "Don't get any bright ideas," he warned.

Sithias was too busy admiring the wand to respond. "I like the weight in this one. A good solid mahogany." He tapped the thick base of the wand on the table. "My, my, my, the craftsmanship is exquisite." He stuck it out toward Finn to get a better look. "Sssee? It's fashioned with a cluster of silver wings around the crystal. Note the clarity of the stone. Not a single imperfection."

"Aye, I see it just fine, Sithias. Now put the wand down."

Sithias held it up to the light. "I can't explain it, but this wand feels like it was made for me." Holding the wand like he was someone's fairy godmother, or something along that line, he twirled around none too gracefully and then came to a stop in front of the spell book, wavering dizzily in place.

Glancing down at the page, he smiled. A sneaky smile. Before Finn could question what he was doing, Sithias tapped the bowl of ground herbs and spoke the first line of the spell. "*Memoriam quoque terribili facie prodire–*"

"Sithias! What do you think you're doing?"

But it was too late. The bowl of herbs burst into flames, igniting the same fiery light within the wand's crystal. Startled, Sithias veered back as the crystal's light left a trail of red mist shot through with glittering sparks.

"Never interrupt a spell!" Sithias admonished him. "Don't you know anything?"

Dumbfounded, Finn stared at him. "But Gerdie's not even in the room to benefit from the spell."

Sithias smiled ruefully. "Oh dear. How could I forget?" He shook the wand as if to blow out the crimson glow emanating from the crystal like he would with a match. But the wand's light only increased and the sparkling vapors thickened and pooled all around him.

"Stop it!" Sithias's command was more of a nervous quaver.

Finn moved away from the thickening mist. "Say it like you mean it!"

"I did!" The wand shook in his hand as he stared in horror.

"Speak in that other language," Finn suggested. "Maybe the magic doesn't understand English."

"Yesss, the spell is in Latin. What's the translation?"

"You're asking me?"

Sithias frantically searched through a stack of books. When he found the one he was looking for, he flipped through the pages, wild-eyed and panicked. He finally settled on a page and gulped as he scanned for the answer. "Oh! I found it!"

He waved the smoking wand with a dramatic sweep. "*Hiberent!*" he shouted, his voice more of a frightened squawk. But all that did was generate an even larger, red glittery cloud. "Oh no!"

"Oh no indeed." Finn crossed his arms. "When Brune gets back she's going to be furious with you."

Gerdie skipped back into the library with the doggit hopping beside her. When she saw the mist swirling around the table, she ran forward clapping her hands. "Look at the pretty sparkles! What is it?"

"A terrible mistake," Finn grumbled.

"Maybe not." Sithias stared at Gerdie intently. "I'll just finish the spell now that Gerdie's here."

Finn stepped in front of Gerdie. "Not on your life."

"Trussst me, I can do this." Sithias didn't sound confident at all.

Finn opened his mouth to argue, but before he could draw his next breath, shapes formed from within the scarlet mist. There were twelve of them, each one drawing in the swirl of vapors to become distinctly female shapes. Sithias's eyes widened with fear as the shapes transformed into the same woman–one with long ebony hair, fair skin, cold but beautiful features and a long gossamer gown.

"No, no, no, it can't be!" Sithias cried.

Finn was equally shocked. "Is that who I think it is?"

Sithias bobbed his head up and down with an audible gulp. "Elsina!" He turned slowly in a circle, his mouth hanging open as he stared at each duplicate woman. "H-how did this happen?"

Gerdie peeked around Finn's leg. "Who's Elsina?"

Before Finn could answer the question, the twelve Elsinas swarmed around Sithias, trapping him within a tight ring. He shrank in on himself.

"Where have you been?" one of the Elsinas demanded to know.

Another rubbed up against him, making Sithias stand ramrod straight with terror. "My bed's been miserably cold without you." She tickled him under his chin, flapping his white, wispy goatee. "Where's my muscular, handsome Mr. Romance? You know that's what I like," she crooned with a pout.

"Thisss is the r-real me," he stuttered.

"How could you leave me?" another shouted.

An Elsina slapped Sithias across the cheek. He shrieked with pain as he touched the crimson handprint on his pale cheek. "All you left was a note!" she yelled.

"You coward!" one of them sobbed. "You couldn't tell me to my face. You snuck away!"

"He's a snake!" another Elsina said. "Never trust a snake!"

One of the more affectionate Elsinas pushed the one who'd slapped

Sithias. "How dare you hit him! You know how sensitive he is," she scolded.

"And artistic," another agreed as she sidled up next to Sithias. She stroked his arm, holding tighter as he drew back in horror and tried to wriggle free. "An artist needs his space."

A fourth loving Elsina flanked Sithias from the other side. "Artists need to experience the world. That's why he left."

A fifth Elsina from the hostile team conjured a fireball and hurtled it at the Elsina draped on Sithias's arm. "Tell that to my broken heart," she seethed as she stood over the ashes of her target.

Sithias yelped and tore lose from the Elsina petting his arm. "She's armed! They're *all* armed. Run for your lives!"

"Does he mean us?" Gerdie asked Finn.

"Aye, but don't worry yourself, lassie," Finn assured her. "They're only after Sithias."

Gerdie watched the women chase Sithias through the library. "Are they gonna hurt him?"

"I don't think so." Finn scooped her up in his arms and edged toward the door. He wasn't actually certain of anything, but he trusted the five Elsinas, who still loved Sithias, to protect him from the scorned Elsinas.

Sithias raced ahead of all the dangerous sorceresses, weaving in between the many islands of tables. He faked a right, then took a left to try fooling them, but it didn't work. They quickly cornered him and his screams echoed throughout the high ceilings before he disappeared behind their flailing, grasping arms.

Several fireballs launched from the mob and a battle broke out with the protective Elsinas shielding Sithias against the angry ones. Two of his protectors disintegrated into piles of ash next to his feet. With a frightened shriek, he morphed into a dragonfly and zipped high above the chaos as they hurled their deadly fireballs at each other.

The scary fight was over within a matter of seconds. Smoke drifted on the air above the ashen remains of each Elsina Sithias had mistakenly conjured.

The buzz of wings whisked past Finn's ear and Sithias landed on his shoulder. "Whew! That took some clever maneuvering on my part to avoid dying."

Annoyed with his friend, Finn swatted Sithias away and set Gerdie down. "You survived out of sheer dumb luck and nothing more."

Sithias hovered in front of him for a second before his form suddenly elongated and returned to his previous form. "Maybe so," he agreed ruefully.

Brune entered the library and stopped just outside the door when she found them huddling near the entrance. She glanced around suspiciously. "I smell smoke." Her gaze fixed on Sithias. "What did you do?"

Gerdie smiled up at her sister, her brown eyes twinkling with excitement. "There were a whole bunch of pretty ladies chasin' Sithias around the library. They were mad at him and tryin' to kill him. But then they–"

Sithias guffawed loudly, like he'd heard the funniest joke ever. "Leave it to a child to come up with the craziest things." He flapped a long skinny arm dismissively in Gerdie's direction and inched toward the door.

Brune's eyes turned to angry slits. "Sithias... you tried doing the spell, didn't you?"

He slumped with shame. "I only read the first line."

Brune marched over to the table. A quick survey of the red smoke wafting from the bowl of scorched herbs and a glance at the first line of the spell was all it took to understand what had taken place. "Do you even know what the first line says?"

"Not exactly," Sithias murmured.

Brune scowled at him. "*Memories too fearsome to face come forward.*"

Sithias nodded like he should've known. "Sssay no more. It's all making sense now."

Brune huffed. "Go get me more hawthorn leaves and berries. And this time you'll be the one grinding them. Hear me?"

"Thunderingly ssso." Sithias lurched for the exit and disappeared behind the doors.

"I take it I'm no longer needed." Finn patted Gerdie on the head and moved to leave.

"Finn." Brune's voice had lost its sharp edge. "Thank you for keeping Gerdie safe."

He gave Brune a friendly salute and left abruptly, his spirits lower than ever. Apparently, the destroyer of destroyers was only good at babysitting anymore. That simply wouldn't do. Not with Mahelia making threats to force Fate into returning to Biraktar. He needed his powers back if he was going to help her make a stand against Mahelia.

Whether Fate wanted his help or not.

7
RADIOACTIVE

JESSIE FLOPPED INTO A CHAIR and propped her feet up on the curved arm. "Are you going to tell me what you and Finn were fighting about back there? I only just saw you both together a few hours ago and everything seemed perfectly copasetic between you. What the heck happened?"

Fate sat down in the chair next to the box Brune had given her. "He's been lying to me, Jess." The rage ignited, heating within her solar plexus. "They've *all* been lying to me."

Jessie dropped her feet on the floor and sat straight. "About what?"

Grief dampened the fury somewhat as Fate's gaze landed on the bestiary lying open to the picture of the black unicorn. "Eustace is... gone." She couldn't say the actual word. Not when there was still hope. The 'D' word was too final.

Jessie stared back in confusion. "What do you mean gone? Where'd he go?"

Fate swallowed the lump in her throat. "The Eustace you chatted with today was Sithias."

Jessie blinked in silence for a few seconds. "Are you saying Sithias was pretending to be Eustace? Why would he do that?"

The flames of anger blazed hot, scorching Fate's insides, rising to her chest. "Because Farouk killed Eustace months ago." Molten heat poured up her neck, making her hair fly around her face.

Jessie's face went slack. "Eustace... died?"

Fate clenched her fists and nodded.

"Oh no." Tears brimmed in Jessie's eyes, but her shock had turned to fear because she stood and backed away from Fate.

"Why are looking at me like that?"

"Because your eyes are glowing white. You look radioactive! And there's enough heat coming off you to melt my face off." Jessie hugged herself as she frantically looked at the door. She didn't move though. Fate was standing between her and the exit. "I'm so sorry about Eustace. I loved him too. He was like family to me, but please don't take it out on me. I-I know we had our differences when I was Kaliena's personal assassin and I did horrible things to you."

Fate sucked in a deep breath to cool her fury. Her best friend was terrified of her, looking at her like she was a monster. Feeling awful about giving Jessie such a fright, Fate allowed the rise of shame to fully dowse the fire raging inside her. "Sorry, Jess. I really didn't mean to scare you like that. Please, sit back down."

Jessie dropped into the chair, more out of obedience than choice.

"Relax," Fate told her. "I'm cooled off."

Jessie nodded nervously.

"Am I still looking radioactive?" Fate asked.

"No."

"See? I'm fine. You can stop digging your nails into the arms of the chair now."

Jessie let her arms hang stiffly at her sides, staring back at Fate like someone cornered by a rabid dog.

"You can leave if you want," Fate offered sadly. "I wouldn't be upset if you did."

Jessie's gaze traveled to the door. Fate was certain she'd take the opening, but she surprised her by remaining in her seat. "No, I'll stay."

Fate let out a shaky sigh of relief. "Well, now that you've glimpsed the dark side of my otherwise cool powers, what do you think?"

"That I never *ever* want to piss you off." A nervous smile formed on Jessie's lips. "And that we probably shouldn't talk about Finn for awhile."

"Agreed. We'll focus on more positive things, like bringing Eustace back to life." Fate turned the book around so Jessie could see the picture. "And I'm going to do it with this."

Jessie leaned forward. "With a unicorn. A black spooky looking unicorn?"

"Yup, Brune says it has the ability to make what's dead alive again."

Jessie made a face. "As in necromancy?"

"It's not the same."

"But–"

"Trust me, this isn't that."

Jessie nodded. "Okay. I want to help then. I've never been much for research, but now that I'm back to being ordinary again, I don't have much else to offer."

"Yes! I'll love you forever if you can help with that. Have you seen how thick these books are?"

Jessie looked at the four large tomes and stacks of scrolls with dread. "Yeah, not exactly quick reads."

"It'll go faster with the two of us working on this."

Jessie settled back in the chair. "What about your unpleasant mother-in-law? She seems to have other plans for how you're going to be spending your time. Then again, I suppose you could pull that radioactive card out of your pocket and send her packing."

Fate lifted her foot and pointed at the soul ring. "You're forgetting about this ball and chain strapped to my ankle. Believe me, if I could fight this, I would. But I've experienced how this thing overrides my powers enough times to know I'm at Mahelia's mercy. What's worse is, she knows it too."

"What was all that arguing with Azrael's mother if you've already given up?"

"There's no way I'm going to kowtow to Mahelia. I might've been throwing empty threats at her, but I can at least make her life uncomfortable if she's going to insist on my presence."

"What about saving Eustace? Is that all of a sudden on the back burner?"

"No way, I'm taking all this stuff with me. If I have to sit vigil next to Azrael's sick bed, then I'm going to have my nose in these books and make good use of my time."

"Wait, how am I supposed to help with the research then?"

"You'll go with me."

Jessie stared back, surprised and hesitant.

"Unless... you don't want to." Fate's need to have Jessie with her during the most difficult time of her life intensified. The thought of being without a single friend in Biraktar left her more hollowed out than she already was.

"I'm not sure I should." Jessie's gaze dropped to the floor.

"Why?"

"Because I'm normal now, completely ordinary. I don't have super strength and speed anymore, or invincible armor to protect me. If there's any trouble, I won't be able to do anything about it. I'm weak and helpless in this world."

Fate reached out and laid her hand over Jessie's. "You have me to protect you. I promise, I'd never let anything bad happen to you."

Jessie shook her head. "You can't make that kind of promise and you know it."

Fate did know. She certainly hadn't been able to prevent Jessie from being enslaved by Kaliena. Was she being selfish for wanting Jessie by her side? Of course she was. The best thing she could do for her friend was let her go.

"Jess, do you want to go home?" Fate's chest tightened as she waited for

Jessie's answer.

"As in all the way back to Seattle?"

Fate nodded.

Jessie stared past her as she considered the question. Time agonizingly stretched out. Unable to sit still a second longer, Fate stood and walked over to the large wooden wardrobe holding her favorite personal belongs. She pulled out her desert garb and laid the items out at the bottom of the bed.

"It's settled then, you're going home," Fate announced, doing her best to sound cheerful.

Jessie stood as if in a daze and started toward the door. She stopped with her hand on the doorknob and looked at Fate. "What's Biraktar like?"

"It's beautiful, actually. The streets are paved in gold with towers built in solid jewel-toned glass that glitters in the sun as the city floats within puffy clouds of ranemist high above the desert."

"The city floats in the sky?"

"Held up by the ranemist," Fate confirmed.

"What's ranemist?"

The horrible memory of Moulghazel being slaughtered by Kaliena's fleet flashed in Fate's mind, but she pushed it aside to hold the cheery smile she was forcing for Jessie's benefit. "The ranemist is made by a sacred sky whale, and it's what keeps Biraktar from sinking into the hungry desert and makes the Biraktar ships fly. The ranemist is what gives life to the people of Biraktar." Those were Azrael's words, but there was no better way to describe how vital Moulghazel and the ranemist was to his people.

Jessie leaned against the door. "Sounds fascinating."

"More fascinating than Seattle?"

"I'm thinking... definitely." Excitement sparked anew in Jessie's eyes, but sadness quickly moved in to dull her gaze. "I do miss my parents though, especially my mom. She must be out of her mind with worry about me." She covered her face to stifle a faint sob.

Fate crossed the room and hugged her friend. "Shh, it's okay, Jess. You're forgetting about the ginormous time difference between here and home."

Jessie pulled back to look at her. "Time difference?"

"You know about this," Fate reminded her.

"Pretend like I don't."

Fate stared at Jessie with concern. Maybe her memory wasn't as intact as previously thought. "When we were at gran's bookstore, I told you I'd been gone for six months from the time I'd left the book signing. But you said it had only been a few hours since I'd left Seattle. That's how differently time runs here, so there's no need to worry. You haven't been gone nearly as long, so it's safe to say your parents think you're still partying at the bookstore right now."

"Oh yeah, and I remember telling mom I'd go home with you and Eustace to spend the night since I didn't know how late the whole thing would go. That means I've probably got a decade here before they'd ever notice I was missing."

She wiped her eyes dry and smiled. "Whew, I completely forgot about all that! I suppose that's because my strongest memory is thinking you were totally batty back then when you mentioned the whole time-warp thing."

Fate recoiled. "Ouch. Call me nuts, bananas or crackers, I don't care. Anything but *batty*. Jeez, you know how I feel about that awful nickname the entire student body stuck me with. I swear, if it ends up in the school yearbook, I'll–"

"Sorry, sorry! Blame it on Kaliena. She must've scrambled my brain." Jessie smiled mischievously. "But that whole mention of nuts and bananas has me jonesin' for a hot fudge banana sundae topped with candied nuts."

"Ooh, I could munch on that." Fate followed her friend back into the sitting area and made herself comfortable while Jessie worked her magic with the food simulator. "How close do you think you can come to the yumminess of the real thing? Should we make a bet?"

"You'll lose." Jessie smiled smugly as she typed in the description and turned each dial to whatever mysterious specifications she somehow knew to choose. Pressing the last button, she glanced back at Fate. "Get ready to wipe the drool off your chin."

The machine dinged and Jessie opened the door. Her smile vanished as she stooped to have a look. "Hmm, I must be off my game. This looks like baby food slop." Pinching a nut between her fingers, she tasted it and made a face. "Ew, that's not candied nut. I think I made dirt."

"Darn." Fate sighed. "I was really looking forward to slobbering all over myself."

Jessie removed the dish of runny yellow and brown mush. "I'll try again. Using the simulator is just like making pancakes. The first pancake's always a throwaway because it comes out burnt and ugly until you get the temperature right." She returned to adjusting the dials, but before she could hit the 'make' button; there was a demanding knock on the door.

Fate's granny-faced chamber bot emerged from her closet and tottered across the room.

"Tell whomever it is I'm asleep and not to be disturbed," Fate instructed.

She and Jessie kept quiet while the chamber bot repeated the order.

"I do not care what she says, wake her." It was Mahelia's voice.

"I cannot," the chamber bot replied. "Thank you for visiting. I will deliver your message when Fate wakes."

The door slammed into the chamber bot, throwing Fate's mechanical granny off balance before the bot could stop the door from hitting the wall with a loud bang. Mahelia stormed into the room, her face stone cold as she laid eyes on Fate lounging comfortably in a chair. "Azrael has been moved onto the ship. Pack your belongings. We are leaving."

Fate stood. "I'm almost done. Go back to the ship. We'll be out shortly."

Mahelia frowned. "We? If it is Finn you are referring to, he cannot come."

"It's not. I'm bringing Jessie with me."

The quick glance she gave Jessie was cursory at best. "Fine, bring your slave. We have plenty of well-trained servants to attend to you in Biraktar, but if you insist on bringing your own, you may do so."

"Jee thanks, you're too generous." Fate clenched her jaw.

Jessie's mouth fell open as she watched Mahelia leave. "Slave? Why didn't you correct her? I am not about to start wiping your—"

"Don't worry. I'm not going to start ordering you around. Believe me, it's best if you're unimportant and basically invisible to Mahelia. She'd have a major problem with you if she knew you were Kaliena's personal assassin and helped with the slaughter of her sacred sky whale and the destruction of more than half of Biraktar's fleet."

"Well, don't tell her."

"She won't hear it from me," Fate promised. "I was more worried about you getting too comfortable around Mahelia and spilling your guts, as you so often do if you're upset. Or drunk on chocolate."

"Oh please." Jessie scowled at Fate, but finished with a shrug. "Okay, I admit I've been known to over-share."

"Glad we got that straightened out." Fate changed into her desert garb. After cinching the straps holding her quiver and saber, she wrapped an airy white cotton scarf around her neck and tucked it inside the neckline of her lightweight hooded jacket.

"So where are my cool desert duds?" Jessie asked.

"I'll have to outfit you after we board. For now, we'll just stop by your suite and grab your usual uniform and fighting gear on our way to the ship." Fate grabbed the books and scrolls Brune had given her, stuffed them inside her pack, slung it over her shoulder and grabbed her bow.

"You seem weirdly at ease with all this. Aren't you at all tense about being ordered around and held prisoner by that horrible woman?"

Fate thought about it a minute, surprised by how calm she'd become. "Hmm, I know I should be nervous about this, but to be honest, I'm glad to be getting away from here. Away from Finn and Sithias and everyone who lied to me about Eustace." The fire flared in her belly, shooting through her veins.

Jessie stepped backward. "Wow, you really *are* furious with them."

"More than you could ever know. And that's why I need 'my slave' along." Fate clarified with air quotes. "You know, to keep me from going radioactive."

"Got it. Now back to Mahelia. What if she keeps you from going after the unicorn to save Eustace?"

Cold anger triggered a determined smile as Fate strode to the door. "She can't stop me. Nobody can."

8
REJECTION AT EVERY TURN

FINN ENTERED THE KEEP GARDEN and followed the path winding through the thickest foliage. He breathed deep of the rich dewy scent of earth mixed with the sweetness of exotic blooms perfuming the air. The tension he'd been locked into ever since Fate had made it clear she wanted nothing to do with him lifted ever so slightly. He'd almost forgotten how soothing the garden was on his nerves, but spending time in nature wasn't why he'd come.

He was looking for Tove. After asking some of the Beldereth knights he'd seen her keeping company with of late, he was told she should be in the garden. So far, there was no sign of her.

He thought about calling out, but quickly decided against it. She'd only escape being in his presence before he caught up with her. He was no longer a match for her speed, but he hoped to beg her forgiveness and ask if she would consider inking him with the Elder race runes again.

Soft rustlings to each side of the path indicated the presence of the small, scurrying creatures inhabiting the garden. He wasn't familiar with the fauna in the garden the way he was with the animals living in the highlands back home. These were especially shy and elusive. He'd only glimpsed a few of them during his more frequent visits to the garden, when he'd first arrived in the Keep. Their leafy skin and twig like limbs blended too easily with the surrounding flora.

The appearance of several large mushrooms signaled the outer edge of the giant mushroom forest. Finn immediately recognized the small clearing carpeted with blooming moss. Arching fern fronds and dense thickets enclosed the space. He walked over to the tallest mushroom and kneeled down to touch the soft dewy moss, his blood pumping hard as he remembered the one and only time he'd made love to Fate, here in this exact place.

The memory of her bare skin against his, flushed him with heat. The sight of her lying beneath him with her hair splayed over the moss and eyes shining with unbridled passion had been dizzying. Never had he felt more connected to her than in that one precious span of time. The merging of their bodies had been the very fusion of their hearts and souls into one.

But Fate didn't share the memory of their union. She would never know the elation of finally being truly and completely together. If she had even an inkling of the most sacred moment of their relationship, there would be no way she could turn her back on him. Because the love they'd expressed together would be etched on her soul, just as it was with him. That alone would override her present inability to forgive him.

Fighting against the agony clawing inside, Finn stood. "Don't give up, boyo. You'll win her back. You have to."

He strode away from the clearing, stepping back onto the stone path. The further he went, the larger the mushrooms became. Many of them grew in clumps, looming over him as tall as mighty oaks. The ridged underside of their expansive caps glowed with soft bioluminescent light in hues of azure and green.

As Finn moved deeper through the mushroom forest, he decided Tove wasn't in the garden. He started to turn back when he heard a muffled *thwap* up ahead. He crept forward, stopping behind a stand of palm fronds blooming with red flowers that smelled like boiled cabbage. Wrinkling his nose, he parted the fronds slightly for a better look.

Tove drew the string of her bow back, her gaze focused on a group of hanging vines, all of which had arrows spliced through each slender tendril. She was dressed in a sleeveless tunic and leather breeches. Elder race runes marked her face and bare arms. Her long ebony hair was tied back from her fine elfin features. The glow from the canopy of mushrooms cast her olive skin with a blue-green sheen. Her beauty had always been otherworldly to him, and still stirred a special place in his heart.

Finn stepped to one side, but his foot slipped on the moist earth. Grunting as he caught himself from falling, the sound disrupted Tove's concentration, sending her arrow flying straight past the thin target of another vine.

She turned her head in his direction, squinting into the dim light. "Finn. What are you doing here?" The hateful edge in her voice was plain.

Finn pushed through the palms. "Looking for you."

Tove drew her knife, marched over to the vines and sliced through the tendrils holding her arrows. "We have nothing to say to each other."

"That's not true," Finn argued. "I understand your feelings, but we're family, and families work things out."

"My family is dead, and you know nothing of how I feel. I have nothing left." Tove's fury shifted the green of her eyes to a shade that was almost black.

"Tove, you have me. I've given you the space you've needed since the war ended, but you have to know I'm here for you. *Always.*"

She laughed harshly as she ripped the arrows from each vine. "I don't have you. Not since you left me for Fate. And when you finally showed your face again, you asked us to lay our lives on the line." Her hand shook as she returned the arrows to her quiver. "You might as well have killed my mother and brother with your own hands."

Finn took her by the wrist, turning her to face him. "How can you say that? I mourn their loss every bit as much as you do."

Tove jerked her wrist free of his grip. "You'll never know the pain of what I've lost. *Never.*"

"That's where you're wrong. I've lost an entire life filled with people I love. People who don't exist, except on paper. I have no home in Scotland. No past that's real. My memories of my family are all based on fiction. Yet I mourn every single one of them, even though I know they were never truly real. But I've learned to value the relationships I've built here. You and Grysla, and Rudwor and Sithias, and..."

"Fate," she finished for him.

"Aye, and Fate. Please believe me when I say you all mean more to me than I could ever describe. I consider each of you my family."

Tove's expression hardened all the more. "None of that matters to me. I will never forgive you for involving my family in your war."

"It wasn't my war, it was–"

"Fate's."

"No, you have it all wrong. It was everyone's war. Kaliena had to be stopped."

Tove slung her quiver over her shoulder and picked up her bow. "The war is over. *We* are over. Do not speak to me ever again."

"Don't do this, Tove. Please forgive–" But she was gone in a blur of motion before he could finish his sentence.

More hopeless than ever, Finn trudged out of the garden. He was barely through the door when Sithias came running up to him, flushed and out of breath.

"Fate's leaving!" He turned back in the direction he'd come, gesturing for Finn to follow. "Hurry, Mahelia's ship is about to disembark!"

Finn's heart pounded out a sudden burst of panic. Fate was leaving without so much as a single word to him? Catapulting into a run, he passed Sithias like he was standing still and skidded around the sharp corners of the long corridors, banging into the walls as he did so.

He burst through the door of the sanctuary to find Brune standing by the open hatch. Finn rushed across the room, stopping to hold onto the rounded edges of the opening as the gangplank withdrew. "Stop them!" he rasped, too out of breath to say the words with any real volume.

Brune shook her head. "Sorry, the wheels are in motion. There's nothing I can do."

Finn stared helplessly at the retreating royal flagship as the whole of the Biraktar fleet turned and followed. Jessie, Mahelia and the crown prince stood next to Fate on the stern of the ship. The desert sun blazed down, lighting the red highlights in Fate's hair as the wind whipped her wavy locks behind her back. He waited for her to turn around. To take one last look at what she was leaving behind.

Seconds dragged out into minutes as he watched her go, face forward with nary a glance over her shoulder, until at last, he lost sight of her altogether and the entire fleet became dots against the blue expanse of the horizon.

The strength in Finn's limbs abandoned him. Gritting his teeth, he locked his knees to hold himself upright.

A hand rested on his shoulder. "Don't torture yourself any longer, sssir." Sithias's voice was little more than a sad whisper. "Come away from there."

Finn turned stiffly away from the empty sky. "We can't just let this happen. We have to go after her."

Brune frowned. "And do what, besides get yourself killed for the effort?"

"Mahelia forced Fate against her will," Finn argued. "I won't stand by and let that evil woman get away with this. Not again."

"Fate agreed to go." Brune let out a weary sigh. "I tried to talk her out of it, but she wouldn't listen. She was eerily at peace with the whole thing. In fact, I had the distinct impression she would've done anything to be anywhere but here."

"With me," Finn added.

"And me. You're not the only guilty party here," Sithias reminded him.

"I'm just as unhappy about this latest development," Brune said. "Fate at least solved one major problem for us. We no longer have the Biraktar army threatening to blast us out of existence."

Brune made her way to the door before stopping to look at them. "I'm counting on you two not to do anything rash. Use your heads and realize maybe it's best Fate's gone for now. She'll have time to cool down without the constant reminders of losing Eustace to trip the switch on that ticking time bomb she's become."

Sithias worried his hands together as he watched the door close behind her. "I hate to say it, but I have to agree with–"

"Don't say it."

"But–"

Finn held up a hand. "If you think I'm going to let Fate go to Biraktar all alone, then you don't know me at all."

"She's not alone. Jessie's with her."

"What can Jessie do to protect her?"

Sithias opened his mouth, but nothing came out.

"That's right, nothing. Jessie can't keep Fate from harm now that she's back to normal."

"Fate's not exactly harmless though. Or powerless for that matter." Sithias muttered the last part. "After all, we've both ssseen what she's capable of if pushed."

"Do I really need to remind you that losing herself to Ananke is the very reason we lied to Fate in the first place?" Finn paced back and forth.

"No you don't." Sithias sighed. "You're right, we have to do something. But what? Do you have any ideas?"

Finn came to a stop in front of Sithias. "Aye. You and I will go to Biraktar and bring Fate home."

Sithias visibly quaked. "How? I can't fly a ship. Can you?"

"We don't need a ship. You'll get us there with the Words of Making."

"Uh... I suppose I could. A simple trip from one place to another shouldn't backfire on us."

Finn smiled for the first time in a long while. "Good, but before we do that, I'm going to need my powers back. I won't be any more helpful than Jessie if I have to go without the Elder race runes."

Sithias squirmed with obvious discomfort. "Oh, I don't know, sir. That'sss much trickier than a straightforward trip to Biraktar. Wasn't Tove the one who inked the runes on you? You should ask her."

"I did. She refused."

"Oh."

Finn waited for Sithias to give in to his request, but when he remained silent, his anger erupted. "Are you actually going to deny me?"

His voice came out like a vicious growl, which made Sithias jump. Finn regretted his tone immediately. "I'm sorry, my friend. I didn't mean to lose my temper. I had no right to speak to you like that. I'm at my wit's end... I feel useless to Fate without the Elder race runes."

"It's all right, sir. I understand."

Finn sat down in the nearest chair, tired but still determined. "Let's plan to leave tomorrow at first light. I'll need the rest of the day to pack my gear and weapons. I'm sure I can get Brune to supply me with some gadgets to give me some sort of advantage, without letting on that we're going on a trip."

Sithias nodded apologetically. "I think that would be bessst, sir. I'll go and gather my things as well."

Rejection at every turn.

Leaning back into the chair, Finn closed his eyes, listening to the shuffle of Sithias's departing footsteps. As soon as he knew he was alone, he looked out at the sprawling desert beyond the open hatch. "I won't give up on you, Fate," he whispered. "Please don't give up on me."

9
AN UNBREAKABLE SPELL

THE GOLDEN SPIRES OF BIRAKTAR shimmered into view. Fate had to shield her eyes against the sun flashing off the glass, jewel-toned towers. Jessie leaned against the ship's railing and gasped at the marvel of the floating city surrounded by a sea of thick, swirling clouds.

"Unbelievable," Jessie muttered. "The city really does float."

"Did you think I was making it up to get you to come?"

"You have been known to exaggerate." Jessie elbowed her playfully. "Wow, that's one of the most beautiful places I've ever seen."

"True, Biraktar is spectacular," Fate agreed, her dread building as the fleet spread out around the lower docks, while the flagship climbed to the landing dock on one of the upper tiers of the palace.

Mahelia and the crown prince emerged from the captain's suite and signaled for Fate and Jessie to join them on the main deck below. Two guards followed, carrying Azrael on a stretcher between them.

Fate took her proper place beside him as they walked across the wide gangplank. Mahelia had made it quite clear that her need for fresh air would be brief after being cooped up in the suite silently sitting vigil next to Azrael and his mother for the whole trip. Five minutes was definitely brief.

A huge staff of servants, otherwise known as slaves, stood in lines off to one side as the king and the entire royal family, comprised of Azrael's brothers, their many wives and brood of children, walked out onto the deck to greet them. The king's face grew stern when his gaze fell on Fate and then onto his unconscious son.

Ignoring his open dislike of her, Fate lifted her chin proudly. But she quailed on the inside. How had she thought being in Biraktar would give her a respite from her grief and anger? Her spirits sank deeper into the mire. Foolish to think she could outrun her feelings. The pain of losing her father would follow her wherever she went. The same went for the sting of betrayal by Finn and Sithias.

They paraded through a cavernous chamber of ornate, gilded walls that led to a winding staircase. After climbing several flights, they entered a suite; bare of the previous opulence. A wall of doors stood open to the fresh air and a terrace overlooking the city. Filmy curtains fluttered in the breeze. Palms and flowering plants added color to the otherwise sand colored walls. Several servants dressed in white stood silently by, each staring straight ahead, awaiting any order uttered by their masters.

Azrael was laid onto a narrow bed placed in the center of the room. Mahelia covered him with a soft white linen sheet and sat down in a chair next to him. She glanced at Fate, indicating that she take the only other seat available next to her.

The king and his sons entered a few minutes later. He stood over Azrael, glaring down at his son's peaceful, sleeping expression as though he should wake because the king willed it. Azrael's brothers gathered around the foot of the bed. They too glared, but not at Azrael. Fate was their target.

Feeling very much alone, she glanced around for Jessie, realizing with a start that she wasn't in the room. As much as she wanted to know where her best friend was, this wasn't the time to inquire. Dropping her gaze to her lap, Fate fidgeted with her hands, hoping Azrael's father and brothers would soon leave.

The sharp voice of his father cut through the silence. "What did his hateful wife do to my son?"

Fate tightened every muscle, willing herself not to openly react to the insult. None of them knew she wore a transmodulator in her ear and could understand their native tongue. Unlike the last time she'd been held captive in the palace, when they'd purposely excluded her, knowing she only spoke English.

She quelled a smile. Let them assume she remained ignorant to their words. It would undoubtedly work to her advantage if they felt safe to speak freely in front of her.

"Azrael was injured in the war, my husband." Mahelia spoke in a tone even more soothing than the one she'd used to subdue the crown prince upon their arrival at the Keep. This time her voice was musical and entrancing.

Fate chanced a sideways glance at Mahelia. Her skin was softly illuminated with an inner light. If Fate didn't know better, she would say Mahelia looked like an angel. A being come down from heaven.

But Fate did know better. Mahelia was wrapping her Djinn illusions around the king, because his dark scowl had softened into love and trust. The brothers weren't smitten in the same way as their father, but their demeanor definitely eased.

"Have patience," Mahelia crooned. "Azrael is in my care now and he will wake soon enough."

The king smiled peacefully. "Very well." He gestured to the family to follow and they all took their leave, all within a few minutes of weaving her spell.

Fate relaxed her rigid posture. "What was all that about?"

Mahelia looked at her with a raised brow. "I think you know."

Fate played dumb. "Mmm, not really. It was all gibberish to me." She wasn't about to let on she'd understood a single word. Nor would she thank Mahelia for saving her from certain death for being the 'hateful wife' of the king's wounded son. She was the innocent in this. It wasn't her fault Azrael had forced her into marrying him. She certainly wasn't to blame for the damage Farouk had done to his heart.

Mahelia narrowed her gaze on Fate.

Time to deflect. "I will say you have a way with your husband. Does he know you're part Djinn and able to manipulate his feelings with your witchy ways?"

"He knows what I am."

"And he's fine with that?"

"Of course. He considers my considerable powers an asset to our kingdom."

"Except that he doesn't know when he's being snowed over whenever it suits you."

The bright sunny room suddenly darkened with shadows. Long, writhing shadows that emanated from Mahelia. "Do you think it suits me to save you from harm? If I did not need *you* to save Azrael, I would have allowed my husband to drop you into the desert, where if the fall did not kill you, the teeth beneath the sands certainly would."

Fate ignored the nasty remark. "You think I can save Azrael? If I could, don't you think I would've by now?"

"No, I do not. I think you have been hoping for Azrael's death so that you would be free of his soul ring. All so you could return to that peasant boy you say you love."

"First off, Finn is not a peasant." She was surprised by how quickly she came to his defense, considering how upset she was with him. "Secondly, I would *never* wish for Azrael to die. I care about him too much for that."

This seemed to appease Mahelia because the slithering shadows receded, allowing the sunlight to wash the room with golden hues again. "I am pleased to hear that." She stood and walked over to a table filled with dried herbs, bottles of various colored liquids, as well as bowls of gemstones and crystals. Mahelia returned with something in a silk bag, which she quickly untied.

When Fate spied the contents, she held up her hands and shook her head. "No way. We're *not* doing this again."

Mahelia grabbed Fate's arm, her fingers digging into her flesh as she shoved the tablet with its pliant wax surface into her hand, followed by a rolled sheet of gold and a stylus. "*You will.*" The outer edges of her body distorted, wavering in and out of view as those threatening shadows emerged again. "Refuse once more, and you will feel the wrath of a desperate mother's love for her son."

Fate nodded. "All right, I'll do it. But only on one condition."

The shadows flared from Mahelia. "There will be no conditions! You will write what I tell you to write."

Fury blazed hot and mercurial inside Fate. The desire to test her own wild, unpredictable power against Mahelia's was becoming dangerously close to irresistible. She needed Jessie there to calm her down. Her bestie was the only one in her life who didn't make her want to go berserk.

"I'll do what you want, Mahelia." Fate seethed through clenched teeth. "Just get me my servant."

"We have no need for others to be here."

"Refuse me, and you'll feel *my* wrath." The inhuman growl in Fate's voice as she spat Mahelia's words back at her triggered unexpected fear on the woman's face.

"I will return in a moment."

Mahelia left the room while Fate focused on deep breaths. She looked at Azrael. "I really hate her," she grumbled. "But I'm happy you have your mother back, Azrael." Her throat tightened. "I know how happy I'd be to have my dad back."

Fate blinked back unwanted tears as Mahelia ushered Jessie into the room.

"You asked for me?" Jessie's frown and probing gaze showed the worry on her face.

"I need... my medicine." Fate kept her expression blank, the way she'd seen Mahelia, whenever she spoke to her servants.

"What ails you?" Mahelia asked.

You. Everything, Fate wanted to say. "A sour stomach and a massive case of heartburn."

"I have tonics to ease such conditions."

"No, not like my medicine. This stuff is the bomb. Works in seconds," Fate assured her.

Jessie didn't move, panic formed in her eyes knowing she didn't have any medicine and didn't know what to do.

"Did you forget where you packed it?" Fate asked.

Jessie nodded.

Fate huffed with feigned annoyance. "Check my satchel." She rolled her eyes as Jessie hurried over to Fate's gear, moving aside her sword, quiver and bow to get to the canvas bag lying underneath. "She's not usually this unorganized. I chalk it up to having to leave in such a rush."

Mahelia's stare was impatient. "She can be replaced."

"Thanks, but no thanks. I keep her out of sentiment more than anything else."

Jessie coughed. Loudly.

Fate looked over her shoulder, mouthing a silent apology to Jessie. "Have you found them yet?"

Jessie squinted at her, a sign she was peeved. She'd nearly emptied the bag, when she looked inside a container, openly surprised by the contents. "I believe I have. How many do you need this time?"

"Four should do it." Fate was getting a little hungry.

Jessie promptly delivered Fate's 'medicine' and dropped four chocolate truffles in her palm. "Enjoy."

Fate sighed. "As much as I can." Popping one in her mouth, she closed her eyes as the rich, dark chocolate melted over her tongue. Fate looked at Jessie and smiled. "It's working already."

Jessie's forced smile spoke volumes. Besides having to play the dutiful servant, her friend had discovered Fate had hoarded the chocolate truffles Sithias had given her in the hopes of being forgiven.

Heat warmed Fate's cheeks at having been caught in a fib. She'd told Jessie she'd thrown the chocolates out. But how could she? Sithias was a master at writing up the most delicious truffles with the Words of Making. She'd often tried to do the same, but could never come close. When it came to chocolate his descriptive skills had surpassed her own.

"May we begin?" Mahelia's patience had run out. The light in the room had dimmed again.

Dread turned her stomach, and Fate's appetite vanished. Taking dictation from Mahelia was perilous at best. She remembered the woman's doomsday solutions for ending the war. Death and destruction were all Mahelia knew.

But then again, it was Farouk she'd been dealing with at the time.

Maybe this could work after all. She handed the remaining three truffles to Jessie. "One was enough." She winked at Jessie. "Toss these back."

"Trust me, I will." Her friend retreated to the edge of the room with truffles in hand.

Fate smoothed the gold sheet over the waxed side of the tablet and held the stylus. "You know, I really don't need your alchemized gold sheet to amplify the Words of Making. I can do this without the extra magic."

Fate's thoughts slammed back to her most successful use of the Words of Making. There had been no fancy writing tools. She'd used Kaliena's blood to spell out the words to save Finn from utter destruction. Her heart throbbed out a dull ache at the memory of how close she'd come to losing him. And yet she couldn't see past her rage to forgive him. She was literally torn in half.

Mahelia shook her head. "You will follow my direction."

"Fine. We'll do it your way." Fate agreed more out of wanting to stop thinking about Finn, than from the irritation of arguing with Mahelia.

Mahelia sat next to Fate, but her attention was on Azrael. Tension tightened the corners of her blue eyes as she leaned forward and placed a hand on his arm. A mother's love weakened even the strongest of women.

A father's love was no different. How many times had Fate tortured Eustace with the same worry and fear? Too many. If only she could go back in time to save him from what she'd put him through.

She made a silent pledge do better when she had him back.

Mahelia spoke. Her voice quavered with emotion as she recited the words, surprising Fate as she inscribed them onto the gold sheet. When Mahelia finished the dictation, Fate stared at the moving message for a few seconds. This was going to work. She knew it deep down. Just as she'd known when Sithias had recited the words that had peacefully ended the war.

Tears pricked Fate's eyes as she read the words aloud. Slowly. Lovingly. "*My Azrael, the boy with eyes brighter than the bluest sky and a smile more radiant than the sun, I remove the dagger piercing your grieving heart, and make you whole and strong, by pouring all the love I have to give, from my heart to yours.*"

Fate held her breath as she watched Azrael's face. His chest rose and fell just as before, but with greater movement. His breathing was no longer shallow and barely visible. His smooth brow furrowed as he moved his arms up over his head and yawned.

Mahelia and Fate stood at the same time, each moving closer to him.

Azrael groaned and stretched as he opened his eyes, freezing in place when he saw his mother and Fate leaning anxiously over him. His bewildered gaze moved back and forth between them. "Am I to believe a miracle has taken place?" he asked, defaulting to his native language. "My mother and my wife have become friends?"

Fate pretended not to understand as Mahelia laughed. Her eyes were shining, her smile relaxed as she stroked his hair. "The only miracle today is you opening your eyes."

"I hoped for too much then." Azrael sat up, directing one of his rare, disarming smiles at Fate. The rakish flash of his white teeth against his mocha skin stole her concentration. Seeing the brilliance of his blue eyes, filled with mirth and something akin to desire, froze her in place.

Her heart pounded and she blushed.

Azrael swung his legs over the edge of the bed and stood. Taking a deep breath, he stretched again. "I feel stronger than ever." He turned to his mother. "Did you slip one of your tonics into my food before I went to bed last night?"

Mahelia was about to answer when Azrael looked around the room. "Why are we in the healing room?" He scrutinized his mother, and then Fate. Her blush intensified when his gaze lingered on her. "You are both well, are you not?"

"We are perfectly healthy," Mahelia assured him. "Let us walk the garden and I will set all your questions to rest. There is much you have missed and I think it best you hear it all from me." She tucked her hand in the crook of his arm and guided him toward the door.

When they were halfway out the door, Fate spoke up. "Hey guys. Where are you going?"

Azrael leaned toward his mother, whispering something that made Mahelia chuckle, but with much less humor than before. She obviously wasn't all that happy with whatever he'd said. Mahelia patted him on the arm and gestured for him to continue on without her.

Azrael's gaze shifted to Fate. Was that amusement and excitement in his departing glance? Or had she imagined all that? He'd always been guarded around her. Barely letting her know his true feelings. He'd been especially closed after he'd seen her with Finn and had come to understand the depth of how they felt for each other. Of course, that had all been right before he'd witnessed Farouk peeling Mahelia's skin off his beastly form. That was enough to throw anyone into the deepest, darkest pit of despair.

She should know.

Mahelia stood within the doorway, studying Fate. "Thank you for restoring my son to me."

"I didn't do it for you. I did it for Azrael."

"Not for yourself?" Mahelia asked. "Not even in the smallest way?"

"Maybe a tiny bit."

Mahelia's expression remained flat, unreadable. "I am sure you will understand my desire to spend some time alone with my son after our long separation. He will be all yours afterward. Azrael is anxious to make you his wife."

More uncomfortable than ever, Fate glanced at Jessie, whose mouth hung open. "He won't feel that way once he remembers everything. He knows my feelings for Finn. I can't believe he'd force me to be with him against my will."

"Ah, but is it against your will? You made Azrael whole and strong by pouring all the love you have to give from your heart to his."

"Those were your words, not mine!"

"Maybe, but those words came from you, words woven together into an unbreakable spell. One that was made for you and for Azrael." She closed the door, leaving Fate to absorb the shock of having stepped into yet another one of Mahelia's traps.

10
ALL THAT GLITTERS

THE DIMLY LIT SURROUNDINGS of Finn's bedchamber swirled into a gray blur before reconstructing into a burst of lustrous gold. He shaded his eyes, blinking as he adjusted to the brilliance of the sun glaring off every gilded surface. A rainbow of colors bounced off glass domes, splashing sparkling diamond patterns over the exotic landscape of stunning architecture.

"Oh my!" Sithias gasped. "Biraktar looks like a veritable treasure chest of the finest jewels. I don't think I've ever seen a city as magnificent and luxurious as thisss!" He waved a long, skinny arm in the dancing light, amused with how bright tints of rose, plum and tangerine added color to his pale skin.

Finn made a face. "You don't think it's all a touch over the top? I mean, even the streets are paved with gold. It's a wee flashy for my taste."

Sithias looked horrified. "Who doesn't like the sparkle and glitter of fine things? What's wrong with you?"

"Nothing." Finn frowned at the splendor. "I choose to refrain from being easily impressed. Remember that wise old saying, *all that glitters is not gold*. That advice applies *here* especially. Fate being bamboozled into marrying Azrael by that conniving witch, Mahelia, is all we need to know about how these people operate."

Finn crossed his arms when he noticed Sithias wasn't listening. Instead, he was kneeling down digging the point of his dagger into a gold cobblestone in the road. "What are you doing?"

"Checking to see if this is solid gold or not." Sithias grunted with the effort of standing, but he was smiling as he did so. "It's solid. Proving all this glitter *is* gold."

Finn stared up at the sky and sighed. "You've missed my point entirely."

"I understand completely, sir. But that won't stop me from appreciating the scenery while we're here." Sithias rounded the corner and disappeared.

Finn chased after Sithias, bumping into him the moment he came around the corner. The only thing standing between them and a busy street filled with Biraktar citizens was a topiary clipped into the shape of a whale with wing-like fins. "You wrote up a secluded spot for us to land in to *avoid* being seen, Sithias. If we go out there, we'll stand out like two tourists for sure," he whispered. "Come back before someone notices us."

Sithias nodded and they hurried back into the empty alleyway.

"That was risky," Finn scolded. "Don't let your curiosity get the best of you."

Sithias reached into his satchel and drew out a pen and notepad. "That wasn't curiosity. Well, maybe slightly," he muttered quickly. "But I needed to get a feel for the culture here. It's the only way I can write up some appropriate attire. These people love color. My distinguished gray tweeds and your humdrum, monochromatic beiges will not do."

Tapping his pen on his chin, he eyed Finn up and down. "Hmm, I think I'll put you into a silk robe of bold emerald, finished off with a ruby red sash and elaborate gold trim."

"Really? You've just described a Christmas tree ornament," Finn grumbled.

"Oh stop. You'll love it." Sithias scribbled the description.

The second he finished speaking the words aloud, the cool swish of silk slipped over Finn's skin, a sensation that was both startling and disturbing. He glanced down at the flowing robe and blousy trousers that gathered at his ankles and frowned. "Satin slippers? Is that really necessary?"

"It is." Sithias was busy writing his own description, but he kept scratching words out and rewriting them.

"You didn't take this long to write mine," Finn pointed out.

"We both know that's because I'm much pickier about my wardrobe." Sithias studied his description and smiled. "Thisss will do. Prepare yourself for the reveal."

Finn stared blankly back as Sithias took a big breath and spoke.

"*I am now dressed in the finest and latest creation of the most sought after tailor in Biraktar. Royal blues are my color. Lustrous pearls fastened with gold thread are woven into the most intricate symbolic designs of importance, using the best silks, which clothe my skin, now the color of caramel. A turban of the same silks, with a peacock feather at my brow covers my head.*"

With the words spoken aloud, Sithias transformed his pasty countenance into a dark skinned, long and lanky young man. The royal blue robe gleamed with deeper hues of indigo and azure highlights. Tiny pearls fashioned into shapes of stars trimmed the cuffs and hemline of the flared robe like the constellations of the night sky. He certainly looked like a nobleman, except for one thing.

Sithias held out his arms and gasped with wonder. "It's breathtaking!" He twirled in place. "What do you think? I can't see the whole thing without a mirror. Is it as amazing as I imagined?"

"Not sure." Finn stifled a laugh.

"What's so funny?"

Finn pointed and burst out laughing. "Your eyebrows. They're white!"

"Oh dear. Well, that's what I get for being rushed about it."

"Why didn't you just shift like you always do?"

"I wanted to make sure I had every detail perfect, but I left out the hair color! I should've known imagination trumps words every time." Sithias closed his eyes while Finn watched the white hairs of his eyebrows darken to black. "How's that?"

"A much better match, except that the same problem remains. What are we going to do about my pale face? No one's going to buy that I'm from these parts merely because I'm dressed like them."

"Right. That is a problem. Should I change your looks altogether?"

Finn disliked the idea. He didn't exactly trust that Sithias could undo a dramatic change in appearance. "I'd prefer to hang onto my original face."

Sithias paced a few minutes, deep in thought. "I have it!" He grabbed one side of his robe, sweeping it majestically as he turned to face Finn. "If anyone asks, I'll say you're my guest."

"That could work. If we knew for sure that pale-faced guests are a common thing in Biraktar."

Sithias's amber eyes lit up. "Even if that hasn't always been the case, it wouldn't be suspicious now. Not after Biraktar fought with foreign allies in the war against Kaliena. I'll say you're an ally on your way back to Oldwilde. To Beldereth. Or Asgar. That would be believable."

"Aye, that could work. I'm impressed."

"Thank you." Sithias held his chin high. "Well then, shall we find our way to the royal court, where we'll be one step closer to finding Fate?"

Finn's pulse raced with the thought of seeing her. Would she be relieved they'd come for her? Or would they feel the sharp sting of her rage? He pushed his doubts aside. Best to follow his heart. His heart believed they would find a way back to each other, even if his head kept telling him it was over.

He picked up his satchel to retrieve the transmodulators he'd nicked from the Keep sanctuary and handed one to Sithias. "Remember to hit the switch for two-way translations. We wouldn't want them unable to understand us when we're speaking to them."

Sithias turned it over in his hand. "Where's the switch?"

"Here, let me do it." Finn ensured the setting, then pulled Sithias's turban back a bit to install the tiny device behind his ear.

"Ow!" Sithias yelped. "You never said it would hurt. And please be careful not to messs me up."

Finn pressed his lips into a tight smile as he pulled the material back in place. "Everything's where it should be." He kept smiling to avoid the grumpy frown he was feeling on the inside and pushed his transmodulator into the cleft behind his ear. The jab of the pins as it clamped in place was more startling and painful than expected, but he acted like it was nothing.

"Ready?" Finn asked.

Sithias smoothed his sleeves with a pleased smile. "I do believe I am." They turned to go, but then came to an abrupt stop. "I take that back. How could I forget?"

Finn looked him over. "There's nothing forgotten, Sithias. We're all set to go."

"No, we're not. We have your back-story, but nothing for me. I don't even have a name. I can't go out there and give the performance of my life without knowing my character's name and backstory!"

Finn's impatience was wearing thin. "This is the performance of your life?"

Sithias grabbed his chest as if Finn had mortally wounded him. "I am a seasoned thespian and playwright. I have standards to which I must adhere. Which means every new performance mussst be better than the last."

"Fine. Make up a name and story. *Quickly*."

Sithias stroked his chin, his dark brows narrowed in concentration. He muttered musings under his breath, then frowned and stomped his foot. "There's too much pressure. I can't think of anything. It would help if I could research the culture first. I don't even know what sort of names are popular amongst these people."

"We don't have time for you to do a sociological study. Just figure this out now," Finn pressed.

"Not helping!"

"All right, let's go with what we know."

Sithias pointed at him. "Yesss, that's the first rule of writing. Go with what you know." He stared at Finn. "What do we know?"

"We know Azrael. Sort of. It was a brief encounter, but from what I observed, I'd say he's an entitled, misogynistic mama's boy with an over inflated superiority complex."

"Still not helping."

"Aye. Well, we've both been around Mahelia. I'd say she's even worse than her son, but there has to be something we can–"

"That's it!"

Sithias had a manic look in his eyes, but Finn decided to remain hopeful.

"Mahelia's part Djinn and I know all about them. Remember when I did all that research on the Djinn back when we first entered the Marajaran Desert?" Sithias nodded excitedly with his hands out like he was about to catch a rock falling from the sky. "It's coming to me... yes, yesss." He let out a relieved sigh and looked at Finn. "I have the whole thing."

Finn waited, but Sithias just stared into space with an amazed smile. "Well? What are you waiting for? Let's hear it."

"Hold on. I'm taking a moment to bask in my genius."

"Sithias, don't test me right now," Finn growled.

Sithias turned to Finn with a regal bow. "You are looking at Mahelia's distant cousin, who has come to check on the well-being of her son, Azrael, after hearing word from family relations he had fallen into a mysterious malaise. I have brought with me the renowned Druid healer, Finn McKeen. That would be you."

"I know my own name."

Sithias blinked, as if coming back to the present moment. "Oh, yes of course you do. I was immersed in my new role. What do you think?"

"Actually, I like it, because you won't have to worry about trying to be a Biraktar native. There's only one thing missing. What's your name?"

Sithias straightened his spine and smiled. "Aradif."

"As in *the* Aradif who tested our character when we were in the desert to see if we should live or die?"

"The very same." Sithias closed his eyes, his features swiftly morphing into that of the dark-skinned young man they'd met. When Sithias opened his eyes, they were the same brilliant blue that both Mahelia and Azrael shared.

Finn smiled with a soft chuckle. "Nice to see you again, Aradif. Will you still be wearing the royal blue, or should you be changing into the white robes you were wearing when last we met?"

"I'm keeping the blue. We must dress to impress if we want to be taken seriously here in Biraktar."

"You seem awfully sure of that."

"Did you not see how the people here dress? Phfff, you really must learn to pay closer attention to fashion. Remember, women love a well-dressed man."

"Noted. Now let's go."

They strolled out onto the busy street, merging into the thick crowds with little notice. Understandable, as the place reverberated with vendors shouting their wares.

"Ha! Look at that, sssir!" Sithias trotted over to a small booth of carvings and held one up for Finn to see. "Does this remind you of anyone you know?"

Finn stared at the carving, careful to hide his surprise. The small statue was of a white snake with golden brown wings. Sithias could have posed for the artist.

The merchant stepped forward eagerly. Ignoring Finn, he smiled at Sithias and launched into his sales pitch. "You will not find finer effigies of our great Guiding Star than these. I only buy from the best carvers and painters Biraktar has to offer. Note the grace and divinity in the curve of the lines."

Sithias nodded in agreement, his newly changed blue eyes bright with amazement. "The grace and divinity is *exactly* what caught my eye. I am *most* impressed." He grinned at Finn. "Wouldn't you agree?"

"Aye, it's grand, but we should be going."

"Agreed, but I cannot leave without first purchasing one of these outstanding works of art."

Finn fumed silently, watching Sithias rub his hands together while perusing the selection.

"This is a difficult decision," Sithias told the merchant. "Why don't you give my foreign friend here the history behind the Guiding Star. That way, he'll be able to appreciate what an important and auspicious purchase this is."

"Of course." The merchant's expression grew pinched, but it was clear he wasn't about to jeopardize a sale. "Our Guiding Star is the sacred constellation that is the great winged serpent in the sky we call, Aradif."

Sithias glanced back at Finn in shock. Finn kept a straight face as he listened to the merchant, though he was every bit as shocked as Sithias. What were the odds?

"Aradif controls the primal forces of both creation and destruction. We call upon the great sky serpent for protection, as well as the necessary wisdom to use our own creative and destructive powers for the good of all, in this humble life we live beneath the stars."

"I couldn't have said it better myself!" Sithias struggled to lift the largest statue in the collection. At three-feet-tall, it was a tad cumbersome.

Finn knew exactly who would end up carrying it. "You don't want one of the smaller ones?" It was a couched statement on Finn's part, not a question.

Sithias hugged the statue to his chest. "Oh no, Aradif has guided me to this one." He handed it to the merchant. "Have this packaged for me. I will send a servant to retrieve it for me before sunset."

The merchant set the statue on a bench behind his display. When he turned back, Sithias dangled a pouch of coins and dropped it in his hand. The man seemed a bit confused, but then tested its weight with a few shakes and bowed his head with a smug smile Finn didn't care for. "It was a pleasure doing business with you."

Sithias tilted his head. "And you, kind sir."

Finn let out a tense sigh as they made their way through the bustling marketplace, his gaze fixed on the pearlescent palace gleaming bright in the sun high above the surrounding buildings. "Was all that absolutely necessary?" he said, unable to hold his temper any longer. "We agreed we wouldn't draw undo attention. Yet you put us under a magnifying glass back there."

Sithias huffed and stopped to face Finn, clearly offended. "I'll have you know that was an amazing display of sleuthing at its best. I finessed useful information from that man without him suspecting a thing."

Finn laughed sourly. "I'll admit it was quite the coincidence that we happened upon a deity with your looks and the exact name you chose as your cover while we're here, but from where I stood, the whole thing looked more like you admiring yourself."

Sithias tsk, tsked as he shook his head with disappointment. "I'll forgive you for your small thinking."

"Will you now?" Finn caught the suspicious stares of passersby. Their argument was drawing attention. "Let's keep moving. And remember, we only stop if someone speaks to us."

"Fine." Unhappy with Finn's admonishments, Sithias turned on his heel and marched ahead of him.

When they reached the end of the marketplace they took a less busy road, one that gave them full view of the palace. They were halfway there when several guards strode purposely in their direction. The merchant they'd paid, hurried along beside them, pointing at Finn and Sithias.

Finn clenched his fists at his side. "He didn't suspect a thing, huh?"

Sithias sighed. "Oh dear. How did I miss the signs?"

"You were too busy worshipping your tiny idols, that's how."

The guards stopped in front of them, holding their spears crossed to block their path. The one with the most plumes on his turban stepped forward. "What is your business here?"

Sithias tipped his head in a slight bow. "We have come to see the king's wife, Mahelia."

The guard searched his face probingly and then held out his hand. "Your royal pass."

The merchant snickered. "If he did not have the commonwealth trade pass, I'd wager he does not have a royal pass either."

"Remove him," the lead guard said, signaling for the man's dismissal.

"What about my reward?" the merchant shouted as he was promptly escorted back to the marketplace.

"Of course I have my royal pass." Sithias dug inside his satchel, searching for something Finn knew he did not have.

"It was here, along with my commonwealth trade pass." Sithias gasped, looking thoroughly victimized. "I seem to have been robbed! Probably when we were in the marketplace."

The guard raised a hand, making two swiping motions. Within seconds, the other guards descended on Finn and Sithias, gripping them roughly by the arms.

"What are you doing?" Sithias demanded authoritatively.

The guard smirked. "Lock them up."

II
A SEA OF CONFUSION

AZRAEL GUIDED FATE UP an ornate serpentine staircase that seemed to have no end. Traversing the steps in the long gown she was wearing proved difficult. She had to lift the hem to avoid tripping, while also holding the top part of the gown in place, which was little more than two gathered strips of silk covering her breasts. Thin straps wrapped over each shoulder, extending all the way down to meet the long elegant train at her waist. Thankfully, Jessie had tamed Fate's hair into lovely loose ringlets to help cover most of her naked back.

As far as Fate was concerned there was far too much skin exposed. This was one gown she never would have chosen, regardless of how much she liked the gossamer fabric, the color of a rose sunset, and voluminous skirt that flowed around her with the slightest movement.

"Do you approve of the dress I chose for you?" Azrael asked, as if reading her mind.

Fate hid her surprise. She'd assumed Mahelia had chosen the dress. "I do." She smiled shyly. "It's a bit on the... airy side, but very beautiful."

He seemed pleased. "You will be glad to have air on your skin once we arrive."

So that was why he was wearing a sleeveless tunic instead of his usual long-sleeved attire. Fate's curiosity increased. She couldn't imagine where they were going that wouldn't be cooled by the chill of the desert's night air.

"Are you going to at least give me a hint of what I'll be walking into?" she asked.

"There are no words to describe what is best experienced."

They finally reached the top step and entered a room lit with hundreds of candles set along the walls. A line of servants stood in attendance on the other side of the room. The scent of exotic foods, Fate couldn't begin to identify, wafted in from an open door. She glanced through the doorway, spotting cooks filling bowls with a decadent amount of meats, grains and colorful vegetables.

She was hungry, but not that hungry. It seemed wasteful to be preparing so much food for only two people, but she held her tongue. She was determined to win Azrael over. To make him understand that holding her hostage in a marriage she'd been forced into, was unfair to both of them. The sooner she won her freedom, the sooner she could turn her full attention to resurrecting her father.

"Is this the dining room?" Fate asked. "I don't see a table."

"We will eat on the veranda." Azrael gestured toward a bank of doors. They were closed, and it was then that Fate noticed the stained glass panes. Every other suite she'd been in, including her own, didn't have glass. They were simply openings in the walls and the terraces were more of an extension to the room, with no doors, only curtains to block the light.

A pulsing glow outside the doors lit the stained glass. Azrael held one of the doors open for her. Golden light poured into the room, warm and brilliant, but unnatural in the way it gleamed and waned.

Fate was only a few steps from the veranda when cloying heat and humidity swarmed in, drenching her skin. The air was heavy, yet invigorating. Each breath seemed suffused with life-giving energy. Azrael closed the door behind him as she strolled further out onto the balcony.

Following the sound of a fountain, Fate wandered to the edge and leaned out over the balustrade. She let out a small gasp. At the center of a huge pool was a golden ring in the shape of a cog. At the open center of the cog stood a gigantic tree. Water pooled around its massive trunk. Below the water, its tangled network of roots snaked all the way down to the larger pool below. The tree's lush canopy was the light's source. Each silvery-gold leaf was illuminated and pulsating in a symphony of light.

Rain poured from the leaves, filling the small pool around the trunk, cascading over the gold ring into the bottom pool and shimmering with effervescent bubbles.

"What is this?" She was breathless with wonder. When Azrael didn't answer, she turned to look at him.

He was taking in a different view, watching her delight with great interest. "This is Aulbhala, our sacred tree of life. Without her, there would be no life for us here in the desert."

"It's amazing. I never really thought about where all the water comes from, but it has to come from somewhere." Unable to face the intensity of his gaze, she glanced back at the tree. "So... is there a whole forest of these water-making trees, or is it one of a kind? I can't imagine it's native to the desert. Is it from here?"

"You have an inquisitive mind." Azrael's eyes lit with amusement. "I like that about you."

"Uh, thanks." Needing something to do with her hands, she twirled a lock of hair around her finger. "My friend Jessie's the exact same way. Probably even more curious than me. The only difference between us is that her hair wouldn't be frizzing in this humidity and turning into a crazy mess the way mine is." She bit her lip, unsure why she'd said that.

She was searching for another idiotic topic of conversation, when the servants walked out onto the terrace with platters in hand.

"I like the wildness of your hair." He ran his fingers through one of her curly locks. "It is a reminder to me that deep down, you are wild at heart." Azrael took her hand. "Come, our dinner is served."

He waved the servants away before guiding Fate down onto one of the many silk pillows arranged around a short-legged table. Azrael sat next to her, reached for the flat bread and tore off a piece for her, which she nibbled while eyeing the opulent display of enticing dishes.

Using his own piece of bread, Azrael scooped small strips of meat drenched in a dark orange sauce. Instead of eating it himself, he offered it to Fate, holding it close to her mouth until she took a bite.

Blushing under his relaxed, yet molten gaze, she glanced away, when an explosion of flavors filled her mouth. Any awkwardness she'd been feeling was replaced with her enjoyment of a mixture of sweet and sour infused with the taste of smoked orange and tangy herbs. "Mmm, that's *delicious*! The meat's so tender it practically melted in my mouth. I've never tasted anything like it. What kind of meat is that?"

Azrael gave her a pleased smile. "It is a sulayfir. I put it on the menu special for you."

Fate coughed. "A desert dragon? Are you saying I just ate a hundred-foot-long scaly snake thing with enough fangs to make minced meat of a megalodon?"

Azrael's smile widened. "Ah, you remember."

"How could I forget? I was nearly eaten by one within minutes of landing in Dunebala!"

He nodded. "But I saved you from it."

Fate wouldn't have used the word 'saved' exactly. She remembered all too well how she'd had to beg him for a ride on his boat.

"We might not have met, had it not been for the sulayfir. I thought this a most appropriate ingredient for the occasion."

"How thoughtful." Fate stared at the dish of meat, her appetite dwindling rapidly. "This isn't the same one, is it?"

Azrael chuckled softly. "Not likely. Dunebala is teaming with sulayfirs."

"And this is one of your staples here in Biraktar? Like chicken is to us?" Fate gulped down a rising nausea.

"I am not familiar with chicken. But yes, sulayfir is a common food source for us. One feeds thousands of people. We use many useful parts of the sulayfir. Nothing goes to waste."

"Great. Super resourceful." Fate struggled to put a smile back on her face. "Are there any vegetable dishes here? Maybe one or two without meat?"

"You are displeased." The guarded expression she'd become accustomed to seeing on Azrael's face returned.

"No, not at all," she replied hastily. "The food is incredible. I appreciate all of this." She gestured at the beautiful setting. The movement reminded her of the extreme humidity making her dress cling to her body in places ordinarily hidden.

"I am relieved to hear that." His tension eased somewhat as he poured dark purple liquid into her goblet.

Fate took a tiny sip, then swallowed more when she tasted sweet, rich berries. There seemed to be no hint of alcohol so she finished it and asked for more. After a few more glasses, her many concerns faded into the background, along with her reservations toward the meal. She dug into each dish, enjoying the culinary magic that had created them, while resisting the urge to ask the ingredients.

Azrael leaned back into the cushions with his hands behind his head, smiling as he watched her eat to her heart's content. Fate had never seen him this relaxed, which made it easier to let her own guard down. Maybe a little too easy, because she caught herself staring at his bare sculpted biceps with a quiver of delight.

She quickly dropped her gaze, searching for something to say. "Uh, I think it's about time I told you I've been a little upset with you, and for quite some time now."

Azrael sat straight with concern and she rushed to ease his mind. "Relax, I'm not seriously upset." She forced a chuckle. "I just wanted to give you a hard time for leaving me on a cliffhanger with Sarayna and Kalael's story."

He gave her a wry smile before sinking back into the pillows. "Where did I leave off?"

"Well, let's see..." She tapped her chin. "Oh yes. The demon king, Dregkaan, fell in love with Sarayna and stole her away from Kalael to make her queen of his underworld kingdom. That's where you left me, high and dry."

"Ah, it is true. There is more to the story." Azrael's gaze drifted to the silvery-gold lights dancing over the domed ceiling as he collected his thoughts.

"Time passes differently in the demon realms. What is a year in our world can equal a thousand years in the underworld. As time marched on, Sarayna came to know no other existence than the life she lived with Dregkaan. Her brief marriage to Kalael grew to be a dim, yet cherished memory. She even came to wonder if Kalael had been a figment of her imagination and he might have faded away altogether, if not for the strength of her love for him. The heart remembers, even if the mind forgets.

"Sarayna's life with Dregkaan may not have been of her choosing, but she never resented him, and in fact, came to love him. For she was a shining spirit, blessed with celestial gifts and incapable of hatred. This very goodness is what held Dregkaan under Sarayna's spell. And so he was caught within an unbreakable thrall, powerless to be anything but kind, protective and loving to his angelic queen.

"The day Kalael invaded the underworld with his army became a nightmare for Sarayna. Dregkaan was unprepared for the brutal attack. Just as Kalael had been too enchanted by his alluring wife to leave and fight a war against the demon infestation, Dregkaan had been equally unwilling to leave Sarayna's side. The demon king had long since ceased setting his swarms upon the human race and Dregkaan himself had grown soft.

"Kalael slashed his way into the castle, leaving behind him a wide swath of blood as he forced his way into the throne room. When he saw Sarayna trembling with fear in the arms of the demon king, he went berserk and slaughtered the royal guard until all that was left was the demon king.

"Dregkaan set her behind him and drew his sword in time to block Kalael's strike. But Kalael wielded the scimitar of the gods and the demon king's blade shattered with a force so strong it knocked him to the ground. Kalael's divine weapon was designed to destroy that which was corrupted by evil and nothing could withstand its deadly blow. Kalael lifted the scimitar above the demon king's head.

"Sarayna's scream stopped Kalael. He turned to her, bewildered by her tearful pleas to spare the demon king. Dregkaan used this distraction to take up the sword of a fallen guard and was ready to drive the point through Kalael's ribcage, when Sarayna put herself in the way. In that moment, Dregkaan knew she was willing to die for Kalael. Her heart had chosen, and in turn, broke his heart.

"The unbearable pain of losing her love and devotion consumed Dregkaan. Yet he could not imagine forcing his gentle queen to renounce Kalael and stay with

him. Had Sarayna been willing to die for him, he would have fought Kalael with all the strength of his love for her, but she had made her choice. And so, Dregkaan dropped his weapon and fell to his knees, consoled by one thing. That Sarayna weeped for his demise as Kalael brought his scimitar down and cleaved him in two."

Fate waited for more, but apparently the story was over. "That's a horrible ending! I can't believe I waited all this time just to have it end on such a downer."

Azrael laughed softly. "That is the way my mother told it to me. There is no other ending that I am aware of." He rose from the pillows and leaned toward her, his blue eyes sparkling with amusement. "Would you have preferred that Sarayna had stayed with Dregkaan?"

She glanced down at her glass and took another sip. "No, not if she loved Kalael more. I just don't see why Dregkaan had to die like that. It's sad. He was good to her."

"He loved her very much and wanted only to see her happy." Azrael drew a silk pouch from his pocket, untied the satin cord and spilled the contents onto his palm.

Fate recognized the pendant embedded with sapphires in the shape of a winged serpent immediately. It was the protective talisman Mahelia had promised to give her after she married Azrael. She'd said it would stabilize her powers enough to keep her from becoming weak and disoriented when she was in Farouk's presence.

The thin gold chain glinted as Azrael clasped it around Fate's neck. His fingers lingered on her skin, sending an involuntary thrill through her. Steadying her breath, she lifted the pendant, studying the dazzling piece with more interest than she actually felt. But her heart was racing beneath his touch. He withdrew his hand when she shifted her shoulder. "I'm surprised Mahelia's letting me have this," she murmured.

"Mother told me she promised the necklace to you as protection against the Hinn. You must realize, it was the Hinn who switched the necklaces on the day of our wedding."

"That's what Mahelia said. If her story's to be believed." Fate muttered the last part under her breath.

"I understand your distrust, Fate. You trust me, do you not?" His gaze was probing in more ways than one.

Heat rose to her face anew and she quickly dropped her gaze back to the food. "Can you believe I'm still hungry?" She scooped up a big bite of noodles, which she chewed with delight.

"Mmmm! These are heavenly. How does your chef get those crunchy little bits inside the pasta?"

"Come, I will show you." Azrael stood and helped her rise. Suddenly lightheaded, she teetered into his muscular chest.

She giggled. "Sorry about that."

"I am not." His passionate gaze stirred an avalanche of emotions she feared she'd never dig her way out of.

Another blush warmed her cheeks and she stepped back none too gracefully. "Weren't you going to show me the secret to making those yummylicious noodles?"

"Follow me." She caught the disappointment in his eyes before he steered her over to the edge of the balcony. "Your noodles are in the water. Do you see them?"

Fate leaned over the railing and squinted. "Them, as in those tiny yet long, squirmy worms?" Her stomach churned.

"Pearl eels. If allowed, they will grow to be almost as large as a sulayfir. The chef harvests them frequently and marinates them in marked casks for months to soften the bones until they arrive at the perfect texture."

"Oh." Fate swallowed an immediate rush of bile in her throat and fought to keep her food down. They'd been getting along too well to have everything spoiled with an offensive vomiting of her entire meal. The matter of her freedom was too important.

All this thinking and staring at the darting eels made her dizzier than ever. Fate turned away from the pool, tipping backward. Azrael caught her by the waist and pulled her against him. He rested his chin on her shoulder as she stared straight ahead. "Stop denying what you feel for me." His mouth caressed the delicate shell of her ear. The heat of his breath sent tantalizing shivers down her spine.

Her heart thudded, pumping a deafening roar of blood into her ears as she fought the urge to turn and lift her face to his. She shouldn't be having these feelings. Feelings like this had always been reserved for Finn, and Finn alone. Yet here they were. An overwhelming desire to yield to Azrael. To touch her lips to his. To be held within his strong muscular arms and be kissed deeply.

A chaotic storm of thoughts swirled in Fate's fogged mind. She couldn't think straight.

That berry juice!

There must have been something in it. And it didn't help that she couldn't get a grip on her pounding heart and rapid breathing. Unable to trust herself with Azrael a second longer, she pushed his hands away, backing up until she bumped against the balustrade. When Azrael moved toward her, she held up her hands. "Don't come any closer!"

Azrael's dark eyebrows creased into a pained frown. "You are my wife. I am your husband. It is time for us to be together."

Her transmodulator vibrated, indicating he'd reverted to his native language, and she was thankful she could pretend she didn't understand him. "I don't know what you brought me here for, but I'm not ready for whatever it is you want to do with me."

He repeated what he'd said in English.

Fate shook her head. "No! I've already been forced into a marriage with you, but you will *not* force me to be with you in *that* way against my will!"

Azrael's jaw tightened as his gaze fell to her chest, where her silk dress clung thinly to her breasts. Fate crossed her arms and covered them with her hands.

"You mistake me for a brute. Why?" Hurt clouded his eyes. "I have not laid one unkind hand on you since our wedding. All I have done tonight is demonstrate my love for you."

Fate was stunned. While a huge part of her wanted to open to his unexpected declaration of love, there was a strong stubborn part holding onto the anger and resentment she'd felt for too long at being held hostage.

She lifted the hem of her gown, revealing the soul ring on her ankle. "You call this love? This is bondage. It's called enslavement."

Azrael pointed at his own soul ring. "I belong to you, just as you belong to me. There is no difference."

"No difference?" The power at her core surged, clearing her head of the intoxicating fog she'd imbibed. "You *chose* to have me put that soul ring on you. I was never given that choice. I was told I was too valuable to your people for what I could do with the Words of Making. I'm a prize to you. One you happen to like, at least for the moment anyhow. Well, let me tell you something, that makes *all* the difference to me."

His eyes widened with shock when he saw the veins in her arms and chest light with the girdle's power. "You are upset. I will have you escorted back to your bedchamber."

"So that's it? You won't release me?" Fate yelled at his back as he marched toward the door. "You're worse than the demon king! At least he was willing to let Sarayna go!" Her voice pitched to a raging snarl that filled the huge, enclosed space and echoed back at her.

Azrael closed the door, leaving Fate to seethe alone, lost in a sea of confusion. Was she actually angry with him for refusing to free her, or was she furious with herself for not surrendering to him?

12
PERMISSION GRANTED

"UNHAND ME, YOU BUFFOON!" Sithias demanded. "I will *not* be manhandled! Do you have any idea who I am?"

"No, but we have ways to force you to reveal your identity," the lead guard said.

"There's no need for any of that," Sithias insisted. "I can tell you now. I am Mahelia's distant cousin. She sent me the royal pass, which I had in hand, until it was ssso rudely stolen from me. If you're going to arrest and torture anyone, it should be the thief who robbed me!"

Seeing that his words were falling on deaf ears, Sithias resisted going with the guards by pulling in the opposite direction, which resulted in their grips tightening around his arms as they lifted him off the ground. Wincing in pain, Sithias flailed his feet.

Despite his discomfort, he couldn't help admiring the way his royal blue robe flowed elegantly around his kicking legs. His lavish wardrobe was being wasted. He'd envisioned a grand entrance into the palace.

Sithias craned his neck to glance back at Finn. He was still knocked out cold, his head hanging and his feet dragging between the two guards who were carrying him.

Poor Finn had put up a valiant fight, just as he always did, but he hadn't stood a chance against six armed men without the supernatural speed and strength he'd once possessed.

Sithias felt terrible, fearing he'd been too hasty in denying Finn his request to have his Elder race runes restored. He would correct that mistake as soon as the opportunity presented itself. Though for the moment, their survival was solely his responsibility, and Sithias knew exactly what to do. In fact, he relished his plan so much, he laughed quietly to himself.

The lead guard scowled at Sithias. "This is no laughing matter. You would do well by showing contrition for your illegal trespass into Biraktar."

Sithias sobered abruptly and sneered at the man. "It is you who will be sorry when I reveal my true might."

It was the guard's turn to laugh. "I will not hold my breath."

Sithias shifted into his natural state, a transformation that took little to no concentration for him, with the exception of one slight change in mind. As his arms sealed to his sides and his brown skin paled to ivory and hardened over with glistening scales, he focused on size.

The guards holding onto him screamed and backed away as Sithias expanded in girth and rose high above them. He stopped growing when he was level with the second terrace of a nearby building. Spreading his massive feathered wings, Sithias cast his long sinuous shadow over the men cowering on their knees and bowing with their foreheads touching the gold cobblestones.

"It is Aradif!"

They were all suddenly shouting, making it difficult to understand what they were saying. The noise drew the attention of those in the streets and at the marketplace, until they were surrounded by droves of people, all on their knees, praying and worshipping at the top of their lungs. Sithias hadn't intended to gather such a large audience, but all that really mattered was proof of the fear and respect he needed to move onto the next phase of his plan.

"Sssilence." Uncoiling slightly, Sithias lowered his giant head in front of the lead guard. "I will sssee the king's ssson, Azrael, and hisss mother, Mahelia." He concentrated on adding hisses back into his words, which didn't come as naturally as it used to. But this worked to great effect, because the man visibly shook as he stared up at Sithias in terror.

"*Now*!" Sithias demanded.

Startled from his fright, the guard fell over, then scrambled to his feet. "Forgive me, Aradif. I was blind to the truth."

Sithias breathed in the satisfaction of pure power, an intoxicating sensation he could easily get used to. "My mercy musst be earned. Do as I demand, and I will consssider your requessst."

The lead guard nodded anxiously and turned toward the palace. "Follow me, your holiness."

The other guards rushed in behind him, leaving Finn flopped in the middle of the road. The crowds followed the guards, swarming past his unconscious friend carelessly. If he didn't do something fast, he feared Finn would be trampled.

"*Ssstop*!"

Every face in the crowd turned in unison. Sithias slithered forward, abruptly clearing a path until he reached the guards. "You left my companion behind to be trampled. Retrieve him, and tell my worshipersss to go to Temple, where they will pay their respectsss to me… for two daysss…

without food."

Having recovered from his shock, the lead guard bowed. "I understand, Aradif." He signaled to his men to pass the message onto the crowds, which had been growing in increasing numbers with each passing second. He looked up at Sithias with a concerned frown. "Forgive me, your holiness, but why have you taken favor with this lowly *Earth* dweller, when he is not worthy of being in the presence of those who have fought against all odds to live in the sky with you?"

Using silence to unnerve the man, Sithias remained quiet. This was almost too easy, but mostly because he'd been mistaken for Aradif before and was familiar with his effect upon the deity's worshippers.

He'd nearly forgotten his encounter with Sabirah, the beautiful yet wicked sorceress who'd poisoned Finn with a branch from the bloodthirsty oak controlled by Mugloth. Her hatred of Finn, the Druid earth lover, had been frightening. Yet Sithias had stumbled onto a way to control Sabirah by appealing to her utter devotion to Aradif, the great winged serpent in the sky.

"You take libertiesss with me that have not been granted to you." Sithias thought back to the exact words he had spoken to Sabirah, remembering the perfection of her response when she'd shown suspicion over his concern for Finn. "My mercy isss broad and mysteriousss, and not for you to judge."

The man cringed openly. "Forgive me, Aradif. I am the one who is not worthy. I will see to your companion myself."

Sithias nodded. "Sssend word ahead to the palace and tell them of my return. I will not sssuffer anymore offensesss from my people."

The lead guard barked an order to one of his men and sent him running in the direction of the palace. Once Sithias was assured of Finn's safety and care, he took to the air for a quick sightseeing tour of the city. Circling overhead several times as he marveled at the unusual architecture and array of colors and materials used in the towers, domes and buildings. The streets were mostly empty, and any people left were rushing in the direction of the Temple.

Sithias flew lower when he saw that Finn was being carried through the palace gates. He landed in the garden just as the royal family hurried out to greet him. Spreading his wings wide, he hissed to show his displeasure. The king and his many sons stood still, though not without fear in their eyes, while their wives and children hid behind the men.

Two women remained in place. Mahelia and Fate. Unlike all the others, who were awestruck and in shock, they were not afraid in the least. Fate knew exactly who he was. Mahelia didn't recognize him, having never met him in snake form before. He would have expected her to react to his mighty appearance with the same awe, had he not been aware she wasn't entirely human.

A man moved in next to Fate and whispered in her ear. It took a few seconds for Sithias to realize it was Azrael. He'd been healed, and by the way he stood with a possessive arm around Fate's waist, Azrael still considered himself very much her husband. Sithias hoped for an indication she was uncomfortable with Azrael's open claim of her.

All the delicious power Sithias had enjoyed up to that point drained away when Fate did nothing to dissuade Azrael. Sithias had hoped for a sign she was relieved to see him. She might think her agreement to be there was voluntary, but Sithias knew better. As long as the soul ring was controlling her, Fate was a prisoner of these people. Still, that shouldn't be getting in the way of showing concern for Finn's bloodied and unconscious state. But Fate showed no emotion at all. *Nothing.*

Sithias was almost glad Finn wasn't witnessing this. He would be devastated, and Sithias hated to think how much lower Finn's spirits might fall.

The king stepped forward, a tall regal man whose white beard marked his age. He kneeled and raised his face to Sithias. "Aradif, I am honored by your glorious presence. May I ask why you have chosen to bless us in this way?"

Sithias used all the disappointment and indignation he felt about Fate to fuel his performance. He loomed over the king and hissed loudly. "I am here to right an imbalance. An egregious injussstice has been perpetrated here."

The king's face grew tight with fear. "What injustice, your holiness?"

Sithias lowered his head until his gaze was level with Fate and Azrael. "You allowed a wrongful marriage to take place between your ssson and thisss woman, who belongsss to another."

Azrael drew his saber and pointed it at Sithias. "Lies!" he shouted. "Do not listen to this, father. This is not Aradif. This is a deceiver!"

The king threw his son a sharp look. "Azrael. Be quiet!"

His brothers descended on Azrael, knocking the saber from his grip as they struggled to pin him down. Fate put a hand to her mouth, watching as they subdued Azrael with both concern and something else. Excitement maybe? Sithias could only hope.

"Take him away from here," the king ordered. "Mahelia, go with your son. Subdue his rage by whatever means necessary."

Mahelia glanced up at Sithias, her eyes narrowed with suspicion. "Come with me," she told Fate. "Your place is by your husband."

Sithias hissed at Mahelia. "*She* must ssstay."

Mahelia stared back. "*I see you.*" Shadows darkened her face for a brief moment before she turned and followed them inside.

"Aradif, please forgive us." The king held his palms together in supplication. "Please help us to correct this imbalance."

"I have brought the man who isss the rightful husssband, whom *your* guardsss have beaten, merely for being a visssitor here. I am greatly dissspleased."

Confused, the king looked at Finn, and then at his guards. "I will have them punished," he assured Sithias. "Executed if you wish."

"Punishment will sssuffice."

The king gestured for his palace guards to remove the offending guards immediately. "Your holiness…" He trailed off, clearly conflicted and in great turmoil.

Sithias moved in closer to the king, pleased with how he visibly quaked in such close proximity. "Ssspeak."

"Our laws are clear and based on your holy scriptures, Aradif. Written in honor of you, our Guiding Star…"

"Yesss," Sithias pressed.

"My son and his… I mean this woman, were wedded in the Temple and sealed together. As you know, this means they are truly married under the eyes of the law, regardless of this other man's claims. To add to that, they are bonded together by soul rings."

Sithias hissed in the man's face, making him shrink with fear. Based on how everything had unfolded thus far, Sithias hadn't expected any such resistance. He would have to tread carefully so as not to add fuel to Azrael's accusations. This could blow up in their faces if he went against their firm beliefs.

"There isss nothing unbreakable in my presence." Sithias held his breath, hoping he'd been vague yet forceful enough to make the king consider breaking the sacred laws.

"I understand," the king replied after a prolonged pause. "We must perform the Sumnara Trials."

Sithias didn't know how to respond to that since he didn't know what that meant. Not even with the help of the transmodulator. Fortunately, the king continued speaking.

"With your permission, we will prepare the three trials for my son and the claimant to compete in."

Sithias raised his head and peered down at the king. "Permission granted."

13
TIME TO FORGIVE

THE FIRE IN FATE'S BELLY burned hot and painful as she fought to contain it. Hearing the king and Sithias talk about her like she was some prized cow up for auction, rather than a person with every right to choose her own destiny, galled her beyond belief. Out of everything she'd suffered and fought to hold onto, she'd never felt more insulted than in that moment. The beauty and sparkle of Biraktar and the many wonders she'd come to appreciate, would be forever marred by the filth of discrimination.

She wanted to surrender to the raging, indwelling power more than ever before and show them what a powerful, liberated female looked like. But would she be free, or consumed by something else altogether? She suspected the latter. There had been little time to search inward, but her insides vibrated with cautious fear, telling her this was no time to lose control.

Fate clenched her fists and held her expression blank as the king announced the competition between Azrael and Finn. She glanced at Finn, her heart aching at his injured and comatose form. Why had he come after her? She'd been clear about her need for space. That she couldn't look at him without seeing lies in everything he said and did. It hurt too much then and it hurt too much now.

"See that the claimant is ready to compete by tomorrow's sunrise." The king made a dismissive wave in Finn's direction as the guards gathered him up off the ground and carried him into the palace.

Sithias tilted his giant head as he addressed the king. "I trussst his woundsss will be dresssed and that he will be well cared for."

The king bowed. "You have my word, great holy one."

"I will return at sssunrise." Sithias flapped his huge wings, stirring a strong gust of wind that swept over them as he lifted off and flew away.

Fate returned to her bedchamber, where she found Jessie pacing the length of the room. She stopped and ran over to Fate. "I'm going bonkers with boredom here. If I'd known you were the only one having all the fun, I never would've come along. Please tell me something interesting before I lose my mind!"

"Ha! You think any of this is fun for me?"

Jessie stared cautiously at the fiery glow lighting Fate's skin. "Whoa, cool down. I didn't mean *actual* ha-ha fun. But you have to admit getting dressed up like a princess and having a romantic dinner with a real prince–who's hotter than this desert–is way better than sitting around doing nothing."

"It wasn't romantic."

"Come on, a candlelit dinner by a pool and a waterfall coming from a tree with leaves that make rainwater? Nooo, that's not romantic at all."

"Yeah, but I didn't get the chance to tell you about the food. There were wormy eels in the pool and I ate them thinking I was slurping back noodles." Fate made a face. "And did I mention the main course, desert dragon on a bed of rice?"

Jessie made a gagging sound. "I suppose that's where the mood took a nosedive."

"There was no mood."

Jessie raised a skeptical brow. "Your red face says otherwise."

"The whole thing was confusing and awkward, and I don't want to talk about it anymore." She plopped down on the bed. "Besides, there's more important stuff happening now. Starting with Sithias and Finn's very unexpected arrival."

Jessie sat on the bed next to her, crossing her legs as she leaned in. "Finn came after you? Oh, now *that's* romantic."

Fate's heart thumped harder. "It is," she admitted. "But he never should've come. The guards beat him up." She swallowed. "He's in bad shape, Jess."

"Will he be all right?"

"I think so. Biraktar has excellent healers."

"What about Sithias? Did they beat him up too?"

Fate laughed sourly. "Uh, no, Sithias showed up in his original snake form, only super-sized, and now he has the king convinced he's their god."

"What?"

Fate rolled her eyes and filled Jessie in on the history of Aradif, the Guiding Star the people of Biraktar have worshipped for centuries. And then she went on to tell Jessie about the upcoming competition.

"That's crazy!" Jessie laughed. "And brilliant."

"Maybe, maybe not. There's so many ways this could go sideways. One being, Finn getting killed." Fate chewed on her bottom lip. "He's a normal human now."

"I know what that's like." Jessie pouted. "Being normal sucks."

Fate understood Jessie's frustration, but she'd rather have her best friend discontent than not at all. "In Finn's case, yes. I can't see how he can win against Azrael without the strength and speed the Elder race runes gave him."

"Isn't Azrael a normal human too?"

"No, he's part Djinn, which means he's got enough supernatural mojo to do real damage to mere mortals."

"Have you seen him in action?"

"Oh yeah. He made quite the heroic entrance when he saved me by taking down a desert dragon." Fate frowned with the memory of when he'd tried to kill her shortly after that. "He's swift, agile and skilled with a sword. Especially when he tried to kill me that one time. I had a way of bringing out the best in him when we first met."

Jessie's expression turned dreamy. "I'd like to see that." She shook out of the stare. "Not the trying to kill you part."

Fate's frown fixed on Jessie. "Wow, you've got it bad for Azrael."

"Sorry! I'm so sorry! I know I shouldn't be drooling like this, but he's *hot.* I honestly don't know how you're resisting him. I'd be all over that one in a heartbeat if it was me."

"I'll admit I've had my moments of weakness, but I can't let myself go there. Not when I'm chained to him this way. If I'm going to be with anyone, it has to be by choice. Not force." Fate sighed. "And then there's Finn. Even though I want to hate him for lying to me about Eustace, I can't. I still love him and I always will."

The sorrow she'd been holding back since learning of Eustace's death flooded to the surface. Fate buried her face in her hands, unable to keep from sobbing. The dam had broken and the tears could not be stopped. Jessie hugged her, holding her trembling shoulders until she was too spent to cry anymore.

She handed Fate a cotton cloth to dry her face. "Maybe it's time to forgive Finn. Holding onto all this anger is bad for you. And bad for everyone if you keep stuffing this in until you blow your stack."

"True."

"A step in the right direction would be to use your Words of Making to give Finn his powers back. At least then you wouldn't have to worry about Azrael killing him."

Nodding, Fate wiped her eyes dry as she walked over to her bag and pulled out a notepad. She held the pen poised, deciding not to overthink what to write. Otherwise, she risked talking herself out of it with what might go wrong if she didn't do this right. A few minutes later, she was ready to speak the words aloud. "Here goes nothing," she said. "*The Elder race runes originally inked into*

Finn's skin are now returned with his powers restored exactly as they once were."

Jessie stared back in silence. "How do you know if it worked or not?" she asked after a few minutes.

"There's no way to confirm without Finn in the room."

Jessie slumped into the generous mound of pillows on the bed. "I suppose that means we're stuck here for the rest of the day until the competition tomorrow morning."

Fate set the notepad down and walked out onto the terrace. The colorful, sparkling city below did little to lift her spirits. A gilded cage was still a cage. She hated the thought of Biraktar being her home, but as long as the soul ring anchored her to Azrael she was powerless to leave.

She certainly didn't expect him to remove it. Not after last night. She'd been stupid to think she could sweet talk Azrael into releasing her. He was incapable of understanding why she would never be happy being enslaved in a marriage, even if it was couched in the finest luxuries imagined.

Finn was her only hope now. Her rage had blinded her to his warnings. And yet, he'd come to challenge Azrael and the royal family, despite knowing she had deliberately put as much space as she could between them and might never forgive him.

The hard shell around her heart cracked. Finn loved her enough to fight for her despite all the odds against him, knowing he might die in the process. She couldn't let that happen.

Fate rushed back into the room and grabbed the notepad.

Jessie rose from the cloud of pillows and sat straight up. "What're you doing?"

"You and I are going to check in on Finn." Fate wrote hastily. "I have to make sure he has his powers back."

Jessie clapped. "Yay!"

Fate read the words aloud. "*Jessie and I are now standing next to Finn's bed.*" She waited for her surroundings to blur and shift the way they always had in the past, whenever she'd used the Words of Making to move from one place to another.

Nothing.

Jessie glanced around. "Isn't something supposed to be happening right about now?"

"Yup. Maybe I was too vague." Fate wrote out several sentences with more description and read each one aloud. Not a single line worked to transport them to Finn's side.

"What's the deal?" Jessie asked.

A heavy weight of despair settled in on Fate. This could mean only one thing. Finn's injuries were far more serious than she'd thought, and he must be...

She broke into a fit of tears.

Jessie rushed over and patted her back. "What's wrong. Why are you crying?"

"I think Finn might be–" a sob choked off Fate's words. She couldn't catch her breath.

"Dead?" Jessie asked. "*No*, why would you think that all of a sudden?"

"Because the only way the Words of Making stopped working like this before between us was because our connection was completely severed. Back then it was because he'd been poisoned by Mugloth, but that's not the case here. This has to be something more... final. I know Azrael and Mahelia would love nothing more than to see Finn out of the picture. They probably had him–" Sobs returned to consume her.

"No. No way." Jessie grabbed her by the arms. "Look at me. That's not what's happening here. After everything you told me about how the king reacted to Sithias, he will see to it that Finn lives to see sunrise. Don't forget, he's too afraid of this Ardoof dude he thinks Sithias is pretending to be."

Fate took in a long shuddering breath and clung to that. "Oh yeah."

"Let's think about this logically. There has to be some other reason your words didn't work. Could it be the girdle that's stopping you?"

Fate wiped her wet cheeks with the back of her hand. She shook her head. "I don't think so."

"What about that fancy ankle bracelet you're wearing? Didn't you tell me it burned your skin when you and Finn were getting too hot and heavy?"

"That's it, Jess! The soul ring won't let me do anything against Azrael's wishes. How could I forget that?"

"Because you're too emotional to think straight, that's why." Jessie crossed her arms and fumed. "How primitive are these people? I mean, this soul ring business is worse than a chastity belt! And those were horrid. Azrael's hotness factor just cooled to subzero. I can't believe I crushed on him. What was I thinking?"

"There's no denying he's photogenic," Fate muttered. She sat on the bottom of the bed, suddenly drained of energy.

Jessie sat down next to her. "You okay?"

"No, because if I couldn't do a simple thing like get us into Finn's room, that means he didn't get his powers back either." Fate trembled. "If I know these people, this is a competition to the death, and one Finn won't survive."

14
THE SUMNARA TRIALS

FINN WOKE FROM a mercifully deep, dark sleep to a pounding headache. He opened his eyes to discover he could barely see through the narrow slit of his bruised, swollen lid. Rising onto one elbow, he groaned from the ache of cracked ribs. He glanced around blearily at a plain room with no windows or furniture besides the bed he lay on.

Pain drilled throughout his tenderized back and abdomen as he slowly rose to a sitting position to check the full range of damage. They'd stripped him of his clothes, leaving him in his under shorts. Bandages covered his injuries. Purple bruising spread past the strips of cloth, an alarming sign there might be internal bleeding.

He shifted his legs over the edge of the bed and gingerly set his feet on the floor, wincing as he stood. A bout of dizziness had him grappling the air for support. Fearing a fall, and the added pain that would cause, he dropped back onto the mattress, panting from the effort and cursing his weakness.

He wouldn't be anywhere near this broken if he still had the Elder race runes and he'd be healing twice as fast as well.

The door opened and an elderly man in a white linen robe entered the room, followed by three women in beige-colored robes. He gestured to his female attendants. "Dress him for the trials."

Finn grimaced as the transmodulator vibrated in his ear, a harsh sound that shot a jolt of pain through his throbbing brain.

The women helped him stand. He swayed in place. Two of the women prevented him from falling over, while the third slipped a black garment over his head and guided his arms into the sleeves. She lifted his feet into the bottoms and tied it at the waist. A sash of the same dark material was wrapped around his waist. He grimaced but made no sound when she cinched it tight.

The man opened the door, speaking in a low tone to whomever stood outside the room. The three women left and Finn was about to sit back down when two guards entered. Gripping him by the arms, they escorted him out into a narrow corridor toward an enclosed staircase.

Finn's heart hammered with panic and the exertion of keeping pace. This was all too similar to when he'd been a prisoner of Asgar and had been delivered to the chopping block. He'd known then that he was being taken to his doom, and he knew it now. Fortunately, in this go around, Sithias was fully aware of the situation and was no doubt working on getting him out of this sticky predicament.

But shouldn't the rescue have happened already? His blood pumped faster with even more fear. There was always the chance something had gone horribly wrong while he'd been unconscious. If Mahelia had confirmed Sithias was an imposter, he might not have escaped in time.

Finn tried to to dispel his growing doubts but it was useless. His thoughts darkened all the more, especially when he wondered if Fate would stand by and allow him to be slaughtered in whatever manner decreed by Azrael and his people.

The thought provoked an ache in his chest more agonizing than all his injuries combined, sapping what little strength he had left. By the time they reached the top of the long stretch of steps, Finn was out of breath.

The guards pushed through two huge doors. Finn welcomed the fresh air on his face, cooling the sweat pouring off his forehead. It was still night everywhere he looked, except for a wash of light in the sky peeking over the rooftops. The sun was just beginning to rise.

He staggered forward as the guards tugged him across an alleyway leading into a long dark tunnel. After a few minutes they emerged back into the open air once again, where the stone ended and sand began. Finn squinted to see his surroundings within the dim light of dawn, slowly realizing they stood on the outer edge of a vast coliseum.

At the center, dozens of slaves stood next to three round platforms laid out in a straight line. They were massive in size and covered with mosaic tiles. Countless tiered levels surrounding the arena were filled with people. From what he could tell, the entire population of Biraktar was in attendance. They sat silent; the general mood was somber.

At one end of the oval coliseum stood a high platform lit with torches. An elaborate throne stood front and center. Finn assumed the man sitting on it was the king. Standing to one side of him was the crown prince, as well as a line of men who could be his brothers. Their ages ranged widely but he could see the strong family resemblance to the crown prince and Azrael, who Finn noted was absent. A large group of women stood opposite the king's sons, most likely their many wives with a horde of children. Fate and Mahelia were not present among them.

He couldn't think of anything more barbaric than to bring children to an execution. Further dispirited, Finn hung his head in defeat.

The king stood and addressed his subjects. "Centuries have passed since our people have gathered for the Sumnara Trials. Our people have faithfully followed the sacred laws handed down to us by our Guiding Star." He paused solemnly. "Until now, when the great winged serpent, Aradif, appeared to me with a message."

Awed gasps rippled across the sea of people. Equally surprised by the announcement, Finn lifted his head, suddenly alert and hopeful.

"Aradif appealed to me to undo a great imbalance mistakenly perpetrated here in our city," the king continued. "It would seem–unbeknownst to us–that Azrael's wife belonged to another man who claims they were husband and wife."

Shock and outrage rose from the crowds.

Claimed?

Finn scowled at the king who raised his arms to silence everyone.

"Do not blame Prince Azrael," the king continued. "He knew nothing of this and is innocent."

"*Liar,*" Finn growled under his breath. Pain bloomed across his back from the blow a guard delivered from behind.

"My son is deeply hurt by this unfortunate discovery, yet he wishes to honor the vows he made to the woman he considers to be his wife by entering into the Sumnara Trials. We now obey Aradif's decree that the three trials take place at sunrise."

A chill raced along Finn's spine as he wondered what these trials involved. Anger rushed in to banish the chill when he realized this was *Sithias's* decree. What in bloody hell did he think he was doing?

The king gestured to the guards standing next to Finn. "Bring forth the claimant."

The guards walked Finn into the center of the courtyard. Hisses of disapproval resounded from the audience, a disturbing sound that pushed his nerves over the edge.

"I now present my son, Prince Azrael." The king bowed with a grand sweep of his arm as Azrael entered the arena.

Dressed majestically in a crimson uniform embellished with gold trim and a golden breastplate to match, Azrael strode into the arena to join Finn. He did not meet Finn's pointed gaze, and instead, turned to face the king with his saber drawn and held skyward. "I dedicate my blade to reclaiming my family's honor on this holy day of the Sumnara Trials!" Azrael shouted.

The citizens of Biraktar cheered and clapped. The noise reverberated throughout the coliseum. The king allowed them to go on for several minutes before silencing them again. He signaled a directive to a guard standing offstage. "Bring forth the woman in question."

Finn tensed every sore muscle in his battered body, thoroughly incensed by the king's dismissive references toward Fate as 'the woman'. The guard escorted Fate onto a platform set directly beneath the king and the royal family. Mahelia followed in her wake and came to stand beside her. More spine-tingling hisses issued from the crowds.

Finn clenched his jaw, his outrage so great he wanted to shout his indignation for how they were treating Fate like a lowly possession to be sold off. He caught her gaze and swallowed hard. There were tears in her eyes as she stared back. Were those tears of concern for him? Or for her own plight?

He knew he must look a terrible sight and hoped she still cared a little about what happened to him. But he'd certainly understand if she was mainly frightened by her circumstances. Azrael had her locked up tight with that damnable soul ring. For all the power she possessed, she was unable to use a single drop of it to free herself.

Finn balled his hands into fists until his arms shook with fury. He would fight for Fate's release, regardless of how weak and powerless he was in his current state. It would no doubt be the death of him, but at least the final act of his life would be for the worthiest of causes.

"Bring forth the Morning Star," the king announced.

A procession of what appeared to be thirteen priests entered the arena. Twelve of them followed behind the priest holding a tall gold staff crowned with an egg-sized diamond encased within an intricate circlet of metalwork inlaid with sapphires. They stopped in front of a white marble plinth with a hole bored into its center. The twelve priests divided and stood to either side of it while the priest slipped the bottom of the staff into the plinth.

Finn waited for something to happen, though nothing did. The priests merely turned in the direction of the sunrise and chanted. Azrael sheathed his saber and did the same, chanting in time with the priests, his gaze fixed on the sun's light growing in strength above the coliseum walls. The crowds joined in the chanting until they were all of one voice.

Finn on the other hand, remained silent, his tension nearly unbearable as he wondered where Sithias was hiding. What was his plan for ensuring his survival throughout whatever horrors these three trials had in store for him?

A ray of sunlight slivered over the top wall of the coliseum and a hush fell over everyone. All eyes stared at the light as the sun slowly climbed higher into the sky, chasing away the last remnants of night. A small slice of the sun's full brilliance struck the diamond in the priest's staff and a rainbow of colors splashed across the stadium, piercing the early morning shadows with what looked like an entire universe of stars.

The beat of many drums cut through the silence, a clamorous interruption that fired painfully through Finn's tortured nervous system. Hundreds of drummers marched into the arena. The harsh beat continued until the sun cleared the coliseum walls. The drummers stopped and silence returned.

"With the light of the Morning Star, comes the Sumnara Trials," the king announced. "Let them begin!"

A man in heavy armor holding a whip stepped forward and shouted an order. "Heave!"

The sound of grinding stone echoed throughout the stadium as the slaves strained against the heavy chains attached to the first round platform. Finn figured the slab must weigh a ton to account for so many men assigned to pulling on such thick chains. There was no firm ground to walk on and their shackled feet slipped in the sand. When one of them fell, the slave master whipped the man savagely until his back dripped with blood.

Rage skimmed alongside Finn's mounting fear. The injustices these enslaved men suffered was intolerable. But he was in no position to help. If anything, he was presently in more trouble than the slaves, a thought that turned his full attention to the huge hole opening up beneath the platform being hauled aside.

A guttural snarl resounded from somewhere down inside the hole, raising the hairs on Finn's arms. Azrael strode to the edge, his expression unflinching as he stared down at the source of the menacing sound.

Finn's guards shoved him forward, nearly knocking him to his knees. Hiding his pain, he regained his footing and joined Azrael near the edge of the pit.

The ground below was a graveyard of human bones. Most were picked clean but some still had flesh clinging to them in bloody strands. Terror iced along his veins as he scanned for what had created the carnage. Within the recesses of the wall of hard clay was an iron gate, adjacent to the next covered platform, no doubt the only way out of this gruesome pit once he was trapped down inside. He didn't even want to think what horrors awaited him in the second trial. If he even survived the first.

Another roar echoed from the hole, but there was still no sign of the monstrous thing down below. But then a gruesome bear-shaped head edged out into the light. Sharp, curved horns protruded from its gnarled forehead. Torn ears twitched and turned like a horse warily listening to its surroundings. The massive head tilted to one side as it looked up, revealing a wrinkled fleshy snout and black lips curling away from drooling fangs.

Finn's breath stalled in his lungs when its feral eyes stared back at him. He took a step backward, bumping into the guard behind him. "I don't suppose I could borrow that sword of yours?"

A fleeting glimpse of compassion crossed the guard's face before his expression turned blank and emotionless. "You go in with what you came with."

"I arrived unarmed because I came here in peace." Finn glanced at Azrael with his saber and armor. "I don't see the fairness in my opponent being fully prepared while I'm expected to go in defenseless."

Azrael turned toward him, his first acknowledgment of Finn's presence. "The law is the law."

"Aye, the law." Finn frowned at Azrael's righteous tone. "This law of yours seems to bend easily enough for you and your family."

Azrael stepped forward, his blue eyes cold and unfeeling. "You further shame my family honor with your false accusations."

"You and your family shame *Fate's* honor by treating her like a possession in this dodgy charade of yours."

Azrael's grip tightened on the hilt of his saber, but Finn's guard was quick to intervene. "Prince Azrael, it is time for you to take your place on the other side."

Azrael leaned in toward Finn, his voice an angry hiss when he spoke. "I promise, you will die down there." He turned abruptly, marched around the hole and stopped in front of a rope ladder put in place while they were arguing. There was a ladder for Finn as well. Each one hung halfway down inside the pit.

The king's voice rang out. "Begin your descent," he ordered.

The drums pounded out a tense, rhythmic beat, matching the slam of Finn's heart as he lowered himself onto the ladder. The stench of diseased flesh filled his nose the further down he climbed. When he reached the bottom rung, he twisted around to check the monster's position.

Azrael was already on the ground, his saber drawn as he slowly approached the creature. It stayed against the wall, watching him from the shadows. The monster's guttural growl filled the pit, before pitching to a roar when Azrael swiped his blade and moved forward. Without wasting another second, Azrael lunged at it, his movements a swift blur before he found his mark.

The beast howled, reacting with a vicious swipe of its massive claws.

Azrael was faster and used the opening to strike again. A bloodcurdling shriek rang loud in Finn's ears as the monster stood on its hind legs and lumbered fully into the light.

Finn gripped the rope, staring open-mouthed at the giant–a hulking wall of pure muscle covered in patches of matted fur. Any exposed flesh was gray and shot through with dark bulging veins. Tumorous growths covered its shoulders and arms. Barbs grew from the knees of its hind legs and deadly spikes jutted from the forearms.

Finn couldn't tell if these were deformities or if the beast was diseased. He suspected the latter. The simple act of standing had left the beast panting and hunched over, allowing him to see a rounded back with a row of bony spikes protruding from its spine.

He spied blood dripping from fresh cuts across its mottled torso. Azrael had wounded it.

The rope ladder jerked upward without warning. Finn lost his grip and fell, the wind knocked out of him when he slammed into the ground. Pain drilled through his sore body. Gasping for breath, he glanced up just in time to see both ladders pulled completely from the pit. He rolled to one side, a move that saved him from being skewered by a spike in the beast's arm.

Adrenaline fired through his limbs, fueling him with unexpected energy. He jumped to his feet, drawing backward as the beast loomed over him. Thick strands of mucus dripped from its nose and mouth, vibrating grotesquely from the growl rumbling in its throat.

The beast lurched at Finn, aiming the long spike in its arm directly at his chest. Finn dodged to one side, barely escaping the deadly strike by inches. Propelled forward and in full swing when it missed, the monster drilled the point of its spike deep into the hard clay wall. Its growls became an enraged shriek as it struggled to pry the spike free.

Taking full advantage of this, Azrael made a running leap with his blade arching down on the monster's neck. The beast's ears prick back in Azrael's direction as it twisted around, blocking the blow with its free arm. The impact sent Azrael flying across the length of the pit. He smashed into the other side, head first. When he fell to the ground, he didn't move.

The beast tugged frantically to free itself. Finn sidled over to Azrael's saber and picked it up. Hearing his movements, the monster growled, locking Finn in its sights.

Gripping the hilt of Azrael's saber, Finn inched forward, ducking low to avoid being beheaded. He backed out of reach and rushed to the other side of the monster. Howling, it thrashed wildly, trying desperately to loosen the spike, twisting against its trapped arm to see where Finn stood. But it couldn't turn far enough. Finn stayed in its blind spot.

He moved in, ready to strike the killing blow, when he noticed the slick red pool of blood soaked over the patchy fur of its back. Azrael hadn't inflicted any wounds that high up on the giant and this stopped Finn. Mahelia must've seen to it that the monster was wounded to make it easier for Azrael to survive long enough to kill it and win the trial.

Finn knew damn well it hadn't been done for his safety, since he'd never stood a chance of killing it without a weapon. It would've worked and no one would be the wiser, except she hadn't foreseen Azrael being knocked unconscious. He couldn't resist a smug smile as he relished exposing Mahelia's dishonorable attempt to help Azrael cheat.

The beast's raging howls dwindled to a hoarse snarl. Panting hard, it crashed to its knees, too weak to stand any longer. That's when Finn saw the blood gushing from one of the bony spikes jutting from its rounded spine. The spike jostled loosely within the red, pulsing fountain with each ragged breath the creature took.

Finn slid the saber inside the sash at his waist and climbed onto the beast, using the bony spikes on its lower back to climb higher to the wobbly spike near the base of its skull. The creature growled and writhed weakly. When Finn reached the spike at its neck, he wrapped his hand around the base, curious as to how cold the bone felt in his grip, compared to the other spikes, which had all been warm. Something was off. Maybe this was the equivalent of a loose, rotten tooth needing to be extracted. He pulled gently on it, testing to see exactly how rooted it was.

The monster's pained screech was deafening. Finn clamped his hands over his ears until its tortured cry faded into rasping gasps. He couldn't help feeling sorry for the beast. Despite the human bones littered over the ground, this was a creature merely trying to defend itself against its captors. And now it was dying in an unfair fight, which meant he needed to work fast. Otherwise, they would credit its death with the wound Azrael had dealt it.

Crouching with both feet on either side of the wound, Finn gripped the spike and gave it a hard yank. The spike dislodged with such surprising ease, Finn lost his balance and fell off the creature's mountainous back. He hit a pile of human skulls. Arching his sore back, he rolled off them, quickly checking to see if the beast had risen, but it hadn't moved and the spike in its arm was still trapped in the wall.

Rising to his feet, Finn searched for the bone spike lying amongst the bone graveyard. Panic pumped in his veins when he didn't spot it right away.

He sifted through the bones, tossing them aside in his frantic search, then stopped over a flash of bloody metal. The bony spike was attached to what appeared to be a metal rod. Grabbing the spike, Finn pulled an incredibly long spear free of the debris. It was as tall as him.

He swore under his breath. Mahelia had certainly disguised the spear well by making the end look like one of the creature's spikes on its back. Finn glanced at the beast, unmoving but breathing shallowly. He wondered how it had survived as long as it had after being impaled by a spear of such great length.

A groan from behind had Finn turning toward Azrael, who rose to a sitting position. He rubbed his head and squinted at the monster. "Is it dead?" He frowned when he saw his saber strapped to Finn's waist and then his eyes widened when he noticed the spear. "How? You came unarmed."

"Don't play dumb with me. We both know what your mother did to save her precious boy."

Azrael shook his head. "I do not know what you mean."

"We're playing it that way, are we?" Finn laughed harshly. "Fine then. She stuck this thing in the creature's back to make it easy for you to finish it off, all while keeping everyone from suspecting you weren't good enough to win on your own." He gestured to the stadium of rapt, silent citizens. "I'd say they know now though."

Azrael stood, but much too fast and was forced to hold onto the wall to maintain balance. "I will cut your tongue out the moment I take my saber back," he threatened.

"I'd love to see you try, mate."

Azrael's face paled and he backed away. "It appears I will not have to."

Finn stiffened against the hot, fetid breath suddenly hitting the back of his neck. He turned slowly, his knees weakening as he stared into the monster's slavering maw.

15
THE WARLOBEAR

FINN SQUEEZED THE HANDLE of the spear, his arm shaking as he took a careful step backward. The beast's gaze flicked from him to Azrael and back again with a warning growl. It was hunched low, but not from weakness this time. Finn had the distinct impression it was measuring his intentions regarding the offending spear.

A hundred thoughts raced through Finn's mind all at once. The main one being that he should never have pulled the spear out. He could clearly see the monster was healing swiftly. The large tumors had already shrunken to the size of pebbles and its dark brown fur, now smooth, was growing back over skin, which was no longer gray but a healthy pink. The row of bony spikes on its spine had shriveled and fallen off, though the sharp barbs on its knees and the sword-like spikes in both arms remained sturdy. Unfortunately, with the return of its strength, the beast had pried itself free of the wall.

"Pass me my saber," Azrael said from behind him. "If we work together, we can bring it down."

Roaring at the sound of Azrael's voice, the creature rose to its full, immense height. Finn didn't move, though his body trembled as he stared up at the giant, knowing it could kill him with a single strike.

Finn waited for exactly that to happen, and yet with every second that ticked by, the beast did not attack. Standing tall and majestic, it roared at the sky with justified rage. A king in its own right, the glossy black horns curving from its forehead like a crown only confirmed its eminence over them, a sight that struck Finn with a nagging familiarity.

The creature had been unrecognizable in its former state of erosion, but seeing it now, Finn knew he'd laid eyes on this same beast before. In the Twisted Bone Forest when he'd hunted with Tove. She had called it a warlobear. Just as the lion is king of the jungle, the warlobear is king of the northern-most mountains of Oldwilde.

Finn remembered seeing it in the distance, a giant bear armed with fangs, horns, claws and spikes. Its dark fur had made it stand out against the snow. When the warlobear had spotted them across the snowy hills, it had risen onto its hind legs. An action that transformed a beast into a giant warrior, because from a distance, those spikes protruding from its arms had looked like swords. Its mighty roar had caused an avalanche in the highest region of a nearby mountain.

Tove had immediately kneeled in the snow, telling Finn to do the same. He'd done as instructed; fully expecting this would appease the warlobear. But instead of leaving, the beast dropped back onto all fours and charged swiftly toward them.

"Stay very still," Tove had told Finn when he'd made a move to escape. "We must gain his trust by demonstrating our submission and respect for entering his kingdom."

"His kingdom? I don't see a castle anywhere nearby."

"This is his castle. The mountains are his walls, the peaks his towers. This forest is his courtyard, and the animals that dwell here, his citizens."

Watching the beast gallop toward them made it all the more difficult to hold such a vulnerable position. "I suppose his citizens are food as well."

"The warlobear eats only fish. He is built to cut through the ice and spear his catch."

Finn relaxed only slightly. "At least he won't *eat* us."

"Only a warlobear struck by the sickness would kill and eat us." Tove had given him a sidelong glance when he'd visibly tensed. "Stay. This one is not sick."

Finn had many more questions to ask, except that the warlobear was upon them before he could speak another word. He'd shaken in the presence of the enormous beast, despite the supernatural strength and speed Tove had given him with the Elder race runes.

The warolobear's massive head had loomed over them. White puffs of air plumed from his nostrils as he sniffed the space between them. All the while measuring them, an intelligence in its eyes Finn could never have guessed at. After a moment of prolonged tension and fear, the warolobear had turned and left them unharmed.

The warlobear's gaze returned to Finn, its enraged roar dwindling to a low, seething snarl. Finn stared back, seeing the same intelligence as before. There was only one thing to do.

Azrael spoke again, his voice hushed and nervous. "Finn, you must use the spear. Kill it."

The warlobear's eyes snapped on Azrael, growling as its muzzle quivered with malice. Finn dropped the spear, drawing the beast's attention away from Azrael. Slowly, Finn loosened his sash, allowing the saber's weight to slip from his waist before it fell to the ground with a heavy thud.

Azrael voice was incredulous, louder than before. "What are you–"

"Kneel." Finn kept his tone even and calm and as he lowered to his knees.

The warlobear watched Finn warily, then its gaze shifted to Azrael.

Finn glanced over his shoulder at him. "If you want to live, kneel."

Azrael stubbornly stood and Finn feared he was about to witness him being torn apart. The warlobear would only wait so long before it took the gesture as an outright challenge.

Just when it looked as if Azrael would rather die than submit to what he no doubt viewed as a vicious, mindless beast, he followed suit and kneeled. The warlobear fixed his gaze on Azrael, a relentless snarl in its throat as it waited him out, its muscles coiled and ready to defend itself if Azrael reached for the saber.

"What now?" Azrael whispered after several minutes had passed.

Good question. There was no place for the warlobear to retreat. They were all trapped inside the pit together, until the guards either threw the rope ladders down low enough for them to reach, or lifted the mysterious gate in the wall, which likely opened into the next pit where the second trial would take place. Why hadn't they done so yet? The only reason Finn could think of was they still fully expected them to kill the warlobear.

There had to be another way. Finn refused to be a party to murdering this noble creature. They'd not only ripped him from his natural domain, but had tortured and poisoned him until he'd mutated into something monstrous.

Finn reached into his pocket. The warlobear's gaze moved to Finn and his growl grew louder. Finn slowly pulled out his Druidic inscribed wooden flute. The Elder race runes he'd once carved into it had been erased just as they'd been erased from his skin, when he'd been remade by the Orb of Aeternitis and returned to his original self. But he remembered how to play the rune notes Tove had taught him. The power behind the runes would be absent, but maybe there was a slim chance the warlobear would recognize them.

Finn blew the first rune notes of the wind song. The soft melodic music put an immediate end to the warlobear's growls and wary gaze. Encouraged, Finn continued to play, his own thoughts taken back to his time with Tove and Grysla in the Twisted Bone Forest. The exhilaration of living in those harsh, yet beautiful snowy mountains, the reverent discovery of his elemental powers and his deep, sacred connection to the earth returned.

Tears of joy blurred his vision, further flooded over by tears of grief at knowing he would never experience such freedom, or sense of family ever again. The last tree troll was gone. He would never again hear the deep rumbling voice of his dear friend. Nor would he know the warmth of Tove's friendship. She hated him, and he would forever hate himself for bringing about the cause of Grysla's death.

The warlobear lifted his head to the sky and howled, a mournful sound that resonated within the earthen walls. All the sadness and longing Finn felt for his time in the Twisted Bone Forest mirrored the warlobear's sorrowful howls. An eerie call that echoed within the stadium, over and over, until his howls multiplied, as if they came from a whole pack of warlobears.

The warlobear's howls ended with an abrupt bellow of pain. Finn stopped playing, momentarily disoriented before he saw Azrael withdraw the full length of his bloody saber from the warlobear's belly.

Pure, blind fury propelled Finn into action. Dropping his flute, he picked up the spear and lunged at Azrael, who blocked the attack with more speed and skill than Finn possessed. Astounded by his strength, Finn nearly lost his grip on the spear, but managed to hold onto it and block Azrael's returning blow.

A deafening roar put a swift stop to the fight and Azrael edged backward until he bumped against the gate. Snarling, the warlobear dropped to all fours and advanced toward him.

Azrael looked at Finn. "You have my word that I will not fight you throughout the remainder of the trials if you call off this beast."

"This is no beast." Finn shook his head. "He is a king, and as you know, there's no telling a king what to do."

The growling warlobear's muzzle drew back from a row of long fangs as it came within inches of Azrael's face. Azrael instinctively slipped to the ground to get away from the mouth. "Please," he implored.

Before Finn could answer, the grinding of metal filled the pit. The gate opened and Azrael slipped through. Finn ran up to the opening in time to see Azrael rush down a tunnel toward light at the other end.

That's when Finn noticed the warlobear's labored breathing. He didn't need to look any further than the pool of blood on the ground beneath him to know what was wrong. Finn felt sick with remorse. By losing himself in the music, he'd given Azrael the opening he'd needed to deliver a cut too deep to staunch.

Finn put a hand on the warlobear's neck and ran his fingers through the soft fur. The warlobear turned its head, staring back with gentle eyes.

"Forgive me." Finn choked on the words.

"Move through the gate!"

Startled by the voice, Finn glanced up to see a guard, his bow drawn taught with an arrow aimed at this chest.

"Now!" the guard ordered.

Finn stared defiantly at the guard. He wasn't going to leave the warlobear to die alone.

The swift shot of an arrow whistled past his ear, hit the wall and vibrated in place. "Move, or the next will be buried in your head," the guard yelled.

The warlobear nudged his muzzle against Finn's arm, pushing him toward the opening. Finn took the spear with him in case Azrael went back on his word and took a few steps forward before glancing back. "Goodbye, my friend."

He turned away quickly and forced himself to continue and remember why he was doing this. To free Fate from bondage.

Finn reached the end of the tunnel and hovered warily inside the opening. Azrael stood on a narrow platform just outside the gate. The covering had already been pulled aside, allowing sunlight to pour in. A hissing noise rang from below, an incessant sound that bounced off the walls.

"Please don't let that be what it sounds like," Finn muttered under his breath, as he took a half step forward and stood on tiptoe. "Bollocks!" He retreated back inside the opening.

Azrael glanced over his shoulder. "I take it you do not care for snakes."

Finn wasn't about to share his deeply rooted disdain for snakes ever since a rattler killed his mother on a hike in the mountains. It didn't matter that the memory had been manufactured by Fate when she'd created him on paper. The feelings were brutally real.

He glowered at Azrael. "As a matter of fact, my best friend happens to be a snake." He refrained from sharing that he'd been severely distrustful of Sithias when they'd first met.

Azrael scowled back. "You mean the snake who claims to be Aradif." A cruel smile formed on his lips. "Where is this snake now? What sort of *friend* would put you in harm's way and then abandon you in your greatest hour of need?"

Finn had been wondering the very same thing. "I don't need rescuing. I can take care of myself."

"You are fooling yourself if you think you can survive this next trial. Unless you can fly, your only way to the next gate is to wade waist deep through a vat of blue vipers, the most poisonous snakes in all of Shalamoraize." Sheathing his bloodstained saber, Azrael stepped to the very edge of the platform and jumped.

Stunned by the bold move, Finn fully expected Azrael to land somewhere in the middle of the wide pit. But that's not what happened. Judging by the sheer height of his jump, Azrael obviously possessed even more supernatural strength than he'd initially realized, because he easily cleared the distance and landed safely on the other side.

A loud cheer rose from the citizens of Biraktar. They'd been silent since the trials began, a presence Finn had almost forgotten about, what with his main focus being survival. Azrael, on the other hand, took a bow, which stirred another wave of applause louder than the last.

When the stadium quieted after a few minutes, Azrael leaned against the locked gate, crossed his arms and smiled at Finn. The air of confidence he exuded infuriated Finn.

"What are you waiting for?" Azrael could have kept his voice low to keep the conversation between the two of them, but he clearly wanted everyone to hear. "No one would blame you if you surrender your claim on my wife."

If Finn could still fly he would've bolted straight into Azrael with both fists and knock him into the snake pit. Unfortunately, that handy power was gone with all the others. If he hadn't been so distracted with keeping the big ugly secret about Eustace from Fate, he would've had her restore everything he'd lost. And she gladly would have.

Finn sighed. Truth be known, he hadn't asked because his guilt wouldn't let him.

"Do you surrender?" a guard yelled from above.

Finn glared at the guard whose arrow was aimed at his aching heart. "Never!" he growled. He wouldn't be able to live with himself if he gave up.

Not that he expected to live much longer. He didn't see any way across that didn't involve getting down there with the snakes. The clay walls were too smooth and sheer for climbing. Even if there were enough handholds in the wall to make it worth trying, he doubted his stamina would last in his weakened state.

All he had was the spear.

Steeling himself, Finn stepped out onto the lip of the platform and looked down at the writhing, slithering pool of thousands of snakes. Deep blue in color, their iridescent scales shimmered beneath the sun in shifting hues of sea green and turquoise. If he weren't so repulsed and terrified, he'd take pleasure in thinking they'd be better used for shoes and purses.

A shiver of revulsion passed through him the longer he stared at the vipers. "Well, stabbing them all is definitely out of the question," he muttered to himself. "Pole vaulting, it is."

Finn held the spear horizontally in both hands, measuring the weight and length as best he could. The spear was long for sure, but he had no idea if the length was mathematically correct for leaping the distance. Nor was he certain if there would be enough flexibility to gain proper momentum.

"All I can do is try. But I'll need to take a good run at it." He heaved another big sigh and turned to go back inside the tunnel.

Finn stopped when he saw the warlobear shambling toward him. His entire girth filled the large tunnel, making it a tight fit as he pushed his weight past the walls. When he finally reached the end, the warlobear halted just inside the opening. He was breathing hard and his large head hung low, as if the weight of it was too much to carry.

"You should be resting. Not moving around. You need to give yourself a chance to heal." Finn stroked the side of the warlobear's head, just under the ear.

The warlobear moaned and blinked wearily. His panting eased somewhat, but only increased as he pushed himself further through the opening until his paws rested on the edge of the platform. Then he lowered himself flat on the ground and nudged Finn's shins with his nose.

Finn kneeled down next him. "I don't understand."

Thrusting his muzzle against Finn more roughly, the warlobear growled weakly.

"I'm sorry, my friend. I could help if I had my medicines with me." Finn winced at the smears of fresh blood spreading from beneath the warlobear's underbelly. No amount of medicines could help that fatal wound. Finn's anger toward Azrael flared anew.

The warlobear growled more forcefully, swiped a paw at Finn's leg, knocking him over onto his shoulders. Finn started to move off, but the warlobear pushed up onto all fours. Twisting to one side, Finn was forced to coil his fingers into the warlobear's fur with his free hand, while holding his grip on the spear to keep it from falling into the pit. He started to slide down to get off, but had to hold fast again when the warlobear stood on his hind legs and jumped off the platform.

"*Nooo!*" Finn cried out, his heart breaking as he held onto the warlobear's head.

The warlobear wailed in pain as it pushed through the snakes, each step a pained, shaky struggle. Every snake in the pit slithered with horrifying speed toward him, biting each other to reach the thick, meaty legs they knew were ripe for sinking their venom into.

Finn stabbed frantically at the vipers, hitting some with the spear, but missing most. The snakes were too fast, and when he saw how many of them struck the warlobear with jaws open and fangs dripping with yellow venom, he wept.

They were more than halfway across the pit when the warlobear staggered. He let out a mournful wail as he sank to his knees.

Finn hugged the warlobear's head and stroked his fur. "It's all right. You've done well, my friend. You can go to sleep now. Be at peace and rest your eyes."

The warlobear's wail faded into a soft whimper. No longer able to withstand the vipers' massive poisoning, the warlobear fell forward. Jostled by the impact, Finn held on to keep from falling in. The vipers swarmed in around the body, covering the head and limbs, biting and biting.

Finn stood and stepped onto the highest part of the warlobear's back. But some of the vipers raised their heads and slithered up over the large furry mound toward him. Panic shot adrenaline through Finn's limbs. Without thinking, he ran the length of the warlobear's back, drove the spear down into the snake pit and vaulted himself into the air with his legs aimed at the platform, where Azrael stood waiting for the next gate to open.

Finn held tight to the spear as he catapulted through the air. Pain bit into his heels when he hit the hard surface and slid across the platform with so much momentum, he slammed into the gate. His grip loosened on the spear, which rolled back to the edge of the platform. Finn dove for it, his waist going over the edge before he caught the spear, but there was nothing to keep him from pitching headfirst into the snake pit.

16
THE SPEAR OF KARTHALA

FINN STABBED THE SPEAR straight down into the writhing viper nest to stop the fall, his body ramrod stiff and feet hooked on the edge of the platform. Sweat poured off his nose as he balanced in a rigid plank position, his arms shaking with the effort of holding onto the rough, bone handle of the spear. He shifted his hips, hoping to move his feet backward to regain a few more inches on the platform but nearly lost his balance in the effort when the spear wobbled beneath him. His shoulders, torso and legs quaked with the strain of holding his body straight. Pain pulsated through his muscles all the way down to his aching hands.

Nothing could save him now. He only hoped the venom would bring about a swift death. Defeat loosened his grip on the handle and Finn slid inexorably toward his doom.

A streak of absolute terror renewed his will to live. Finn clenched the handle as hard as he could, stopping the slide, but he'd lost the strength to hold his balance any longer. The spear tipped to one side. One leg slipped from the platform. The next foot came loose. Squeezing his eyes shut, Finn waited for the inevitable swarm of cold scales and the venomous sting of countless bites.

A hard yank on his ankle jerked him upward, making him crash into the wall. Confused, Finn opened his eyes and angled his head to see who was holding him. To his surprise, it was Azrael who hauled him up enough to bend his legs over the platform. Finn clutched his spear, uncertain if he was being saved out of mercy or to be ultimately killed in battle.

Azrael pulled him all the way onto the platform before letting go of his legs. Finn rolled over quickly and stood, checking to see if Azrael had his saber drawn. When he confirmed his weapon remained sheathed, Finn leaned his back against the wall, gasping to catch his breath.

Finn looked him in the eyes. "Thank you. I know you didn't have to do that. You could've let me die and you would've won."

Azrael tilted his head slightly in acknowledgment. "You won the first trial and you had already won the second as well. If I am to win this, I want it to be because I passed the final test over *you*," he seethed. "It is the only way to prove I alone am worthy of claiming Fate."

Finn chose to ignore that last remark. He was too preoccupied by what Azrael had said. "I don't get it. Why would you think I won the last two trials? I didn't kill the warlobear and I didn't make it across the pit without help."

Before Azrael could answer, the grinding sound of the third gate being drawn had them both turning toward the widening crack of the opening.

"Move through the gate," the guard ordered from above.

Finn glanced at Azrael and gestured for him to go first. "After you."

Azrael didn't move. "To be clear, the help I gave you in no way makes us friends. Understood?"

Finn nodded. "Abso-bloody-lutely."

Azrael stared back as though he was daft, then turned into the large tunnel and Finn followed. The air was cool within the dim passageway. As they moved closer to the end of the tunnel, the temperature dropped sharply, chilling the sweat dripping down his back and chest to the point of making him shiver.

Azrael stopped just inside the opening, his saber drawn as he warily scanned the huge pit. Finn stepped in beside him, wrinkling his nose at the unpleasant odor of mold and mildew filling the space. Unlike the other two open pits, this one was covered with fine netting, which filtered the sunlight. It appeared more like dusk inside the deep well, making it easy to forget it was a clear sunny morning outside in the stadium.

Finn's jagged nerves ramped back into high gear. He disliked the indigo shadows hiding whatever awaited them. Another chill shuddered through him, not from the frigid air he sucked into his lungs but from his inability to see what lurked in the dark.

"I don't suppose you have any idea what's in there, do you?" Finn whispered.

Azrael was quiet a moment. "I have my suspicions."

"Which are?"

"I will not voice them until I know." Azrael spoke a strange word Finn didn't understand, and smacked his hands together. Golden light flared bright, illuminating the interior for a split second, but with all the harshness of a strobe light.

Finn witnessed pure horror in that brief flash. A tall, sinewy bat-like creature awoke from a perch close to the opposite wall, where it hung upside down. It was reptilian with features that could almost be mistaken for human, if not so hideously distorted. Hissing at the light, the creature craned its neck, baring needlepoint fangs designed to pierce soft flesh. And that soft flesh was to be Fate's.

She was lying, still and unconscious, on a stone plinth in the center of the pit.

Finn's heart pounded with sheer terror and undiluted rage. He shoved Azrael against the wall, ramming his forearm into his throat. "How could you do this to her?" he growled. "Wasn't it enough that you enslaved her and forced her to marry you?"

Azrael gripped Finn's arm but refrained from using force. "I had no idea they would do this," he confessed. His gaze moved to the center of the shadowy pit, where they'd glimpsed Fate. "If I had, I would gladly have freed her from both the soul ring and her vows. I would *never* risk her life in such a way."

"It's a mite late for that now, isn't it?" Jerking his arm away, Finn turned and stared into the darkness. A querulous groan and rustling came from above. The creature was stirring. "We have to get Fate off that dinner plate down there and into the tunnel. After that we can work on killing the thing."

Azrael shook his head. "She cannot be moved. Did you not see? They have her chained down."

"Then we get down there."

Azrael's eyes filled with fear as he cast an upward glance into the shadows.

"This is no time to lose courage," Finn seethed.

Azrael lowered his gaze. Something in his eyes unnerved Finn. He knew something Finn didn't. "What aren't you telling me?"

"My mother used to tell a story about a cursed, blood-thirsty creature called a Necrofa. She said it was an ugly scaled thing, but that it retains the remnants of a human, even though its arms were webbed to its sides like the wings of a bat. The face is most unsettling, because it is there, that you will see the man it used to be."

Finn grimaced. "No way. That thing was never human."

Azrael exhaled a heavy sigh. The warmth of his breath threaded the icy air like wisps of steam. "I recognized the man in its face. He was my father's personal bodyguard and good friend. There is no mistake. I have known him since I was a child."

Finn stared at Azrael in disbelief. "But how could he have turned into *that*?"

"He was turned because of the curse."

More rustling and mewling sounds had Finn peering back in the general area he'd caught sight of the creature. He gripped his spear in both hands, ready to jump down into the pit with Fate. "This is sounding more like a meaningless myth than anything else. It doesn't matter what it's called. All we should be concerned with is protecting Fate by killing the bloodsucker."

"You do not understand." Azrael pushed away from the wall and stood beside Finn. "The curse passes onto whomever slaughters the creature."

Finn frowned at him. "Wait, are saying one of us is going to turn into *that*, depending on who kills it?"

Azrael nodded. "Yes. That is how my father's friend became the creature."

Finn was horrified. "That would mean your father ordered him to slay the first one. Why would he do that to his friend?"

"I believe he asked his friend to sacrifice himself so I would recognize him and know not to be the one to kill the creature."

Finn looked at Azrael, puzzled and surprised. "Why are you telling me this? You could've kept this key piece of information to yourself and let me do the deed. You'd be guaranteed to come out the undeniable winner."

"I told you. I want to demonstrate my worthiness to Fate." Azrael winced visibly. "She still has feelings for you. If I have anything to do with your demise, she may never forgive me."

"She's asleep, drugged or something." Finn bit down on his anger. These people continued to treat her like a meaningless object. But this wasn't the time or place to press the issue. "How would she ever know?"

"All that happens within the trials is being transcribed by the priests. Every action we take and every word we speak is becoming a part of public record for all to see."

"Oh." Finn shook his head. He should've known Azrael's motives weren't entirely altruistic. "Transparency is the only reason you're being... forthright."

"There are other reas–"

A hair-raising shriek drowned Azrael's words. They both bolted off the platform. Unable to see the depth of the jump, Finn's feet hit the dirt sooner than anticipated. Pain shot through his shins and his knees caved beneath him.

The pit filled with the sounds of flapping leathery wings overhead. Frosty blasts of air gusted in Finn's face as he rose achingly to a standing position. The Necrofa swooped low. Finn ducked when the cold touch of its wing grazed the back of his neck and head. He jabbed frantically into the dark with his spear.

"I can't see a bloody thing!" Finn yelled. "We need light!"

"The light will expose Fate," Azrael shouted from the other side of the pit.

The Necrofa made another pass, this time so close Finn heard a low hiss in his ear and smelled the reek of its moldy breath. He stabbed the air in a frenzy, hoping to wound it enough to ground it. "We're fighting blind here! And I think it can see us!"

"So be it." The commanding sound in Azrael's voice coincided with an explosion of light above them. A ball of golden flames hovered in place, banishing the thick shadows in an instant.

The Necrofa's ear piercing screech seemed amplified as it thrashed against the walls, its clawed feet scrabbling the smooth surface, searching for its perch. When it finally grappled onto the perch, it swung upside down, twisting its head toward the inside of the pit.

Just when Finn was beginning to think the light had blinded it, the creature's shrewd gaze fixed first on Azrael and then moved to Finn, before landing on Fate. The blindness had only been momentary. Finn sprinted over to Fate and stood in front of her. The moment he raised his spear and aimed the point at the Necrofa, it hissed at him.

Azrael positioned himself on the other side of Fate and ran his hands over the chains pinning her down. "I think I may be able to remove the chains. If I can free her, we must work swiftly. The Necrofa will be more vicious than ever when it sees its sacrifice being taken." He spoke in a hushed tone so as not to provoke the creature.

Finn kept his eyes locked on the Necrofa. It stretched its neck to see what Azrael was doing. "Do what you need to do," Finn told him.

He listened to Azrael uttering a strange sounding incantation. The first set of chains slipped away, falling to the ground with a loud clamor of metal.

A shriek filled the pit as the Necrofa thrust itself off the perch, sweeping its thick membranous wings downward, whipping up a cloud of moldering dust in its wake.

"Hurry," Finn said. "It's up to you to get her out of here."

Azrael unlocked the last set of chains and lifted her into his arms. Her head lolled to one side, her body limp as he backed away from the plinth. The Necrofa dropped down, its wings flapping furiously with clawed feet ready to clutch Fate from Azrael's arms.

Finn drove the spear at its talons, a move that only nicked it with a mere scratch. But the creature screeched in pain and flew higher to escape Finn's reach. Finn glanced back at Azrael, who jumped easily onto the platform with Fate and retreated inside the tunnel.

The Necrofa saw them, plunged downward and landed on the platform. It hopped forward and lowered its head to fit within the tunnel's opening.

Finn couldn't see Azrael, but he could hear him yelling and fighting. The Necrofa's wings twitched and jerked from each blow of Azrael's saber, but his blade obviously wasn't delivering any serious wounds because it continued to push deeper into the tunnel.

Finn raced over to the platform, but it was too high. He no longer possessed the same ability as Azrael to jump such a height. Panicked, he glanced around, searching for something to stand on, or climb with. The only thing available was the stone plinth, which was far too heavy to move. His gaze dropped to the chains. They weren't all that long, but they had hooks on the end.

"It's better than nothing," he growled under his breath.

Grabbing two lengths of chain, he hooked one to the other and ran back to the platform. He had to make this work. There was real fear in Azrael's shouts. Finn swung the chain and tossed the hooked end up onto the platform. He pulled slowly on it, hoping to catch the hook on the edge but the hook was lying on its side. It slipped over the edge and fell to the ground.

Finn shook with frustration. "Calm down, boyo," he told himself. "You can do this."

Taking a deep breath, he tossed the chain back up onto the platform. This time there was a slight drag as he gently pulled on it. "That's good. It's digging into the clay." He tugged the chain carefully, clenching his jaw as he watched the end of the hook tip over the edge. He gave it a hard yank and the pointed curve of the hook caught hold.

"Got it." Finn hastily anchored his spear within the sash at his waist and pushed it behind his back. Gripping the chain with both hands, he set his foot on the wall, then the other and tested his weight against the pull of the chain.

By some miracle it held. Finn continued to move his feet higher, one at a time. He grabbed the next length of chain and pulled himself up. By the time he reached the top, his tunic was soaked through with sweat, despite the glacial temperature.

Azrael yelled again. There was pain and abject terror in his voice now. The Necrofa must be winning the battle. Finn climbed fully onto the platform. All he could see from this angle was the creature's backside and wings filling the tunnel. It had Azrael and Fate cornered all the way down at the other end, where there was no place to go but into the snake pit.

Finn loosened his sash and freed the spear, squeezing the bone handle tightly with both hands. He had the advantage here. The tunnel was a tight fit for the creature. It wouldn't be able to turn around easily. All he had to do was drive the spear into its back.

Finn gulped, knowing full well the curse would pass onto him. He would become the Necrofa, the very bloodsucker they were trying to save Fate from. But she was everything to him, as vital as the air he breathed. The thought of living in a world where she no longer existed was unbearable to him.

Finn charged forward, a roar of fury, sorrow and love tearing at his throat. He was upon the Necrofa within a few short seconds, plunging the long tip of his spear into its scaly hide. It carved through bone, muscle and organs as easily as cutting a slice of cake.

A bone-chilling shriek echoed through the confines of the tunnel and the Necrofa stiffened, its hard scales rapidly decaying around where the spear pierced its hide. Black mold spread over its scales, filling the air with the stench of rot. The mold spread over its wings, shriveling them until they were so thin they shredded like tissue and flaked away. The Necrofa's body buckled in on itself, as if its insides had been hollowed out. Dark flecks drifted over the floor, until all at once, there was no substance left to its form.

The spear dropped to the ground. The bone handle made to look like one of the bony spikes in the warlobear's back broke away from a steel handle of fine metalwork. Finn picked it up and wiped the dust of ground bone from the wrought grooves in the handle.

Azrael waved away the dust particles. His arm was bleeding and there were cuts on his face. Fate lay frighteningly still near the edge of the platform.

Finn couldn't tell if she was breathing or not. "Is she all right?"

Azrael nodded tiredly. "I managed to keep it away from her."

Finn breathed out a sigh of relief, but didn't move. "Thank you."

Azrael lifted Fate off the ground and walked back through the tunnel toward the third pit. Finn wanted to follow, but he didn't know when the curse would start changing him. It could happen at any second, and he suspected the transformation would be as swift as the creature's demise.

"You may've won the trial, Azrael, but you should do the right thing and free her," Finn called out. "If you truly love Fate, you'll let her decide if she wants to be with you."

Azrael stopped and turned around. "Do you not understand what happened here? Fate is free to be with you."

"What? But the curse. I dealt the killing blow. I'm cursed now."

Azrael shook his head and walked out onto the platform. Thoroughly confused, Finn trailed after him and stepped out into welcome sunshine. The netting had been pulled away and two rope ladders hung down with the ends generously draped over the platform.

Azrael carefully shifted Fate over one shoulder and started to climb up the rope ladder.

Finn caught him by the arm. "Hold on there. Are you saying I'm *not* cursed?"

"You are not cursed." Azrael frowned at Finn's hand. "Release me and I will carry your wife up the ladder. Unless you wish to risk dropping her in your weakened condition."

Finn let go and Azrael resumed his climb. Hearing him call Fate his wife sent a jolt of energy through Finn. He slid the spear into his sash again and quickly scaled the other ladder to catch up with Azrael. "I don't get it. How is this possible?"

Azrael didn't stop climbing. "You had the Spear of Karthala from the very first trial. I always believed the spear was a myth. I was wrong, especially in my approach to the first test. The priests designed the trials to be a karmic test. You showed the... warlobear, as you called it, compassion by removing the spear, which was the very key to winning the next two trials, while also protecting you from the curse."

The clenched muscles in Azrael's jaw betrayed his anger. "I should have known. I thought this was a test of force and relied too easily on my Djinn powers."

"Well, I for one am grateful for those powers. I wouldn't have survived if you hadn't kept me from falling into the snake pit," Finn reminded him.

When they reached the top, the guards removed Fate from Azrael's shoulder. Finn watched them carry her away. "I should go with her." A row of guards blocked his way. He glared at Azrael. "What is this? You said I was free to be with her."

"I assure you, Fate is safe. Let us finish the ceremony and then you will be taken to her." Azrael dismissed the guards and gestured to Finn to face the king, who now rose from his throne.

One of the priests walked over to Finn. When he reached for the spear, Finn held tight. Not out of greed or any real desperation to possess it, but because the weapon had been critical to his survival and he felt bonded to it.

Azrael leaned toward him. "You must release the spear. It does not belong to you."

Finn shook his head. "I'm not comfortable handing it over. Not after what I've seen you people do with a weapon such as this."

A loud, sibilant hiss came from the vast audience as two guards grabbed Finn by the arms. Knowing he was outmanned and pushing his luck, he released his grip on the spear and let the priest take it.

The king glowered down at Finn before raising his stern gaze to everyone in the stadium. "Let it be known that the claimant is the victor," he declared.

An air of bitter resentment came from his citizens, all of whom hissed that much louder.

The king raised his hands, silencing them immediately. "The priests have decreed that Prince Azrael's marriage to the woman is annulled. She is free to leave with the claimant."

Finn cared little about the king's disrespectful reference toward him as claimant, but he hated how the man continually refused to use Fate's name. Finn couldn't wait to get her out of this awful place, where people expendable.

His gaze landed on the slaves who were pulling the heavy platforms back over the pits, entombing the warlobear inside with the horrible nest of vipers. Finn was outraged. If there was any justice at all, the body should be returned to the Twisted Bone Forest, where the warlobear had been born.

One of the slaves fell to the ground. Finn recognized him by his blood-soaked back as the man who'd been whipped for falling when the trials had first begun. The nearest guard lashed his whip over those fresh wounds. Finn winced as the man shuddered and cried out.

Unable to stand by and watch any longer, Finn bolted over to the priest, grabbed the spear from him and charged the guard with the whip. "Stop this!" he growled.

Several guards descended on Finn all at once. He fended off their strikes with the spear, but he was sorely outnumbered and they quickly disarmed him. A blow from behind had him hurling forward. Finn tripped and hit the sand, where he landed next to the beaten slave. The slave looked at him with sad amber eyes Finn knew all too well.

Sithias had been present since the trials began.

17
FREEDOM FOR ALL

"THE CLAIMANT HAS DISGRACED this sacred ceremony and himself as victor. Lock him away!" The king signaled the guards with an irritable wave of his arm.

The guards jerked Finn roughly to his feet and dragged him off toward the entrance they'd used to deliver him to the ceremony. Exhaustion had taken over. Every ounce of energy Finn had managed to hold onto throughout the trials had evaporated.

His bewilderment at discovering Sithias had sat by and allowed him to go through all that misery further depleted him. As to why Sithias had posed as a slave and allowed himself to be beaten was utterly baffling. Had he been taken prisoner as well?

Finn was too exhausted to think on it any longer. All he wanted was to sleep and deal with the fallout once he'd regained a modicum of strength.

"Ssstop!" Sithias's sibilant voice filled the stadium and seemed to come from every direction.

The guards dropped Finn, each of them turning slowly in fear. Too weary to stand, Finn scraped his knees through the sand as he turned around. The shock of seeing Sithias as a beaten, bloodied slave was one thing, but seeing him transform from a victimized man to a winged snake that grew to be ten times his normal size was a whole new level of shocking.

A cacophony of frightened screams and gasps came from the audience.

"The only disgrace that hasss taken place here today isss in the way you treated my companion, whom I placed in your care." Sithias loomed high over the royal platform, making the king look small and insignificant by comparison.

The king cowered beneath Sithias's furious gaze. "We treated his wounds, your holiness!"

"That isss all you did," Sithias hissed. "You sssent him into the trialsss weakened, unprotected and unarmed, while your ssson, who isss endowed with unnatural ssstrength, wasss wearing armor and bearing hisss own weapon."

The king dropped to his knees. "We merely followed the rules. Each competitor goes in with what they came with. It is not our fault your companion came with nothing but–"

"Sssilence!" Sithias stared at the trembling king. "I am gravely disssappointed. Thisss man not only endured the trialsss, he conquered each tessst exactly as they were desssigned to be won. And yet you would imprison and punish him for defending a downtrodden ssslave becaussse he showed the very compassion your priesssts designed the trialsss around."

Sithias slithered onto one of the heavy discs covering the pits and spread his feathered wings to an impressive length. "Having personally sssuffered the lashing of massster to ssslave, I will no longer ssstand by and allow anymore wanton abusse. Citizens of Biraktar, I decree that ssslavery is abolished from thisss day forward. There will be freedom for all!"

Shouts of resistance rose from the people. A deafening hiss from Sithias silenced them. "Anyone caught practicing ssslavery in Biraktar will sssuffer the punishment of death!"

"Your holiness, Biraktar needs its slaves to survive." The king's quavering voice was as powerless as it sounded.

Sithias turned to look at him. "Correction. Biraktar's survival now dependsss on finding a way to live without ssslavery. You may begin by paying your laborersss and ssservants."

The king rose to his feet but kept his head bowed. "Only citizens of Biraktar can be paid."

Sithias rose into the sky with a mighty sweep of his giant wings. Clouds of dust and sand radiated out in powerful gusts, hitting the faces of everyone on ground level. He landed back in front of the royal stage, causing the king to drop back to his knees. "I suggessst you make each and every former ssslave in Biraktar a citizen."

"Your holiness. I regret to say it is not within my power to do so."

"You are king, are you not?"

"As king, I must follow the laws written in your holy book, that the people of the stars shall be given domain over those of the earth. All our slaves are *earth lovers*." The disdain for 'earth lovers' was more than apparent in the king's tone.

"Then I repeal thisss law here, now and forever," Sithias decreed. "I alssso revoke the ussse of sssoul ringsss. No man or woman should be indebted to the one who sssaves his or her life."

Another burst of angry hisses and shouts came from the audience.

Sithias lowered his gigantic head until he was close enough to the king to bite his head off. "Thisss appliesss to Prince Azrael. He will releassse the claimant'sss wife from the sssoul ring he placed upon her." Sithias turned to look at Azrael, who stood on the lower stage next to Mahelia.

They both stared up at Sithias with open malice.

"I will sssee it done now!" Sithias demanded.

Azrael stepped forward. "I released Fate the moment I lost the trials."

"Show me. Bring her out!"

Mahelia slipped through the curtains of a tented room at the back of the lower stage. A few moments later, she stepped back outside, holding the curtain aside. Fate poked her head through and glanced around sleepily before her eyes widened in surprise at the sight of the colossal Sithias who lowered his head from a great height to scrutinize her.

"The sssoul ring isss removed?" he asked, keeping his tone distant and aloof, as if he were speaking to a stranger.

Fate lifted the hem of the simple cotton shift she was wearing and exposed both ankles. The soul ring was gone. Finn smiled. Fate was finally free of Azrael's control. Every horrible thing he'd suffered during the trials had been worth it. He'd accomplished what he'd set out to do.

Sithias raised his head, directing his gaze to the king. "I am satisssfied. Do I have your word that my companion and wife are free to leave Biraktar sssafely?"

"You have my word, your holiness." The king rose shakily to his feet. "To demonstrate my promise, I will have my precious son, Azrael, escort them safely home."

Mahelia stiffened with an enraged gaze burning up at the stage, where her husband stood.

Sithias tilted his head with a distrustful glint in his eyes. He remained silent to allow the tension to build. "And what of the ssslaves?" He slithered back into the middle of the arena. "They are ssstill in chainsss."

The king made one authoritative clap. "Release the slaves at once!" he ordered his guards.

The slave masters held onto their whips and stood still, refusing to obey.

"Arrest them!" the king shouted.

The wall of guards lining the stadium walls stormed the slave masters, swiftly relieving them of their whips before taking them away. All the remaining guards worked quickly to unchain the numerous teams of puzzled slaves.

The king gave Sithias a nervous glance. "Are you pleased, your holiness?"

Sithias weaved his way back to the royal stage. "My pleasure remainsss unfulfilled."

"What can I do to make you fully pleased?" the king asked.

"Deem thessse emancipated sssslaves and all othersss within Biraktar your cherished citizensss."

Finn watched in amazement, impressed by how far Sithias was pushing things, but anxious his friend was getting close to stepping over that hairy edge between winning and blowing his cover.

The king cleared his throat as he addressed the full stadium. "Let it be known by the omnipotent authority of our great and holy Guiding Star, that all freed slaves are deemed citizens of Biraktar."

The audience hissed their disapproval.

"With the sssame rightsss the original citizensss of Biraktar have alwaysss enjoyed," Sithias pressed.

"Careful, Sithias," Finn murmured under his breath.

For the first time, the king frowned at Sithias. "Your holiness, I fear that would be asking too much of your people, who have been nothing but loyal and devoted to you and your word. This sort of equality would mean a freed slave could hold office, or even marry one of us. The people bitterly tolerated Azrael's marriage to the earth woman because of the soul ring. I implore you. Do not ask them to bend to the point of breaking. There will be civil war."

Sithias increased his size until his coiled body threatened to squish the small humans near the edges of the arena against the walls. They cleared the area in a hurry, crying out in alarm. "You dare to defy me?" His booming voice resounded within the stadium and shook the ground.

Fear energized Finn, pushing him to rush over to Sithias, who was now a towering coil of ivory scales with wings that eclipsed the sun. He yelled and jumped to gain his attention. Sithias lowered his head enough to be able to hear Finn.

"What isss it? I'm in the middle of negotiating here," Sithias whispered.

Finn suppressed a repulsed shudder. Seeing Sithias in serpent form at fifty times his normal size was more than even Finn could handle. "Don't you think it's good enough that you've freed the slaves here?" Finn whispered back. "Maybe it's best you let them handle the particulars so we can be on our merry way."

Sithias stared back, the irises of his eyes like two huge limpid orbs of cerulean. At least he'd remembered to shift his eye color back to match Aradif's.

Sithias blinked. "I pushed it too far, didn't I?"

"Oh just a wee bit. Let's hope it's not too late to do some backtracking. Go at it carefully," Finn warned.

"Leave it to me." Sithias winked, and Finn actually heard the wet slap of his lids closing before the snake lifted his head high into the sky.

"In the ssspirit of peace, my companion hasss bessseeched me to take mercy upon you." Sithias lowered his head, stopping above the king so as to force the man to look up at him. "I will allow the original citizenry of Biraktar to decide upon the rightsss given to the new citizenry of freed ssslaves."

The king bowed to Sithias. "Thank you, your holiness."

Finn let out a sigh of relief.

"Uh-uh, I wasss not finished. I have ssstipulations to my retraction."

"What are you doing?" Finn growled.

"I decree that every new citizen be given fair pay for fair work, decent shelter and food, and the right to sssave their hard earned pay without penalty."

"It is done, your holiness." The king's expression had gone flat. Fear no longer had him in its grip. If Finn had to guess, he would say the man was growing... annoyed.

It was time to leave.

Sithias spread his enormous wings. "I will take my leave. But be warned. I will return at a time of my own choosssing to confirm that you are obeying my new lawsss."

"As you wish, your holiness," the king replied.

The sweep of Sithias's wings generated a blast of wind that had everyone covering their faces to avoid being pelted by sheets of sand. Finn held the collar of his shirt over his nose and mouth to keep from inhaling the fine dust billowing around him. When at last the dust settled, Sithias was gone and the citizens of Birakter were already clearing the stadium. Finn sensed the general attitude of the population was one of anger and disappointment. He wanted to leave more than ever.

He walked over to the lower stage, searching for Fate. His spirits plummeted. Was she still so angry with him she couldn't wait around to face him?

Azrael emerged from the tented room and waved him inside. It was a small space with a bed, which Fate was sitting on. She was still sleepy and disoriented. Finn's heart pounded with a tortured mixture of relief and apprehension. But when she glanced up and took in his beaten state, her face filled with concern. She stood but didn't move. "Finn?"

He nodded, hopeful but without any further expectation. "Aye, I'm here, love."

She rushed over, her body colliding softly into his as she wrapped her arms around his waist and put her head on his chest. Finn leaned into her, pulling her close as he nestled his face into the silken curve of her neck. *Pure heaven.*

After a few precious minutes, Fate crooked her head back. Her forehead creased with worry as she looked up at him. "You're hurt."

"Just a few scratches and bruises is all. Nothing a hot bath and a good night's sleep won't fix," he assured her.

Mahelia let out an impatient huff from behind them. "Azrael, remove these *earth lovers* from our sacred city. Their presence here has become intolerable." The look she shot them as she parted the curtains was filled with contempt.

Fate stepped back from Finn and turned to Azrael. It was only a slight move, but Finn felt the separation of their bodies as keenly as the combined injuries he bore from the trials and the beating he'd taken from the guards the night before. Keeping one arm around her waist to show that she was his, he reluctantly turned to Azrael.

"My ship is waiting." Azrael held his chin high and stared at the back wall.

Fate bit her bottom lip, confusion filling her eyes. "What happened? I can't remember anything from the time you both climbed down into the first pit." She touched her head. "I don't feel right. Why do I feel so woozy?"

Finn's chest heated with instant rage. "They drugged you, Fate, and they put you down there with a blood-thirsty monster."

Fate's mouth fell open. "What? Why?" She looked at Azrael in disbelief. "You allowed this?"

Azrael's noble and guarded expression crumbled when he looked at her. "I did not know. If I had, I would have taken you away before I would allow such a thing."

Fate swayed dizzily and Finn stepped in behind to hold and steady her. "Was this Mahelia's doing?"

"Yes, she administered the potion," Azrael confirmed. "To be fair, the trials were designed by the high priests. She was merely doing as she was told."

"My guess is she gladly did what she was told." Fate sucked in a deep breath and pulled away from Finn's embrace. He swallowed down his disappointment as she tested her balance, walked over to a wooden post and leaned against it.

"Which one of you saved me?" she asked.

Finn said Azrael's name at the same time Azrael said Finn's name.

Fate's gaze flitted between them both in surprise. "Wow. You're both being rather gentlemanly toward each other. I really missed out, what with being drugged out of my mind and all. Are either of you going to tell me how you came to this mutual love fest?"

Finn made a face. "There's no love fest going on here. We were forced to work together down there. If the truth be known, I came to respect Azrael. Only in the moment, mind you."

Azrael nodded sternly. "Yes. I would agree with that."

Fate smiled. "You two became friends?"

Finn shook his head vehemently, as did Azrael. "No, we're not friends," Finn confirmed.

Fate watched them both with a puzzled frown. "Okay, throw me a bone here, guys. Did you both win the trials? Was it a tie or something?"

"Finn was the victor," Azrael replied quickly.

"Hmm." Fate dropped her gaze to her bare feet. "So that's why my soul ring slipped off."

There was no missing the pain in Azrael's eyes. "Yes. Finn won the right to take you as his wife."

"Did he now?" Fate raised a brow at Finn. "I suppose this means you expect to toss me over your shoulder and drag me back to the Keep."

What just happened? Finn gulped. "Did you have other plans?" he asked.

The veins in Fate's neck lit with an inner fire and shot to her temples, lighting her skin with an unnatural gleam. "I do actually." She spoke in a low, angry tone but there was an eerie amplification to her voice, like another voice had joined hers. "I plan to go to Feldoril Forest to find the black unicorn so I can undo what was done to Eustace."

Hot air radiated from her body. Heat waves blew her long hair away from her face. All the anger and resentment she'd harbored against him had returned. She was both beautiful and terrifying in her rage. And now with the soul ring removed, Azrael's will was no longer a force that would keep her from going wherever she pleased.

Finn couldn't believe he was actually wishing for the soul ring to be back in place. He held his hands up and took a step toward her. "That's fine. I'll come along and help you with that."

Fate was breathing hard, her eyes lit so bright they stared straight through him. "I don't need your help." The volume in her voice consumed the small space as heat scorched the air.

Jessie ran into the tent and something zipped past Finn's ear–an amber-eyed white dragonfly. "Good call, Sithias," Jessie said. "She's about to detonate again."

Sithias hovered in place. "Oh my! Are we too late?"

Jessie inched toward Fate. "You guys back off and let me talk her down."

"How did you know what was happening?" Finn asked Sithias as Jessie distracted Fate. "You weren't even here."

Sithias zagged closer to Finn. "I've been here the whole time. You were too caught up with your reunion to see the little mouse in the corner."

Azrael edged in next to Finn as they both backed away from Fate, speaking in a whisper. "I've always known Fate is god-touched, but this, I have not witnessed from her before."

The air in the tent was sweltering. Finn wiped his brow. "She's more than god-touched," he whispered back. "She's the descendant of Ananke, an ancient god who's waiting to fully emerge. We'll lose Fate if Jessie can't calm her down, and it's likely we'll all be destroyed in the process. Maybe even the entire universe along with us."

Azrael frowned with concern. "What changed? What made Fate so angry?"

"Me. I did," Finn confessed.

"Not just you, sir. We're both guilty of lying to her," Sithias added.

"About what?" Azrael asked.

Too tired to explain, Finn stared at Fate as Jessie distracted her with a story of one of their shared childhood memories. She was animated and purposely loud to ensure Fate focused solely on her.

Somewhere in the background, Sithias quietly told Azrael about how Fate witnessed Eustace's murder and the sudden emergence of Ananke before Fate was thrown through the portal into the desert and lost her memory. Finn focused back in on Jessie's efforts when Sithias came to the part about them lying to Fate. It hurt too much.

Finn let out a sigh of relief when he felt the air cool. Jessie had saved the day. The fire in Fate's veins vanished and her eyes returned to the warm, inviting brown he loved to drown himself in.

Fate wobbled in place as Jessie stepped in to hug her friend. Tears trickled down Fate's face as she glanced at Finn over Jessie's shoulder. He nodded to her, but she quickly closed her eyes against him.

Jessie kept one arm around Fate's shoulder and looked at Finn intently. "I told Fate we need to go back to the Keep so we can hit the books and help her figure out what's causing her to go radioactive. Something's gone haywire with the girdle. You know what I'm talking about?"

"Aye, we do." Finn couldn't be more thankful for Jessie's involvement.

"Should I use the Words of Making to get us there?" Sithias asked.

"Sounds like a plan," Finn replied hastily. "That way Azrael won't have to put himself out by flying us back in his ship."

"No, I want Azrael to come with us." Fate's voice sounded small after the unnatural volume only moments before. But Finn knew that tone in her voice. She wasn't about to be talked out of it.

He turned away, silent in the knowing that Fate had feelings for Azrael, which in his worn out state, made him wish he'd died in the trials.

18
MORE LIES

FATE FELT MORE LIKE her old self after a peaceful night's sleep in her own bed. Even with Jessie sprawled out next to her, kicking and hogging most of the space. She'd insisted on spending the night in case returning to the Keep triggered any lingering resentments Fate might still be harboring.

Jessie strolled back into the room, freshly showered and dressed for the day. They strode out into the hall and headed for the sanctuary. "Are you ready for this?" Jessie asked.

"Ready to hit the books?" Fate nodded. "Absolutely."

"No, I meant being in the room with Finn and Azrael at the same time."

Fate's pulse quickened. Her skin still tingled from the touch of Finn's arms around her from the day before. Sinking into his embrace, soaking up the heat of his body pressed against hers was as natural as breathing. Most of all, being held by him eased the constant agony of missing Eustace. Finn was as much home to her as her father had always been.

Which was exactly why she had to stay away from him. Her grief was the fuel she needed to drive her quest in finding the black unicorn. She couldn't risk allowing Finn to comfort her. She would become content and might even be willing to accept her loss. That simply wasn't an option. Not if she intended to do everything within her power to revive Eustace.

"It's no big," Fate replied. "The real question is, can Finn and Azrael handle being in the same room together without coming to blows?"

"That'll only happen if you start making eyes at Azrael after everything Finn went through to free you." Jessie gave her a sidelong glance. "You wouldn't do that though. Would you?"

Guilt plagued Fate as she bit her bottom lip. She'd known Azrael would return with them when she'd asked him. He'd declared his feelings enough times for her to be convinced of his sincerity. The very fact that he hadn't refused only proved it. Azrael was definitely a complication she could do without, but he was also the wall she needed to put between her and Finn right now.

"Did you see the trials?" Fate asked.

"Oh yeah and it was awful. Finn went through hell. He literally went in with *nothing*. Zip, zero, nada. Unlike Azrael. Who walked in with his fancy armor, saber, super strength and Djinn magic. He pretty much breezed through the whole thing. There were so many times when I thought Finn was going to die, but he survived on his wits and courage alone. I suppose there was that one time when Azrael saved Finn." She rolled her eyes. "I'll give him points for that."

Fate wasn't surprised. Azrael was ruthless toward anyone he considered his enemy, but he was also capable of showing mercy when motivated. She'd certainly experienced that when they'd first met. "Huh... I wonder why he did that?"

"Azrael said you'd never forgive him for allowing Finn to die."

"Did he say that after the trials?"

"No, that was during. The priests used some sort of magic to broadcast everything they said and did down inside the pits." Jessie let out an exasperated huff. "You should also know Azrael deserves big points for risking his life to defend you against the monster that wanted to suck your blood."

"If that's the case, how was it that Finn won?"

"It turns out the spear he removed from the rabid beast in the first trial was the only thing that could kill the bloodsucker without the curse passing onto its slayer." When Fate didn't say anything, Jessie grabbed her by both arms. "Don't you get it? Finn knowingly sacrificed himself when he killed the monster to save you. And he had no idea that was the only way to win."

"Finn did that for me? *Again*?" Fate choked out the last word. It physically hurt to think about what could have happened to him. Finn's love knew no bounds. And yet she had taken this long to forgive him for the lies. Even now, the burn of resentment flowed through her veins, but at least she finally understood he'd only wanted to protect her. It pained her to know how much she'd punished him for it.

She didn't deserve him and she feared all she would ever bring Finn was anguish.

Jessie shook her gently. "Why are so sad? You should be happy knowing how much Finn loves you." She let go of Fate's arms and sighed. "And Azrael probably loves you just as much. He's already proven he'd die for you."

"I'm evil. Just plain evil."

"Don't be so silly." Jessie turned Fate in the direction of the library again and pushed her forward.

"I'm being serious here. I'm totally wicked. I asked Azrael to come with us because it felt too amazing to be with Finn yesterday. He made me forget how sad I am about Eustace. I can't afford to become complacent. Nothing can get in the way of going to Feldoril and finding that black unicorn."

Jessie fell in step beside her, waving her hand at Fate. "Pfft, you're not evil or wicked. You're just messed up in the head. And who wouldn't be after everything you've been through?"

Fate wanted to believe it was that simple. It would be so much easier to blame her behavior on traumatic events, but she wasn't buying it. There was something wrong with her, something had begun to stir from a hidden place inside, driving her every action without regard to others.

Jessie stopped and stood in front of the sanctuary door. "Back to my original question. Are you ready for this?"

Before Fate could answer, the door opened and Gerdie grinned up at them. "There you are. I was just comin' to get you two."

"You remember us?" Fate asked.

Gerdie's grin turned quizzical. "Of course. You're Fate and you're Jessie."

Fate searched Gerdie's eyes. Sure enough, the wise, centuries-old spirit she'd first come to know gazed back at her from within the six-year-old child's face. "Your memory's back."

"That's what everybody keeps tellin' me. Things don't seem much different to me, except I don't have any interest in playin' with this bouncin' tin can." The doggit hopped in place next to her. "I can't seem to get it to go away. It follows me everywhere. I wouldn't mind so much if I could get it to help me with my work."

Fate smiled. "Straight back into research mode, I see."

"Yup, and there's lots to cover." Gerdie waved them inside with her little arm. The quick march of her shoes clicked over the stone floor as the doggit jounced beside her, its metal feet banging loudly and out of time with her steps.

Brune and Darcy were bent over a large tome at the big table in the middle of the sanctuary. Sithias was with them in rapt attention, stroking his chin pensively and looking every bit the studious librarian he favored being. Finn paced back and forth on one side, while Azrael perused the many books filed within the bookcases lining the back wall.

Her heart raced as they each turned to look at her. Finn's tense expression softened with love and longing, while Azrael's gaze heated with desire. Her face grew instantly hot and her gaze fled to the table piled high with books. This was going to be much harder than she'd first imagined.

Gerdie climbed up onto a chair and stood on the seat to peer at the open book the others were studying. Fate took the chair next to her. Finn headed over to sit beside her, but Jessie sat down before he could get there. Azrael sat on the opposite side of the table, which to Fate was worse than if one of them sat next to her. She'd have to work doubly hard to avoid his gaze.

Brune closed the book that was of so much interest to everyone and stood at the head of the table. Darcy and Sithias took seats on the other side with Azrael. Brune slid a leatherbound journal across the smooth polished surface.

Fate stared at it. "What's this?"

"Your great, great, great, great, great–" Sithias ran out of breath and sucked in more air before continuing. "Great, great-aunt on your mother's side. She was a Keep Guardian and in charge of logging the family tree."

"Wow, really?" Intrigued and happy for the distraction from her muddled emotions concerning Finn and Azrael, Fate flipped through the pages of handwritten notes.

"Go to the bookmarked page," Finn instructed. "That's where you'll find the reason for what's been happening to you."

The weight in his tone worried Fate, but her curiosity was greater than her trepidation. What could the writings of an extremely distant relative have to do with her present condition?

Jessie scooted in beside her to read the elegant handwriting. Fate leaned against her friend for comfort as she began reading. The entry was all about the discovery of an ancestor who was purposefully seeded by an ancient deity named Ananke. However, the culmination of this seeding was not to come to fruition for many generations.

Fate almost laughed at the ridiculousness of the story. It sounded like all the other farfetched myths she'd read throughout her childhood. Then again, she'd fought too many creatures of myth to discount the possibility entirely.

"Whoa, this is wild," Jessie muttered, under her breath.

Fate nodded as she turned the page. The hairs on the back of her neck stood on end when she read the last paragraph describing the prophesy of Ananke's descendent–time of birth unknown–who would become the vessel strong and worthy enough to house Ananke's full presence and immense power.

"Holy crow. This totally sounds like you!" Jessie stared at Fate like she was a circus freak.

"No, uh-uh. That's not me." Fate pushed the journal away.

Jessie grabbed the book. "Did you read the part about fortuitous and unfortunate happenstance? Your entire life has been filled with nothing but the best and worst luck."

"*Everybody* has good and bad luck," Fate argued.

"Not like you. I don't know anyone else who's had a meteor demolish her brand new birthday present car. Or anyone who scored a collector's edition comic book at a yard sale and sold it on Ebay for a few thousand bucks, only to find out it was worth a half million."

"It was actually $10,000 I sold it for, and I could've gotten a quarter, not a half mil." Fate stared her down. "Exaggerate much?"

"Who's exaggerating? Your school essay landed you an unheard of publishing deal, and the book was an instant best seller with book tours and huge fans, such as Darcy here."

"Um, ex-fan, just to be crystal clear." Darcy stared flatly at Fate. "It didn't take more than an hour of knowing you to be thoroughly unimpressed."

"Exactly," Jessie continued. "All that dream-come-true stuff went poof the moment you were thrown into the *Book of Fables*. See? It's all adding up." Jessie chalked several points in the air with her finger as Fate scowled at her. "Should I continue? Or do I need to remind you about the worms?"

"*No*, you've made your point," Fate grumbled.

Azrael extended a hand. "May I read the passage?"

Jessie hesitated for a split second before shoving the journal across the table toward him. He had to lean across the wide surface to reach it. "Thank you," he said.

Everyone was quiet, but all eyes were on Fate, except for Azrael who was busy reading.

"Okay," Fate conceded, "let's say this distant relative was onto something and my family bloodline is actually tainted by this Ananke deity. Why wouldn't Brune or Gerdie be chosen as vessels? They're at the tail end of the exact same cursed family tree too."

Frowning, Brune crossed her arms. "Did you even read what's written there, or did you skim like usual?" She exhaled impatiently. "It says the vessel will be given the name of Ananke's daughters, known as the *Fates*. You're the only one in the family with *that* name."

The truth stirred from deep within, but Fate resisted admitting it out loud. That would mean she truly was the definition of her given name: "*The development of events beyond a person's control, regarded as determined by a supernatural power.*" She'd memorized those words at an early age when she'd begun to notice her luck was either extraordinarily amazing or outstandingly horrible.

But there was no denying it any longer. Something far bigger than her had been working from behind the scenes all along. Every action she'd taken had been driven by fear. Her terrifying tumble into the vicious storybook realm of the *Book of Fables* had not only tested her sanity, but had made her feel helpless and powerless. Her decision to enter the Keep had at least been hers. She'd done that thinking it was the only way to rescue Finn and maybe in turn, take back control of her life.

But from everything she'd learned in the last five minutes, her life had never been hers. It had all been a cruel illusion.

Fate covered her face to hide tears she could not stop.

Jessie wrapped her arms around her. "Oh no, I'm so sorry, Fate. I was way too hard on you. I shouldn't have rubbed your nose in the facts the way I did." Jessie's grip tightened. "And you, Brune! You're always so mean to Fate. She's your niece. Can't you go a little softer on her once in awhile?"

"I suppose I can be a bit harsh at times." Brune sounded chastised. "I only do it to toughen you up, Fate. If it makes any difference, I respect how skilled you've become. If you ever want your position as Keep Guardian back, I'll hand it over without any argument."

"I suppose that's as close to an apology as you're ever going to get from her," Jessie muttered.

"Fate, if you need some time to let all this sink in, we'll understand if you'd like to take a break." Finn's voice cracked with emotion. "I can go with you..."

All Fate wanted to do was run into his arms, to be held by him and lose herself within the warmth and safety of his embrace. She wiped the embarrassment of tears away with the sleeve of her shirt and leaned forward to see around Jessie.

Finn's green eyes shone with hope.

She shook her head, resisting the temptation to run to him. "No, I need to stay and see this through." The disappointment in his eyes killed her and she drew back behind Jessie. "I want to know everything. Did something happen to wake this Ananke up?"

"Well, yesss." Sithias fiddled nervously with his bow tie. "Remember how I helped you locate Hippolyta's magic girdle? Apparently, wearing the girdle is what's transformed your body into a vessel strong enough to house Ananke's full emergence."

"Hold on. Are you blaming me for doing what I had to do?" Fate frowned to fight off another wave of stinging tears. "Hippolyta's girdle is exactly what I needed to fight the war against Kaliena and survive. Without it we would've lost the war and you all know it."

Sithias surrendered with both hands held high. "No one's disputing your reasoning. But we've all noticed how wearing the girdle hasss changed you."

"I know it did. I have a penchant for war because the girdle was made by the god of war." Heat flared from her core, and Fate had to breathe deeply to keep it from rising. "That's why I have such a short fuse, but I fight it every time to keep it under control."

"Do you really believe you have it under control?" Finn asked. There was no accusation in his tone. Fate sensed he genuinely wanted to know if she believed it.

She sighed. "No, it's getting harder and harder to contain."

"We know the reason." Finn leaned forward with both elbows on the table, attempting to see around Jessie, who Fate continued to hide behind. "Your spirit broke when you witnessed Eustace's death. That was when Ananke took over. You weren't you anymore. You were gone. I know you don't remember, but we've all seen it with our own eyes and it's time for you to see what happened too."

Fate's stomach coiled tight as Brune called up a holographic image. That awful sense of being surrounded by lies swarmed back in. They'd been keeping so much more from her than she ever could have suspected. She was suddenly terrified of what she was about to see, yet furious she was only now discovering this.

Everyone, except Jessie, Gerdie and Azrael were liars. She wanted to die inside knowing Finn had been part of this elaborate conspiracy of lies.

Volcanic heat erupted at her center, shooting through her veins like quicksilver. Fate stood and hammered her fists against the table's surface. The sheer force of the blow left a crack in the hardwood. Startled, Jessie backed away and banged into Finn. Gerdie fell off her chair, her arms flailing. Sithias caught her, but not without falling himself, though he managed to cushion Gerdie from hitting the floor.

"MORE LIES!" Fate's voice thundered against the walls of the sanctuary.

Brune and Darcy recoiled from the waves of heat pulsing from Fate's body. Finn and Jessie stayed where they were, but lifted their hands to protect their faces from the scorching heat.

Azrael was the only one who seemed unaffected. He rose from his chair and spoke in a dulcet tone that calmed her. "I understand your anger, Fate. You have every right to be upset with them."

Nodding, Fate hung on his every word.

"As someone who was not part of this deception, I can clearly see why they chose to protect you from the truth throughout the aftermath of your father's death." Azrael placed his hand on the closed journal. "I say this because these writings confirm what I have always seen within your maraja, that you are the descendant of a god. Otherwise, you could never be the vessel for the power Hippolyta's girdle has endowed you with. An instrument of a god such as this would have destroyed you on contact had you not already been god-touched."

The intensity of Fate's rage waned, but she didn't want to let go of it completely. Fury was the only thing standing in the way of of abject despair and shattering into a million pieces. Despite her resistance, she was locked within Azrael's gaze, listening with renewed trust yet terrified of the truth.

"It is time for you to set aside your misgivings and face what you have become," he urged her. "Allow your friends to show you and we will all be here to help you along the way."

Fate surrendered her anger and collapsed into the chair, spent. Jessie sat down and took her hand. Finn and the others resumed their place at the table. Brune hesitated before hitting the button on the control panel and looked at Fate. "Are you ready?" she asked.

"Play it," Fate croaked as butterflies crashed in her stomach.

The vast landscape of the Keep surface came into view as the lens zoomed in on a gigantic coliseum with a gleaming blue lake at its center. Fate knew without question it was a vast store of the elixir of life Kaliena had amassed. A bright light suddenly appeared at the water's edge and took the shape of someone in shining gold armor.

Fate gasped when she realized she was looking at herself. But she was unearthly in her appearance, with skin that gleamed with an inner fire and eyes of bright white light. Fate stopped breathing as she watched herself do the impossible and materialize a sword with a blade of black flames. She wanted to yell at Brune to shut it off, but there was no going back. She had to see this through.

Holding onto Jessie's hand like a lifeline, Fate watched herself plunge the sword into the elixir. The blade's dark fire raced over the surface, killing the life-giving light of the elixir until all that remained was a slimy black sludge.

Fate clutched at the sob in her chest. They could have used the elixir to revive Eustace. She only had herself to blame for robbing him of living and continuing on. But why? What could her motives possibly have been at the time? Had she done it out of sheer wanton desire for destruction?

Jessie squeezed Fate's hand. "Don't blame yourself. That wasn't you. It was Ananke who–" She stiffened suddenly when she saw who blasted across the Keep, a dark blur that slammed Fate into the sludge. "That's me!" she gasped.

Covered in ensorcelled armor, Jessie hovered over the black lake, waiting for Fate to surface. Several minutes passed before Fate exploded from the lake, a radiant being the darkness could not cling to. Huge wings of light suspended her in the air.

Jessie aimed her weaponized arms at Fate, drilling her with lasers. They sliced through Fate's golden armor but she remained unharmed. Sweeping her light wings, Fate hurtled into Jessie, the impact so tremendous, she crashed into the top tier. Fate dove on top of Jessie before she could rise from the rubble.

Fate was sickened with guilt as she watched her gauntleted fist pummel Jessie's head until her exoskeleton crackled with tiny bolts of lightning and went dark.

She put her hand over her mouth and looked at Jessie. "I... I never knew I did that. Jess, I'm sorry."

Tears dripped from Jessie's chin. "No, I'm the one who's sorry." Jessie shuddered. "You asked if I remember any of what I did while I was under Kalilena's control. Well, I remember it all. I knew what I was doing the whole time, but I didn't care. I had no feelings for you, or anything for that matter."

Jessie fell into an inconsolable fit of tears. Fate held her friend, whispering that she understood. They'd both been victims of forces beyond their control. The only important thing now was that they forgive themselves and embrace each other as the sisters they've always been, without guilt or remorse.

The recording played on. She held onto Jessie, watching as Ananke flew over the Keep's expanse and laid siege on Kaliena's armada, using her flaming sword to light them into raging fires. Countless airships plunged to the Keep surface before Ananke landed on the deck of Kaliena's massive flagship. A horde of undead soldiers attacked, but Ananke hacked her way through them. Wodrid charged at Ananke with a fireball, but Kaliena got there first, armed with six scimitars in each of her many hands.

Jessie turned to see what had grabbed hold of Fate's attention. "Oh my god," she whispered.

Ananke's light wings vanished as Kaliena advanced, but something stopped the sorceress, because she dropped her weapons and clutched at her throat. She couldn't breathe. Ananke stood without moving, but it was she who was strangling Kaliena. Wodrid launched his fireballs at her. Ananke deflected them with the same unseen force she was using to kill his lover.

An explosion of light obliterated the scene and turned to static.

"That's all we have," Brune said. "The footage ended when the Keep passed through the portal and crashed here in the desert."

Fate stared into space, dumbfounded and speechless. Her head was reeling. *Ananke was real.* The deity had hijacked her body, and unlike Jessie who remembered what she'd done, Fate had zero memory of any of it ever happening.

"Fate?" Finn stood and walked around Jessie. "I know this is a lot to take in, but there's more you need to know."

"More?" Fate sagged in her chair. "How could there possibly be more?"

He rested his hand on her shoulder. His touch was warm and all too inviting. "We have to remove Hippolyta's girdle. As you now know, it's the only way to prevent Ananke from being able to fully possess you again."

Fate wriggled out from beneath his all too tempting touch. "And how do you expect to do that? There's no getting this thing off once it's on."

"Actually, there isss a key that will unlock the girdle," Sithias interjected. "Dantalion's Key, to be exact." He adjusted the round-framed glasses perched on his nose and gulped. "But first, we have to travel to the underworld to retrieve it."

"Underworld as in Hades?" Fate repeated. "Or do you mean hell with a capital 'h'?"

"That'sss the one."

It was all too much. Fate felt like she was being pulled in a hundred different directions. There was only one direction she wanted to go in. "Nope, no way. I'm not getting yanked off course by some crazy excursion into Hell." She glanced at Azrael. "I've been sidetracked long enough. The only place I'm going is to Feldoril Forest to hunt the black unicorn. Eustace's resurrection is my only mission right now. Everything else will have to wait."

"This again." Finn glared at Brune. "Did you bother to mention you aren't a hundred percent certain this unicorn theory will even work?"

"I was doing damage control at the time. Someone needed to keep her from exploding and turning into Ananke again." Brune's lips pressed together in frustration.

"Hold on." Fate stormed over to Brune. "Are you saying you fed me a bunch of bull?"

Fear moved in Brune's eyes but she stood her ground. "Of course not. The spell book I gave you outlines everything you need to know." Her nervous gaze shifted to Finn. "The uncertain part is whether or not you're capable of performing the spell properly."

Fate nodded. "Well, I think we both know I'm not. It's settled then, you're coming with me to ensure the spell works."

Brune took a defiant stance Fate knew all too well. "I can't leave the

Keep. I have my hands full with the Serpen uprising. I still don't know if we can trust the Asgar army, and Rudwor's been making noises about needing to return to Beldereth." Exhaustion showed in her face as she sighed. "I don't even want to think about what'll happen if I lose the Beldereth knights."

"I'll go with you and do the spell," Gerdie offered.

"No!" Fate and Brune said in unison.

"This'll be a dangerous trip." Fate was quick to explain when she saw how deflated Gerdie looked. "Trust me, you'll have plenty to do here. Brune's going to need your help."

"I'm well versed in spellsss." Sithias blinked at her hopefully.

"Hardly," Brune scoffed. "Need I remind you of your bungled remembering spell?"

"Aye, I'd have to agree on that one," Finn added.

Sithias flapped his arms. "Everyone makes mistakesss!"

"You can come, Sithias, but for very different reasons," Fate assured him. "As for anyone else who wants to come along, all I can say is, I'll think about it."

19
THE REAL ARADIF

FATE SKIMMED OVER the glaring white sands of the Mirajaran Desert without a fixed destination in mind. The heat rising from the dunes would've been intolerable, save for the wind blowing against her face and arms. She couldn't remember the last time she'd flown without restriction. Azrael's soul ring had kept her wings clipped for far too long. The freedom to fly anywhere she wanted was dizzying.

Blissful even.

Nothing could weigh her down at the moment. Not even the horrid visions of Ananke's wanton destruction. Flying lifted her spirits like nothing else had in a long, long time. She could almost convince herself this freedom was real.

Almost.

The heaviness returned. How could she fight an ancient goddess who has ruled over the fates of lesser gods and humans alike since the beginning of time? She was just one girl trying to survive against impossible odds and failing miserably.

Fate landed on the highest peak of a sand dune and sat down. The heat worsened without the breeze of flying, but she wasn't ready to return to the Keep. She needed time alone to think. Yet solitude only seemed to magnify the gravity of her situation. She was a tiny bug being crushed under the heel of a giant.

Tears threatened to come in another flood, when she glimpsed movement in the distance. The slim whirling funnel of a dust cloud whipped its way across the dunes. Shading her eyes, she watched, half interested, until it shifted directions quite suddenly and moved toward her.

She smiled with the memory of how she used to lie in Finn's arms and listen to stories of what had happened to him while they'd been apart. At the time, Azrael's soul ring had prevented them from getting any closer than a hug. Story telling became a neutral way of passing the hours together.

One of Finn's more memorable stories had been his adventures in the desert with Sithias in search of the fiery divide. If she remembered correctly, the Mirajaran was protected by the *jann* sect of the Djinn, whose leader happened to be the *real* Aradif.

From Finn's retelling, he was not the deity the citizens of Biraktar had exalted him to be in their scriptures. He was an immortal who tested if travelers were worthy of safe passage through the perilous desert. Apparently, this Aradif took the form of a white camel or a whirlwind.

Was it possible she was being visited by this same being?

Fate considered launching into the sky while she still could but curiosity got the best of her. Finn had said Aradif had predicted him fighting Kaliena in the Mirajaran Desert long before the war had ever begun.

Maybe Aradif could look into her future and tell her how to prevent Ananke from consuming her body and soul.

Long drifting eddies of dust blew off the whirlwind as it raced across the last dune. It slowed and then stopped in front of her. Strong gusts tossed her hair back, peppering her face with specks of sand. Lifting her arm to shelter her face, Fate squinted as the whirlwind thinned, revealing a robed figure within the center of the funnel.

The sand swirled to a standstill and floated around a young man no older than Finn. He had the same sky-blue eyes as Azrael, as well as the deep warm color of skin, enhanced by his white linen robes. Fate recognized the ancient soul dwelling within, a disturbing contrast to a disarmingly youthful visage.

He bowed his head slightly. "I am Aradif. I could not ignore the call of your soul."

Fate thought about feigning ignorance, but sensed Aradif did not suffer fools who played games. "Yes, I want to know my future."

He considered her request with a look of warning. "Knowing what is to come, before you are ready, can carve your destiny into stone. Not knowing allows for flexibility in the steel point that inscribes the imminent. Are you prepared for your future to become an absolute certainty, Fate?"

Hearing him speak her name surprised her for some reason and only added to her apprehension. "I haven't been ready for everything that's happened so far." She gave a shrug of defeat. "Can knowing my future be any worse? I prefer being prepared. I hate not knowing. I'm tired of being afraid all the time."

He nodded calmly. "Very well, I will show you."

Aradif swept his hand. Shimmers rippled in the air as the dunes changed shape and the Keep's colossal hoops–half buried in the sand–arose into view. Kaliena's defunct titans stood within the hoops like useless iron sculptures that would one day be worn away by the sands of time. The Keep hovered at the center of it all, just above the sand like a silvery jewel. A jewel designed to endure millennia upon millennia.

A vicious battle raged on the ground and fleets of airships littered the sky. Fate hadn't noticed them at first. They were so much smaller in comparison to the gigantic structure. There were as many armies present as in the war against Kaliena, but this time they were fighting each other. It was a wild, frenzied battle for survival.

White-gold light exploded above it all. More brilliant than the sun that surely it would incinerate every living thing. The armies below cowered as the brilliance took on the shape of a giant woman with wings of pure light. Her sword and shield blazed with power. Her skin glowed with the same inner fire. The radiance was brightest at her waist, and in that moment, Fate knew she was looking at herself.

The face and body were hers, but that was all that remained. Her soul had been burned away by Ananke's power. Fate had ceased to exist, because if there was even a small part of her left, she could never do what happened next.

Ananke swept down over the armies, her blazing broadsword slicing through thousands of warriors, men and women alike. The touch of her blade set them afire, consuming them within seconds, scorching the sand to glass. Dark clouds of ash and embers rolled into the air, a thick sheath of death that spread with each strike of Ananke's sword.

Fate clapped her hand over her mouth to muffle the cry of horror climbing into her throat. This was what Finn and Sithias and all the others had feared. Their lies had been to prevent this very thing from happening. There could be no more outrage on her part because she finally understood what words and descriptions could never convey.

"Stop," she pleaded. "Please stop. I can't watch anymore."

"As you wish." Aradif erased the scene with a wave of his arm and the sweeping dunes of the peaceful desert returned.

Fate sat in stunned silence, her eyes clenched shut against the vision, but nothing could blot out those nightmarish images. They were seared in her brain. "This can't happen," she said finally. "There has to be something I can do to prevent it from coming true."

Aradif shook his head sadly. "Unfortunately, the fear this vision has instilled within you is already forging a path to the very destination you wish to avoid."

Terror hammered in Fate's chest. As close as she was to letting it paralyze her, she fought against it. She refused to believe she was completely powerless in this. "No. I won't let this happen. I can change this. I have the Words of

Making. I can rewrite everything."

Frenzied excitement thrummed through her system and her breathing became a shallow pant. Beads of sweat trickled down her forehead, stinging her eyes as she stared at the horizon. She'd been quashing the temptation to use the Words of Making to bring Eustace back. All out of fear she might worsen the situation. But from what Aradif had shown her, they were all doomed as it was.

"Do you wish to see what the power of the Word will do if fear pens this new version of history?" Aradif waited for her answer. His robes fluttered in a breeze, which seemed reserved for him alone, a respite from the oppressive heat she would have greatly appreciated.

Fate stood, nervously pacing, her hope dwindling in the face of witnessing another horrifying vision. But what if Aradif was wrong? What if she really could fix all of it in one fell swoop? She certainly wouldn't do this alone. She'd get Sithias and Finn, and maybe even Brune and Gerdie, to help her figure out every possible way things could go sideways.

She swallowed down her dread and nodded. "Yes, show me."

Aradif moved both arms this time, a gesture that was like opening two heavy curtains. Fate took a step back as he parted the veil between time and dimensions, revealing a sky the color of blood, cloaked in ashen mist. The rolling dunes were gone, replaced by a flat bed of hard, cracked clay that stretched into a horizon blurred by fire on all sides.

The six hoops surrounding the Keep were broken, protruding from the clay bed like the skeletal ribs of a gargantuan beast. The Keep lay shattered and strewn in countless pieces, alongside Kaliena's dismembered titans. The terrible scene resembled once mighty statues lying amidst the debris of a civilization forgotten by time.

The demolished Keep, along with all its precious artifacts of magic, gutted Fate. Was this the final result of Ananke's destruction? How had the desert been turned into a fiery wasteland? Was this hellish world isolated to the deserts of Shalamoraize? Her stomach tightened into a queasy knot. What of Oldwilde? Had this desolation spread to all the magical realms? It sickened her to think of those lush forests razed to the ground, ringed by a wall of eternal fire.

In the distance a gigantic shape lumbered forward, its full form obscured by drifting clouds of ash. It was an unrecognizable hulking thing, yet familiar in its slinking, predatory movements and glowing red eyes.

Fate's blood turned to ice the second Farouk's wolfish head emerged into view. He was massive in size, a hellhound whose kingdom was this desert.

But how? After witnessing Ananke's terrifying might, Fate had a hard time believing Farouk could triumph over that kind of power.

But then a figure swept through the ash, a giant warrior with wings of night fringed in flames and spiked armor as black as ink. The winged knight descended to a mountainous tower of human skulls to land next to a throne set at the very top, composed entirely of human femurs. Fate swallowed bile when she saw the coiled skeletal remains of a large snake adorning the back of the throne in a spiral. Her heart hurt thinking it might be Sithias.

Farouk sidled in next to the gruesome structure, his fanged snout level with the top of the mound. The knight sat on the throne and removed the horned helmet.

Fate's throat constricted and she stopped breathing entirely.

She was the dark, winged knight and she was in league with Farouk, her father's murderer!

Choking for air, Fate staggered backward, lost her footing and tumbled down the dune, the fall so swift and dizzying, she careened all the way to the bottom. Her mind was numb. She couldn't think, couldn't move.

Stars swam across her vision and she had to consciously suck in a lungful of air to keep from passing out. Panting, she stared into the blue sky, shivering despite the sun beating down on her.

Aradif appeared next to her, shading her eyes from the glaring sun. "Do you see now?"

"Yes, I do." Her voice was a parched croak as she rose to a sitting position. "I don't understand how any of that could ever happen. I would *never* be part of making that hellish kingdom. And I most definitely would not side with *Farouk!*" Her mouth filled with the sour tang of hatred when she spoke his name.

"You say that based on what you know in this time and place. But the devil dog hunts you with an unknown purpose, just as Ananke's desire to emerge into this world as a physical entity is beyond our understanding. You could spend a thousand years rewriting what once was into what you desire and still be unable to predict that one turning point, which triggers the final outcome you witnessed here today. There is no rearranging the celestial order to our whims. Our destinies are written in the stars, and always will be."

Fate struggled to her feet. "What are you saying? That I give up? Game over?"

Aradif stared at her with the same placid expression. How could he be so calm about what they'd seen?

"Why aren't you upset?" Fate yelled. "Aren't you worried about your desert being turned into that graveyard? Did you see how many people died to make that disgusting throne?"

"The desert sands are home to more bones than even that. We are mere guests here, regardless of the landscape."

Fate stared at him in disbelief. "You're willing to accept this as your future? You don't have any desire to try and prevent it from coming true?"

Aradif shook his head. "I do not have to do anything. I already know you will not use the power of the Word to rewrite your history, lest you risk the corruption of your soul and the devil dog rising to power."

Fate knew it too. She was more terrified than ever to put pen to paper. "What about the battle we saw? Are you going to just stand by while the world fights over the Keep, only to be completely destroyed by Ananke in the end?"

"Why would I intervene? These are small human matters which Ananke will preside over. Once the battle ends, I will see to it the desert swallows the Keep. Its enticing secrets and seductive treasures will be buried with countless other secrets and treasures once known to humanity."

Rage ignited in her core, a welcome heat that chased the chill of dread from her bones. "Finn told me you helped him and Sithias. Are you going to turn your back on them after saving them?"

"They saved themselves by proving their worth."

"Are you saying I'm not worthy?"

Aradif tilted his head and looked her over, a judgmental gesture she resented. "Your worth is unimportant in this. *You* are unimportant, in the same way it matters not which jar I choose to pour life-giving water into."

20

WE'VE DONE THIS BEFORE, RIGHT?

FATE WAITED UNTIL NIGHT to return to the Keep. After her gut-wrenching encounter with Aradif, she'd flown to the ocean to watch the waves roll in on a white sandy beach. The cool breeze and soothing sound of the water had not provided the peace and respite she'd hoped for. Because Aradif's words never stopped ringing in her head.

You are unimportant. You are unimportant. You are unimportant.

She was Ananke's sock puppet. Always had been. Always will be.

Fate landed just inside the open hatch of the sanctuary and peered inside. The lights were dim and the room empty. They'd all gone to bed, just as she'd hoped. She couldn't handle speaking to anyone right now. Sleep was calling. She couldn't wait to black out and leave the agony behind. At least for one night.

She was halfway across the room when a voice startled her, freezing her in place.

"Fate?" It was Finn.

Sighing heavily, Fate turned to see him lean forward in one of the reading chairs tucked against the shadowy back wall of the sanctuary. "Not now, I need to sleep."

He stood and walked over to her. His green eyes were filled with the same sorrowful defeat that was eating her up from the inside out. "I can help." His voice was little more than a soft whisper. "All you have to do is let me in."

She backed away, shaking her head. "I can't. I-I have to–"

"There's nothing you have to do right now. Not with me, or anyone else." He took her hand and she melted beneath his touch. "You shouldn't be alone. Not with how you're feeling."

"You have no idea how I'm feeling."

Finn gently tapped her breastbone. "Oh but I do, lass. Have you forgotten our connection? Nothing's changed. You know I can feel what's inside your heart like it's my own."

"Don't you have your shield up? I thought you don't like having my emotions mixing you up."

He nodded. "Aye, most of the time I prefer to be dealing with my own rubbish and let you do the same." He pulled her hand to his lips and kissed her fingers. "Since I can't fly after you these days, I couldn't resist checking in on you."

The heat of his breath and touch of his mouth sent the most exquisite tingles up her arm.

"Will you let me watch over you tonight while you sleep?" he asked. "Please don't say no."

"Yes." She was breathless as she turned and pulled him by the hand.

Fate's pulse raced as they walked in silence all the way to her suite. She pushed through the door and stopped when she saw Jessie sprawled in the middle of her bed, sound asleep. They backed up into the hall and closed the door quietly.

"Your room," she whispered.

Smiling, Finn squeezed her hand and they hurried down the hall to his suite. He closed the door and leaned against it. "I don't have any frilly nighties, but I can give you a t-shirt."

She smiled shyly. "That'll do."

Finn retrieved a shirt from the wardrobe, but she picked up the one slung over the back of a chair and headed for the washroom. "I've been in the desert all day and I'm in serious need of a shower."

Finn's gaze heated with desire as she closed the door. Trembling with excitement, she peeled off her sweat-stained clothes and stepped beneath the warm water. What was she doing? Was she really going to spend the night with Finn?

Every inch of her body cried *yes*.

And why not? Her staunch resolution to stay away from him had crumbled in the face of what Aradif had shown her. All the reasons for keeping her distance seemed thin, needless. Her constant grief over losing Eustace would never go away. Nor would her fear of a dreadful, inescapable future vanish.

Allowing herself to be comforted, maybe even strengthened, was better than falling into a pit of despair. Finn was the only one who'd ever been able to accomplish that nearly impossible feat.

The water turned off the moment she stepped out from beneath the cascading faucet. She grabbed a towel, dried off and slipped Finn's shirt over her head. The cotton fabric smelled of his sandalwood soaped skin and she breathed it in deeply. Her heart pounded with anticipation.

Too impatient to do anything with her hair except comb out the tangles, she slipped through the door with her long, wet tresses soaking spots into the moss-green shirt.

Finn's mouth fell open. His gaze caressed the curves glimpsed beneath the t-shirt, which was loose and ended just past her hips. He lingered on her bare legs before returning to stare at her now blushing face.

The heat in her face flooded over her body, lighting her skin afire as he crossed the room. Trapped within the fervor of his gaze, she lost herself in the myriad shades of green in his irises, from the deep forest green around the outer edges, to the bright grassy meadow dotted with gold specks around each pupil.

The warmth in Finn's hands soaked through the t-shirt's thin fabric as he pulled her close. His hands shook with passion. She sensed he was holding back, being overly gentle when she would have preferred a harder grip to match the waves of excitement crashing through her body.

"We've done this before, right?" she whispered into his ear as he kissed her neck.

"Aye, love, we have." The husk in his voice vibrated against her skin, sending pleasurable shivers everywhere.

Finn caught her up in his arms, the desire in his eyes so fierce it was almost savage. "Are you sure you want to do this?" His voice was a hoarse whisper, his chest heaving with every breath. "Tell me now before we move past the point of no return."

Fate swallowed, her throat tight with rampant longing. "*Yes.*" It was all she could say. She was past words. All she wanted was to surrender to him–*to them, together.*

Finn carried her over to the bed and laid her down. The muscles in his jaw flexed as he stood over her. The look in his eyes was so overwhelming in its intensity she flushed with another wave of heat. Fate clenched her bottom lip between her teeth, staring at his muscular arms and broad shoulders. Crossing his arms, he lifted his shirt over his head and flung it to the floor.

A small cry caught in her throat when she saw the bruises covering his torso, the undeniable evidence of his love for her. Saddened, she reached out to touch the purpled splotches but he stopped her with a shake of his head. "Don't think about that. Look past it and be with me, love."

When his hands moved to unbutton his jeans, her heart slammed against her ribcage, skipping beats until she could barely breathe. Finn stripped down to his boxers and climbed on top of her, his hand running smoothly over the crest of her thigh to the dip in her waist.

Fate arched toward him as his mouth hungrily found hers and their tongues met. He tasted like honeyed water and she drank with a thirst she felt would never be slaked. She pressed against him, her body aching from deep within to be one with him, to experience what only Finn remembered from the first time they'd made love. There would be no forgetting this time. Each sweet caress, every delectable kiss was being etched into her heart and soul, never to be erased by anything or anyone ever again.

Finn raised himself up to look into her eyes, his expression filled with more love than she'd ever seen him express. Cupping his hand at the base of her head, he gently brought her neck to his lips. The feathering warmth of his breath over her skin and the hot stroke of his tongue sent shivers of wild desire through her, lighting her nervous system with tantalizing currents of electricity.

"*Now,*" she breathed. "I want you now."

The weight of Finn's body pressed down on her as she opened to him. The warmth of his body soaked into her until she could no longer tell where she began and he ended. They were one, and for the first time since all the darkness had descended upon her, Fate knew pure heaven.

Fate woke the next morning in Finn's arms. She lifted her head to see if he was awake. His eyes were closed and the rhythmic sound of his breathing indicated he was still fast asleep. Resting her head back onto his chest, she snuggled in close, smiling with the memory of the night before.

Her blood pumped with renewed desire as flashes of their lovemaking replayed themselves in her mind. She'd never let herself go like that before and Finn had been more than willing to give her whatever she'd wanted, whenever she'd wanted it.

Two spots of heat burned into her cheeks. She hadn't known she could be so voracious in bed. They'd hardly gotten any sleep because she simply hadn't been able to get enough of him.

Wriggling against him, she tried nudging him awake to see if he might be in the mood for more. When Finn didn't move, she sighed, though with far more contentment than any frustration she might be feeling in the moment.

"You wouldn't be trying to seduce me again, would you?"

Fate lifted her head to find him awake with a sleepy, yet wolfish grin on his face. "Is it working?"

He chuckled. "You're a wicked wee vixen." He pulled her on top of him. "You tell me."

"I don't have to. You have a tell." Nuzzling her mouth against his neck, she tickled him with her tongue. Finn moaned and pushed against her.

A frantic knock on the door startled them both.

"Finn!" Jessie called from the other side. "Open the door, Fate never made it back to her suite last night!" She resumed her pounding.

"You'll have to answer that, love." Finn sat up and carefully adjusted the blankets over his lap. "I'm too compromised at the moment."

Fate laughed as she reached for his shirt and wriggled into it. "Probably best I get it. Jessie's going to be shocked enough as it is."

"Finn!" Jessie shouted. When Fate opened the door, her friend was frowning with her fist raised for another bout of banging. "Uh..." Her face went blank with shock as she stared at what Fate was wearing.

"Sorry I didn't check in." Fate smiled sheepishly. "I've been distracted."

Jessie clapped her hand over her open mouth. "No kidding." Her voice was muffled but her tone was curious. She grabbed Fate by the arm and yanked her out into the hall. "You totally did it, didn't you?"

Fate nodded. "And not just once."

Jessie gasped. "You're naughty!"

"If this is what naughty is, I'm okay with it."

Jessie stared back in wonder. "Wow. So you two are back together. Like *seriously* back together."

"It would seem so."

"And you're past the whole lying to you part?"

Aradif's predictions flashed in Fate's mind, dampening her smile. "After everything I learned yesterday, I understand why Finn and the others lied. I would've done the same."

Jessie bobbed her head up and down stiffly. "Great. I'm super happy you sorted everything out."

Fate wasn't so sure. "Really? Because your face doesn't look happy. What's up?"

Jessie waved her off. "It's nothing. I'm being stupid."

"Tell me," Fate pressed. "If this bothers you, I want to know."

"Well, I was just thinking now that you're back with Finn, and all happy and calm about it, you don't really need me around anymore to help you stay calm."

"Yes I do."

Jessie looked skeptical. "Come on. I haven't seen you this happy since... Jeez, I can't remember when."

Fate was starting to get worried. "What are you saying? Are you thinking of going home again?"

Jessie shrugged. "Is there any real reason for me to stay? I suck at research and I have no super powers anymore. I'm pretty much useless to you and everybody else here."

"That's so not true," Fate argued. "There's plenty for you to do here."

"Like what?"

Fate thought about it, but she was coming up blank.

"See? You know I'm right."

"No, you're not." Fate took her friend's hand in hers. She wanted to return to the blissful state she'd been in before she'd opened the door, but Jessie wasn't the only one who would be intruding. The first order of business was reassuring Jessie of her importance.

"I need you here, Jess, now more than ever. You're the only one who remembers Eustace as far back as I do." Tears stung at the back of her eyes. "You're my anchor to him, and the only family I have left. I can't go to Feldoril Forest without you. I have no idea what we'll be facing there. What I do know is, I'll be needing someone along to keep me on track."

Jessie's sigh was one of relief. "I can do that."

Fate gave Jessie a hug, blinking until the tears abated. She let go and smiled at her friend. "I suppose I should get dressed and let Finn know the honeymoon's over."

"Uh, yup. You *are* only wearing his t-shirt and Azrael's suite is just down the hall from here. I know he's your ex and all, but it's probably too soon to rub the reunion in his face."

The words were no sooner out of Jessie's mouth when Azrael emerged from his suite. He was in mid step when he noticed them and came to an abrupt halt. His eyes locked with Fate's. He visibly winced at the oversized t-shirt she was wearing, which was obviously not hers.

Fate wanted to melt into the floor. Pulling the bottom of the shirt down as far as it would go over her bare legs, she inched backward into the doorway and bumped into Finn, who was fully dressed.

"Awkward doesn't begin to describe how I'm feeling right now," she muttered.

"I got this," Jessie said, out of the corner of her mouth. "Hey Azrael! How's it going?" She strode toward him, though his gaze remained on Fate and Finn standing in the doorway. "Did you sleep good? Aren't the beds here the best?"

Finn stepped out of the way so Fate could slink back into his suite. He closed the door, eyeing her with an air of suspicion. "Your face is redder than a bowl of cherries."

"Well, I'm pretty much half naked here!"

His lips curved into a playful smile. Gone was the tension she'd first noted. "I can make you all the way naked, if you'd like," Finn offered.

Fate held out her hands to stop him. She couldn't possibly relax into bed with him knowing Azrael was standing outside in the hall. "No! If we get back in bed, we'll be in here for the rest of the day."

"I can handle that."

Fate grabbed her dusty pants, hopping as she yanked them up her legs and buttoned the waist. Her sweat-stained jacket went on over Finn's t-shirt and she quickly tucked the ends of it into her pants. She shoved her feet into the dirty boots and headed for the door without lacing them.

Finn caught her by the hand. "Whoa, what's the hurry?"

"I want to get everyone together and figure out who's going with me to Feldoril Forest as soon as possible."

Finn stiffened. "Wait, what's really going on here? Is this about Azrael?"

"What're you talking about? This has nothing to do with him. You know all I can focus on right now are my plans to get Eustace back alive and well. And that means making a trip to Feldoril Forest. Once I have my dad back, I'll be ready to face whatever hell dimension I have to enter to put the kibosh on Ananke's grand plan."

Finn's jaw tightened as he stared at her. "Fate, you're not being honest with me. My gut's knotting from the tangle of emotions coming off you. We need to talk about this. I know you still have feelings for Azrael."

"You're reading me?" Fate fumed.

"I haven't shut myself off, because I didn't think I needed to. I've been open to you, heart and soul, since last night."

Fate was mortified. "Well, don't. You have no right to invade my privacy like that!"

"I... I wasn't purposely trying to–"

"It doesn't matter. Put your shields up, or whatever it is you do to keep my stuff separate from yours."

Finn's mouth angled downward into a pained line, the equivalent of a dagger to the heart. She suddenly felt monstrous and cruel. A new layering of guilt propelled Fate toward the door. "I'll go call the meeting and see you in the sanctuary later."

She closed the door before Finn could say anything more. Thankfully, Jessie had accomplished what she'd set out to do, because the hallway was empty. Azrael was nowhere in sight.

Fate raced to her suite at lightning speed as if to outrun her jumbled emotions. But nothing could stop the tidal wave from crashing in the moment she slammed the door behind her.

Overwhelmed, she staggered into the middle of the room. How could she go from a night of absolute heaven to the sheer torture of being torn into pieces all over again? Drowning in the agony of losing Eustace was an undercurrent she constantly fought against. But seeing Azrael's reaction to her standing outside Finn's room, wearing his t-shirt and nothing else, had added a whole new dimension of confusion and guilt.

Finn accused her of still having feelings for Azrael. Was he right about that?

Fate stared at the floor, pressing her hand over her chest and the increased turmoil her question inflicted. She'd always be grateful to Azrael for saving her in Dunebala, regardless of how much they'd hated each other in the beginning.

She couldn't ignore the fact that Azrael had proved his love–a love she'd thought him incapable of–and had willingly suffered the disgrace of marrying her. He'd even gone through the trials to remain her husband, further proving the depth of his commitment. If there was one thing she knew about Azrael, he was a man of honor.

How had she thanked him? By giving him little to no thought from the time he'd lost the challenge to Finn. Worse yet, the only reason she'd asked him to come with her was to be an obstacle between her and Finn.

So much for that selfishly ridiculous notion.

She regretted her request more than ever, especially after witnessing the pain in Azrael's eyes not less than ten minutes ago. Even now, the shame washed over her like she'd been caught cheating on Azrael.

But how could this be? Being with Finn all night–making love, holding each other, laughing, talking and making love again and again–had never felt *so* right. There was no denying her heart belonged to Finn.

Yet Azrael owned a piece of that precious real estate. As to how much, she didn't know. Fate gulped dryly. Was she in love with Azrael too?

21
TWO LUMPS OF SUGAR

FINN BANGED ON THE DOOR of Sithias's suite with a pent-up rage he could no longer contain. Fate leaving him that way had cut deep–a cut that unleashed a host of frustrations he'd been living with for far too long.

Sithias opened the door, sleepy-eyed in silky pajamas and wispy white hair sticking out in all directions. He blinked at Finn, his long, skinny legs wobbling beneath him as he gripped the door handle for support. "What time isss it?"

"Time to wake up." Finn pushed past him and stormed into the sitting room.

Sithias shut the door, shuffled over to the nearest chair and flopped down. "Is there an emergency? Did Brune call a meeting I'm unaware of?"

Finn paced the floor. "No, but Fate will be calling for a meeting anytime now."

"She's back? Thank goodnesss." Sithias's relieved sigh turned into a drowsy yawn.

"Aye, but she still has it in her head she's going to Feldoril Forest to hunt that damnable unicorn. If it even exists." Finn's laughed derisively. "She might as well be hunting the Easter bunny for all the good of it."

Sithias tucked his chin into his neck, pulling at his pointed goatee with a concerned frown. "Do you think we can talk her into finding Dantalion's Key as our firssst priority? Doesn't she understand it's the only way to remove Hippolyta's girdle and in turn ensure Ananke can't emerge?"

"She understands, but you know Fate. Once she's decided on something there's no changing her mind. Right now she thinks getting Eustace back will keep her calm enough to face what's next with finding the key."

"Hmm, when you put it that way, I think I might have to agree with her. After all, witnesssing Eustace's tragic murder was what destabilized her and unlocked the door for Ananke."

Sithias clapped his hands and his chamber bot butler rambled into the room. "Two cups of strong coffee, please." He gestured to the chair across from him. "Come, sit down with me."

Finn slowed his frantic pacing but his nerves were too on edge to sit still.

"What elssse is bothering you, sir?" Sithias asked.

"Nothing other than being worried about Fate. *As usual.*" He muttered the last part.

The butler bot appeared with a tray and set it on the table in front of Sithias. "My usual two lumps of sugar and a dollop of cream." The bot did as instructed and handed him the cup of piping hot coffee. Sithias took a sip, slurping loudly to avoid burning his lips and smiled as he swallowed. "Perfect as always, Hodgeworth."

The butler bot tilted its head in a bow, its circuits blinking brighter for a split second as if pleased with the compliment. Hodgeworth turned to Finn expectantly.

"Black is fine." Finn sat down begrudgingly and took the cup of coffee Hodgeworth handed him.

"Thank you, Hodgeworth. You may return to pressing my wardrobe," Sithias instructed.

"You named your chamber bot?" Finn watched it trundle out of the room.

"You haven't named yoursss yet?"

Finn shrugged. "Why would I?"

"Because everything needs a name. Naming something gives it spirit. Why do you think ships have been given names down through the ages? It was to imbue that ship with the spirit of good fortune, of course."

"If that's the case, this coffee should be the best I've ever tasted." Finn took a sip of the aromatic brew, surprised by the rich, nutty flavor. "Not terrible," he mumbled.

"An understatement, at bessst." Cupping his hands around his mug, Sithias stared at Finn through the steam swirling from his coffee. "How are you really doing, sir?" he asked after a few moments of silence.

"I've been better." Finn's thoughts turned to the night before. His skin came alive with the memory of Fate's skin against his. She'd been so open, so soft and yielding. They'd never been closer in all their time together than last night. But to have her slam the door on her heart and shut him out again was like having a strip torn off his hide, leaving him with a raw, painful wound.

"How so?"

Finn set his coffee down. "I don't know. I suppose it goes all the way back to when Kaliena used the Orb to dismantle me. Ever since I was remade, I've been lost. I can't fly anymore. I no longer possess the power of the Elder race runes, and Tove hates me too much to ink them back on. It's been pure hell living with the guilt of getting her and Grysla involved in the war. Tove lost her mother and brother because of me. And I know I don't have to tell you how awful it's been lying to Fate about Eustace. All in all, I've been feeling like a rank sack of cow dung."

Finn sighed heavily. "Maybe I'm still feeling the severe beating I took in the trials." He squeezed his hands into fists as he narrowed his gaze on Sithias. "Which *you* tossed me into with zero help on your part, by the way." Unexpressed rage flared hot in his chest. "What were you thinking? I almost died and not just once!"

Finn's sudden explosion startled Sithias so much he jumped and spilled his coffee down the front of his pajamas. Squawking in pain, he called for Hodgeworth to fetch a towel. The butler bot juddered in at a fast trot and wiped him down.

"Thank you, Hodgeworth, I'm fine now." Sithias wrapped the towel around his shoulders. "I had no idea you were harboring such resentments, sir. I thought you understood what was at ssstake with the trials. But please know, I was standing by, ready to ressscue you if it came down to that."

Finn leaned forward, digging his forearms into his thighs. "I rescued myself, for the most part, and once by Azrael. What a shocker that was."

"Exactly! I never had to break character, because you carried your own in there."

"Not helping, Sithias."

"Don't you see? If I had intervened on your behalf, Azrael would've won the trials and possibly everything I'd set into motion as Aradif would have been called into question. If I'd been exposed as an imposter, Fate would still be married to Azrael *and* bound to him by the soul ring."

Sithias drooped in the chair. "Please know how much it pained me to put you through that, sir, but I figured you'd be far angrier with me if you hadn't won Fate's freedom."

Finn's anger cooled, but he wasn't completely satisfied with Sithias's explanation. "Did it occur to you to use your Words of Making to give me the Elder race runes? Even the ability to fly again would've given me what I needed to cross that pit of vipers." Finn shuddered involuntarily.

"I did think of that." Sithias stared back worriedly. "What you don't know is that I snuck into the temple and researched the trials the priests had designed. After translating the texts with the Words of Making, I found out the trials weren't tests of strength and power. As you now know, compassion was the key to winning all three trials and I feared you'd default to using strength and power if you were endowed with the runes again. Once I made that crucial discovery, I knew you'd win. Because who has more compassion than you, sir? No one I'm aware of. You're a druid and can't help yourself.

You're good-hearted to the bone."

Sithias smiled nervously as he worried his hands together. "Can you ever forgive me?"

Finn flopped back into the chair. "Aye, I see it all now. I don't like it, but I understand."

"And you forgive me?"

"That's asking a lot. The cuts and bruises are a wee fresh still. At least I have the satisifaction of knowing you have a few of your own from the lashing you took at the trials."

Sithias squirmed. "Uh... about that. I sort of protected my back with the thick hide of an armadillo."

"What about the blood?"

"You're forgetting I'm an accomplished performer. It was all for show. You of all people should know I could *never* endure that amount of pain."

Finn nodded grimly. "Aye, that should've been my first clue. Either way, you're on warning, Sithias. I'm done being drawn into any more of your disasterous plans."

"Maybe I can make it up to you?" Sithias held his breath.

Finn didn't answer. He wanted to let Sithias sweat for the next several minutes, but Hodgeworth broke the silence with an abrupt and disturbing message, spoken in Brune's voice. Sithias yelped and shrank from the butler bot as it stood over them with all six arms planted on its waist like Brune often did whenever she was being official. Or exasperated, which was most of the time. "*Meeting in the sanctuary. Ten minutes. Don't be late.*"

Sithias clutched his chest as he fought to regain his composure. "Intercom off, Hodgeworth."

The butler bot resumed his normal stance and retreated to the other room.

"What was that?" Finn shook his head.

Sithias fanned his face like he was about to faint. "It's nothing. I simply find it amusing to see Hodgeworth mimic whoever's ssspeaking through the intercom. Brune's usually my favorite, next to Darcy. Not today though." He made a mournful face. "Today, I'm more concerned with forgiveness. Namely yours, and I really mussst know what I can do to make amends."

Finn's anger evaporated completely. He didn't have the heart to punish him any longer. "Well, if you're that intent on it, there is *one* thing you can do for me."

Sithias sat straight, eager as a dog ready for a walk. "Pleassse, tell me what it is. I'll do anything!"

22
THE HUNTING PARTY

FATE ARRIVED IN THE SANCTUARY to a group that looked less than thrilled to be gathered around the table. She, however, was quite thrilled to be putting her plans into motion and eager to begin. Setting her scrolls and books down in front of her, she glanced up, catching Arael's gaze. Being fully dressed in a new change of clothes did nothing to shield her from the embarrassment and shame that shot through her. His stoic expression only increased her guilt.

Finn stood on the other end of the table, as far away from Azrael as possible. Her pulse shifted into high gear as he stared back at her. The moment they locked eyes, the green of his irises gleamed from within.

She hadn't seen that for months. Then she noticed the Elder race runes inked on his temple. The rest of them would be on his arms and back, but were covered by his long-sleeved shirt. Fate's gaze darted to Tove, whom she'd asked Brune to invite. Had Finn gone to Tove to have the runes inked back onto his skin? Jealousy burned in her chest at the memory of the intimacy she'd witnessed between the two of them when they'd been together in the Twisted Bone Forest.

Logic kicked back in. Tove couldn't possibly have inked those runes. That would have taken more than the hour that had passed since she'd left Finn's room. That could only leave Sithias. She would've liked to be the one to return the runes and had certainly intended to, had she not been so completely caught up in the whirlwind that was her life.

Jessie winked and gestured for Fate to stand next to her. Gerdie yawned and looked around sleepy-eyed from where she stood on a stool next to Brune. Darcy didn't appear to be anymore awake. She still had bed head and was holding a tall mug of coffee, staring off into space with a grumpy glower. Her face looked naked without the usual slathering of Goth-style makeup.

Fate suddenly regretted the early hour. It probably would've been best to let everyone sleep a few hours more so they'd be sharp and not this group of zombies. She smiled, hoping to rouse them with a cheery disposition. "Hey guys. Thanks for dragging yourselves out of bed at this rather–"

"Ungodly hour." Darcy aimed her disgruntled frown at Fate.

"This couldn't wait until *after* a shower and breakfast?"

"Yeah, well I suppose I should've–"

"Ssso sorry I'm late," Sithias said from the door as he held it open. "I had a little trouble getting the cinnamon buns ready for the meeting. But you'll all be happy to know they're hot, soft and doughy, and dripping with melted butter. Come along, Hodgeworth."

A chamber bot trundled in, its six spindly arms filled with trays of buns and steaming coffee offering choices of cream and sugar. The room filled with the delectable aroma of cinnamon, butter and coffee as the bot placed the trays down on the center of the table without spilling so much as a drop of the precious morning tonic everyone lunged for all at once.

"Thanks, Sithias," Fate whispered, as he squeezed in between her and Jessie.

"I always have your back, misss." He smiled, though nervously.

"I know you do." A lump formed in her throat, knowing she'd been especially hard on her dear, dear friend. "I should've known better." It was all she could manage to get out.

Sithias patted her hand. "Say no more."

"Can we get on with this?" Darcy took a bite of her cinnamon bun, which did nothing to sweeten her sour disposition.

Fate nodded. "As you know, I've decided to hunt the black unicorn before I go on some wild goose chase to find a key in Hell."

Darcy set her mug down so hard the coffee sloshed over the sides. "If anything's a wild goose chase here, it's this unicorn hunt." She frowned at Hodgeworth as he stepped in the way to sop up the spilled coffee. "I'll have you know I've done *months* of research on all the kingdoms of Hell and how to enter the realm holding Dantalion's Key. As compared to a few choice spell books Brune had me pull from the library with reference to an elusive black unicorn that *might* be the main ingredient to a resurrection spell. Emphasis on might."

Fate counted to three as she took a deep breath. Leave it to Darcy to challenge her in front of everyone else. "Don't worry, Darcy, your research won't go to waste. I fully intend to go after Dantalion's Key, but as I'm sure you can tell, getting my *father* back is my first concern."

Darcy placed both hands on the table and leaned forward. "I know you think the universe revolves around you, Fate, but let me remind you you're not the only one who lost a loved one. Remember Mason? My boyfriend? Or is he just one of the many missing holes in that wedge of Swiss cheese you call a brain?"

"I haven't forgotten Mason. If I could undo what happened to him, I'd do it in a heartbeat." Fate fought to maintain a calm level tone but the heat building in her core was proving hard to contain.

"All right," Brune interjected. "Let's take this down a notch. Arguing isn't getting us anywhere. Whether we like it or not, we're moving forward with Fate's plan to send a hunting party to Feldoril Forest. Darcy, you're free to exit this meeting if you wish, and we'll enlist your help later when it's time to move onto retrieving Dantalion's Key."

Darcy lifted her mug to her mouth without taking her eyes off Fate and took a long, leisurely slurp. She finally set the cup down. With the faintest smile on her lips and a wicked glint in her cold blue eyes, she said, "I'll stay. On one condition."

Fate opened her mouth to object, but Brune spoke first. "Which is?"

"I come along on the hunt for the black unicorn *and* Dantalion's Key."

Fate *hated* the idea. "You're a researcher, not a... field agent or whatever you want to call yourself."

"I've done all the research there is to do, and I've had enough of being cooped up in the library. It's time for me to stretch my legs."

"Even if you get said legs cut out from under you?" Fate asked. "Because that's what'll happen. You have no fighting skills or super strength to speak of. How do you expect to defend yourself?"

"I can hold my own."

Now she was just being cocky. And stupid.

"Care to expand?" Fate asked.

"I'm a fifth generation witch, who's had access to the most powerful grimoires in existence. And while you've been off on all your little 'adventures', I've been studying and practicing my craft." Darcy clawed condescending air quotes at Fate with her black nail polished fingers.

Fate wanted to slam Darcy's talons against the table, even if it meant breaking a few digits. She folded her arms to keep from doing just that. "I get that you're a *witch.*" She grinned at her own personal meaning of the word. "But you expect me to believe you're a witch with powers?"

"That's what I said."

"So you're saying you can blast magic and cast spells at the threats we'll inevitably come up against?" Fate suppressed the urge to laugh outright.

"Yup. *And* I can do that resurrection spell you're in such desperate need of."

Fate's amusement evaporated, suddenly feeling like she was sitting across from a poker-playing card hustler. Time to call Darcy's bluff and get her to lay all cards on the table. "Fine. You can come, but we have to see proof of your so-called 'powers' first." She scratched air quotes back at Darcy.

Darcy's unflagging confidence persisted. "I can do that. Any requests on what you'd like to see?"

"Nope. I'll leave it to you to decide." Fate did little to hide a doubtful smirk. Darcy was an ordinary girl who only wished she had powers. The only thing extraordinary about Darcy was that she was extremely annoying.

"Hmm, what shall it be?" Darcy glanced at the ceiling as she thought about it. An unsettling smile formed on her face as she curled a strand of hair around her finger. "I have one that'll have your attention." She focused in on Fate. "Consider this one tailor made for you."

Darcy inhaled deeply and began a low, breathy chant. The words were foreign to Fate's ears. As far as she could tell the incantation didn't even include the usual Latin that seemed common to most spells. If anything, it sounded like Darcy was speaking gibberish.

Fate wanted to burst into uncontrollable laughter, but her amusement vanished when Darcy's words issued from her mouth in puffs of green mist. In fact, the chant changed the sharp grating of Darcy's voice into honeyed tones that were sweet and melodic even to Fate's ears.

The misty tendrils curled outward, undulating hypnotically toward each of them. Fate blinked sleepily, her defenses down as her muscles relaxed. She was beginning to wonder why she'd ever judged Darcy so harshly. Maybe she wasn't so bad after all.

Then Finn moved in behind Darcy and wrapped his arms around her waist. The green irises of his eyes were lit so bright with desire they were almost white.

Fate jolted to attention as Finn nuzzled Darcy's neck and ran his mouth over her skin. Darcy bent her head to one side, allowing him full access. She let out a soft moan and turned toward him, her lips meeting Finn's in a deep, passionate kiss.

Momentarily paralyzed with shock, Fate watched, unable to find her voice. But as that kiss continued, jealousy exploded within every molecule of her being. She hurled one of her books at the wall, breaking the spell with a thundering bang and furious shriek.

Finn pulled away, glaring at Darcy, confused and outraged. "What the bloody hell?" He wiped his mouth.

Darcy smiled at him with an appreciative gaze sweeping over his body. "Thank you for volunteering, Finn." She directed her self-satisfied smirk at Fate. "I take it I grabbed your full attention. Did I pass?"

Fate glared back, her heart pounding with so hard she could barely catch her breath. "I don't even know what that was," she seethed.

"A siren song spell layered over a true name invocation," Darcy explained. "Not that I expect *you* to understand any of that."

Gerdie raised her hand and jumped up and down. "Oh, oh, oh! I do! I understand! Darcy spoke Finn's true name while she was singing the siren song. There wasn't anything he could do. He was helpless against her."

Fate remembered all too well how Finn had nearly drowned when a siren had called him into the water. And she would never forget how Mugloth had used Finn's spirit name to control him. This was her fault. She should've recognized the name spoken within the incantation and stopped Darcy from making fools of them both.

"How could you possibly know Finn's spirit name is Emrys?" Fate couldn't stop shaking with anger.

"Aye," Finn growled, "I'd like to know as well."

Darcy appeared entirely unfazed by their outrage. "I told you. I do my research. And just so you know, I'm all read up on the black unicorn. Not that there's a ton of info available on the subject. But go ahead, ask me anything."

Heat pumped through Fate's blood stream, burning like acid. Darcy must've guessed Fate's lack of extensive research, given the events of late. The temptation to drill Darcy with questions about the black unicorn was strong but she wasn't about to admit her shortcomings. Not now. She disliked Darcy even more for dangling that carrot in front of her.

"I think we can all agree Darcy is well-suited to join the hunting party." Brune watched Fate with concern, a warning in her gaze as she continued. "She can perform the resurrection spell, while holding her own against any dangers that crop up. Unless of course, you'd prefer to take a vote."

"No, you can come with us, Darcy," Fate conceded begrudgingly. "But if you ever play us like puppets again, I won't hold back."

Darcy nodded, glancing down at her coffee mug to escape Fate's enraged stare.

"All right then. Other than Darcy, I need a show of hands as to who else is joining the hunting party."

Finn, Sithias and Jessie were first to raise their hands. Azrael volunteered after a few seconds of hesitation. Fate gave him a quick, awkward nod before turning to Tove. She'd been watching quietly from the sidelines with an unreadable expression.

"Tove, would you be willing to join us?" Fate asked. To be honest, she wasn't thrilled about having Finn's ex along, but there was no denying Tove would be an asset to the team. She was fast, strong and an excellent hunter and fighter.

Tove shifted her weight from one foot to another. "I am inclined to say no."

"Oh. Can I ask why?"

When Tove wasn't forthcoming, Finn spoke. "Tove won't say it here, but she doesn't want to come along if it means being around me." He clenched his jaw, obviously pained by the tension between them. "I can step aside if you'd prefer to have Tove in the party," he offered.

"No, we need you too." Fate's reaction had been knee-jerk and her face grew hot. She looked at Tove. "Is there anything I can say to change your mind?"

Tove shook her head. "I will be returning to my home."

Fate nodded. "How are you planning on getting there?" The Twisted Bone Forest was a long ways away in the northern most region of Oldwilde.

"Rudwor offered to give me transport when he returns to Beldereth."

Brune cleared her throat. "Sorry, but that'll be a long wait. Rudwor promised to keep peace here until... well, until we can decide how to deal with the Serpens." She retrieved the book Fate had thrown and replaced it on the stack.

"Would you consider joining us if we deliver you to the Twisted Bone Forest afterward?" Fate asked Tove.

The green of Tove's eyes darkened, a sign of the anger seething just below the surface. "I will consider your offer. *After* I know more."

"Fair enough." Fate moved aside the trays of leftover cinnamon buns and coffee to make room for the map. The scroll was long and the parchment thick, making it necessary to place empty mugs on the ends to keep the corners from curling back in on themselves.

"This is Feldoril Forest. As you can see it stretches along the entire eastern coastline of Oldwilde and is completely uninhabited by humans." Fate ran her fingers over the mountain range at the center of the forest. "These are the Glor'ner Mountains, completely impassable on foot, but not a problem for us. Fortunately, we still have an airship and a captain to fly it."

She glanced at Azrael and quickly dropped her gaze to the map, pointing to draw everyone's attention away from her reddened face. "This large clearing here on the coastal side of the Glor'ner Mountains is the Mornavar Valley." She reached for the smaller scroll and rolled it out on top of the main map. "This one maps out everything within the Mornavar Valley, its rivers, waterfalls, lakes and network of caves."

Fate patted the stack of three books she'd brought to the meeting. "If the books are right, this valley is filled with priceless treasures of powerful magic. Several thousand years ago, Serpen legions advanced into the forest in search of Mornavar Valley."

"Figures it was Serpens," Brune grumbled.

Fate agreed with a nod. "It's said they marched for more than ninety days without ever even reaching the eastern base of the Glor'ner Mountains. The trek was plagued by trackless belts of swampy marshlands and constant attacks from beasts of the forest. The Serpen's journey finally ended at a vast grove of enormous oaks. Apparently, the soldiers were overtaken by a terrible gloom, which drove most of them mad. They turned on each other and those who survived being slaughtered by one of their own either became lost or food for wild beasts. The story ends there, because not one of them returned."

"Does anyone ever wonder how such stories were ever recorded if there were supposedly no sssurvivors?" Sithias asked.

"I wonder that all the time." Gerdie rolled her eyes with that wise, lopsided smile Fate had missed seeing. "The books in the library are filled with stories like that."

Fate opened the book recording the forest's history. "According to this, the ancient forest and all its mysteries have lured explorers and historians alike. Many of them never returned. But a few survived to chronicle their findings." She closed the book, resting her hand on the leatherbound cover with its embossed title leafed in faded and chipped gold. "That's as much as I know so far. Who's interested in boning up on the history?"

"Oh, I'll take it!" Sithias was quick to offer.

Fate stacked another book on top of the history book and slid it across the table.

Sithias eagerly reached for them. "What's this second one?"

"A record of every known botanical species in the forest."

Sithias looked like she'd thrown a smelly sock at him. "Ooh, botanicals have never been my bailiwick. I'm terrible at remembering official plant names. I'm even worse at distinguishing the difference between sssimilar species. I once picked a wild orchid for Elsina." He smiled wistfully. "I will say she loves her orchids, and they do perfume a room like no other flower. *Except* when that orchid is a corpse flower. Believe me, nothing kills the mood like the stink of rotting flesh."

"Point taken." Fate glanced around the table. "Any other volunteers?"

Darcy gestured for Sithias to hand her the book, which he sent sliding across the table. She caught the book before it careened over the edge and smiled. "You could say botanicals are my cup of tea. It's a witch thing."

The unsettling glint in Darcy's eyes made Fate squirm inwardly, but with no other takers, she was forced to accept the offer.

Fate tipped the last book on its end, squeezing the thick spine in frustration. "Last, but definitely not least, we have the Feldoril Forest Bestiary. I've only read about the black unicorn, which isn't much. But as you can see by the size of this big bad book, the forest is teaming with magical and dangerous wildlife. There's not much that isn't harmless in Feldoril Forest. Actually, the book suggests not all the creatures are known and recorded in here, so I need someone who has experience with wild beasts to take this one."

"I will," Tove offered. "I know how to speak to animals."

Fate stared back in surprise. "Awesome, we have our very own Dr. Doolittle."

Tove frowned, obviously unfamiliar with the name.

"Pass that down," Fate muttered as she handed the heavy book to Jessie, who struggled to keep from laughing out loud.

"I will assist Tove."

Fate stiffened at the sound of Azrael's voice. "You can talk to animals too?" she asked, her chest tightening at the thought of him working closely with Tove.

"No." Azrael didn't smile, but she noted a spark of amusement in the crinkling around his eyes. "As you know, I am well versed in fighting the wild beasts of Dunebala."

She couldn't argue with that. "Sure. It's settled then. You and Tove are in charge of beast control." Fate avoided looking at Finn, knowing she sounded more upbeat than the conversation called for–a lame attempt at overcompensating for an unexpected twinge of possessiveness. Would she ever get over her insecurities where Tove was concerned?

"Aye, it's settled." Finn's tone was laced with anger. "Can we move on?" His eyes had gone from a brilliant green to a smoky sage as he glanced at Jessie. "There's still a few of us who don't seem to have any particular purpose on this quest of yours."

The sharp edge in his voice snicked her heart and Fate struggled to maintain an unflinching expression. "I'm getting to that," she assured him matter-of-factly. "Since we'll be sailing over the Glor'ner Mountains, therefore avoiding the perils of trekking through the forest to get to the valley, our main concern will be the Falinorin. There's little known about them, since no humans have ever made it as far as Mornavar. All I have are references to them being stewards of the valley. I found references of some ancient texts that should have more information on them, but I haven't had time to look them up."

Fate lifted a sheet of paper she'd written the list on. "I'd like you to find out everything you can on them. If you're willing."

"I can handle that." Finn settled back in his chair, arms crossed and staring straight ahead.

Fate felt terrible for causing him pain. She never should've asked Azrael to come back with them, regardless of his value to the hunting party. She was weak. Torn in half. Unable to fully commit her heart to one person.

"What about me?" Jessie asked. "Should I help Finn?"

"No, I'm putting you in charge of the most important part of this 'quest' of mine." She couldn't resist using Finn's words. Not out of spite, but because that's truly what this was, a quest of the highest order. "You'll have to work with Brune on this, but we'll be transporting Eustace with us and I need you to ensure his body arrives safely and stays that way until Darcy can perform the resurrection spell."

"Sure... I can do that..."

Fate waited for Jessie to say more. When her friend remained uncomfortably silent, Fate looked at the others. "Great meeting everyone. We'll leave first thing tomorrow, so do what you have to do to get ready."

The exodus that followed was shockingly swift, leaving Fate by herself and feeling painfully alone.

23
BON VOYAGE

"A WOMAN'S HEART IS a delicate, complex instrument, laddie." Rudwor swung a burly arm over Finn's shoulders as they strolled the long corridor. "No matter how much you think you've mastered playing her heart until she's crooning beautiful love songs to you, she's every bit as capable of making sounds that'll have your ears bleeding if you happen to pluck the wrong chord."

"Well, I wouldn't go so far as to say Fate's never shrieked at me." Finn smiled knowingly. "But at least not the way you've been shrieked at by any number of maidens you've upset with your off key ways. It's more like I can't keep up with how she's feeling. Fate's constantly surprising me with a thousand other emotions I never see coming. All of which can happen within the run of an hour or less. Why is that?"

Rudwor pulled at his braided beard. "Can't help you there, lad. Why do you think I've never taken a wife? I can't be king and have my head spun around until I can't think straight. That's no way to run a kingdom."

"Aye, but don't you get lonely? Wouldn't you prefer to have someone by your side to help you make those hard decisions? Someone to hold every night and share your future with?"

Rudwor grinned. "I'll never be lonely as long as I have the soft, warm body of a willing lass in my bed to keep the winter chill from seeping into my bones. As for making those hard decisions, that's what my advisors are for. But that's just me. I'm a simple man with simple needs."

They came to a stop in front of the sanctuary door and Rudwor turned to face him. "You on the other hand are cut from a whole different cloth–Fate's cloth. Your bond with her is thicker than blood. Your very soul was carved from her heart. She's as much a part of you as you are of her." Rudwor tapped a meaty finger against Finn's breastbone. "And that's what you keep forgetting. Fate is bound to you in ways she's still unaware of. Regardless of how twitterpated she might get over this desert prince you've been fretting so much about."

Finn's backpack suddenly felt heavier than it should. He shifted it to his other shoulder, tightening his grip on the strap. "Is it that obvious?"

"Only to me. And probably to Azrael. We're men, and we tend to be territorial when it comes to our women. Wars have been fought over the fairer sex, all while the women puzzle over why we men are behaving so badly." He shook his head. "They have no idea what helpless victims we are to their beauty and soft touch. We need them like the air we breathe."

"Truer words were never spoken," Finn agreed. "If nothing else, it'll be an interesting trip. One I wish you were coming along for."

"Ah, I could use an adventure, especially knowing Darcy will be onboard. Now there's an enticing lass who's given me the slip more than once. Can you believe she has no interest in this?" Rudwor waved his hands over his barrel chest with a look of bewilderment.

"Her loss."

Rudwor nodded. "Aye, she has no idea the delights she's taken a pass on. But that's fine. I've set my eyes on Brune of late, and she's in dire need of my help, so I must stay for her sake." His expression took on a faraway look. "Now there's a woman I could consider a life with. After I chip through that fortress of ice she's built around herself, of course."

Finn almost laughed, but refrained when he realized Rudwor was serious. "Well, good luck with that, my friend. You'll need it."

Finn pushed through the sanctuary door with Rudwor behind. The room was filled with activity. Most of the hunting party was there, in addition to Brune and Gerdie. A half dozen bots were passing back and forth across the gangplank, loading Azrael's airship with supplies, weapons and armory. Finn glanced around for Fate, who was nowhere in sight.

Neither was Arael, for that matter.

Fate hadn't come to his room to spend their last night at the Keep together as he'd hoped she would. Had she spent the night with *him*?

Finn scanned the deck of the ship, the burn in his chest increasing when he saw them standing near the helm, deep in conversation. Fate was dressed in desert garb, loose along the limbs, but the hooded leather vest was fitted tight around the seductive curve of her waist. Azrael's long dark hair was wrapped in layers of ivory cloth and he wore a regal robe made of a light filmy fabric. The robe shimmered in and out of view around the edges depending on how the light hit it. He was perfectly suited to the desert, though Fate seemed to have adapted easily enough, thanks to his help.

Finn tried to tell himself Fate and Azrael were going over plans, not exchanging intimacies. But he couldn't calm down. Watching her eyes light up as she spoke to him, combined with Azrael's passionate stare was more than Finn could stand.

Taking in a deep breath, Finn dropped his shields, allowing his awareness to lightly touch Fate. Her essence, while always strong, was stronger than ever before, made worse by a wild flurry of emotions, a force that rocked him off balance.

Rudwor slapped a heavy hand on Finn's back, nearly knocking him over. "Don't do it, laddie." He held Finn steady. "You're only asking for misery."

Finn clenched his fists, calling his protective walls back in around him. "She's all over the place... happy and sad... excited and guilty... wanting and not wanting."

"The lass is a mess," Rudwor confirmed. "You're best to let her sort herself out, while you do the same. Most importantly, trust in the bond between you. I can guarantee, Azrael doesn't have that with her."

"I wouldn't be so sure. They used to share soul rings. That's got to leave a mark of some kind."

"Maybe so, but not the same as you have with her."

Finn wasn't convinced. His fear was overpowering.

Fate marched across the gangplank and stepped through the open hatch. When her eyes met Finn's her carefree expression diminished into a polite smile. "Looks like we're all here."

The air went out of Finn's lungs.

Sithias, Darcy and Jessie set their boxes down on the big table. Tove turned around from where she'd been examining bows and stacking a supply of arrows.

"The necessities are packed. All that's left now is what's in here." Fate glanced around at the last of the boxes filled with spell books and four aeronaut packs with canisters of extra fuel. She instructed the bots to load the remaining supplies onto the airship and stepped inside the sanctuary to allow them passage.

"I guess this is goodbye for awhile." Fate bent low to hug Gerdie.

She nodded sadly. "I don't care how long it takes, as long as you come back."

Fate straightened. "You can count on it. And Eustace will be with us too."

Gerdie's expression brightened. "Yes, I can't wait to see him again!"

Brune held her hand out to shake Fate's. "Be careful. I need you back. For more pragmatic reasons, of course."

"Right." Fate shook her hand, but then held on with both hands, her expression softening. "Thank you for making all this possible. Eustace is coming back to us because of you. And thanks for holding down the fort while we're away."

Brune looked like she was close to choking up, but cleared her throat with a curt nod. "Go. The sooner you leave, the sooner you return. And don't make me have to come find you. You won't like the mood I'm in."

"Yes, sir." Fate saluted her great-aunt with a playful grin. She waved the others onto the gangplank. "Okay, everyone on board."

Rudwor nudged Finn toward the hatch. "Go get your lass, boyo."

Finn waited for the others to board before he moved toward the gangplank. He stopped next to Fate. "We need to talk, love."

The excitement in her eyes vanished. "Later, Finn. Later."

Finn bit down on the urge to press the issue. Instead, he marched across the gangplank and dropped his pack on deck.

Fate followed right behind him, withdrew the gangplank and cast the rope off from the sanctuary. She signaled to Azrael, who steered the airship away in a steady upward sweep. Watching them work in tandem so easily was a painful reminder of how close they'd no doubt become during her time stranded with the desert prince.

Finn turned his back to them, gripping the railing with a sinking feeling of defeat. Brune, Gerdie and Rudwor stood within the open hatch of the sanctuary, waving goodbye. He lifted his hand but it was hardly a wave, more of a flimsy gesture to hide his disappointment.

Sithias rushed in next to Finn and leaned over the railing, his long, skinny arm flapping back and forth. "Bon voyage!" He was dressed in an outfit of cream-colored khakis and a straw safari helmet. All he was missing to complete the look of an intrepid jungle explorer was a monocle.

Finn turned and leaned against the railing. "You do know that's what you say to the person leaving on a trip, don't you? Not the other way around."

"I do, but I like the way it sssounds. Besides, we can use all the good luck we can get. Even if it's from the person who's leaving." Sithias sniffed and wiped his watery eyes.

"Are you crying?"

Sithias nodded sheepishly. "What can I say? Goodbyesss make me weep."

Finn sighed glumly.

"What's wrong, sir?"

Finn glanced at Fate, who was back at the helm talking to Azrael. There was a telltale blush on her face he knew all too well.

Sithias followed his gaze. "Oh, I sssee." He blocked the disturbing scene with his head. "You have nothing to worry about. I can promise you that."

"You can't promise anything," Finn seethed.

"Maybe not in the strictessst form of the word. But if there's one thing I know, it's that Fate loves *you*. Not Azrael."

"She loves him too."

"No she doesn't."

"Aye, she does. Did you forget I can feel what she's feeling?"

Sithias gasped. "You're not doing that right now, are you? That would be considered a grievous invasion of privacy." He glanced over his shoulder at Fate, who looked back at Finn with a troubled expression. "Admittedly, a jussstified one if I was in your shoes."

"No, I'm not spying. Anyone with eyes can see what's going on." Finn tilted his head, rubbing out the tightness in his neck. "Besides, it's too damn painful to open up to her. I'm done torturing myself."

"For the best, I'm sure." Sithias frowned and shook his head. "We're looking at a four day flight to Mornavar Valley, which for you, will feel like four months if all you do is stand around brooding about Fate."

"Is this your idea of a pep talk?"

"I say we team up together and ssstudy to keep your mind off... more volatile matters."

The last thing Finn felt like doing was burying his nose in a book, while Fate and Azrael became reacquainted with each other. "I suppose a distraction would be best," he admitted finally. "I wasn't exactly given much time to do my homework."

"Oh! I had a peek at the literature on the Falinorin while I was packing the books from the library. Fascinating subject matter." Sithias leaned in with a sideways whisper. "Much more interesting than my assignment. I'm already bored with Feldoril's hissstory, given most of the forest is uncharted territory and what's actually recorded seems to be loose guesswork."

"I seem to recall you eagerly volunteering for that one."

"I did indeed. Had I known it would be like eating a stale cracker, I would've held out for a much tastier treat. But, I'm happy to sssink my fangs into your assignment."

"Fangs?" Finn's aversion to snakes remained, regardless of how long he'd known Sithias. Plus the memory of Sithias in gigantic serpent form, while in Biraktar, was still fresh in his mind.

"A mere slip of the tongue. I sometimes forget I'm not dressed in scales."

"That's not the only slip. The hissing has been sneaking back in more and more since Biraktar."

"I'll work on remedying that." Sithias stared expectantly. "Unless you'd prefer I don't help."

"Oh, by all means, have at it."

"Well, there's no time like the present. The books are over here." Sithias gestured for him to follow.

Finn struggled against the temptation to turn his head toward Fate and instead fixed his gaze on the back of Sithias's helmet and wisps of white hair skimming his collar.

Sithias dug through several wooden crates before finding the one he was looking for. "Ah yes, here it isss. Oops, another hiss. Sorry." He sat down on a rolled blanket and put his back to the curved sidewall to take advantage of what little shade there was on deck.

Finn did the same, noting that Jessie, Tove and Darcy had escaped the blazing sun by retreating into the hull of the ship. While he'd prefer to do the same, he wasn't about to leave Fate and Azrael alone on deck. He'd sweat buckets of salt before he did that.

Sithias flipped through the pages before finally settling on the one he was looking for. "Here it is. The Falinorin... Hmm, this is interesting. The name has its roots in the Dark Speech. I wonder what that is?"

Finn leaned in to have a look but didn't recognize it as such. The Druid Order taught their knowledge of the Dark Speech orally. Never in writing. "The Dark Speech is the secret language of Druids," he explained. "We use it to speak to elemental energies and spirits."

"That's intriguing. Is the language related to the Elder race runes?"

"Maybe. Both languages are similar in that they connect with the elements, though I'd say the Elder race runes are much, much older. They're definitely far more powerful than the Dark Speech."

Sithias nodded excitedly. "This is excellent! Do you realize what this means?"

"Not exactly. Just because I understand the Dark Speech, doesn't mean I know what that word means from reading it."

"What if you speak it?" Sithias handed him the book.

Finn stared at the word and took a deep breath. Channeling all his energy into his throat as he'd been taught when using the Dark Speech, he spoke the name aloud. "*Falinorin.*" Power hissed past his lips, charging the air with its potency. Images came in flashes of a regal race, one of light, one of dark, and in that moment he knew who and what they were.

Sithias blinked in shock.

"What?" Finn asked.

"Your voice. It was so loud. Primal." Sithias rubbed his ears. "The force of it pushed me against the walls and shook the boat. You didn't feel that?"

Before Finn could answer, Fate and Azrael came running over. Tove climbed on deck, followed by Jessie. Darcy emerged last, her climb hindered by a sheet she was using to protect her ghost-pale skin from the sun.

"What did you do?" Azrael asked. He was staring at Finn like he was a threat, his hand gripping the hilt of his saber. Fate stood next to him, her face drawn with fear.

"What the heck was that?" Darcy asked. "That quake nearly knocked Eustace's case over."

"He's fine!" Jessie assured Fate, whose fearful expression turned to absolute panic.

Tove was the only one among them who was calm. She stood behind the others, but stared back at Finn. There was a knowing look in her eyes.

Finn rose to his feet. "Sorry for causing a stir. It was an experiment."

"Kindly refrain from any further experiments." Azrael marched back to the helm.

"What were you experimenting with?" Fate held her hand to her chest as she worked on breathing normally again.

"We were studying up on the..." Sithias glanced around nervously before whispering, "Falinorin." When nothing happened, he patted the pages of the open book. "Just as you asked."

Fate's gaze moved from Sithias to Finn. "I still don't get what happened. Am I missing something here?"

Tove stepped forward. "Finn activated the power stored in the Olde name with the Elder race runes. I will show him how to avoid doing that again."

Fate's brow furrowed with something akin to pain or anger, but she didn't refuse Tove's offer. Turning away with a quick glance at Finn, she walked back to join Azrael.

Darcy fanned what little part of her face was showing beneath the sheet. "Well, I'm out of here. If anyone needs me, I'm down below."

Jessie followed. "Me too. See you when the sun goes down."

Tove sat cross-legged next to Sithias and looked up at Finn. "Sit."

He resumed his seat on the rolled blanket, both surprised and confused by her readiness to help.

Tove waved her hands, gracefully scribing runes into the air while she spoke the ancient language of the Elder race. "You have forgotten how to speak the way my mother taught you. The runes were a gift you have taken back without permission." Her eyes darkened but only for a few seconds before they returned to the sage green he'd always found so entrancing.

Her rebuke filled Finn with shame. He'd been so desperate to have his powers back, regardless of who granted them, he never considered how offensive that would be to Tove. He signed back, stammering over the words spoken in the Elder race tongue, realizing he truly had forgotten how to speak as he'd been originally taught. "I… you speak the truth, Tove. I had… no right to ask Sithias to gift me the runes. *You* are the only one who could grant me that gift a second time. For that, I am truly sorry."

She nodded solemnly while flowing her hands toward her heart. "I forgive you." Her eyes filled with sadness. "For everything."

Finn was stunned. He never dreamed he'd hear those words from Tove. Tears welled in his eyes as he smiled and accepted her forgiveness with a gesture that cupped her words to his heart. He couldn't express how much he'd missed this connection that only the Elder race runes could create. No other language linked hearts as intimately. The only exception was the language of making love.

Tove didn't smile, but the stony expression she'd reserved for him alone fell away and there was an acceptance in her eyes he hadn't seen since they'd been together in the Twisted Bone Forest.

"Uh, excuse me." Sithias interrupted, his whisper apologetic. "While the sign language is a beautiful thing to watch, I'm rather outside of the conversation over here. I'm wearing my transmodulator, but it doesn't seem to work for your Elder race language. I wonder why that is?"

Unwilling to break the spell, Finn held his gaze on Tove. "Leave us for a bit, Sithias. Tove and I have much to discuss."

"Oh… certainly. I'll be below when you're ready for me again." Sithias sounded disappointed, but walked over to the ladder and climbed down.

Tove's eyes smoldered, shifting from bright greens before settling to back to an earthy sage. Finn smiled even more. She'd never been one to hide her emotions. Tove was an open book and a pleasure to read when she was happy and calm. She signed and spoke. "Would you like me to explain the error you made when speaking the Olde name?"

"Aye, very much."

The smallest hint of a smile formed on her lips and Finn was grateful to have Tove teaching him the earth magics once again. "The power of the Elder race runes runs in your veins, just as it does within the earth. Words have lost their power over time, namely the words of humans. They have changed the root words by shortening them. In doing this, they have cut away the Olde power. A human can say the Olde name without igniting the magic. When you spoke the Olde name with the power of the Elder race runes on your tongue, the magic erupted because you were not holding or directing the power."

Finn nodded. "Ah, that makes sense. I see what happened now." He leaned forward. "I saw who they are. Did you see them too?"

"I did."

"I had no idea such a race existed."

The breeze picked up, blowing Tove's sable strands across her face. Finn brushed them gently aside and her eyes lit to a fiery green, before dropping her gaze hastily to the open pages placed between them. "This book will never show us what we already know about the Falinorin." She was careful to sign the name, rather than speak it aloud.

"Aye, everything we need to know about them is in the Olde name."

Tove lifted her gaze. The sage color of her irises darkened to nearly black. "They will not welcome us."

"No, they won't." Finn sighed. "It won't matter though. Fate's prepared for a battle."

"Then they will fight us, and they will likely win."

24
RESISTING DESTINY'S PLAN

FATE TRIED NOT TO WATCH Finn and Tove signing and speaking the Elder race language to each other, but her gaze slid continually to them. From where she stood, the rest of the world seemed to have fallen away from them. Leaving them alone in a private place only they existed in.

The ache in her chest increased when Finn reached out to brush Tove's dark hair aside with a gentle, loving caress. Tove stared back at him, her desire lighting the green of her eyes. Her beauty had always been stunning but her otherworldly looks ran so much deeper. Tove exuded a wildness that was as unpredictable as nature itself, an allure Finn was falling for all over again.

Azrael moved in behind Fate, bending his head to speak softly near her ear. "They are close. I see this upsets you."

Fate turned away from the painful sight. "They were together once. It happened because Finn had no memory of me at the time."

The corners of Azrael's lips curled into a quizzical smile. "Strange. Is that not what happened to you when we met?"

"There were extenuating circumstances in Finn's case. Totally different from why I lost my memory." Fate let out a tortured sigh. "I suppose I see your point though. Finn and I seem to have a weird cosmic pattern happening between us."

"Some would say you and Finn are not meant to be together."

This made her frown. "Who exactly are these mysterious naysayers? Let me see. Would *you* be one of them?"

Azrael's amusement faded, though his gaze remained gentle. "I am merely observing the signs. The two of you have had every obstacle thrown in your path. As if destiny itself has been purposely separating you from one another. Yet, while you were apart, you each found someone to love." He swept his arm, gesturing at Finn and Tove, the airship, and then at Fate before bringing his hand to his chest. "Now we are all here. The four of us, together, resisting destiny's plan."

This was an unexpected change of subject that caught Fate off guard. They'd managed to keep their conversations to the trip and basic matters at hand, regardless of how embarrassed she still was about Azrael catching her outside Finn's suite in a compromised state only the day before. She hadn't been able to stop blushing in his presence because of it. "I don't want to be cruel here, but do I really need to remind you that Finn and I are together? And I mean *all* the way."

Pain snatched the warmth from Azrael's blue eyes. "No, I need no reminders."

Regret pounded in Fate's heart. "I'm sorry. I never should've asked you to come back with us. What was I thinking?"

"Only you can answer that question. Maybe you should take the time to do so." Azrael returned to his station at the helm and untied the wheel, gripping the handles until the white of his knuckles showed through his skin.

Fate searched for something to say that would make up for her grave mistake and came up empty. She turned from Azrael's cold expression, only to be confronted anew with Finn and Tove speaking their silent, intimate language.

Overwhelmed by a deluge of emotions she couldn't begin to separate, her pulse skittered chaotically. "Screw this," she muttered and launched into the clear sky, all too willing to fly too close to the sun and let it incinerate her.

Fate's flight didn't last long. The noonday desert sun was unbearable, forcing her to return to the ship within an hour's time. After that, she avoided both Finn and Azrael for the remainder of the trip by busying herself with necessary research, which was more than enough to fill the hours of a day.

Unfortunately, she could only sit and read for so long before she grew restless and had to find other tasks to fill her time. If she wasn't discussing details for the spell with Darcy, she was cleaning the hunting rifles and sharpening the blades of every sword and dagger in the arsenal.

After a while, there was nothing left to be done. With this extra time on her hands, she took to sitting next to the case holding Eustace's body–something she'd been unable to do when Brune had first revealed the truth to her. It had been too painful, knowing she was looking at an empty shell floating inside a cloud of multidimensional magic.

All that had changed since then. Now that she was on her way to finding the key ingredient for calling his spirit back into his body, Fate found great comfort in viewing her father's peaceful face, because he would soon be opening his eyes. Her excitement grew with each passing day, knowing she was another step closer to setting her world right. Everything would be so much better with Eustace there to guide her.

Nothing would get in the way of that. Her love life could wait.

At night, she slept on one of the beds near the other girls. Partly to keep one eye on Tove to make sure she remained in her own bed, but mostly to maintain the distance she'd put between herself and Finn.

She caught him glancing her way more than once, and always, his green eyes were filled with more pain than she could face. Everytime he approached her, she'd find someone to call out to and draw into some offhand conversation–one of the few advantages of being on a small ship.

Azrael on the other hand, was doing a fine job of keeping his distance. If he spoke to her at all, it was merely to instruct her on the course to keep the airship on when they traded shifts at the helm. Those were the times, when the question he'd posed would return to nag at her.

Fate had rationalized her reasons for asking Azrael to return with them more times than she could count. But there was some truth in what Azrael had said. His presence had an undeniably strong effect on her. Not as powerful as what she shared with Finn, but it was there all the same. And it wasn't fair to Finn if she couldn't give her heart to him completely.

A horn suddenly blared from above deck, startling Fate from the book she was blankly staring at. Sithias yelped and dropped his book. Jessie woke from a nap, drowsy and disoriented.

Darcy swore under her breath when she spilled a bottle of purple liquid she was pouring into a bowl. "What the devil was *that*?" she grumbled.

"Azrael must have spotted land." Fate jumped to her feet, tipping over the stack of books on her mattress. Without stopping to pick them up, she rushed to the ladder. They'd been flying over the ocean for the last day and a half and she was anxious to see the lush green forests of Oldwilde after having been in the deserts of Shalamoraize for so very long.

The scent of cedar and pine perfumed the moist, cool air as she stuck her head above deck and climbed all the way up. When Fate saw Finn and Tove leaning over the railing, she turned sharply and walked over to Azrael. She stopped beside him, speechless when she saw snowcapped mountains in the distance and the emerald green of an ancient rain forest rising on the lower hills to each side of them.

She inhaled the earthy scents and moved over to look at the map pinned open on a board next to the helm. They were on the southern most spear of Feldoril Forest. The remainder of the flight would be to follow the spine of the Glor'ner Mountains until they reached Mornavar Valley.

"How much longer before we get there?"

"I estimate a few hours after sunset," Azrael replied, his tone clipped and matter-of-fact.

Ignoring the sharp pang she felt every time she bumped against his chilly exterior, Fate nodded. She should be relieved he wasn't pressing her anymore, but she wasn't. "I'll get the crew together so we can go over all the research and finalize our plans."

Jessie, Darcy and Sithias were already topside and admiring the view. Fate marched over to join them. "Gather around, everyone." She stared pointedly at Finn and Tove. "We have until sunset to go over the last of your findings and carve our best plan of action into stone."

Azrael tied off the wheel and joined the circle. Finn and Tove approached hesitantly, exchanging a secretive glance that bothered Fate. She set her hands on her hips. "Am I sensing something wrong here?" she asked Finn. "You've finished your research on the Falinorin, haven't you?"

"Aye, of course we have." Finn stared back defiantly. "What is it you think we've been doing all this time?"

Fate laughed cynically. "How would I know? You two have been huddled up talking in sign, and when you do speak out loud, nobody can understand what you're saying."

"We've been speaking the Elder race language." Finn clenched his jaw. "Much of it's in sign, however."

"Right." Fate resisted the urge to sign something of her own. "Well, Darcy's already briefed us all on the plants she needs to add to the spell. Sithias has mapped out exactly where we need to parachute into the valley. And Azrael has filled us in on which creatures to look out for. All on his own, I might add, since Tove's been working exclusively with you on researching the Falinorin. So how about you share what you two have discovered about them, assuming you can pull yourselves away from your rather engrossing conversations."

Finn pressed his lips into a tight line and nodded. "Tove and I wanted to be thorough in our research before we shared what we've discovered *outside* the books you provided."

Fate frowned. "Explain to me how you could possibly discover anything about the Falinorin outside of the books, especially since you've never *seen* them."

"As you know, I accidentally triggered the power in the name because of the Elder race runes. What I didn't tell you is that Tove and I instantly knew the meaning of the name and were given visions. They are not what the books tell us they are, which is why I took the time to read through them all to see if

I could find any similarity to what Tove and I saw." He shook his head. "I didn't. At least nothing of any real importance."

Fate didn't like the reluctance she was sensing from him. "I'll admit I skimmed over those books. All I know is the Falinorin are stewards of the valley and possibly a shy, elusive yet harmless race of elves." She'd pictured small, pointy-eared people wearing clothes made of leaves but decided to keep that to herself.

"Elven is what they are," Finn confirmed. "They are anything but harmless."

"Finn will not say the words, so I will." Tove stared at Fate, her expression cold and guarded. "We cannot enter the valley. If we do, your so-called stewards will kill us."

Fate glared at Tove. "First off, that's not your call to make. Secondly, everyone on this ship is a force to be reckoned with, in one way or another. So let me be clear. We're going into the valley and we'll get what we came for."

"Finn told me that is what you would say." Tove's gaze swept over Fate with what she took to be pity. "Are you prepared to be the reason for all your friends dying?"

The air went out of Fate's lungs. She already blamed herself for losing Mason and Lincoln, and ultimately for what had happened to Eustace. Heat exploded in her core, shooting through her veins, bursting bright beneath her skin.

Sithias covered his mouth. "Oh my, she's going to pop!"

Jessie rushed forward, locking eyes with Fate. "Keep looking at me," Jessie told her. "Breathe. Just breathe. Remember why we're here. We're doing this for Eustace. Nothing's going to get in the way of that."

Fate squeezed her eyes shut, imagining the moment when Eustace would wake and wrap his arms around her–the safest place in the entire universe. Peace washed over her. Taking one last deep breath, Fate opened her eyes. "Thanks, Jess," she whispered.

Everyone else had retreated to the furthest edge of the deck, all except Finn and Azrael. They both stood next to Jessie, each tense with concern. Fate walked over to the railing and held her face to the wind, welcoming the crisp, fresh air on her skin. A few minutes later, she turned back to the others. "I'm fine now. I didn't mean to scare everyone."

Darcy rolled her eyes. "Uh, more like terrified us. You really need to get a grip, girl."

Anger sparked again, but Fate countered it by putting a smile on her face. Albeit a fake smile. "Maybe you shouldn't talk right now, Darcy."

Darcy opened her mouth, probably to say something even more inflammatory, but Fate cut her off before she could utter a peep. "Finn and Tove, please tell us everything you know about the Falinorin. That way we can proceed with knowledge." She glanced at the others. "Is that fair?"

Everyone but Darcy nodded.

Finn signed something to Tove and followed with a quick translation. "I'll take the lead on this one."

Tove's only response was to spring onto the railing, light as a bird. Her long dark hair streamed on the currents of air as she balanced with ease and stared out at the forest. An old sense of inferiority returned, pretzeling Fate's stomach into knots. Tove commanded attention, whether or not she uttered a single word.

"The most important part to know is that this elven race is as ancient as the forest itself," Finn began. "They know every inch of the land, from its mountains to its rivers and lakes. Most of all, they are connected to the forest and everything living there. They can see through the eyes of every creature, great and small. They communicate with the beasts and the trees in the same way Tove and I can, because they speak the Olde language."

Fate didn't like what she was hearing. "So what you're saying is, there's no sneaking past them into the valley."

"If what Finn says is true, they will already know we are here," Azrael added.

"Aye, that's exactly what I'm saying and it gets worse. They jealously guard Mornavar Valley."

"Then we'll hunt at night when they're sleeping," Fate pressed. "That's when the black unicorn comes out."

Finn shook his head sadly. "That won't work. They are elvenkind, but there are *two* races: the Elrinye and the Darfal. The Elrinye live in the light of day. The Darfal live in the dark of night." He was careful to say each race's name with a hush in his voice. Tove had obviously taught him how to control the power when speaking the Olde language aloud.

"Oh joy. Round the clock guardians." Fate paced. "That's a problem."

"Sounds like game over to me." Darcy shrugged when Fate shot her a frown.

"We're not turning around," Fate insisted. "We'll just have to go at this... differently than we first planned."

"Which isss?" Sithias asked.

Fate scrambled for an answer. "Uh... Well, we have two people here who speak pretty much the same language as the Falinorin." She looked at Finn.

"You and Tove will have to be our official ambassadors and ask them if they'll allow us into the valley."

Finn raised his eyebrows in surprise. "You really don't understand how the Elder race runes work. There'll be no hiding our reasons for coming to the valley, because the words transmit our intentions through visions."

Fate's frustration tripled. "Then I guess we'll have to throw ourselves on their mercy and hope they grant us permission to trap the unicorn. Surely they'll let us take a single hair from its mane so we can–"

"I thought we needed the–"

"Darcy, I'm well aware of exactly what we need from the black unicorn." Fate stared Darcy down, her core bursting with molten heat as she silently imposed her will. "Maybe you should hit the books and refresh your memory."

Darcy stared back and remained surprisingly quiet.

Tove jumped down on deck, landing without a sound. "I promise you, the Falinorin will *never* grant us permission. We are best to turn back."

Fate stepped toward her. "I guess you were too busy day dreaming to hear what I said. We're not turning around."

Tove remained silent but stood her ground in spite of the heat radiating from Fate.

Finn moved in between them. "We'll figure something out." The fear in his eyes unsettled Fate. He was afraid she was going to hurt Tove.

Fate felt like a monster. Hurt and angry, she turned her head, unwilling to face him any longer. The peaceful, open sky called to her more in that moment than it ever had. "I need some time to think about this." Her breath hitched in her throat as she choked back a sob. "*Alone*."

Fate launched skyward, every muscle in her body tightened to increase her speed. When she came to a stop and looked down, the airship was a tiny dot against the dark green of the forest blanketing every peak and valley.

Turning to face the sun, she closed her eyes, soaking in the life-giving rays like someone who'd lived in a cave for the last year. Ironic, since she'd spent so much time in the desert, where she'd had to hide from the same harsh, burning rays.

Fate lost all track of time as she floated high above her problems. They seemed so far away and she wished she could stay there until they worked themselves out without her. Sadly, that was a child's wish. No one else was driven enough to figure out the solutions and make the hard decisions. Her very sanity depended on making this work, because if she failed, Eustace would be truly gone. Forever.

Tears brimmed in her eyes. The sunlight caught within them, casting a prism of colors across her vision. For the first time in a long time, she let them fall freely down her cheeks without worrying who would see her crying.

"Fate."

The sound of Finn's voice startled her. Fate lost all concentration on flight and dropped. Before she could right herself, he caught her in his strong arms. A slow, easy smile formed on his beautiful face. "Sorry, love, I didn't mean to give you such a start."

Shock, anger and relief churned within her, the peace she craved shattered in an instant. How was it possible she wanted to kiss him and slap him all at the same time?

Anger won out.

"What part of, *I need to think alone*, didn't you understand?" Fate pushed away from him.

Confusion chased the smile from his lips as he hovered in place. "I thought you'd welcome some support. I know how torn up you are at the thought of failing Eustace."

Fate couldn't keep her chin from trembling as she fought back another wave of tears. "I won't fail. I *can't*."

"Aye, I know. I know that better than anyone here." He thumped his chest with his fist. "There's only so much I can wall out, but there's no keeping your pain from coming through the cracks. It's too strong."

The understanding in his eyes melted through her defenses. Fate flung herself against him, resting her head on his chest as he pulled her close. Sobs shook her, torn from deep inside as she released the sorrow and frustration she'd been stifling for too long.

Finn kissed the top of her head, holding her in his safe embrace as she shuddered with tears she feared would never cease. "Don't you worry, love. We'll figure this out. We always do."

Hearing him say that filled her with renewed strength. She lifted her head to look into his eyes. "Do you really think we can?"

Finn gently wiped the tears from her wet cheeks. "Honestly, I have no idea. But when has that ever stopped us?"

"True." She started to smile but doubts moved in. "This time feels different though. Like I'm on my own in this. Mostly because I seem to be the only one who has any real motivation for wanting Eustace back. And... I know everyone's afraid of me. I've seen the terror in their eyes. In yours too."

Finn nodded reluctantly. "Aye, I won't deny there's a healthy dose of fear, but it's not of you. It's Ananke we're afraid of."

"No, they're afraid of me too. I'm beginning to think I forced everyone into coming here. They were frightened of what I would do if they said no."

Amusement danced in Finn's eyes as he shook his head. "Don't be silly, lass. We all love you. That's why we're here. We want to help."

"Darcy doesn't love me."

"Well, no. You've got me there."

Fate stared at the shadows of the mountains stretching over the landscape, made long by the setting sun. "I'd bet serious coin Tove doesn't love me either."

Finn didn't reply, but his silence spoke volumes.

"She still loves you."

The troubled look in Finn's eyes scared her and Fate instantly regretted opening that door. Was he about to confess being torn between Tove and her again? She didn't think her heart could take hearing him say that.

"I can't speak for Tove, but I don't love her that way anymore." Emotion filled his voice. "*You* have my heart. *Forever.*"

Fate dropped her gaze. "But... Watching the two of you together these past few days... the way you communicate..." Blinking back tears, she shook her head. "There's a closeness in what you and Tove share that's beyond anything you and I have ever had."

Finn tipped her face upward with a gentle nudge under her chin. "Aye, I won't deny the Elder race runes connect Tove and I in a way that transcends all the usual forms of communication."

Fate tried to turn away but he wouldn't let her. "Look at me, Fate." The green of his irises turned to a fiery emerald gold. "None of that compares to what *we've* shared when our bodies have become one. Intimate doesn't begin to describe the union of our hearts and souls when we're together that way. What you and I have is *sacred.* Have you forgotten we're married?"

Fate's chest constricted with a thrashing storm of emotion–deeply passionate love riddled through with threads of ambiguity. She could hardly breathe. "Technically, yes. I still don't have any memory of that. Or the wedding night, for that matter."

"We're married, Fate."

"Are we really?"

"How can you ask that?" Finn's voice dipped into an angry growl.

Her heart hammered behind her breastbone. "I lost the hand fasting bracelet you made me."

"I don't care about that. I can make another." He looked stricken, like she'd stabbed him in the heart. "Are you trying to say you don't think of us as married?"

She closed her eyes and Azrael's face flashed in her mind. Opening them, she drifted backward, unable to voice an answer to Finn's question.

"You don't," Finn said flatly, when she remained silent for too long.

"Finn, it's not that simple."

"It is for me." Sorrowful lines etched themselves over the handsome plains of his face. He turned away, sinking downward into the dimming light of dusk. "I'll see you back at the ship."

Fate watched him leave. If there was any one time to stop him, this was it. But she let him go, and in that moment, her heart cracked in two.

25
THE POWER OF NIGHT

FINN'S HEART ROARED in his ears, drowning out the voices of the others as they discussed the last few details of Fate's plan. He'd been unable to look at her after she'd returned an hour later. The sound of her voice–back to business as usual–tortured him. It was clear to see she'd spent the last hour hatching out this new plan, with no further thoughts toward where they'd left things between them.

How could she move on so quickly and easily? He'd been tempted to drop his shields and open himself to what she was really feeling deep inside. He suspected her uncertainty and ambivalence was centered on Azrael. Confirming that would wreck him completely.

Finn moved to the railing with a drag in his step then leaned his elbows on the edge. He stared at the forest, black and featureless beneath the night sky. He and Tove were to descend near the edge of the valley and allow the Darfal elves to make first contact.

Normally, a situation like this would fill him with nervous energy. He was literally putting his life in danger with the possibility of being killed on the spot. Despondency had destroyed all sense of self-preservation and the thought of being put out of his misery was not upsetting.

ove put her hand on Finn's shoulder. "I am ready."

Finn turned his head to look at her. Tove's quiver was filled with arrows and she was packing a sword and several daggers. The green of her eyes shone dark with the threat of danger. She was ready to put her life on the line. He pushed away from the railing to face her. "I want you to stay behind until I've made first contact with the Darfal."

"No. We go together."

He shook his head. "Tove, I'm firm on the subject. I can't ask you to risk your life all over again."

"You did not ask. Fate did."

Finn exhaled his frustration, slowly, angrily. "Even more reason you shouldn't do this."

Tove glanced over at Fate, where she was still talking to the others. She signed and spoke one word. "What happened between you two?"

"It doesn't matter," he replied in English.

Tove gestured with her fingers raking the air between them. "Speak to me only in the Elder race language. Do not use the words of humans. That is how we will survive down there."

Finn folded his arms, refusing to sign. "You're not going with me."

"What's going on?" Fate asked, startling Finn.

Tove held up a hand. "Settling a difference."

Fate searched Finn's face. "Why don't you want Tove to go with you?"

"I think it's best I go first." Finn swallowed down the instantaneous rise of anguish just looking at Fate caused. "We have no idea how the Darfal will react. At least, if you lose me, you'll still have Tove to communicate with them."

Fear flashed in Fate's eyes before she quickly glanced down to hide it. When she raised her gaze to Tove, she'd taken control again. Or maybe he'd imagined what he'd seen. "Do you agree with him on that?"

"No, I do not," Tove answered.

"Then it's settled. You'll both go down. Are you ready?"

"Ready as I can be when I'm outvoted by two stubborn lasses." Finn swept Tove up into his arms. Her breath hitched as she stared at him in surprise. "How else do you expect to get down there?" he asked Tove.

Fate cleared her throat and held up an aeronaut pack. "With this. That's what I came over here for."

"She'll be fine without it." Finn lifted off, hovering a few feet off the deck as he watched Fate. He enjoyed the look of outrage on her face, even though he knew he shouldn't.

Fate flushed with color. "Put her down, Finn." Her voice shook. "What happens if you get separated from each other? Tove will need this to fly back to the ship."

"Aye, I can't argue with that." Finn dropped back to the floor and set Tove down. She swayed and started to tip. He grabbed her by the waist to steady her. "Whoa, lass. I guess you still don't have your sea legs under you yet."

Tove nodded without looking at him. She slipped off her bow and quiver to allow Fate to help her strap the aeronaut pack onto her back. Finn had never seen Tove–or Fate, for that matter–move so stiffly.

Fate stepped back to let Tove finish buckling the straps. "Do you remember everything Brune taught you about flying the aeronaut pack?"

"I do." Tove pulled on the last buckle, checking the tightness, before turning on the ignition. The metal dragonfly-shaped wings whirred into a glinting, silvery blur of motion.

Satisfied, Fate returned to business and wrapped a headphone behind the shell of her ear. "Let's test your comms."

Finn was already wearing his, but Tove fumbled with hers. Sensing Fate's impatience, he brushed Tove's hair aside and helped her position the delicate brass instrument. When it was in place, he shot up in the air, putting at least ten yards distance between himself and the girls. "Can you both hear me?" he asked quietly.

"Crystal clear," Fate replied.

"Yes," Tove added.

Finn dropped and landed beside them. "We'll be off then." He stared at Fate, wanting more than anything to be sent off with a kiss, but she didn't move. If anything, her expression hardened even more.

Sithias hurried over, worrying his hands together when he saw they were about to leave. "I can hardly believe the mission begins now after all that studying." He lurched at Finn and gave him an awkward hug. "Be extremely careful down there, sir. Both of you."

Jessie joined them. Azrael and Darcy trailed behind, each keeping their distance.

"Yeah, you have to watch out for elves," Jessie said excitedly. "From everything I've read about them, they're superior fighters because they're lightning quick and can hear stuff from miles away." She pulled on her ear. "Because of the points on the ears. Must work like antennas or something."

"And you're getting this from the books we brought with us?" Fate asked. "Because Finn said there wasn't anything in them that was accurate."

Jessie frowned. "Hey, I trust Tolkein knew what he was talking about." She looked at Finn. "The Falinorin had the pointy ears in your visions, didn't they?"

"Aye, they did. And you're right about all the rest. They're fast and they can fight better than any human."

"See?" Jessie gave Fate a satisfied smile. "I always knew J.R.R. didn't make that stuff up. I'd bet my entire leatherbound collector's editions that he traveled to a place like this. Whoa, do you think he came here to Oldwilde? That's got to be what happened! I wonder where the hobbits live?"

"I must know all about this Tolkein character. Tell me about him." Sithias winked at Finn as he whisked Jessie off in the opposite direction.

Finn was thankful for that. He was growing tenser by the minute. There was so much more to the Falinorin than the few things Jessie had mentioned. While he understood the two elven races on a deeply intrinsic level, that knowledge certainly did not ensure their safety. They would have to tread carefully.

"Ready?" he asked Tove.

She answered with a twist of the gears and launched into the black, starry sky. Finn gave Fate one last parting glance. For the briefest second, he saw his sweet bonnie lass in the gentle softening of her face. In that tiny fraction of time he thought she would run into his arms. But that slightly cracked door, slammed all the way shut.

"Come back." Fate straightened her shoulders. "Both of you."

Crushed by disappointment, Finn leaped over the edge of the ship and chased after Tove.

They landed where the thick of the forest ended and the open, sweeping meadows of the valley began. There wasn't much light under the crescent moon. From where they stood, the moon glow hit the peaks of the grassy hills, which rolled away from them in a steady downward descent. A dark lake glinted beneath the stars at the very bottom of the valley. Beyond the lake and even further away, a fire burned.

Finn signed and pointed. "That must be the Eternal Flame of the Great Oak."

Tove gestured by tapping her fingers in the air. "The Elrinye dwellings are lit. They are awake. Their powers will be weak without the sun. We should go there first."

Tempted to agree, Finn signed a contrary answer. Something told him that would be a deadly mistake on their part.

"Why not?" Tove asked.

"We will be seen as aggressors. We are best to wait for the Darfal to come forward."

The moonlight grazed off the frightened crease of Tove's brow. "They are at their strongest at night. I do not like what I have seen of them." She placed a hand over her heart. "They scare me the most."

Finn made a slicing gesture with the side of his hand. "The Darfal are the more hostile of the two. That is why we must face them first."

Tove didn't argue, but he could see her struggling with her fear. Her eyes were dark orbs, alert as she stared into the shadows of the forest behind them. She quickly unbuckled the straps of the aeronaut pack and slid it beneath some thick bushes. Tove barely had her quiver back in place when there was a crackling somewhere within the trees.

Finn reached for his flute, ready to transform it into a wind sword in the span of a few seconds. Then thought better of it. They'd come in peace and they should present themselves that way.

However, Tove crept toward the sound, her bow drawn and arrow nocked. Finn reached out to calm her down enough to drop her aim, when a chilling roar and loud crashing echoed through the night. Finn blew two sharp notes into his flute, every muscle tensed in readiness.

The shadows thrashed, veiling whatever it was that was coming at them. Finn and Tove retreated further into the open meadow. A huge shape lunged from the dense trees and landed a few yards away. Most of it was shadowed within the gray tones of night but Finn saw enough to know it was a giant horned mountain lion. The silver light of the moon flashed in its feral eyes as a deep growl rattled in its throat. A predator at the top of the food chain, the lion slinked toward them, its muscles rippling beneath sleek fur.

Tove pulled hard on the string of her bow, preparing to let the arrow fly. In the split second she released her fingers, Finn pushed her to one side, throwing her aim off course. Her furious look pierced him like he'd been shot with the lost arrow. He couldn't afford to lose her trust again, but he knew without a doubt, killing the beast would bring absolute calamity down upon them.

He signed, telling her to speak to the lion as she had always done with the animals of the Twisted Bone Forest. Her dark eyes widened in disbelief, hesitating for a moment before speaking the Elder race language.

Her voice thundered, ringing out over the forest as sparks flew from her mouth.

Finn hadn't expected her reaction to be so explosive. When they'd previously hunted together she'd always spoken gently to the animals of her native forest. Fear was obviously at the root of the power behind her words.

The lion shrank from the sound. Lowering its large head, the lion laid down on the ground in immediate obedience of her command. Tove edged toward Finn, breathing hard as she stared at the lion. He took her hand and squeezed it, hoping to calm her down.

"What do we do now?" she asked.

"We wait."

"For what?"

Strong gusts of frigid wind whipped around them, sudden and frightening. Something grabbed Finn from behind, tearing Tove's hand from his grasp. Silence wrapped around him. Everywhere he looked was darkness.

The forest and stars had been blotted out.

Finn struggled against the vice-like grip around his waist and arms. Unable to raise his air blade, he twisted around, catching sight of a male face. No more than a silvery smudge imprisoning him within the dark murk. Calling upon the Elder race runes, Finn spoke the invocation for Air to break through the inky vortex.

The sharp point of a blade dug painfully against his neck, cutting his summons short.

"Silence." The word was different, spoken in the Olde language, yet there was no mistaking the meaning.

Panic fired through Finn's veins. The encasement of pitch black was disorienting, making it impossible to think. He needed to get a grip on his fear. This thrashing darkness hadn't been part of the visions he'd seen of the Falinorin. This could only be the Darfal. His captor was definitely drawing on the power of night.

The plan had worked.

It wasn't easy but Finn stopped resisting altogether and let the elven male take him prisoner. His only hope at that point was that the Darfal, as well as the Elrinye, would hear them out before punishing them for trespassing.

He glanced around, hoping to glimpse Tove. The shadow veil surrounding him seemed to have thinned, as a weak source of light now penetrated the cloak. Squinting at the light positioned on a higher plane, he realized they were sailing swiftly toward it. Thick branch-like shapes passed across the light, which flickered like fire.

This could only be the Eternal Flame of the Great Oak.

The firelight suddenly extinguished, plunging Finn back into pitch black. The violent sensation of downward circling motions caused instantaneous nausea. His fear returned full force when he realized they were dropping deep into the underground, where the Darfal lived within the roots of the Great Oak.

This was bad. He'd hoped to be presented to the Falinorin as a whole in the top branches, where the Elrinye lived and attended the Eternal Flame.

They jolted to a stop and Finn's feet touched down on firm ground as the shadow veil dissolved into thinning ribbons of mist. The elven male withdrew his blade and released Finn. Fighting the queasiness in his gut and a skull full of dizziness, Finn widened his stance to keep from falling over. A few seconds later, he regained his equilibrium and glanced around, fully expecting to be locked in a prison cell.

Instead, he stood in a great hall of rough-hewn earthen walls shot through with branching roots gleaming with silvery dust. Soft, diffused light emanated from the roots themselves, the only source of illumination within the vast chamber. The ceiling was high and rounded like a cathedral. A long, stone table stood in the middle with chairs formed elaborately of bent and braided branches lining each side.

At the end of the great hall, the Darfal elven queen sat on a throne carved from a solid block of crystal. The entire royal court stood in attendance just below her throne. More elves arrived in the form of twisting vortexes of black vapor, which they cast off like robes of shredding smoke. Several hundred elves lined themselves at the end of the hall and down along the sidewalls.

The Darfal were darkly beautiful beings. Fine boned with slanted eyes, raven hair and skin that shone with a silvery sheen, as if kissed by starlight. Their long ears curved upward into points like the thick yet delicate bloom of a calla lily. They seemed to embody the night, the moon and stars like nothing Finn had ever seen before.

He turned to his captor, who'd stepped aside, still clenching the dagger he'd pressed to Finn's throat. Remembering the elf's tight, unwavering grip, Finn was surprised by how much slighter in build the warrior was. If he compared weight and muscles alone, he should've been able to take the guy. Undoubtedly, the elf's source of power came from the night, maybe even the infinite night that was home to the stars. If that was the case, this was a power greater than even the Elder race runes could supply.

"Where is my friend?" Finn was careful to speak in the Elder race language and with a tone of respect.

The warrior elf stared back, aloof and unconcerned. He didn't look any older than sixteen. In fact, they were all surprisingly youthful. The oldest amongst them appeared to be in his or her late twenties at most. There wasn't an elder in sight.

An icy gust of shadowy mist whipped past Finn and came to a stop. The night cloak of a female elf split off into misty tendrils fast thinning on the air. She had Tove in her grip, who struggled frantically to be freed. She let go suddenly and Tove fell to her knees, panting, her eyes wild with terror.

Finn rushed over to help her up. Tove thrashed blindly, grazing him on the chin with a clenched fist. Ignoring the hard knock, he moved back in. When Tove recognized him she settled down enough to stand. She shook visibly as Finn signed to her. "Be still. Fighting will not help."

"Come forward." The command came from the queen.

Finn guided Tove past the long table and the hundreds of elves in attendance. When they rounded the top of the table, the queen's guards blocked them from going any further.

The queen's dark dress glittered with crushed black diamonds and her crown was made of smoked quartz layered with moonstones. She held herself regally, like a woman well practiced in her authority. Her eyes–the color of thunderclouds with feline pupils–conveyed the wisdom and experience of untold centuries. Yet she looked all of fifteen, still sporting the peaches and cream complexion of a mere girl.

"Why are you here?" Her voice was also that of a child's, but her tone was supreme, commanding.

Finn gulped down his nervousness. "We have come to ask permission to be here in your valley."

She leaned forward, her slit-shaped pupils enlarging into black discs as she stared at him. Through him. "For what reason?"

"Mornavar Valley is the only place in the world where we can find the ingredients to save a friend's life."

"What are these ingredients?"

"Plants, mostly." Finn's heart began to pound.

The queen straightened her spine, resting against the back of her hard, shining throne. "And?"

Finn stared back. Did the queen already know the answer to her question? Was she testing him to see if he told the whole truth? This was it, the dreaded moment in which his next words would seal their fate.

26
ANOTHER OUTRIGHT LIE

"THEY WILL NOT LIKELY RETURN TONIGHT." Azrael put his hand on Fate's arm and turned her away from staring out over the black forest. "When did you last eat?" he asked.

"I'm not hungry." How could she eat knowing Finn's life was in mortal danger? Especially since she was responsible for throwing him into it.

Guilt and fear knotted in her stomach. She couldn't rid herself of their last conversation. The pain in Finn's eyes haunted her. If only she could have said what he'd wanted to hear. But how could she, when all she felt was lost and torn in half?

Finn deserved all of her. She loved him too much to pretend otherwise.

Azrael sighed. "I will leave you alone if you wish."

When he turned to go, she stopped him. "Please stay."

Azrael looked into her eyes, deeply, searchingly. "Why do you want me to stay?"

Fate dropped her gaze, afraid he'd see what was best left unsaid. She looked into his entrancing, crystal blue eyes. "Your presence comforts me," she admitted, hoping this partial confession would be harmless to everyone concerned.

He nodded with the faintest smile. "This comfort you seek must be why your soul ring remains on my ankle."

Fate was floored. "How can that be? I thought it came off the same time yours unlocked from my ankle."

"No, it did not." Azrael drew his long robe aside to reveal the soul ring. "As you can see, I am still very much bound to you. Because you wish it."

"I don't," she argued. "I'd never want to own you or make you feel tied to me against your will. I officially free you." She waited for the soul ring to drop off. "Why didn't it work?"

"If your words do not align with your feelings, nothing will change. You must truly desire that I am free of you."

Fate swallowed down the rapid thud of her heart in her throat. "But I do."

He ran a finger lightly down one side of her face, sending a guilty shiver over her skin. "I would stay with you even without the soul ring's bond."

"Why?" she asked, breathless as the air stood still between them.

"Because I handed you my wealth, my royal station, my protection and my love on our wedding day. You are my princess. I will honor those gifts I gave you until the day I die."

Fate could hardly believe what she was hearing–this on the heels of Finn asking if she considered herself still married to him. The two of them couldn't be more different from each other, yet they were exactly alike in the commitment and vows they'd made to her.

If she were being honest, it was this fathomless depth of love that drew her in. Who didn't want to be loved and treasured? Sadly, the virtuous traits each of them possessed in equal measure had thrown her into a world of confusion and absolute anguish.

She had to stop torturing them and herself. It was time to make a choice and put an end to this misery.

"We need to talk."

Darcy's voice jolted Fate enough to make her jump. Azrael withdrew his hand.

"About what?" Fate turned around with a frown.

Darcy raised a perfectly penciled eyebrow as she eyed Azrael and then Fate with a smirk on her vivid-red lips. "About the spell. Shall I talk freely, or would you prefer to do this in private?"

Fate glanced at Azrael and gulped. "In private."

"I will leave you two to speak," he replied. "Goodnight."

Fate waited for him to climb down below deck. "Go ahead."

"My, my, how do you do it, Fate?"

"Do what?"

"Get two gorgeous hotties like Finn and Azrael tied up in knots over you? To top it off, they stick around while you play them off against each other. You really must share your secret."

Fate wanted to slap the smug smile off Darcy's face. "Just get to the point. Is there a problem with the spell?"

"There will be, if all we get from the black unicorn is a 'single hair from its mane'. What we really need is its alicorn."

"I'll make sure we get the horn."

"Oh, so you lied to Finn and all the others then." Darcy feigned bewilderment. "Why would you lie about that, Fate? I honestly don't understand your sly motivations."

Fate's pulse jittered with fear-laced irritation. "I think you know."

Darcy's blue eyes filled with feigned naiveté. "I don't. I need you to explain it to me. Unless you'd prefer I bring it up to–"

"*Yes*, I lied and I did it to protect Finn and Tove. They have to believe this hunt for the black unicorn is a harmless quest. That way when they tell the Falinorin why we've come, they'll be more likely to let us into the valley. Obviously, taking the unicorn's alicorn will kill it, and I'm pretty sure the Falinorin will be against that part of the plan."

Darcy nodded with satisfaction. "Thank you for your honesty. Your secret's safe with me. But..." Sucking air between her teeth, she shook her head. "I sure wouldn't want to be you when Finn finds out you lied. Then again, all hell's going to break loose when you do kill the unicorn, so it's anybody's guess what you'll be dealing with when that happens."

"I have contingencies in place for when that time comes." This, of course, was yet another outright lie.

"I suppose one of those contingencies is Azrael, since the odds are good you'll lose Finn after all's said and done."

Fate's heart hammered, this time with abject terror. Would Finn turn his back on her for this? She wouldn't blame him if he did. Not after everything she'd put him through lately. "Are we done here?"

"Sure." Darcy meandered over to the ladder and slowly started climbing below deck. She stopped. "It really sucks when you don't get everything you want, doesn't it?"

When Fate didn't respond, a knowing sneer returned to Darcy's painted lips as she descended out of sight.

27
THE ELRINYE

"WE HAVE COME in search of the black unicorn."

An unsettling hush fell over the elven night court. Finn glanced nervously at Tove. She was still shaken from their capture. He'd never seen her this frightened before and feared she might lash out and bring the entire court down upon them.

The queen broke the uncomfortable silence. "First you trespass into our forest, then you desire to intrude upon our sacred valley and take its gifts?" She stood, a tall lithe figure in the dimly gleaming light. "Past invaders have died for less."

Panic fired through Finn's veins, a response that made holding still a challenge. He would only fight if they forced him. Fate was counting on him. Returning empty handed meant denying Fate of her only chance to bring Eustace back. He simply could not risk the devastation that would bring about.

The queen slowly descended the dais, her movements as graceful and measured as a panther. "Unlike the interlopers of long ago, you continue to live because you speak the Elder tongue." She stopped on the last step to study Finn. "Though you are of the Druidhean line, I see your intentions are honorable."

Finn inhaled, having stopped breathing for several seconds, and tipped his head in a slight bow. "I am grateful for your mercy."

"That is as much as I can grant you," she replied. "You may leave in peace."

Tove tugged on his arm when he didn't move. "Finn, we must leave."

"You go. I will stay."

Tove shook her head. "You are not invited to stay." She glanced fearfully over her shoulder at the queen.

"I will not be the one to tell Fate she cannot revive her father." Finn stepped past Tove. "*Please*, allow me to stay," he beseeched the queen. "Teach me your ways, that I may contribute and trade my efforts for what I have come here for."

The queen eyed him with interest. "For a human, you are more determined than most."

One of the older males stepped in beside her and whispered. She stretched her long neck to listen, then waved him away. "I will allow both of you to stay until the moon's full bloom."

Finn started to breathe a sigh of relief too soon.

"Only if the Elrinye agree," she added. The queen gestured to the warriors who'd been the ones to capture and deliver them into the great hall. "Show our guests where they may sleep until sunrise."

Before Finn could thank her, the queen, and all her court, vanished within swirling cyclones of the darkest shadows. A wintry chill blustered throughout the hall. Finn buttoned his coat and followed his escorts.

They moved through several winding passageways, all lit by the giant oak's glimmering roots. Finn inhaled the ever-present scent of rich soil. He'd missed his deep connection to the earth and the abundance of life that sprang from it after spending months in the Keep high above the arid, lifeless desert. There would be no tears shed if he never returned to the deserts of Shalamaraize.

The female elf opened a slate door engraved with runes similar to the Elder race runes. Only these were far more intricate. Tove rushed past, while Finn turned and signed with both hands to his heart, followed by a tap on his mouth to thank them. The warriors did not return the friendly gesture and left within frosty gusts of black, churning mist.

He followed Tove inside and closed the door. The suite was huge and lavishly filled with silken drapes of every color of the night, ranging from ebony to deep indigos and soft, muted grays. Darkly dyed carpets woven with elaborate patterns of stars and moon phases covered the earthen floors.

There was also one very large bed.

"You can have the bed. I'll take the floor," Finn announced, wishing only to avoid any awkward misunderstandings on Tove's part.

She'd been anxiously circling the room like she was a prisoner instead of a guest. Tove suddenly stopped, glaring at him with something close to hatred. He hadn't seen that look since they'd lost Grysla and Leif in the war. "We agreed not to use human speech here. *Ever*. Our lives depend on it."

"We're alone, Tove. No one is listening."

"You do not know that." Her terror was more pronounced than ever. "This may be a test. To see if we are more *human* than we presented ourselves."

Finn grabbed a pillow from the bed and tossed it on the floor. "Why are you so jittery? You're usually much cooler under pressure than this."

"*You* have got into me!" she yelled, in less than perfect English and with the Nordic accent her brother Leif had passed on when he taught her. "You change the plan when you like, such as bumping my arrow off target. You are unpredictable." Tears stood in her eyes. "I cannot trust you because everything you do is for *her*."

"You mean Fate?"

"Who else? *She* is all you see."

"She's my wife." The sharp pang of doubt in Finn's heart said otherwise.

"Is she?" Tove's expression magnified his doubt. "She does not act like your wife. I have seen how she looks at Azrael."

Finn's chest seized from the cruel slice of her words. But Tove spoke the truth. The energy drained from his limbs and it was all he could do to reach the edge of the bed and sit down.

Tove's anger and fear dissolved as she approached him. Her hands fluttered from her heart to his. "Forgive me," she signed. "I had no right to be unkind."

"You're only saying what I've been denying." Finn hung his head. "I asked Fate if she still considered us married. Instead of saying what she felt, she answered with her own question."

"What did she ask?"

"She wanted to know if we were truly married if she had no memory of the vows and wedding night." The sorrow collecting in his throat had him choking on the last few words.

Tove gathered his pillow from the floor and placed it back onto the bed. She crawled into the middle and rested her head on the satin pillow. Her long ebony hair splayed across the shimmering material as she opened her arms to him. "Come, lie down with me. We must sleep. Sunrise will arrive shortly."

Finn climbed onto the bed, meeting Tove's embrace with his own.

Morning came all too soon and with its swift arrival, came the comforting stroke of fingers raking softly through Finn's hair. Groggy with sleep, he smiled with eyes still shut and pulled Fate against his body. "Ooh, you're a saucy minx. You know just how to wake me." He nuzzled his face into the silken crook of her neck, kissing and biting her skin. She pressed against him with a faint moan that wasn't Fate's voice.

Finn's eyes popped open, his movements stiff as he pulled away to look at Tove. Passion lit the brilliant green of her eyes as she smiled at him.

"Sorry, I must've been dreaming." Finn let go of her waist and rolled onto his back, fixing his sights on the ceiling. "Any idea what time it is?"

Tove sat and swung her legs over the edge of the bed. "Dawn."

Finn surveyed the dimly lit room. The gleaming roots webbed throughout the earthen walls of the bedchamber were slightly brighter, though not by much. "How can you tell?"

Tove stood and adjusted the clothes she'd slept in. "The earth wakes me when the sun rises."

"How does that work?"

"I grew up in a cave with a tree troll for a mother." Her voice was sharp as she gathered up her bow and quiver. "I do not know how it works." She softened her tone. "This has always been the way for me."

The sound of the slate door sloughing over the earthen floor had them both standing at attention. "Right on time," Finn muttered.

Slicing her hand through the air, Tove threw him a warning look. "No human speech!"

He nodded as their appointed guards stood outside in the hall, coldly gesturing for them to come out. Finn and Tove reluctantly followed them through the rounded passageways, which slowly graduated into an upward climb.

Running his hand along the walls, Finn connected with the earth, pushing his dark sight deep within the underground network. The roots of the Great Oak sprawled for miles beneath the earth, a vast network that bled beyond itself into all the trees of Feldoril Forest.

A ceaseless thrum drew his awareness toward the core, where the oak's heartbeat radiated with a power too blinding to look upon. Finn withdrew immediately, forced to use the walls to steady himself. The Great Oak was indeed the heart and brain of the forest, a connection the Falinorin were an integral part of.

They came to many forks in the passageways, all branching off in different directions. Each was marked with large crystal pillars etched with the same unfamiliar runes. Without their guides, he and Tove would be lost within this subterranean maze. Possibly forever.

Fresh air breezed in from up ahead, a sign they'd reached the surface. Diffused light emanated from an opening in the distance. When at last they reached the end of the passageway, their escorts led them through an archway and Finn stepped out into the new day.

The sky was a dusky gray in the west, while the sun blazed in the east behind the jagged tree line, lighting distant clouds with bright rims of orange. They stepped onto a pathway of elegantly intertwined branches, which spiraled around the base of the colossal oak.

Finn had to lean all the way back to take in the sheer height of the tree and the massive canopy that blotted out the sky overhead. The immensity of the tree was astounding. It was at least four times the size of Grandfather Oak on Innith Tine.

Tove let out a small gasp as she stared up at the tree.

They followed the guards on an upward climb along a winding staircase that snaked around the trunk. Finn could save them the long, strenuous trek ahead by taking hold of Tove and flying to the top. Given the circumstances, that was obviously out of the question.

Fortunately, the arduous journey was an interesting one. As they climbed higher, they passed dwellings the size of mansions, made entirely of branches woven tightly together in intricately braided patterns similar to Celtic knots.

Lights from inside lit amber stained glass windows with a delicate glow. While Finn admired the dark beauty within the great hall of the Darfal, the artistry and craftsmanship displayed by the Elrinye was far more dazzling in its gently twisting curves. Unlike the hard, angular designs of stone and crystal the Darfal favored.

Strangely though, he wasn't seeing any of the Elrinye, what with the sun rising in the sky. Even stranger was why they were being escorted by two Darfal elves, both nocturnal creatures plainly out of their element.

Finn could tell their powers had diminished considerably. Their moon-pale skin had lost the lustrous silvery sheen he'd witnessed the night before. The unbending strength he'd experienced when they'd been captured had abandoned them. Their breathing was labored from the lengthy climb.

Finn's questions were answered when they reached the very top and stepped onto a mossy plateau the size of a large field. The Great Oak's branches ringed the open space like giant fingers extending from a flattened palm. Cradled at the very center of the tree's protective grip and leafy canopy was the Eternal Fire.

Stunned by the breathtaking scene, Finn stared at the flames, mesmerized by how they flickered from within and around a towering amber crystal–the source of the Eternal Fire. This was not a killing fire. These were radiant flames of life-giving light.

This was a holy place, a sacred site like no other.

Flaming balls of light suddenly appeared in rows of concentric circles, hovering and vibrating in place until there were hundreds surrounding the crystal. The lights swiftly elongated into illumined, living beings. They exploded from clouds of red-gold sparks before solidifying into dark-skinned elves with hair as fiery in color as the crystal's flames.

They were youthful like the Darfal, though far more vibrant. The Elrinye emanated a life force that pulsed through the air in waves, buzzing over his skin like the touch of thousands of bees' wings. The energy beckoned him, tugging him forward. Their Darfal escorts did nothing to stop Finn and Tove from moving toward the circle of Elrinye. The elves parted to allow them inside their circle.

Finn could not help staring at each elf as he passed by. They watched him back with eyes of luminous gold, each gazing straight into him, reaching into his very heart and soul. Normally, he would have despised such an invasion of his person but he sensed this was natural to them. They could not look at him without knowing his essence in that instance. Just as he could not glance at his own hand and not recognize it as his.

Finn took Tove's hand in his as they rounded the Eternal Fire. They came to a majestic throne comprised of red sapling branches–very much alive and shiny with new bark–braided and woven together into a swirling backdrop outlined by a profusion of tiny orange blooms.

The queen sat on a soft cushion of fresh green moss. She wore a warrior's breastplate of the finest gold over a filmy gown of plum-rose colors. Her long strawberry blonde hair fell in a loose braid down her back. A small gold crown of intricate metalwork began above the line of her fair eyebrows and disappeared beneath her hair. The sunlight pouring in through the branches lit the points of her delicate ears with warm peachy tones. She was both peaceful and frightening in her eerie beauty.

Unlike the Darfal queen, who could have passed for a teen in any other world, the Elrinye queen looked a woman in her late twenties. Which meant she must be ancient.

Her gleaming, impassive gaze rested first on Finn, probing deeper than any of the others who'd taken a look inside. This was invasive. He went rigid as the icy point of her stare raked through his mind, scratched at his heart and ripped into his solar plexus.

She moved onto Tove. Pure terror etched lines into Tove's face as the queen barged in and searched her soul. Finn gave Tove's hand a reassuring squeeze to let her know she wasn't alone. When the queen released Tove, she trembled, though her eyes had gone black with fury. Finn tugged her closer and wrapped his arm around her waist to keep her from lunging at the queen.

"I am told you wish to learn our ways in order to become a contributing member of our tribes," the queen said. "All as a trade for what is sacred and forbidden here in Mornavar Valley."

Finn didn't like the sound of that. He stepped forward, guiding Tove to stand behind him. "Aye, I was the one who made that offer."

The queen's stare seemed even more vacant as she studied him. "We have had interlopers here who cloaked their lies with good intentions. Deception has left a foul taste in our mouths. We will not tolerate lies."

Finn tensed. "How can I convince you of my sincerity?"

The queen looked him over and stood. "Come with me." Taking Tove by the hand, Finn started to follow, but the queen frowned. "Alone."

Finn shook his head. "No, I will not leave my companion behind."

The smooth plains of the queen's face twisted with rage. "You will if you wish her to live."

Fearing for Tove, Finn's heart rammed against his ribs. "Please let us leave. We will not bother you ever again."

"It is too late." The queen turned to a male whose appearance matched Finn's age. "Ethlan, take her away. You know what to do."

In one swift move, Tove had her arrow drawn and aimed but Ethlan was upon her in a burst of fiery gold sparks. Finn started toward the elf, when a sudden flurry of embers and flames wrapped around Tove. She was gone in a blink.

Finn stood there, gutted and stricken with grief. He turned on the queen. "You killed her! We came in peace, but you killed her!"

28
THESE SAVAGE THORNS

"SHE IS NOT DEAD." The queen's serenity infuriated Finn. "Not yet. Do what I ask and Ethlan will return her to you."

Finn shook with rage, wanting to strike back for threatening Tove's life. His own fear and anger would never match what Tove must be feeling. She'd been off center since they'd landed in the forest. He didn't want to imagine what she was going through.

The queen rose from her throne and moved toward him, each step edged with lethal grace. She stopped within reaching distance, pulling Finn into her vast, ancient gaze. Fire blazed within the gold of her irises–flames that flared from the tiny dots of her pupils. It was as if he was staring into the sun, warmed and unharmed by its blinding rays.

Too mesmerized to look away, he stood very still, unable to recall the many concerns that plagued him. He'd never known such peace. Basking in this all-encompassing sunlight was both energizing and relaxing. He craved more.

She reached for his hand. In the instant of her touch, flames of bright sparking embers flew before his eyes, obscuring all else. Absent of heat, the fire consumed every part of him, burning all the way to every molecule and atom. He was without form, yet not unmade. He was part of something greater than even that which he'd connected to within nature.

This was a nameless force, though familiar–the source of life itself. That which permeated everything in existence.

Finn's awareness blended with the queen's. *Nueleth*, that was her name. Her fiery essence merged with his, exploring all that he was. This was not the same painful invasion. This was an open door between them, gentled by vulnerability on her part in the way she allowed the same intimate access to her soul.

Within the span of a few seconds, he traveled back through countless centuries, viewing her life. Born of the Elrinye, she'd been raised to live in harmony with the Darfal, their opposite in all ways, though every bit as vital to the stewardship of the forest. A hierarchy within the Falinorin had been established long ago by earlier generations, leaving the Elrinye exalted above the Darfal.

Dissention between the two races did not exist. The Great Oak of the Eternal Flame united them, blessing each tribe with a home. Two kingdoms governed as one.

The same could not be said of Feldoril Forest. Humans and even those born of magic invaded. Ceaseless battles were waged over the forest's treasures. The sacred realm Nueleth was born to protect hardened her into one of the strongest warriors. She had learned to rule at the knees of her mother, who'd been a just but ruthless queen. Outsiders became a scourge the Falinorin learned to hate.

Strangely, here she was, allowing Finn to see as much of her as he wished. He sensed weariness in her soul. She was tired of fighting, maybe even of living after existing for eons. Though something had woken. His presence as an unexpected stranger had stirred a long dormant inquisitiveness in her. Together, they shared the same thrill of a new and exciting discovery.

Nueleth's fire vanished without warning. He was solid matter again, as if his body had not been transformed into speeding light only seconds ago. Finn was immensely grateful for this more pleasant experience after having suffered the dismantlement of his entire being twice before. Though he found himself yearning for the exhilarating infusion of sun energy.

It took a few seconds to realize he was no longer in the Great Oak. They were standing on high cliffs overlooking a lush green valley with a river winding through it. Towering columns of weathered rock covered in vegetation interrupted the sprawling landscape, walling one side of the river's edge like a colossal, jagged fence. The horizon ended at a large blue lake, where the river ended.

Finn had never seen anything so beautiful and pristine as this valley. "Thank you for showing me this place."

Nueleth's apricot-gold hair gleamed brighter in the sunlight. Loose strands blew around her face as she tilted her head, staring at him with a slight frown. "You are a mystery to me."

Finn didn't know how to respond to that. "I am not hiding anything."

"No, you are not."

Her silence made him uncomfortable. "What are you mystified about?"

"How do you live with knowing you were not born of a mother and father?"

The question stung. "As best I can."

"Do you question your existence?"

"All the time."

Her brow smoothed. "I admire your courage. I do not think I could live without roots. My bloodline flows through me, passing on vital ancestral knowledge. Without that I would have no guidance or purpose."

The old ache returned. Finn thought he'd conquered the trauma of knowing his entire history was a mere fabrication. He hadn't. "I have purpose."

"You have *her* purpose."

"That is all I need."

Nueleth's frown returned, sharp, threatening. "She is a danger to us all."

"No, I can–"

"Do not lie to me. Your fear of her is equal to your love for her. That makes you dangerous as well."

"I would never bring harm to the Falinorin," Finn promised. "I know what you have sacrificed to protect the forest and this valley. If you will allow us to get what we came for, we will leave and never return."

"You cannot take without giving back."

"Aye, as a druid, I understand the practice of fair exchange."

"Let me be clear. You are not here because you are of the Druidhean. The Order has been unwelcome here since Mugloth defiled Grandfather Oak. You are here because you defeated Mugloth and healed Grandfather Oak."

Finn nodded. "What can I give you in exchange for what we came for?"

The ghost of a smile softened Nueleth's face. "You. That is the price."

"Uh... I cannot agree to that." Finn tensed, waiting for her mercurial mood to shift into scorching anger.

She surprised him by remaining calm. "I will give you the time it takes to collect what you need before you give me your final answer. Should you say no, you will leave empty handed."

"Aye, I will take the time," he agreed. "May I see Tove now?"

"No, she will stay with my son until I have your answer. Until then, I will be your guide."

Finn held his tongue for the moment. Whether he liked it or not, this was progress. He reached into his pocket and drew out a rumpled piece of paper. Smoothing it out, he showed Nueleth the two plants Darcy had sketched out. "Do you know these plants?"

The queen drew close until their arms touched. His skin tingled from the vibrant energy she radiated. Smiling at his response, she tapped a long slender finger on the drawing of the thistle. "We know this as neanghaith. It grows in the fields near the lake."

Finn looked out over the valley and the lake off in the distance. He was about to suggest he'd fly and meet her there, but she wrapped him inside her cone of fire before he had the chance to speak.

Her essence merged with his again, this time with a fervor he could not match. She wasn't bothered by his rejection of her open desire. For the moment, Nueleth was content to offer the seduction of being soaked within the calming, expansive energies of the source light, which Finn surrendered to completely.

Nueleth released him. Slightly dizzy from the swift change of scenery, he swayed into the sharp point of a thorn against his bare forearm. The plants were huge–much taller than him–looming like a prehistoric version of what he knew as a thistle plant. The thick, gray-green felted leaves were as wide and long as hawk's wings and the bristled heads were larger than his own. He wiped away the blood beading from a scratch on his skin. "They don't grow them this big where I come from."

"You do not come from anywhere."

Finn frowned. "You have a sharp tongue. Worse than any of these savage thorns."

Nonplussed, the queen drew her dagger. "I will do the cutting. What part of the neanghaith do you require?"

"The down of the thistle is what we need." He rose into the air to see above the plants crowding his view. His spirits dropped when he was met with a field of purple blooms. He slowly descended, careful to avoid being scratched again. "The flowers have not seeded yet."

"Why the seeds?"

"I was not told why," Finn confessed.

"You have no thoughts? No questions?"

"No."

Nueleth watched him with that distant, probing gaze.

Fearing she might grow suspicious again, Finn grasped for what his grandfather had taught him about the thistle. "The thistle in my world takes two years to finally flower. Then it goes to seed and dies. For that reason, I was never impressed with the thistle. Until I learned it is the seed that carries the legacy of its stubborn grip on the land, its defiance to thrive under hostile conditions and even bloom." He looked at his scratch. "Despite its savage thorns. The thistle is a symbol of the creation of life from death. I suppose such characteristics might make the thistle a main ingredient for the remedy of death itself."

Nueleth seemed pleased by his answer. "The seeds come with warmer weather."

"How long will that be?"

"I cannot say, only that they seed during Lithamas."

Finn sighed. The summer solstice. That was at least two weeks away. He would have to find a way to sneak off to the ship to tell Fate and the others about the delay. There was no way Fate would wait any longer than a week without hearing from him before she charged in with both guns blazing. He didn't want to think about the bloodshed that would result from that.

Only one problem. This was his first day and it was too soon to bring up the subject of leaving. He had to cement this tenuous alliance with Nueleth first.

Finn showed her the drawing of the second plant. "What of this one? It has heart-shaped leaves and grows in water."

"Fodhael." Her mouth curled in disgust. "It grows in the dead pools. It has no life giving properties."

"What are the dead pools?"

"Water choked off from the rivers and streams by the vicious growth of fodhael. They suffocate all other plants. They fill the water black with rot. To drink of the pools is to drink death."

"Maybe the fact that Fodhael thrives in an environment of death makes it as potent as the neanghaith for this particular potion we are making for our friend."

Nueleth's demeanor shifted from relaxed to agitation. "It is dangerous to go to the dead pools."

"I can go alone. Please. Show me where to find them."

"No. I forbid you to go to the dead pools."

Where had the conversation gone wrong? Finn did his best to control a rising panic. "Then I must return to the ship I came on. With Tove." Would she call his bluff? His heart hammered with uncertainty.

Distrust moved over her features like the dark clouds of a sudden storm. "Am I to believe you will go away without taking what you came for? I have heard this from humans before. They always lie."

"We will leave empty handed and peacefully." He no sooner made his promise before she swept him inside her blazing energy. This time there was no warmth, no peaceful merging. He was shut out, catapulting through space within a hurricane of anger, pain and hatred.

He had no way of fighting his way out. He had nothing to fight with. He was the smoke riding within the wake of her fiery path.

29
LATE TO THE MEETING

"I'M NOT WAITING A SECOND LONGER," Fate argued. "It's been two weeks. We have to go down there."

"How do you propose we intrude upon the Falinorin without starting a very unwelcome war?" Sithias asked. He glanced at the others for support but no one else spoke up.

Fate squeezed her fists, struggling to keep the heat in her core from exploding to the surface. She was beside herself with worry over Finn. He and Tove should have returned at least a week ago. That was the agreement. One week to negotiate a peaceful transaction with the Falinorin. Giving them an extra week had been torturous enough. Doing nothing was absolute hell. Something had to have gone wrong down there. For all she knew, they were–

No. She couldn't allow herself to think the worst.

Fate looked at Azrael who sat on the floor of the deck sharpening the blade of his saber. He'd been quietly awaiting a return to their last conversation, but she'd taken every opportunity to ensure she was never alone with him. Her concern for Finn had increased to an unbearable level. Her flirtations with Azrael, no matter how unintentional, made her sick with guilt.

"What do you think, Azrael?" she asked.

He set his sword aside to look at her. "I am prepared to fight by your side, should you choose to go to battle."

Her guilt compounded. Azrael was no different from Finn in how willing he was to sacrifice his own life to support her campaign. A campaign she was beginning to think was desperate and futile. Eustace would never want others putting themselves at risk for him. Tove, Jessie, Sithias, and even Darcy, were here because she had wanted it.

All because she couldn't handle her grief and accept her loss.

"That's not an answer to my question. I want to know what *you* think we should do." Fate bit down on her bottom lip to stave off the tears stinging behind her eyes.

Azrael stood. "We are sorely outnumbered by the Falinorin. It would be unwise to trespass onto their land. They will view us as invaders, just as Finn and Tove were no doubt perceived as invaders. If I was in charge, I would abort this mission."

His answer hit Fate like a hard punch to the heart. Tears rushed in to blur her vision. "You would abandon Finn and Tove?"

"A leader must learn to cut her losses in order to save what is left."

Fate's chest tightened. "No. I won't do that. We leave no soldier behind."

Jessie jumped up from the crate she was sitting on. "I agree! We all leave, or we all go down with the ship..." She trailed off, less enthused about the last part.

As much as Fate appreciated her best friend's support, she knew Azrael was right. She wouldn't be responsible for getting them all killed. "We'll wait." She choked on the words. "We'll give them one more week. If they don't return by then, we'll leave."

"Whoa, whoa, whoa." Darcy had been at the stern of the ship, staring out at the forest with her back to them all. She hadn't bothered to add a single word to the conversation up until that point. She turned and strolled forward. "Are you really going to cave like this?"

"You're late to the meeting." Fate struggled to keep her voice even. "The decision's made."

Darcy shook her head. "That's pathetic. Here you are with the power of a god, but you're admitting defeat against a bunch of forest elves you've never even laid eyes on."

"It's not that simple, Darcy."

"Isn't it though?" Darcy's gaze slid to Jessie. "You fought against Fate when Kaliena had you all juiced up. You know what she can do."

Jessie nodded sheepishly in agreement.

Darcy smiled with satisfaction. "That's right. We all saw what Fate can do. She wiped out half of Kaliena's fleet. Tens of thousands of monster soldiers destroyed in less than ten minutes."

"That wasn't me!" Fate shouted this time. "I have no memory of that because it was *Ananke* who laid waste to Kaliena's armies."

"I know." Darcy surprised her by agreeing so easily. "I don't need any reminders. Unlike you, I was there when she took over. It was beyond scary. I'm still reeling from the afterburn of that memory."

"Then you know it's a bad idea to let her out. And isn't that what we're ultimately trying to prevent by coming here?" Fate pointed out.

"No need to state the obvious. Whereas, you seem to be in need of a few reminders yourself."

Fate huffed. "Like what?"

"Well, you have enough super powers from Hippolyta's girdle alone to be seriously dangerous to the Falinorin. Plus, you have the power of the Words of Making. Not just you, but Sithias too."

Fate stared at Darcy without really seeing her. She was playing back the terrifying vision Aradif had shown her and the horrors brought about by using the Words of Making to solve her problems.

"If all we had to do was write up a solution, none of us would be here right now. I'd have Eustace back. You'd have Mason. Lincoln would be alive too. But there are always consequences to using the Words of Making. Do you know why that is, Darcy?"

"No, but I can see you're about to tell me."

"Because I'd have to be a mathematical genius to be able to predict the ripple effect from using them without knowing what all the possible outcomes will be. That's because the remedy for one problem can be what triggers another. One that's even worse than the problem we're trying to fix."

Darcy was quiet. Finally.

Fate let out a weary sigh. "Do you get it now?"

"I do," Darcy admitted.

Fate looked up at the sky. "Thank the powers that be!"

"I get it, but that doesn't mean I'm done."

Fate's energy drained away as if Darcy had stuck a straw in her and sucked it out. "What more could you possibly have to say?" she asked flatly.

Darcy's smile was unnerving. "We use witchcraft. I guarantee you, the Falinorin won't know what hit them."

Intrigued more than she cared to admit, Fate was quiet a minute. "I'm listening."

Darcy's eyes glinted with excitement. "Since we can't just walk into Falinorin territory without stirring up a ruckous, I can cloak us to be invisible. That way we can look for Finn and Tove without being detected."

"I like the idea but I'd feel safer using the visibility disruptors Brune supplied us with."

Darcy stopped smiling. "Those won't work. Just because the Falinorin won't be able to physically see us doesn't mean they won't sense us. I can cloak us so they'd never know we're there. We'll have free rein of the place to walk around right under their noses."

Fate stared without saying a word.

"You'll be able to hunt the black unicorn without interference."

Darcy was making too much sense, something that made Fate more nervous than ever. "Why didn't you offer this to Finn and Tove? You could've saved us weeks of worry by bringing this up *before* they went down there?"

Darcy held up her hand and made the peace sign. Or so Fate thought. "Two reasons," Darcy began. "One: Finn and Tove weren't open to sneaking into the valley. We all knew they weren't going to budge on that. Two: If they knew we had this option, the Falinorin would know we planned to use witchcraft as soon as Finn and Tove made first contact. They made it quite clear any attempt at deception would be reason enough for the Falinorin to kill them."

"True," Fate admitted, though begrudgingly. "I'm not agreeing here, but let's say we do it your way, how do we locate the plants you need for the spell? There's no way to know without talking to Finn and Tove, but it's quite possible they've determined we'll need the Falinorin to show us where to look. Feldoril Forest is massive. These plants could be growing anywhere."

"The thistle grows in the valley near the lake and the marshwort on the other side of Glor'ner Mountains in the swamplands bordering the oak grove you showed us on the map."

"You know exactly where to find them?" Fate glared at Darcy in disbelief. "It sounds to me like there was absolutely no reason to send Finn and Tove to negotiate with the Falinorin." A fever burst beneath her skin as she tensed against her rage. "Are you telling me we could've avoided this? Do you know where to find the black unicorn too?"

"I'm still working on that one." Darcy's self assurance vanished as she watched Fate with a growing fear.

Fate was breathing hard, too filled with hot fury to hold it in much longer.

Jessie ran over, blocking Fate's view of Darcy. "Hey, look at me."

Fate leaned to one side to see around her, but Jessie moved in the way. "No need to lose it just yet. I'm sure Darcy has a perfectly good explanation for all of this." She glanced over her shoulder. "Right, Darcy? Finn and Tove going down there is part of this master plan of yours?"

"Exactly." There was a tremble in Darcy's voice. "We need people on the ground to distract the Falinorin while we sneak in and get what we came for. It's a win-win. The Falinorin will think they protected their land by turning Finn and Tove down, which I can only assume is what's happened."

"Then why aren't they back?" Fate seethed through clenched teeth.

"That's what we need to figure out." Darcy stayed hidden behind Jessie. "That'll be the first thing we do. Once we confirm they're both alive and well–without letting them know we're there, of course–we'll grab the plants and then go after the unicorn."

The raging heat waned enough for Fate to feel the cool air on her skin and clear her head. "Thanks, Jess. I'm good." She took a deep breath.

Jessie nodded and moved aside. Fate took a step forward. Surprisingly, Darcy held her ground. "Finn and Tove better be alive. And unharmed. Do you hear me, Darcy?"

"Loud and furious."

Fate glanced at Azrael and Sithias as she strolled over to the edge of the boat. Sithias was fidgeting, as he always did when he was anxious. Azrael watched her calmly, seemingly unphased by her near detonation. She turned and leaned her back against the railing. "It's one thing to take some plants without the Falinorin catching on, but they'll miss a rare, one-of-a-kind unicorn. And they'll know it was us. They'll kill Finn and Tove for that. We have to free them *before* we go after the unicorn."

Azrael finally spoke. "Freeing them will prompt a search. Our hunt for the unicorn will be over before it begins."

"Then we split into two teams and do both at the same time." Fate looked at Darcy. "How long will it take for your witchy voodoo to locate the black unicorn?"

"A day. Maybe two."

"Can you locate Finn and Tove in the same way?" Fate asked.

"Not likely. It's different with people. I'd need a cutting of hair or an object they're attached to. Do you have anything like that?"

Fate's first thought went to the hand fasting bracelet Finn had made for her. It would've been perfect for what Darcy needed. "No I don't." She sighed heavily. "In that case, Azrael and I will go down with your cloaking spell and look for them while you work on locating the unicorn." She glanced at Azrael. "Yes?"

He nodded. "As you wish."

"I do. We'll leave at first light." Fate turned toward the forest and its majestic mountains. The sun was setting in the west, casting burnished gold rays over the deep green forest. The colors reminded her of Finn's eyes when he looked at her with excitement and love. She turned away with an agonizing ache in her heart she knew would only worsen until she had him back.

30
THE CLOAKING SPELL

FATE WOKE TO THE SOUND of rain hammering over the floorboards of the ship's deck. She groaned and rubbed her eyes. They were swollen from crying into her pillow and a horrible night's sleep. Her imagination had taken her to dreadful places concerning the next day's search for Finn and Tove. She'd been tormented with images of finding their bodies. When she'd finally managed to strike the haunting thoughts from her mind, she'd moved onto the possibility of not finding them and never knowing what had befallen them.

She glanced across the room at Azrael's bed. It was empty and neatly made. The others were sound asleep and there was no reason to wake them. They knew the plan. Besides, she didn't want any tearful goodbyes. She'd shed enough tears the night before.

Fate tiptoed between the mattresses and went about quietly dressing in her armor. She grabbed her weapons and hurried up the ladder. The instant she lifted the hatch and stuck her head out, a sideways wind pelted rain in her face. Ducking back down inside, she put her helmet on before climbing all the way out.

Azrael turned away from the railing as she eased the hatch down quietly so as not to wake anyone. He was dressed in the armor Brune had packed for them. It was odd to see him out of his usual, loose desert wear. Though she had to admit she liked how the fitted leather armor showed off his powerful physique.

Like her, his thick ebony hair was pulled back in one long braid to make wearing the helmet easier. Though the headgear did nothing to prevent the raindrops from dripping from his nose. Not that he appeared bothered by the downpour.

She couldn't help smiling as she walked toward him. "I see you still love the rain."

He nodded. "Water from the sky is a rare blessing I enjoy greatly."

"Mmhmm, we'll see how much you enjoy the rain after the shivers set in."

"The cool air is another welcome blessing I cannot see myself tiring of."

He lifted the aeronaut pack and pushed his arms through the straps, attempting to buckle the wet tangle but with little success.

"You wouldn't say that if this was winter. Icy air mixed with rain is miserable. Well, actually that combination usually means snow, but trust me, it's not nice weather to be out in unless there's a warm fire and a cup of hot cocoa waiting for you after a suitably short outing. Like a walk from the car to the house."

Perplexed by the remark, Azrael went back to untangling the straps.

"Here, let me help with that." She reached around his waist, feeling for the strap she needed to bring to the front center buckle. With so little space between them, she was careful to keep her gaze trained on her hands. When she was finished, she stepped back. Two dots of heat burned in her cheeks when she realized he was watching her with amusement.

"Thank you," he said.

"No problem." She reached for the smelly bag of herbs and crystals Darcy had put together for each of them. They were tied off with long leather strips to wear as necklaces. Fate would've preferred carrying it in her pocket to put some distance between the pouch and her nose.

Of course Darcy had insisted they be worn around the neck and placed over their hearts–something about how they needed to be at the center of their auric fields to be fully effective. Fate had to wonder though. It would be just like Darcy to torture her, even in some small way.

Fate tucked the pouch inside the breastplate of her leather armor, hoping to close off the stink of toe jam and rancid peanut butter. "I don't know about this. Are we actually going to trust that these putrid bags will actually make us invisible? If anything, the Falinorin are sure to smell us, even if they can't see us."

"My mother has worked with herbs and gemstones for as long as I can remember. If used with knowledge, they are surprisingly powerful."

Fate nodded reluctantly. "Are you ready?"

Azrael hit the ignition button, triggering the slender metal wings into a vibrating blur. Fate had considered using the Words of Making to give him the ability to fly, just as she'd originally done with Finn. When it came down to doing it though, she couldn't bring herself to follow through. Maybe it was guilt, but for some reason it seemed like it would be disloyal or shallow to give Azrael the same power she'd given Finn.

She needn't worry about Azrael though. He couldn't fly exactly, but he had the ability to leap to incredible heights and was astoundingly strong and fast. Azrael was more than equipped to take care of himself. However, if circumstances demanded it, she would certainly give him the power of flight.

Fate jumped onto the railing before dropping off the edge. Raindrops stung her face as she leveled out to skim over the treetops. The early morning air had a cold bite as she sped toward the valley with Azrael keeping pace.

After covering a fair distance, the thick crop of trees began to thin, eventually opening up into grassy fields dotted with clusters of trees. Mornavar Valley stretched out before them, cut through with a branching river. The gray gloom of storm clouds hung low as if heavy and swollen with rain. Off in the distance, a massive lake shrouded in patches of misty fog reflected the dull sky.

Fate slowed to a stop, hovering in place when she saw the titanic oak tree rooted into the very center of the valley. The Great Oak of the Eternal Flame. Its size astounded her. The tree made Grandfather Oak look like a sprout. "Wow, the etchings in the book don't begin to do the tree justice."

"I have never seen such a sight." The amazement in Azrael's voice brought on another smile.

"You're enjoying this way too much." She gestured at the pouring rain and shook her head like he was crazy.

"Having lived my whole life in the desert, I will admit this trip to a land of marvels is a welcome adventure."

"Says the guy born in a bejeweled city that floats over a desert full of sand monsters."

Azrael smiled wide–not something he did often–an intoxicating treat that made her heart thud haphazardly. She quickly turned to look straight ahead. "Shall we test this cloaking spell with a fly by?"

"A most wise and cautious choice." Azrael zipped ahead of her in the direction of the Great Oak.

Fate propelled herself forward, her pulse shifting to a more chaotic beat. This was the true test of Darcy's magic. Would they be shot out of the air by Falinorin arrows? Or would they fly safely past?

Fate scanned the ground for movement as they approached the Great Oak. There didn't appear to be anyone out. Probably because it was raining. Who in their right mind wanted to be out in this dreadful weather?

Azrael rose higher in the sky to clear the massive tree. Fate hadn't expected to fly directly over the canopy, but she could clearly see he planned to. "Azrael." She spoke softly into the mouthpiece in her helmet. "Don't go that way. Let's circle around first."

His voice came through the helmet's earphones, low but determined "You circle. I will fly straight over."

"No, wait." But it was too late. Azrael was already racing over the oak. Frightened for him, Fate circled the outside, matching his speed, watching him carefully.

As she moved past the tree, the warm amber light of the massive crystal distracted her. Awestruck by the flames licking the glassy sides, she slowed down, fighting the urge to fly toward the beckoning light offering shelter from the cold, persistent rain.

She couldn't resist coming to a complete stop when she saw figures gathered around the crystal. They looked small from her vantage point, made miniature by the huge fiery crystal. She drifted forward, curious to see the mysterious Falinorin.

The outer branches of the Great Oak were as thick as regular tree trunks, swelling in girth as she slowly floated deeper beneath the leafy canopy, where the rain thinned into a light shower of gentle raindrops. Massive branches cradled a mossy plane with the crystal at the center, creating a breathtaking cathedral-like setting completely sheltered from the elements.

Fate touched down on a branch as large as a two-laned bridge, where she could finally see the faces of the elves. They were beautiful and otherworldly. Their eyes lit bright with the same amber-gold flames burning from the crystal. In much the same way Finn's eyes brightened from an inner fire whenever he was excited. Though with these beings, the luminosity in their eyes was made all the more startling by skin the color of dark ash warmed with tints of terra cotta.

There was no sign of the hostile race Finn and Tove had feared they might be. They were peacefully at work. Some were stringing lush flowers and summer greenery together, while others were hanging the finished garlands around the outer edges of the soft, mossy plateau. Lanterns with sparkling lights hung in the lowest branches and glowing crystals were being placed around the very edges. There was even laughter and conversation amongst the elves, though the transmodulator was giving Fate such confusing translations, she finally turned it off.

Whatever was happening down there, it appeared the Falinorin were preparing for some sort of festive celebration.

Fate relaxed slightly. Had her worries been for naught? She scanned the different clusters of elves, searching for Tove's sable hair and Finn's dark gold, wavy locks amongst the varied shades of flame-colored hair the elves all had in common.

She stifled a gasp when she saw Finn sitting away from the others. He was situated to one side of a throne of flowering branches braided into elaborate designs. The woman sitting on the throne could only be the queen. She watched the activity with an air of pleased detachment.

With a hand resting on Finn's head.

Bewildered by the sight, Fate's chest constricted painfully as she tried to make sense of what she was looking at. She floated toward him, unable to stop herself until she landed softly next to him. Holding very still, she waited for a reaction, but neither Finn nor the queen noticed her presence.

The cloaking spell was working.

Kneeling next to Finn, Fate stared at his blank expression. His eyes were aglow–the same as the elves–as he stared vacantly at the crystal's flames. She frowned as the queen raked her long delicate fingers through Finn's hair, affectionately. Petting him like a dog.

Or a lover.

Rage fired in Fate's chest, making her breath come in short, ragged bursts. What had the queen done to him? Was he under some sort of spell? Fate clenched her fists, her arms shaking as she watched the queen stroking Finn's head. He, on the other hand, seemed oblivious to her touch. Nothing changed in his expression. He was caught in an unending stare, as if trapped within the very crystal he seemed incapable of tearing his gaze away from.

The warring energy burst from Hippolyta's girdle, burning hot against her ribcage. Fate channeled the destructive force into her fists and drew one arm back.

"Fate." Azrael's voice made her freeze in place. "Do not do this. A sudden severing of the enchantment may harm Finn."

The heat churning in her core held her there, demanding she attack.

"Wait for me." The roaring in Fate's ears dampened Azrael's voice. With her gaze fixed on the queen, she moved in. Azrael rammed her to the ground as her fist swiped within a hair's width of hitting her target.

Furious, Fate pushed him off with such force Azrael slammed against one of the oak's massive limbs, crushing the wings of his aeronaut pack.

The queen stood abruptly, calling out a command that had the entire tribe's attention. Narrowing her luminous eyes in Azrael's direction, the queen stalked toward him with sword drawn. She swiped her long blade and would've cut him, had he not leaped to a higher limb in the same instance.

Fear chilled Fate's anger. She'd lost herself in the power again.

Thanks to her runaway fury, the Falinorin knew they were there, even if they were unable to see them. She glanced at Finn. He hadn't moved at all. His eyes were trained on the crystal's flames, lost in a dream and completely unaware of his surroundings.

The queen called out another command. Fireballs suddenly appeared, becoming warriors armed with bows and arrows in bursts of light. The queen drew a circle of sharp glittering light, which streamed outward in concentric circles. Before the ring of light hit Fate, she flew up into the canopy. The light washed over where she'd stood, revealing a glowing impression of her footprints next to Finn. The light flooded over where Azrael had struck the branch, illuminating the sharp cuts in the bark left by his aeronaut pack, along with his footprints.

It took no more than a few seconds for the warriors to figure out she and Azrael had jumped to higher branches. They aimed up into the canopy and let their arrows fly.

Weaving through the gigantic branches, Fate flew higher into the tree while Azrael leaped from one limb to another, climbing to the topmost regions of the oak. Then she heard a grunt of pain through her headphone. Her heart nearly stopped as she glanced back and saw him fall with an arrow lodged in his chest.

Fate dove after him, straining her muscles to gain speed. Too many branches blocked her view and he dropped swiftly out of sight. The moment she cleared the canopy, she saw him plummeting toward the ground. Propelled by pure panic, she plunged, her arms outstretched, closing the distance between them with sheer will alone.

When she reached him near the bottom of the oak, she latched onto his waist and yanked upward. But it was too late to pull out of the fall completely and she slammed into hard earth, twisting her body beneath him in time to absorb the impact.

Rain drilled into her eyes as she scanned the oak's canopy, praying the elves would think they were still climbing upward and not realize they'd fallen. They appeared to be safe for the moment, but that would not last.

Turning her attention to Azrael, Fate spoke his name. He didn't respond. She wriggled out from beneath the aeronaut pack, careful to prevent his limp body from rolling over and snapping off the stem of the arrow. His eyes were closed as she removed the pack, laid him gently on the wet ground and put her cloak over his lower half hoping to keep him a little warmer.

The arrow sticking from his chest made her faint with fear. She prayed his armor had kept the arrowhead from going too deep. He was still breathing and would survive as long as she delivered him back to the ship immediately.

Fate started to gather Azrael into her arms, when dozens of fiery balls appeared, sizzling in the rain as the lights elongated into tall, slender warrior elves. She held still as they disbanded in all directions, spraying out in a methodical pattern so as not to miss any ground. A sure sign they knew they were searching for invisible intruders.

Others moved to the base of the tree, their backs turned to her and way too close to notice if she disturbed the ground. Waiting for them to leave wasn't an option. She needed to get Azrael out of there and fast. It was a miracle he'd survived the fall at all. But she feared any sudden movement might kill him. Moving him would have to be done very carefully and slowly, only that would likely give their position away before she could make their getaway.

If it wasn't raining she could pull her notepad out to use the Words of Making for a safe escape, but the ink would smear as soon as she put pen to paper.

An hour passed as she shivered in rain, watching the warriors search for them in small, repetitive circles. She leaned over Azrael to protect him as much as she could from the relentless downpour. The usual dark warmth of his skin had turned ashen. He was fast running out of time.

Another hour passed before the dark clouds shredded apart and the rain ended. Sunlight poured in, dissolving the gray, foggy gloom, revealing the vibrant colors of the forest, yet still the warriors remained steadfast in their narrowed search. If anything, the sunshine seemed to have increased their urgency, because they scanned the ground as if expecting to find them at any moment.

Tense and even more on guard, Fate fumbled with freezing fingers to unsnap one of the pockets on her utility belt. She retrieved her notepad and pen, her hands shaking as she scratched out the words that would transport Azrael to safety.

Azrael went rigid with convulsions, his heels digging into the mud, knocking the notepad from her feeble grasp into a puddle. Fate glanced at the nearest warriors. They stared straight ahead, but it wouldn't be long before one of them noticed the muddy ground moving.

The warrior directly in front of them turned, as if on cue. Fate's pulse thundered in her ears as the elf glanced at the ground. He called out in a sharp yet strangely fearful tone. Within seconds of his outcry, every single warrior vanished within fiery balls, leaving nothing behind but thin drifts of smoke and embers.

As baffled as Fate was by their sudden departure she wasted no time wondering about what had just happened. Bending over Azrael, she scooped her hands beneath his body to lift him off the ground, when something cold and slippery wriggled against her skin.

Fate jerked her hand back. At the same time, Azrael's seizures ended and he went frighteningly still, all while something moved beneath the cloak she'd tucked in around him. The hairs on the back of her neck stood on end as she grabbed hold of the cloak and whipped it off.

Fate jumped to her feet, frozen in terror.

Azrael was covered with earthworms the size of small snakes. Only these weren't like the ones from home. These oversized worms had round, gnashing mouths lined with rows of needlepoint fangs. Azrael's hands and neck, where the armor didn't cover his skin, were riddled with red, inflamed punctures.

Fate shuddered and glanced from side to side. The worms were everywhere, rising up through the mud, slithering toward them.

That's why the warriors had left so quickly.

Instinct pushed her to take flight, escape these horrors, but she wouldn't leave Azrael. She bent down to lift him up and stopped. The worms were all over him. Her childhood phobia crashed back in, paralyzing her.

Fate noticed her pen sticking out of the mud and grabbed it. She pressed the point into her palm and cried out in frustration. The ink wouldn't stick to her wet skin. She rubbed her hand over her damp pants, then flapped frantically to dry it off. She pushed the pen hard into her skin, ready to draw blood if necessary. Thankfully, the ink stuck this time.

Fate scribbled a message and shouted it aloud. "*Azrael and I are safely aboard the ship, NOW!*"

Her nightmarish surroundings mercifully shifted and blurred from sight as the ship's deck quickly came into sharp focus. She jumped into the air, hovering above the floorboards as the worms slithered off Azrael, their fanged mouths snapping in search of new victims.

Drawing her sword, Fate landed, slashing at the worms with a wild frenzy, slicing through their fleshy, gelatinous hides, spilling their gory innards over the deck. The high-pitched shrieks of the worms roused the others from below deck. Sithias, Jessie and Darcy slowly approached the gruesome scene, careful not to step in the carnage.

Sithias kneeled beside Azrael, shaking his head at the arrow and the deathly pallor of his skin. "Oh dear." He looked at Fate and stood. "What happened down there?"

Shaken and weak with worry, Fate dropped her sword. The loud clatter made her wince. "It's all my fault, Sithias. We never should've come here."

31
Where the Marshwort Grows

"MISSS, YOU MUSTN'T FRET ANYMORE." Sithias fluttered his feathered wings. "Azrael is mending nicely from his wound, and the venomous worm bites, thanks to the supplies from Farouk's rescue kit."

"Don't speak that name to me!" Fate didn't mean to snap, but if she never heard the name of her father's murderer again, it would be too soon. "For all we know he could be behind this entire debacle I've roped us all into."

They landed in the middle of the field of giant thistles. Sithias used his tail to hand her a canvas bag for collecting thistledown. He was in snake form due to his need for wings to fly there. "I hardly see how that could be. *He* would have had to somehow alter the ancient texts we've been using as guides to get us this far."

"Why go to all that trouble, when all you have to do is point someone in the wrong direction? Finn certainly thought this plan was a farce. Maybe this is all one big joke orchestrated by Farouk and he's sitting back having a good laugh about it right now."

"You said his name." Sithias cringed when she scowled at him. "Sorry, misss."

"No, I'm the one who's sorry. Every nerve in my body is on a razor's edge." Fate sighed. "You didn't see Finn. He was in some kind of trance. Spelled, or something. As for Tove, I have no idea where they were keeping her. And we almost lost Azrael. Honestly, Sithias, the guilt is killing me."

He tilted his head with a sorrowful look in his amber eyes. "You didn't force any of us to come here. Each of us agreed of our own volition."

"I should've come alone."

"Don't talk like that, misss. We're in this together and we will see it through together. One day at a time. One task at a time."

Nodding wearily, Fate rose into the air and reached for the downy tufts crowning the closest thistle plant.

"Careful there," Sithias warned. "Stay away from the thorns. Being scratched by one of those will cause you to go into a stupor."

Fate couldn't help smiling at that. "Hmm, a stupor sounds kind of nice right about now. Much better than being a frazzled mess most of the time."

"Not if it means you'll be in one for weeks, months, or possibly years."

"Right, duly noted." Fate moved over the tops of more thistles, gathering the down until the sack was full. She dropped down beside Sithias. "Do you think this is enough?"

"More than enough. We'll be distilling all these seeds down to one drop of oil. I would say there's at least four drops worth here."

Fate managed a thin smile. "One task down. Three to go."

"That's the spirit, misss. Ready to return to the ship? I certainly am. I don't know how much longer I can stand to wear this cloaking spell around my neck. It positively reeks."

"Yup, I'm pretty sure Darcy chose the worst smelling herbs on purpose to torment me."

"If she did, that would be dastardly indeed."

"Indeed." Fate straightened her shoulders. "You know, I'm actually geared up to move onto the next task. Thanks for the pep talk. I needed that."

"I'm relieved to hear it." He smiled through watery eyes and sniffed. "I wasn't sure we'd ever fully return to how it used to be between us."

"It's all good, Sithias. You and me, we're solid."

He blinked away the tears and nodded.

"Race you back?" Fate launched into the sky like a rocket, leaving Sithias flapping furiously and squawking about the lack of warning she'd given him.

She beat him to the ship by a good five minutes. Jessie was wearing shorts and a tank top, sunning herself on deck and reading one of Sithias's books from his collection of classic literature. She looked up from the pages and yawned. "Back already? That was fast."

Fate dropped the sack of thistledown onto the floor. "Yeah, it was easy for once. Things have gone so incredibly wrong lately, easy makes me nervous. And suspicious."

"Take the win." Jessie gave her a dismissive wave. "At least you're not dying of boredom."

"Boredom? What's that?"

"Sitting around with your thumb up your–"

Sithias swooped in, skidding over the floorboards before coming to a wobbly stop. "I refuse to acknowledge you as the winner on the grounds you cheated." Thoroughly disgruntled, he morphed swiftly into the tall, gangly librarian they'd all grown accustomed to and promptly yanked the rank invisibility charm from his neck.

Fate stifled a laugh by clearing her throat. "I admit I cheated."

"I forgive you." He flung the charm down in disgust and straightened his bow tie.

Darcy poked her head up from below, squinting with the pained expression of a vampire about to be incinerated by the sun. "Is that the thistledown?"

"In all its abundance." Sithias retrieved the sack and handed it to Darcy. She took it without a word and retreated back into the shadows.

"Do you need me to go with you to the swamps?" Sithias asked, unable to keep his revulsion of the idea hidden. "Or should I assist with the distilling?"

"Supervise Darcy," Fate told him. "I'm taking Jessie on this next run."

"You are?" Jessie jumped to her feet like an excited puppy ready to play.

"Go get your gear on. And bring the Dragon Eye, just in case."

"Are you sure?" Jessie asked. Neither of them needed to voice the trouble it had gotten them into with Kaliena.

"Absolutely. I want uber Jessie by my side if things get hairy down there."

Jessie stooped to pick up Sithias's discarded invisibility charm. "I suppose I'll be needing this."

"Not where we're going. The swamps are far from Mornavar Valley on the other side of the mountains." Fate held her breath as she pulled the charm out into the air and dropped it next to the other malodorous charm.

"Good, because that stinks worse than a skunk in the backyard." Jessie scooted past Sithias and climbed below deck.

"Shouldn't you give yourself some rest and wait until tomorrow morning?" he asked.

"I'm fine. Besides, I think it's best to keep things moving along while I'm on a winning streak."

Sithias plucked at the chain of his pocket watch and flipped the brass lid open. "It's nearly three o'clock." He snapped the lid shut and tucked it back in his pocket. "It's far too late. You can't risk being caught in the swamps after sundown."

"This is summer. Sunset's more than five hours away. That's plenty of time."

Jessie burst through the hatch in full armor, startling Sithias with her sudden appearance. "How could you possibly change that fast?" He grabbed his chest and fanned his face.

"It's not like I was getting ready for a fashion show, Sithias." Jessie rolled her eyes as she strode over to the aeronaut packs. She strapped the pack on without any trouble and turned to Fate with an eager light in her eyes. "Come on, let's go already."

Fate gave Sithias a sheepish glance. "I'll use the Words of Making to get us there and back. We'll save time that way."

Sithias gave her a tentative nod. "If you insist. Please make sure you're back by sunset. I really don't want to have to come looking for you in the swamps. You know how I feel about getting mussed."

"I do." Fate winked at him then wrote out a simple message. "See you in a few hours," she assured him and read the words aloud. "*Jessie and I are together in the swamplands, where the marshwort grows.*"

The blue sky and gentle flutter of the ship's sails spiraled away in a blur of motion fast turning to gray mist blanketing silhouettes of tangled trees. Sunlight sifted through a thickly webbed canopy of leafless branches, diffused and weakly reflected within still ponds of dark, brackish water carpeted with patches of marshwort.

The stench of decay wafted on the dank air. With the exception of the disgusting odor, the place seemed peaceful enough. Nothing moved. There was no indication of life, other than the vivid green of the marshwort against the drab, muted colors of their surroundings. Even the trees appeared to be dead. Their roots no doubt drowned and choked off by marshwater.

Jessie teetered and Fate reached out to steady her. "Look, the marshwort's right here. See? Sithias was just being paranoid."

"Easy peasy." Jessie pressed a hand over her diaphragm and gulped. "Which means I can avoid this sick stomach by flying back."

"Sure, if that's what you want. We'll have the time." Kneeling, Fate stuck her hand in the slimy water and grabbed a fist full of slippery marshwort stems. "Ew, gross," she muttered as she gave it a hard yank. But the plants stayed stubbornly rooted. "What the...? Hand me one of your knives, Jess."

A breeze gusted in, bringing with it the sound of dry leaves blowing over the ground.

"Whoa, what's that?"

"Huh?" Fate withdrew her hand, shaking off the slime and stink. "I didn't hear anything, except a bit of wind."

Jessie shook her head. "I'm pretty sure I saw something. Over there." She pointed to the other side of the pond.

Fate searched the edges of the pond and was about to dismiss Jessie's concerns when she caught sight of a small head misshapen by branchlike protrusions. It seemed to see her at the same time and vanished within the shadows of the trees. Chills raced up her spine. Had her decision to leave the invisibility charms behind been unwise?

"I guess we're not as alone as I thought we'd be," Fate confessed.

"What should we do?"

"Slap the Dragon Eye on. My vision's exponentially improved since my upgrade, but I can't separate details from the dark like the Dragon Eye can. Remember?"

"No need for reminders. I know exactly what it can do." Jessie extracted the headgear from her utility belt and slipped it on over one eye. Her spine straightened the second the Dragon Eye locked into her brain and nervous system. She moved her head smoothly, almost robotically as the intricate mechanisms revolved around the reptilian looking gemstone eye and scanned the shadowy trees across the pond.

The memory of when Jessie had been Kaliena's personal cyborg assassin hit Fate harder than she'd expected. She shook her head, pushing away the heartache that came with it.

Jessie gasped. "I see them," she whispered.

"There's more than one?"

Jessie nodded. "Yeah, they're all over the place." She cringed as the Dragon Eye brought them into sharper focus.

"What are they?"

"I don't know. Ugly little tree gremlins?"

Fate frowned at the vague description. "Do they look dangerous?"

Jessie studied them. "No, I think they're more afraid of us. They're doing their best to stay hidden. It's almost funny how clear I can see them without them knowing it."

Fate unsheathed one of her daggers. "Keep an eye on them while I get what we came for." Taking the blade, she reached under the water and sliced through the stems.

Chaos erupted in the same instance of cutting the plants. Splitting, breaking sounds like the rending of trees echoed through the air. The earth quaked beneath her knees. The still surface of the pond shivered and rippled.

Huge creatures made of gristly wood and bark peeled away from the dead trees–an army of them, spindly and tall as buildings. Their cracked wooden faces were skeletal in shape with mouths bearing long fangs. They waded into the pools, their long gnarled legs sinking all the way to their knotted knees as they pushed through the slime.

Stuffing the marshwort into her satchel with one hand, Fate stood and drew her sword with the other. Jessie already had her sword out, her stance battle ready for when they crossed the pond.

A hard strike from behind sent Fate flying through space. Before she could right herself, she slammed into one of the creatures. It grabbed hold, its fingers elongating, snaking like vines around her chest.

"Jessie, get out of here! Get help!"

"No way, I'm not leaving you!" Jessie dodged the lashing swipe of a tree creature and struck back, shearing off its arm–a useless injury, because the arm grew back almost as swiftly.

"I can take care of myself!" Fate screamed. "I'm right behind you! Go–"

The creature constricted its grip, cutting off her air.

Jessie weaved between the grasping tree creatures, her moves made perfect by the Dragon Eye's enhancements on her nervous system.

Fate's indwelling power ignited, pulsing heat and fury through her bloodstream. Pressing her arms against her bindings, she yelled in an effort to break them. The creature's grip loosened enough to give her hope.

A hideous thing of slime and slurry lunged from the water, clamping onto the tree creature with sharp claws. Dripping with greenish black sludge, its gruesome face moved close to Fate's. Horror slithered in her gut as she stared into globular eyes the color of sickness and death. Its mouth opened, a dark maw held together by strings of glistening ooze.

And then it exhaled–a fetid, sickly green mist that caught at the back of Fate's throat and burned with a frightening, ripping sensation. She felt the cells and tissue inflame with infection. Her throat closed, making it next to impossible to breathe. Her skull throbbed with fever. The pounding fogged her brain over.

The swamp monster twisted its ghastly head, fixing its poisonous stare on Jessie, who slashed her way through the tree creatures, hewing limbs fast growing back. The monster leaped in Jessie's direction, grappling onto another tree creature before bounding to the next.

Jessie had her back to it with no clue of what was coming.

Fate opened her mouth, screaming out a warning that was all but a faint gurgle. A wave of nausea overtook her as she struggled to rise. The effort only weakened her further. Her head was suddenly too heavy to lift, her limbs leaden. She lost sight of Jessie and collapsed into a quivering heap. Everything had become a blur of dark, fuzzy motion.

Fate's thoughts turned to every failure that had brought her to what was undoubtedly the end of her life. Where had she gone so terribly wrong to have lost her way this completely? When she looked into her past, all she saw was a path of obstinance and rash decisions. She'd certainly paid for her mistakes, though not as dearly as those closest to her. Now Jessie would die alongside her in the swamp.

Her greatest regret would always be Finn. His love for her had never wavered, while her love for him had been flawed, impure. She longed to tell him how horribly wrong she had been. That she loved him and would never, ever stop loving him. Not in this world or the next. He was the one she belonged with, *always and forever*. Her soul cried out to tell him what should have been said all along.

But she was too late to change anything. Unbearable sorrow weighed upon Fate, sinking her into the deep, dark grave of her mind. All she could do was surrender to the cold, black tide that rose to swallow her.

Fate let go and knew no more.

32
THE GLYNDAER DRYADS

FINN DRIFTED BLISSFULLY WITHIN the light of the Eternal Flame, warmed and comforted. This was home. He belonged to this glittering ocean of amber-gold fire. The light was all that existed and his awareness was part of it, expanding over the earth, the whole of nature itself and all living things.

At the same time he was above it all, distant as the sun was to the planet. Free of sorrowful memories and the broken heart that remembered the battles he'd fought to hold onto what had never been his. Loss was foreign on this lofty plane. Here, there was only belonging.

"*Finn.*"

He turned his awareness toward the familiar voice.

"*I'm sorry.*"

The pain and regret in her voice tugged at him, drawing his spirit from where he wished to remain. There was no resisting the pull of desire. Love and longing had awakened.

But returning meant the promise of anguish.

"*Finn, I love you. I'll love you forever.*"

Finn's heart cried out, demanding to answer her call. Yet the lure of being part of a greater whole was stronger. This was the path of least resistance. The old path had been nothing but struggle, loss and heartache. He didn't want the pain anymore. He wanted peace.

"*You are who I belong with.*"

Her voice was so faint now. Alarmingly so. Something was terribly wrong. Finn could no longer fly above it all, no more than a bird could resist the force of gravity when its wings tired.

"*I'm yours. I've always been y–*"

The connection snapped and Finn was falling. Falling into an abyss of dark, roaring fear.

He jolted awake, clutching at the pain ripping through his chest. "*Fate,*" he hissed under his breath.

A hand brushed over his hair, a gentle touch that startled him enough to jump to his feet. The elven queen smiled coolly from her throne. "You have finally woken from the neanghaith scratch."

Finn glanced around, taking a minute to realize where he was. Festive garlands of flowers were wrapped around the thick limbs of the Great Oak. The elves were busy weaving more and stringing them from the higher limbs. The addition of hundreds of lanterns indicated a celebration of some kind.

"Lithamas is nearly upon us," the queen explained when she noted his confusion. "I believe the Druidhean refer to it as Alban Hefin."

"Light of Summer," Finn confirmed. The longest day of light, when the sun is in its greatest strength. Closing his eyes for a second, he remembered the euphoria of bathing within the sun's energies. As beautiful and sacred as this place was, it paled in comparison to where he'd torn himself from only seconds ago.

Finn looked at the queen. "You said I was asleep? I assure you, I was not."

"You are strong." She stood with a look of longing in her luminous eyes. "I have not known anyone who was freed from the dream this soon."

"How long was I... asleep?"

"Time has no meaning here. We let the earth, moon and sun show us the passing of time through the change of seasons."

Desperation tightened the muscles in Finn's chest and arms. He was still in a fog. There was no telling how long he'd been dreaming. He certainly wasn't new to the concept of lost time. All the legends of old told of humans being caught in the faery realm for what felt like a day but had been a lifetime or more. Many had returned to find the weathered graves of their families.

Finn was riddled with doubt and confusion. Had he heard Fate's voice only moments ago? Or had it been centuries ago? "Has anyone come looking for me?"

Nueleth's affectionate expression shifted to scorn. "They did. We sensed two intruders."

"Sensed?"

"We could not see, hear or smell them."

"Are they prisoners now too?"

"No. We pierced them. They fell. We believe the luhgmoors ended their lives."

The Olde language flashed visions of large, fanged worms in his mind. Fate would have been one of the two the queen mentioned. He knew her terror of worms. These must have been a nightmare. If there was one thing he could count on, Fate was too stubborn to have been done in by a phobia. At least that's what he was going to tell himself until he knew otherwise. Fate was alive and currently in trouble.

He still needed to know exactly when this had happened, while somehow skirting around the queen's abstract sense of time. "Did they come here on this day?"

Nueleth shook her head.

"The luhgmoors come out after the rain. Was that one sleep ago?"

The queen looked bored, her expression bordering on irritation. "Enough questions. I have my own. We know of your ship in the sky. How many more will come for you?"

Finn's first thought was to lie and say no one else would come. Unfortunately, the Olde language was transparent. There was no room for deception. "Three, unless Tove escaped. Then there would be four." He waited for her to voice more questions. When she didn't, he pressed for more answers of his own. "Did Tove escape?"

"No. My son has taken a liking to her."

"If he lays a hand on her, I will–"

"She returns his feelings." Nueleth obviously spoke the truth as she understood it.

Tove would never settle into the arms of a stranger that quickly. He coiled his fingers into fists, wanting to punch something. "I find that hard to believe, given how fearful she was of your kind."

"We are not unjust." She stepped forward and brushed a hand through his hair. Finn tolerated her touch only because he wanted more information. "Like my son, I have softened to you, even though you are both lowly humans. Should you choose, you could make a home here. With me. With the tribe and the Great Oak."

Her unexpected invitation held a certain appeal. The peace he'd known since arriving in the forest beckoned to him even now. He could easily see himself adopting a life with the Falinorin. The intimacy he'd known with Nueleth when she'd transported him to the thistle field had been almost as strong as his connection to Fate.

Could he trust his feelings? Or was he under some kind of spell? Doubts swarmed back in to cloud his thinking. As he struggled for clarity, the teachings of his grandfather returned. "*True love is never tainted by fear and confusion. The heart always knows the truth. It is the mind that chooses to ignore its honest promptings. Trust your heart to show the way.*"

"If I choose to stay with you, will I be free to go wherever I please?" he asked.

Nueleth traced a finger down on side of his face. Warm tingles pulsed beneath her touch. A promise of more sensory delights, should he wish it.

"Yes, you will be as free as any Elrinye here," she replied.

Finn nodded. "What happens if Tove and I wish to return to our people?"

The faintest lines of displeasure disrupted the smooth surface of her lovely face. "We cannot allow you to leave."

Her words generated images of darkness. Of nothing. "You offer me no free will. Either I live here or die if I refuse."

Nueleth swept her arm at the beauty all around them. "I offer you a life of far greater value than anything you have previously known."

"Aye, you do," Finn agreed. "The life I have known was of my own creation at least."

"Was it?" Her question cut deep. She enjoyed returning to his painful origins too much.

"None of us chooses how we enter this world. Our choices are what make our lives our own." He shook his head. "You have been a queen too long if you expect others to abide by your choices alone."

Nueleth stared back, seemingly stunned. "You would hurt me with insults?"

"I have no wish to hurt you. I am speaking my truth. If you truly want me to stay with you, then the choice must be mine to make without fearing for my life."

She was quiet a moment and he knew she was seeing what was in his heart. That his concern for Fate and helping her was all he could see at the moment. "You plan to leave."

"I *must*. I am needed."

"What of Tove? Will you return for her?"

This manipulation had to stop but he was in no position to scold the elven queen. This soft spot she had for him was likely temporary and would not necessarily transfer to Tove. "Aye, I will." He would never leave Tove behind.

Nueleth seemed appeased. "Then you have my permission to leave."

Finn glanced skyward. Nueleth's hand on his arm drew a reluctant gaze back to her. "I will expect an answer upon your return." All tenderness had gone out of her voice.

"And you shall have it." With that he shot through the canopy, climbing into the azure sky, where he was finally free. For the moment.

He flew far, waiting until he was well past Mornavar Valley before landing on a ridge, where the forest stretched beyond him as far as the eye could see. Kneeling, he placed his hand on the ground, digging his fingers into moist soil as he pushed his senses deep into the earth, through solid rock and underground caves run through with fresh, crystal clear springs.

Usually his connection with Fate was immediate, but there was nothing. His concentration stuttered as fear crept in. "Keep looking," he told himself. "She's alive."

Finn probed deeper, wider, radiating his awareness in waves, craving her spirit essence. He skimmed across the dense forest, over its vast mountain range. The forest was massive, thick and full of wildlife, most of it feral and deadly. Fearing the worst, he pushed onward through territory too perilous for anyone to traverse on foot.

Finn slowed his search when he reached a grove of mighty oaks. He'd never seen this many sacred oaks covering so much land before. He was about to move on, when the connection to Fate surged up his arm, blasting into his chest in an explosion of molten heat and flame.

The force of it was staggering, shocking his system as her essence churned inside him, a storm of searing fire, smoke and ash. The sparkling light of her sweet innocent soul had dimmed, stained by the darkness of grief, sorrow and guilt. The heaviness of it all soaked into every particle of him until he felt as though he were drowning.

Finn jerked his hand from the earth, severing the connection. Trembling from the onslaught of Fate's emotions, he fought to shake them off and clear his head. He knew she was hurting, but he'd had no idea how consumed by pain she had been.

She was plagued by the same agonizing guilt Mugloth had infected him with. The power Mugloth had wielded over him had pushed him to commit dark deeds he regretted to this day. How could he not have realized Fate was going through the same thing? Ananke was forever thrusting her will upon her, forcing Fate onto a path not of her choosing.

Finn lifted off into the sky, breathing deeply in an attempt to clear his lungs of the weakening anguish he'd nearly drowned in. Flying slowly at first, Finn eventually picked up speed, his determination to find Fate stronger than ever as he headed for the oak grove.

After flying for longer than expected, he landed again, briefly reconnecting to ensure he was still aimed in the right direction. It wasn't until he'd cleared the mountain range and headed north that he finally spotted the grove, a vast woodland of gigantic oaks surrounded by swampland of black pools and dead trees of cedar, pine and alder. The swampy landscape was a puzzling circle of death around the thriving green grove, as if designed on purpose, like a moat around a castle.

Finn flew over the grove, hunting for a clearing somewhere amongst the oaks, where he would have a view of what he would be flying into. He finally found an opening at the very center of the solid canopy of lush leaves.

Slowly, he descended, glancing in all directions, watching for the slightest movement. The woods were still when his boots touched the ground, an eerie stillness that raised the hairs on his arms. There wasn't a sound to be heard. Where was the birdsong he'd heard from overhead?

Bending to one knee, he dug his fingers into the soft soil beneath a blanket of last summer's acorns and dry, brittle leaves. His awareness raced through the earth, questing for Fate. He prepared for another deluge of emotion but the violent tidal wave never came.

Pushing further, he widened his search, radiating his dark sight to the very edge of the oak grove. It was there at the border, between grove and swamp, life and death, that he heard her thin, shallow gasp. He let out a strangled cry when he saw Fate's face, pale-gray as a corpse. Something monstrous leaned over her, exhaling poisonous fumes into her open mouth as she fought to breathe. She was dying.

As soon as Finn broke the connection he felt a painful restriction around his ankles. Roots lashed him to the ground and he was furious for being too distracted to notice.

Taking out his flute, he blew two sharp rune notes, transforming it into his wind sword. He slashed at the roots, slicing them at the quick. More snaked from the earth and grabbed hold to bind tightly around his legs. Finn hacked at them, cutting clean through, only to have others replace the ones he'd sheared off. Hundreds of roots burst from the ground, writhing around his torso, wrapping his arms until he couldn't move.

Finn invoked the element of Earth. Fiery sparks surged from his mouth but was gagged before he could summon the ground to harden around the invading roots. Dirt scraped his face as the root squeezed, forcing itself over his tongue to make it impossible to complete his command.

Growling with rage, he struggled to break the roots through sheer strength and force alone. This only made them tighten their grip until he feared his ribs would crush into his lungs. Starved of oxygen, stars danced across his vision.

Finn finally stopped fighting and the roots loosened enough to allow him to breathe again. That's when they finally revealed themselves.

Beings of wood and leaf stepped away from the trunks of the giant oaks. They'd been there the entire time, blending into the trees as if born of them. They were such a part of this place Finn hadn't sensed their presence.

They were well shaped, especially the females, with fine, pleasing features and supple bodies. Any similarity to humans ended there. Their eyes were large, like those of a deer and warmly dark in color, varying from chestnut to ebony, and every hue in between.

Their smooth, polished skin possessed woodgrained whorls, though pliant and soft enough for movement of expression. The elegant lines of their pointed ears matched the sweeping curves of the branchlike horns growing like crowns from their heads. Thin, tendrils of vines with tiny green leaves hung thickly like hair and cascaded over their shoulders.

Dryads. Finn knew of them from grandda's teachings. They were known to be peaceful as long as the trees and land they tended to remained pristine. Any desecration, such as axe to tree, or harvesting plants without fair exchange, incited their wrath.

A regal male strode forward, his head impressively crowned with huge curved, barbed thorns. The leaves framing his face were large and clustered, like a rich mane. He was muscular and thicker limbed than most of the other males. When he reached Finn, he stood a head taller, a formidable figure as he stared down his proud, aquiline nose.

Elder race runes carved into his skin, radiated from an acorn embedded in his chest, as green as the day the seed had fallen from the oak. Likewise, the dryad eyed the runes inked on Finn's temple. He made a small gesture, which loosened the roots from Finn's mouth and around his chest. Though, not enough to free him. Finn coughed, forced to swallow an unwanted amount of dirt.

The dryad's deep voice cracked like the bending of wood as he signed and spoke in the Elder race language. "I am King Lorberos of the Glyndaer. Why have you trespassed into my domain?"

"Someone I love is dying in the swamps outside your grove and I came to help her. Please, you *must* release me."

The dryad's broad forehead furrowed into an imposing frown. "You are a trespasser, as is the other, and under the rule of my authority."

"You know she's here?"

"The Shrilgresh have the intruder. Punishment is being meted out."

"Execution is what it is."

"As is our way. Though killing this trespasser proves difficult when it should not."

Finn was all at once hopeful, but unsure how long Fate could survive a steady bombardment of poison, even with her regenerative powers. "Will you do the same to me?" he asked, hoping to be taken to the Shrilgresh, and in turn, to Fate. "If trespassing is reason for punishment, then I demand to be given the same treatment."

"Trespass is not the transgression. This is about taking from the land without giving back."

The more the king spoke in the Elder race tongue, snatches of information and images sank into Finn's conciousness. A story was fast coming together, a very different history of Feldoril Forest and the Great Oak than what he'd initially gathered from Nueleth.

An ageless time ago, the Glyndaer dryads were born of the Great Oak. The tree connected these highborn dryads to the Shrilgresh, the wild dryads born of the many and varied trees of Feldoril Forest. Peace and harmony was all they had known.

Until the Falinorin came to Feldoril Forest.

The elven race invaded the Great Oak by driving the crystal of the Eternal Flame into the heart of the tree. The introduction of this fiery crystalline energy changed the oak tree, making it impossible for the Glyndaer to inhabit their home any longer.

Death comes to dryads who leave the tree of their birth, yet to stay, meant death as well. The Glyndaer had no other choice but to abandon the Great Oak. To survive and stay bonded to the tree, each dryad embedded a living, fertile acorn within the soft wooden skin of their chests.

The Falinorin staked their claim over Mornavar Valley and the Great Oak by using shadow magic to cast a gloom over Feldoril Forest's borderlands, including the oak grove. These places turned to swamps. While the Glyndaer were unable to banish the gloom, their presence imbued the oak grove with enough strength to prevent the woods from becoming swampland like all other infected areas of the forest.

The gloom infected trees withered and died, which should have taken the lives of the wild dryads. The Shrilgresh lived, but were changed by the shadow magic, made monstrous in form and more feral than ever. The wild dryads continued to answer to King Lorberos, though they kept to the swamplands, making them a treacherous place for anyone foolish enough to cross into Feldoril Forest.

Which is exactly what the Falinorin wished to achieve.

"Allow me to mend this transgression," Finn offered. "I will give back to the land in her place. But only if you release her."

The ferocity in King Lorberos's dark eyes remained. "Why would I trust a Druidhean who allies himself with my enemy?"

"I have no allegiance to the elves. I was taken prisoner."

"You sought parlay with them, did you not?"

"Aye, I did. I came to ask permission to harvest the seeds of thistle and a wee clipping of marshwort from the swamps." He started to explain that was what Fate had come for, but King Lorberos's frown deepened.

"That is not all you seek. You dare insult me by hiding your intention to hunt the Brairdul through omission?"

Brairdul.

The Olde name of the black unicorn slammed into Finn's skull. Disturbing visions and a history he should have been told about unraveled into a nightmare.

33
HOW THE BRAIRDUL CAME TO BE

LONG BEFORE HUMANS EXISTED, when the air was infused with magic, harmony reined amongst the firstborn of the world. These were the Elder race–known as giants and ancestors of all living things–the shapers of the land and wise keepers of Earth's most ancient knowledge.

Then came the First Trees, the Grandfathers of the forests and voice of the Earthmind. The land itself birthed magical, fae beings known by some as dryads, sprites, pixies, fauns, gnomes and nymphs who tended to the emerging flora and pristine bodies of water. As magic increased, more creatures came into being. One such creature was the unicorn.

Born in a time of purity and innocence, the unicorn embodied these qualities and more. The pinnacle of its power resided within its alicorn, that of healing and absolute immortality. The unicorn was the wildest of beasts, untamable and impossible to capture. Led by the stallion king, great herds of unicorns galloped the wide-open ranges, sacred and free.

Death was not a part of this golden age of magic and oneness. Not until the Eldritch Gloom emerged into the world. Suddenly, there was darkness where there had been only light. No one knows whence it came, only that peace could become chaos and magic could become distorted and sinister.

The Eldritch Gloom spread, corrupting that which had once been pure into hideous things. An evil horde was born, bringing forth the vilest of monsters, bloodthirsty creatures that lurked in the shadows and preyed on the innocent.

The unicorn king lost much of his herd to the Eldritch Gloom. Those that could not outrun its tainted reach devolved into kelpies, sea creatures hungry for the flesh of anyone foolish enough to be tricked into riding their wicked backs and dragged to a dark, watery death.

A council was held between the fae folk, the Elders, the First Trees and the unicorn king. Many days of deliberation passed before they arrived at one terrible solution. The Eldritch Gloom must be contained within a living vessel powerful enough to hold the darkness and stop the spread.

The unicorn king stepped forward to be this vessel.

Sorrow fell across the land the day this brave, noble steed raced headlong into the pitch black of the Eldritch Gloom. When all that remained was darkness it was thought the unicorn king had sacrificed himself for naught. Seasons rolled by one after the other before it became clear the Eldritch Gloom was dwindling, little by little. Until the day came when all that was left was a unicorn, black as night and horrifying to look upon.

His brown glistening eyes had turned to milky orbs and his mighty hoofs were cleaved and diminished in size, like the feet of a goat. Its flared nostrils issued a crimson fiery smoke that slithered around its sharp, spear-like alicorn. Gone was the majestic ivory stallion with its gently spiraled alicorn and smooth mane.

This was how the Brairdul came to be. A savage black unicorn that galloped between the folds of twilight, where few could follow. And so, the Brairdul ran wild, king of the night, as unattainable as the stars.

The First Trees sent a call throughout the Earth to any fae strong enough to catch and corral the Brairdul. By then, humans were conquering the wilderness and might one day happen upon the Brairdul and kill it, as was their way. This was unthinkable. Destroying the vessel would release the Eldritch Gloom, allowing it to finish sweeping the world into darkness and all the evils it would create in its wake.

In answer to the call, the Falinorin sailed across the seas from a far away land. They hunted relentlessly, with the Elrinye covering the land by day and the Darfal stalking the Brairdul within its own dark domain of night.

At long last the Falinorin trapped the Brairdul, but they demanded a reward for their efforts. They desired the Mornavar Valley and the Great Oak as their new home. The Great Oak and the council of First Trees agreed. This was a small price to pay for ensuring the safety of the world. Sadly, the Glyndaer paid the heaviest price by being forced to abandon their birth tree.

The story of the Brairdul faded away as King Lorberos's furious face came into sharp focus. All the pieces had fallen into place. Finn understood both sides. Though he was upset with Nueleth for never speaking the Brairdul's name. If anyone was guilty of lying through omission, it was the Elrinye queen. She'd never intended to take him anywhere near the black unicorn and this infuriated him.

"I did not come here to hunt the Brairdul," Finn said. "I came to take a single hair of its mane."

King Lorberos's expression sharpened. "Your intention for wanting what you think is a small thing, is noble, yet no good will come from any part of the Brairdul. I will not hold you accountable for the other's transgression. You may leave." The dryad turned to leave.

"I cannot leave her behind."

King Lorberos glanced back at him. A faint hint of regret showed in his eyes as he faced him fully. "Very well. We will hold the prisoner until you have given back what was once ours."

Finn stared at him in disbelief. "You want me to give you the Great Oak?"

"These are my terms."

Finn's dismay was so great he could hardly think straight. "How do you expect me to make the Falinorin leave the Great Oak? They will never surrender the tree."

"These are my terms," the king repeated. "I trust you will find a way. After all, you defeated the wayward Druidhean who called himself Mugloth and once possessed Grandfather Oak."

If there was ever a time when Finn disliked the Elder race language and sheer inability to keep his entire past private, it was now. Arguing with the king would only make things worse. "If those are your terms, then I agree to them," he finally conceded. "Though I will expect you to help if need be. We are sorely outnumbered."

"You have my word we will help, if necessary," the king promised.

"You will stop the poisoning now?" Finn asked.

"It is done."

"I have to see her with my own eyes."

"You distrust my word?"

"Take me to her," Finn insisted.

The king paused, then motioned for his release. "Follow me."

King Lorberos's stride was swift and steady as he led Finn through the grove. The other dryads in attendance seemingly disappeared behind them. Along the way others made their presence known by moving away from the trunks of the massive oaks to watch them pass by. The Glyndaer were everywhere within the grove, but chose to remain mostly hidden.

When they reached the edge of the oak grove, they came to a wall of fog. The trees behind the misty curtain were twisted and bare. A festering stench hit Finn in the nose the moment he crossed the threshold and followed the king into the murky swamp. His boots sank and sucked into mud, impeding his step as he focused on keeping pace with King Lorberos.

The sounds of wet, shifting earth and the rippling of water alerted Finn to movement all around them. Distorted shapes rose from the earth in acknowledgment of their king. Bog creatures of rock, moss and tangled branches bowed stiffly as Finn moved deeper into the swampland. Huge serpents of slimy bark with spines of spiked branches emerged from the black pools to slither onto land, watching their king with eyes of gleaming red.

The further they traveled, the more the quiet pockets of the swamp crackled from every direction with the sound of breaking wood, as countless wild dryads peeled away from lifeless trees to make themselves known.

The Shrilgresh towered over them, gnarled, spindle-shanked giants of deadwood. Sickly green eyes stared from faces skeletal in form and mottled with lichen. Fierce by nature, they were subdued in the presence of their king.

From within the dimming light, a yellow-green glow appeared in the distance as King Lorberos guided him onward. They stepped onto a path of large bare roots rising ever higher and away from the muddy bog, one that snaked toward an enormous column of tangled, spiraling roots.

They entered the tower, where Finn's attention was drawn upward by the brilliance of light overhead. The inner walls were covered with the fluttering, luminescent wings of millions of moths, the source of the yellow-green glow he'd seen from further away.

His gaze dropped to the ground and his heart nearly stopped when he saw Fate. He raced over and knelt beside her. He inhaled pure terror when he saw her face. Her skin was bone-white, her lips colorless. He held his ear next to her mouth. When he heard the faintest sigh of breath, his lungs filled with relief.

"Fate, I'm here," he whispered.

No response.

He brushed aside a swath of wet hair covering half her face and winced at the bluish hollows of her eyes. Placing his hand at the nape of her neck, he opened his senses, gauging her life force. The weak thread of life he touched on brought back another wave of fear. Finn glared at the king. "The bloody poisoning may have stopped, but she's hovering on death's door!" he yelled in English.

King Lorberos stared back in confusion. Finn repeated himself in the Elder race language. "Unless you allow me to heal her before it is too late, our agreement is off."

"You cannot heal her. Only the dryad who poisoned her can."

"Then do it!"

"Fulfill the bargain and it will be done."

"And if she dies before I can do my part?" It killed Finn to even say the words.

"You have my word she will be kept alive and fully healed upon the fulfillment of our agreement."

"Your word," Finn grumbled in English. He leaned down and kissed Fate's lips, his chest aching at how cold she was to the touch. "Stay alive, love.

I'll be back for you."

Finn stood and narrowed his eyes on the king, who took a step backward. Finn knew his eyes had darkened as they always did when he was feeling murderously angry. "Remember, your home depends on her safe return."

Whatever inkling of fear King Lorberos had shown was now gone. The same unyielding expression returned as he gave Finn a resolute nod, made dismissive by an abrupt departure.

Struggling against the desire to gather Fate in his arms and escape with her, Finn reluctantly left the tower and leaped into the air. His heart burned with rage as he barreled through the fog and broke free of the tangled canopy holding the swamp in shadow.

His mind raced with questions as he shot over the forest, flying faster and faster to reach the ship. How was he going to wrestle the Great Oak from under the Falinorin's tenacious grip without bloodshed? And what of Tove? She was innocent in all this, caught in the middle of what would undoubtedly become a bloodbath. He needed the others to help him think. To help figure out a solution that wouldn't end in the complete annihilation of either side.

Finn had no idea how much time had passed when the ship came into view. Only that the sun was beginning to set by the time he landed on deck behind Sithias, who was pacing and muttering to himself.

Sithias turned around upon the light tap of Finn's boots and yelped. "Oh my! Sir, where did you come from? You're the last person I expected to see!"

"Nice to see you too, Sithias."

"I didn't mean it that way." Sithias patted Finn daintily on the arms. "I'm relieved to see you, of course. We've been frightfully anxious about you and Tove." He glanced around. "Is she with you?"

"No, she's being held by the Falinorin until I return. But that's not why I've come. Fate's in trouble."

"I knew it!" Sithias quaked. "She and Jessie went to the swamps and they promised to return before nightfall." He glanced at his pocket watch. "Which is less than an hour from now."

"Jessie went with her?"

Sithias bobbed his head frantically.

Another person to worry about. "I didn't see Jessie. Only Fate. She's been poisoned."

"Oh dear." Sithias stared back utterly bewildered. "Then why didn't you bring her back with you? I'm certain I could create an antidote to whatever poison it is. You must go back and–"

"Sithias, please." Finn let out a weary sigh. "It's more complicated than that. I'll explain, but it's best we include Azrael and Darcy. We're going to need everyone's best thinking on this."

"We'll need to go below deck then. Azrael's better but he's still recovering from venomous worm bites."

"Then he was with Fate when she came looking for me."

"You know about that? Fate said you were in a trance or something. She feared you were enchanted, maybe even in love with the beautiful elven queen." He winked conspiratorially. "I reassured Fate your heart belongs to her and her alone."

Finn found comfort in knowing Fate was jealous. Probably more than he should, but he was fine with that, given the circumstances. "Thank you, Sithias. You're a good friend."

"You can always count on me, sir." Sithias beamed with affection as he climbed down the ladder before Finn. "Look who's back!" he announced cheerfully.

Azrael rolled over, struggling to rise to a sitting position. When he saw Finn a split second of disappointment crossed his face before he nodded a curt greeting. Darcy looked up from the tarot cards spread on the coverlet of her bed, mildly surprised but definitely not excited.

Finn took a seat on one of the mattresses circling the open middle, now piled with books, backpacks and weapons. "I've come with urgent news."

"About Fate?" Azrael asked.

"And Jessie," Darcy added, shaking her head like he was an awful person for forgetting.

"Aye. I can't say what's happened to Jessie. Only that I didn't see her there. But Fate was caught and poisoned by the Shrilgresh, the wild dryads of the swamplands."

"You left her there?" Azrael rushed to stand, but his legs gave out and he fell back onto the mattress. He scowled at Finn. "You are a coward."

The accusation angered Finn, especially since Azrael had been there when he'd been willing to sacrifice himself to save Fate during the Sumnara Trials. "If you'll calm down, I'll explain. It's true. I could've escaped with Fate. But it wouldn't have done any good since the antidote to the poison must come from the dryad that poisoned her."

"Then we go there and make it heal her," Azrael argued.

"You don't understand. The Shrilgresh are everywhere in the swamplands and they're vicious. They won't be forced. We'll only end up dead for our efforts."

Azrael's glower darkened. "Death does not scare me. Better I die trying to save Fate than to live and never try."

"Does it scare you to know that Fate will surely die if we fight them?" Finn asked.

Azrael's rage vanished in the face of his worse fear.

"I thought as much." Finn leaned forward. "Trust me, Fate's as safe as she can be for the moment. I made an agreement with the dryad king." He went on to tell Azrael, Sithias and Darcy about his discovery of the Glyndaer and their history with the Falinorin.

Sithias blinked at Finn. "How do you plan to oust the Falinorin from the Great Oak? From what you've described they're firmly rooted to the tree."

"That's what I'm here for. We have to put our heads together on this and come up with a foolproof plan."

Darcy burst out laughing. "Men! I can't believe you. You're willing to start a war with an elven race, who can either ride the shadows in a blink or move at the speed of light?" The smile on her face became a blank stare disturbingly fast. "All to save a girl we all know the world would be better off without."

Sithias gasped in horror. "How can you say that? Fate is our friend!"

"Am I the only one here who's willing to speak the truth?" Darcy looked at each one of them. "An ancient goddess who's been determining destinies from the weakest to the most powerful, throughout time itself, has possessed Fate and waits to emerge so she can destroy the world as we know it. Fate's barely able to keep a lid on it. She's a ticking time bomb. Who needs enemies when you have friends like that?"

Finn caught Azrael staring at the wall, his expression tortured–every bit as tortured as Finn was feeling. As harsh as it was to hear, Darcy was voicing what they'd all been thinking for months. But that didn't mean he was willing to give up on Fate. She never gave up on him when Mugloth had been polluting him with hatred and influencing his thoughts and deeds with darkness. Her belief in him had given him strength when he'd needed it most. If not for Fate, he would've lost the battle against Mugloth.

"Friends don't give up on friends." Sithias crossed his arms, looking ready to burst into tears at any second.

Darcy shrugged. "I'm just saying."

"You're not wrong, Darcy," Finn conceded.

Sithias's mouth fell open. "Sir, you can't be–"

"It's all right, Sithias. Agreeing with what is doesn't mean I'm giving up." Finn leveled a heated gaze on Darcy. "Fate's stronger than *you* could ever know. A weaker person would've lost the fight to Ananke long ago. The fact that Fate's held out this long is astounding. Do you know why she hasn't succumbed yet?"

Darcy stared back unflinchingly. "Oh please, enlighten me."

"It's because Fate's surrounded by people who love her. Which is why we've come on this quest to help revive Eustace. Fate will be that much stronger once she has her father back. After that, it's only a matter of time before we free Fate of Hippolyta's girdle and end Ananke's threat for good."

"That's a lovely sentiment." Darcy glanced down at her tarot cards, the flash of a secret in her eyes as she studied the layout. "It's too bad the cards say differently."

"Those don't mean anything," Sithias scoffed, before gulping loud enough for everyone to hear.

Finn wanted to agree, but he found himself curious. Azrael's gaze shifted to Darcy. "What do they say?" he asked.

Darcy touched a card of a woman on a throne. It was upside down. "This is the Empress in the reversed position. It represents Fate's loss of willpower and strength." She moved to the card sitting to one side of the Empress. "Fate's influences are the Moon, also reversed, and the Devil on the other side. These two cards together mean Fate is cloaked in illusion. She sees only what the Devil wants her to see. You could say she's being deceived by the wrong angel sitting on her shoulder."

Sithias moved over and sat down next to Darcy, drawn in by his own curious nature. "Could the Devil card be Farouk?"

"Possibly, but the most common meaning is one's own self-deception." Darcy glanced at Finn. "What do you think? Is it Farouk, or has Fate been lying to herself?"

Finn shook his head. "That's for Fate to answer."

Sithias tsk-tsked. "I'm unfamiliar with the Tarot, but these cards appear to be the opposite of good fortune. Look at this poor fellow, he's been stabbed through by..." He trailed off and counted softly under his breath. "Ten swords!"

"Complete and utter defeat," Darcy explained.

Sithias winced. "And this?" He pointed at the skeleton riding a horse.

"Death."

"As in Fate's going to die?" Sithias's chin quivered.

"Not likely. The Death card is more about an end to something and a rebirth of something new."

"Oh!" Sithias went from relief and then back to worry again. "As in an end to Fate and the rebirth of Ananke?" His voice squeaked high at the end, punctuating the same reasoning Finn arrived at in the same moment.

"That's how it's looking to me."

"Put those away!" Finn's voice sounded sharp and startling within the enclosed space, even to him. "We have to be more constructive than this. Fate's life hangs in the balance here. As does Tove and Jessie's."

"Did I hear someone say my name?"

They all turned to see Jessie climbing down the ladder. She was caked in dried mud, moss and twigs. Sithias ran over and gave her hug. He abruptly released her when he smelled the bog on her. "Ew, you're a smelly mess!" he said, wrinkling his nose as he backed away.

"Uh huh. We got down and dirty in the swamps. Where's Fate? She said she was right behind me. There's no way I beat her back here." Jessie glanced at Azrael and Darcy, surprised when she saw Finn. "Whoa, Finn, you're here!"

"Aye." He smiled sadly. "Happy to see you're safely back."

"Me too. It got real hairy in the swamps, but we have the marshwort." Jessie shed her gear and uniform, stripping down to shorts and a tank top. Touching her stiff, muddy hair, she made a face, cracking the dry mud plastered on her cheeks. "Ugh, I need a bath." She gave Sithias a sweet smile. "Would you be a darling and write one up for me?"

"I'll do one better than that." Sithias pulled out his notepad, scratched out a sentence and read it aloud. "*Jessie is now clean and fresh as an ocean breeze.*"

"Ooh! That tickles!" Jessie giggled as the mud vanished from her face and her hair returned to a lustrous sheen.

Sithias handed her a silken robe. "Now then, you'll want to have a seat. There's much to discuss."

As Jessie slipped her arms into the robe and tied it at the waist, she finally noted the solemn mood of the others. "What's wrong?"

"It pains me to tell you that Fate never made it out of the swamp." Sithias watched Jessie with concern as she wobbled and dropped onto the mattress across from Finn.

"Are you sure?" she asked Sithias.

Thankfully, Sithias spared Finn the anguish of explaining the complex circumstances of Fate's condition. He didn't have the heart to listen, let alone tell the story all over again. Nor did he have the patience. Not when he was battling this urgent need to leap into action.

But this was no time for reckless behavior. They had to be strategic about this. One move in the wrong direction could mean the possible destruction of one or both of the ancient races he had become entangled with.

If that happened, Fate's death would no longer be a possibility. It would be inevitable.

34
THE BLACK UNICORN

FATE WOKE FROM A SLEEP devoid of dreams or self-awareness. Agony slammed in. There wasn't a part of her body that didn't scream with pain. An insurmountable weight smothered her. She couldn't open her eyes, utter a sound or lift a finger. Her blood seemed thick, unable to flow and she knew it to be true by the sluggish beat of her heart, which was a loud, struggling swish in her ears.

This must be what it is to die, Fate decided. In that same horrifying moment of revelation, she remembered the swamp monster and its fetid breath choking her. Poisoning her.

She wanted to fight, but she was sick, too sick to summon even a drop of will power. Was this really how her life was going to end? Alone in a cold, dank, smelly swamp. Or maybe she wasn't alone. Was Jessie laying somewhere nearby dying... or dead?

Fate would rather die alone than to have that be the truth.

Sorrow squeezed her weakened heart and she drifted toward welcoming death. She was tired of fighting, weary of trying to undo every terrible thing that had happened and exhausted by self-recrimination. Better to let it all go and allow the end to come.

Then she heard Finn's voice, speaking in the Elder race language. The other voice sounded disturbingly inhuman to her. She didn't understand what Finn was saying, but his tone sounded tense and desperate.

His presence stirred her blood into flowing a little faster. His touch was a balm upon the raw wound that was her body as he whispered in her ear. "*Stay alive. I'll be back for you.*"

Why was he leaving her there? Had Fate been able to speak, she would have pleaded for him to take her. But he left. Finn left her behind.

Surely she must have dreamed the entire thing. That was the only explanation.

Fate waited for merciful sleep to return but she was left awake, racked with pain in body and spirit. The fury she'd held caged for too long erupted. Divine fire raged from the deepest part of her, coursing through her bloodstream, burning the sickness from her system.

Her eyes opened to a cone of gold-tinged emerald light. She squeezed her lids to be rid of the oily film blurring her vision. Her surroundings came into sharp focus. She was enclosed within rounded walls stretching to great heights. Every surface undulated with the enchanting glow. It took a moment to realize she was looking at the luminous wings of countless moths. Their flickering wings flared bright, ebbing to a glimmer like the twinkling of stars as they rested upon the gnarled roots of the hollow tower. It was a beautiful sight despite the ugliness of the dim swamp.

Fate slowly turned her head to one side, careful not to alert her captors that the paralysis had worn off. When she didn't see anything, she glanced in the other direction, relieved to discover she was alone. She rose to a sitting position and waited a second before standing. The creatures that had put her there obviously thought her incapacitated.

The thirst for bloodshed drummed through her veins. She'd been suppressing her true power for far too long. All because she hadn't wanted to scare her friends. This was the price she'd paid for playing it small. She possessed the power of a god. She was an invincible warrior, not some defenseless victim.

Fate vowed she would *never* be made weak and helpless ever again.

The nape of her neck pricked with a sense of danger creeping from behind. She twisted around in time to dodge from a vicious swipe of the swamp monster's clawed, bony hand. Its mouth stretched back gruesomely wide and toxic fumes flowed between viscous cords of yellowed slime.

Fate leaped over the creature, careful to avoid being stabbed by the many spikes protruding from its spine, shoulders and head. Grabbing hold of the longest barbs on its head, she planted her boot on its back and yanked hard. The swamp monster shrieked, releasing thick green clouds of poisonous gas into the air. The shrill, otherworldly sound of its pained roar was deafening, an alarm that no doubt echoed throughout the farthest reaches of the swamp.

Fate ended the ear-splitting noise by ripping its head from its spindled shoulders. Black, clotted blood splattered her face as she chucked the head against the wall, scattering moths into the air, until all at once, the entire number lifted off in a chaotic flurry.

Drawn by the light blazing at her core, the moths swarmed her, the sharp points of their wings slicing her skin with thousands of stinging cuts. There were too many and the radiant glare of their wings was blinding. Fate touched the curved walls, feeling for an opening amongst the tightly tangled wall of roots. At last she found one and shot through, half running, half flying over the ground.

She crashed into a giant creature made of deadwood. It lashed out, ready to rope her in its grip. Fate grabbed onto its stretching growth of vines, holding firm as she rocketed upward. In one vicious jerk, she tore the arm from the creature's torso, dropping its appendage on its head before weaving up through the thick canopy of branches holding the swamp in shadow.

When Fate burst free, she fixed her gaze on the dimming sky. Exercising her newfound freedom, she climbed higher and higher. She thought about breaking the atmosphere but finally leveled out when the air grew icy and thin in her lungs. Losing consciousness and falling down into that horrid swamp was the last thing she wanted.

Slowly, Fate let herself sink until the air warmed to a more tolerable temperature. No longer fueled by adrenaline, she welcomed the peace and quiet the lone skies always provided. She considered returning to the ship, where Finn had most likely gone after abandoning her.

She wanted to believe he'd had no other choice, but she couldn't begin to guess the reason. There was a time when Finn would have died before leaving her in harm's way. What had changed? Was it possible he was still under the Elrinye queen's thrall? If that were the case, he would have returned to the Great Oak, not the ship.

Fate quivered with rage. She had to break the enchantment.

Azrael's warning returned. Ending a spell without knowing what she was dealing with could harm Finn. She took solace in the fact that he wasn't in any immediate danger. There was only one thing left to do now. Move forward without Finn and deal with safely extracting him from the elven queen's grip afterward.

Fate reached into the satchel at her waist, grateful to find the damp marshwort cuttings tucked inside. There was only one ingredient left to complete the resurrection spell.

The alicorn.

This she could do alone. She possessed limitless powers, ready to do her bidding. It was her fault for believing she couldn't control them. She'd become too reliant on others and had allowed their fears to confine her actions.

The sky was ablaze with the golden, tangerine light of the sun sinking behind black mountain peaks. Fate rotated in a circle until she spotted the light of the Great Oak in the far distance, a bright pinprick amidst the long shadows stretching over Mornavar Valley. The black unicorn was down there somewhere. But where?

Fate opened to the indwelling power, unlocking its prison door to fully embrace it. The energy uncoiled in a sudden burst, surged along her spinal cord to her brain stem. Stars shattered across her vision as her neural network activated to a heightened state of awareness, radiating in all directions, questing for the unicorn.

Feldoril Forest teemed with life. Fate's sightless gaze touched on each and every one of the forest's creatures–some gentle, others savage–though none held the magic she was searching for. She knew not what it was specifically, only that it would be unique, unlike anything else in Feldoril. Widening her reach to the very edges of the forest, her attention narrowed on the pounding of hooves from a place not of this world.

As twilight strengthened, the gateway between night and day opened, where sandy shores met the wild crash of the ocean, and the magic Fate sought flooded the air.

Dark rolling waves filled her vision, the glittering crests broken by the silhouette of a galloping stallion, black as coal. Throbbing beneath its sleek coat was a web of veins glowing scarlet with magic. The eyes were a milky white, vacant as death itself. Its long mane flowed into smoky embers carried on the wind. Its deformed hooves dug into the wet sandy shores with a loud thundering.

Fate inhaled the salty ocean air, welcoming the spray off the waves against her skin. She opened her eyes, thrilled and a little frightened to discover she was standing on the dark featureless beach through intention alone. She gazed into the night, where only the movement of the water caught silvered chips of light from the last glimmer of sunlight burnishing the sky in the far west.

The drum of the unicorn's gallop grew ever louder, bringing with it a sickening nausea to the pit of her stomach as she scanned the darkness for its presence. The steed was one with the night here on this side of twilight and was upon her without warning. Rearing onto its hindquarters, the unicorn let out a shrill cry. Fate drew back in surprise as two leathery wings spread from its sides like the ragged black sails of a pirate ship. Its pale eyes rolled in horror at being caught unawares.

A power unlike anything Fate had ever encountered radiated from the creature–more immense than the ocean lapping at her feet. It was fathomless. There was no end to how deep and dark this magic ran. As infinite as the universe and every bit as cold, empty and inhospitable to life, this power pressed down on her.

The immense presence within Fate reacted instinctively, pulsing through her like quicksilver. In a blink, her leather armor rearranged into sculpted, silvery-white armor of pure platinum, melded to her body like a second skin. She wasn't sure how she knew no sword could penetrate this armor, only that it was true.

Only it wasn't.

Hard, piercing agony ripped through her torso. Fate rose into the air, not of her own volition, but from the unicorn lifting its massive head. Struggling to breathe, she looked down the long tip of its alicorn, glistening with her blood and sticking out the other side of her ribcage.

Shocked and dismayed, Fate stared at the stars.

What had happened here? No sword could pierce her armor. But this was no sword. She'd been gored with the horn of a beast filled with corrupt magic. The god force power at her center railed against its demon energy. Made of the same foul emanations Farouk had used to weaken her. Only this was stronger, an absolute concentration of pure evil.

A wave of darkness swallowed her within a sea so black and complete she wondered if she had ever existed at all. Her past was blotted out, like ink spilled over the pages of history. She grasped at her dearest memories, clinging to fast fading images of Finn and Eustace, Jessie and Sithias, but their faces slipped away into the shadows.

She was alone again. Forsaken. Lost in a void, a terrible place emptied of warmth and love. Desolation soaked into Fate's soul, sinking her into a black bottomless pit, stagnant and malevolent. This was all there was, an infernal existence that stretched out into an eternity.

You would accept defeat so easily?

The question would have sounded like an accusation had the soft, feminine voice not possessed a motherly concern.

I made you invincible, my daughter. Nothing can harm you unless you allow it.

Fate had no memory of a mother's love, yet the thought of being a disappointment to a mother she had never known was unbearable. She sank deeper into the black.

Take my strength. Use it to rise and fight. Let this be my greatest gift as your mother.

Hope returned, the first glimmer of light in an endless dark.

I will be with you. Together, we will rid the world of this evil.

The promise of a mother's support chased Fate's loneliness away. Until this moment, she hadn't known she'd been living with a gaping hole in her heart. A mother's unconditional love was all Fate had ever wished for. She wasn't alone. This, above all else, filled her with strength.

Jagged light scratched across Fate's vision, and with it, the stabbing, grinding pain of the horn lodged in her ribs and vital organs.

The unicorn bucked violently. Fate screamed in pain as the length of its horn tugged from her body, the sharp tip raking her torn insides. She dropped onto the wet sand, coughing on the blood gushing into her mouth as she rolled into the crashing waves to avoid a cloven hoof from splitting her skull.

Rise!

Fate heeded her mother's command by launching into the air to escape being trampled. Pulsing heat poured into the stab wound, easing the raw, tearing anguish that had her gasping with every breath. Life force energy flowed into her damaged cells and tissue, staunching the flow of blood filling her lungs. She was healing and growing stronger, faster than ever.

Kill the unicorn!

The jeweled hilt of a sword filled her grasp. The blade stretched into a sharp taper, shining in the moonlight as it coalesced from nothing into solid form. Setting her sights on the monstrous steed, Fate dove, aiming the broadsword where the root of its alicorn protruded from the forehead. The blade collided against petrified bone with the clash of steel striking granite. The beast bellowed, a hellish shriek no doubt heard to the very ends of the forest and maybe even across the waters to distant lands.

The unicorn staggered, its head sagging as oil-black blood oozed from the stub. The throbbing glow of its crimson veins dimmed as the horse struggled to stand, its thick reptilian wings flapping lamely. When the effort of taking flight proved too much, the unicorn collapsed. Waves splashed against its back in glittering sprays of foam, the tides moving its lifeless wings in a rhythmic push and pull.

The black unicorn was dead. Darkness streamed from the fatal wound, rushing to fill the sky, consuming the stars in its rapid spread.

Fate kneeled next to the head, repulsed by the creature's vacant, globular eyes and the stench of sulfur emanating from the bleeding stub. She grabbed the alicorn and lifted off the ground to get away from the horrible odor.

The ebony horn was heavier than her broadsword and as long as a spear. Raising it to the moon, she admired its sleek, slightly curved form all the way to the deadly tip that had come so close to killing her. She swung it back and forth, drawn in by the dark, wild power humming through its stock.

This power is ours to conquer and harness, my daughter.

Fate released the broadsword, letting it disintegrate into stardust before scattering on the gentle breeze in a twinkling.

Gather the power back into the alicorn. Take it all.

Fate flew to the darkness spreading overhead and plunged the alicorn's severed end into the black, depthless substance. The tip of the horn vibrated so forcefully she had to clutch tightly with both hands. Her arms quaked as the power flowed back into the severed end. The surging energy thrummed loudly, a deep resonate sound that chilled her to the marrow. She ignored the baleful notes, telling herself she was looking for trouble where it shouldn't be.

When the dark flood above finally began to shrink, Fate pulled the streaming funnel downward until the comforting sounds of the ocean dampened the menacing roar of power. What had been a torrent of dark matter, dwindled to a trickle, until a few last wisps of the sinister energy writhed stubbornly, as if to evade full containment.

The alicorn stilled and the energy calmed to a steady hum. Fate turned the horn around, wondering how to seal the cut end, but the thick base suddenly narrowed, molding the raw edges into a smooth hilt. She wrapped her fingers around the end, smiling at the perfect handhold. At the same time, thin braids of black leather streamed from the ether, weaving into a beautiful scabbard that hung over her back.

Pleased with her bold new weapon, Fate thrust it toward the glittering sky. Peace flowed through her. She had everything she needed to complete the resurrection spell. Her heart nearly leaped from her chest at the thought of her father rejoining the living.

This new gift of the alicorn sword was an unexpected blessing. With this weapon she would remedy every mistake, starting with Finn's release from the Elrinye queen's spell, as well as freeing Tove. Once everyone's safety was assured, she would hunt Farouk and destroy him. Fate knew this without a shadow of doubt, because this time she was under her mother's protection, heeding the wisdom of her guidance every step of the way.

Together, they would purge the world of all its evil.

35
FIRE BREATHING DRAGONS

A SPINE-CHILLING SHRIEK reverberated outside the hull of the ship. Finn jolted to his feet and hastily climbed the ladder. Fear needled his skin as he stepped out into the open air. Something terrible had been unleashed. That much he knew, but what?

He didn't have to look far. A shadow rose from the shoreline, an amorphous body of black mist that snaked across the sky, splitting off like fingers hungrily grasping at the bright expanse of sunlight receding behind the Glor'ner Mountains.

Sithias rushed to his side. "What unholy thing is that?"

Jessie followed, frightened as she stared at the sinister darkness.

Darcy sidled in next to them, nodding in amazement. "The black unicorn is dead and the Eldritch Gloom is loose again."

"What is the Eldritch Gloom?" Sithias looked as lost as Finn felt. "Is that what that frightening darkness is? How is it connected to the black unicorn?"

Finn studied Darcy. "How do you know about the Eldritch Gloom?"

Her eyes darted furtively. "I read about it in the books."

"What books?" Sithias asked. "I never came across any mention of an Eldritch Gloom."

"Actually, I read it in a fable–something about a unicorn king who became the vessel of a threatening darkness that would've consumed the world. I figured it was pure fiction so I didn't add it to the collection." Darcy glanced at the blackening sky. "Apparently, it's real, which means the black unicorn is dead and Fate is most likely the one responsible."

"Why would she kill the unicorn?" Finn asked, unable to keep the angry growl out of his voice. "She did say all that was needed was a hair of the unicorn."

"Oops, looks like the cat's all the way out of the bag." Darcy snickered behind her hand.

Finn's gut twisted with rage. "You all lied to me? To Tove?"

Sithias cringed beneath Finn's glower. "We didn't want to lie, but we knew your lives would be in danger if the Falinorin knew the spell required the animal's alicorn. Of course, this was without knowing the *real* story behind the black unicorn." He glared at Darcy.

Finn fixed his gaze on the floor of the deck as he tried to calm down. "Lies aside," he seethed, "let's look at this logically. Even if that is the Eldritch Gloom, it still couldn't have been Fate who killed the unicorn. She's struggling for her life as we speak."

"Is she?" Darcy asked, one expertly penciled brow arched skeptically.

"What exactly do you mean by that?"

Darcy looked at Finn like he should know. "Think about it. Can she actually be killed while she's wearing that Amazonian wardrobe? I for one haven't forgotten the fact she's had wicked regenerative powers ever since she put that thing on."

"Trust me, Darcy. Fate was barely alive when I left her." Truth be known, his fear had been so great he hadn't put any real thought toward Fate's astonishing ability to rebound from mortal wounds.

Darcy examined her black nail polish. "Didn't you say the dryad king stopped the poisoning to give you time to meet your end of the bargain?" When Finn didn't reply, she lifted her gaze with a cruel smile. "Mmhmm. I'd say Fate got better *real* fast, kicked some dryad ass and went after the unicorn."

Everything he'd discovered about the Eldritch Gloom returned to haunt Finn. He shook his head, unable to find an argument against Darcy's speculations. He should have seen this coming. Once again, his feelings for Fate had overridden sound reasoning.

Even now he was torn. Anger at being lied to about the most critical ingredient of the resurrection spell. Guilt at having played a part in unleashing the nightmare now crawling across the sky. And sheer terror as to whether he'd lost Fate to Ananke forever.

Most of all, untold dread at the thought of being forced to battle Ananke, who wore the face of the girl he loved above all else.

"As much as it pains me to say it, I think Darcy may be right," Sithias admitted, his face drawn tight with sadness.

"You're all wrong," Jessie shouted. "Look, it's going away."

Finn ran to the railing, watching as the gloom streamed downward along the shoreline. The fear prickling over his skin abated. Whatever shroud of evil had been let loose was now contained.

Azrael climbed up onto the deck, out of breath. "What is happening?"

Finn shook his head. "Nothing good."

"Uh, guys, look who's here." Darcy was staring at something high in the sky behind Finn. Fear had wiped the sneer off her face.

Finn turned, his breath locking in his chest as he gaped at Fate hovering above them, a golden beacon of radiant light against the inky backdrop of the night sky.

She was both beautiful and frightening. Dressed in the silvered shining armor of a god, enormous wings stretched from her back, incandescent with a fiery blaze. Heat waves rippled off the wings, blowing her long, auburn hair skyward like wildfire. Her skin was luminescent, gleaming with an inner fire, her eyes lit so bright they glowed white. Her gaze was eerily distant and inhuman.

This wasn't his sweet bonnie lass. It was Ananke who stared down at them through Fate's eyes. The pain it caused him to look upon her face was next to unbearable. Finn's gaze moved to the long spear-like sword in her grip. When he realized it was the unicorn's horn his every fear was confirmed and his heart imploded.

"Fate!" Jessie yelled. She jumped and waved her arms, an action that drew Fate's terrifying gaze onto her. "Get down here, we need to talk to you!"

The smallest frown broke the smooth planes of Fate's blank expression.

Jessie gulped loudly. "What are you waiting for? Hurry up and get your butt down here."

Fate suddenly stood before them on the ship's deck, an imperceptible movement through space that was frightening to witness. Sithias squealed, his knees knocking together as he edged backward. Darcy's mouth hung open as she slipped toward the opposite end of the ship. Azrael didn't move, but he looked every bit as gut-wrenched as Finn felt.

"Hey, I see you have the unicorn's horn." Jessie forced a nervous laugh. "That's awesome. We can do the resurrection spell now."

Fate's cold, remote gaze remained unchanged.

"I bet you can't wait to see Eustace up and around." Jessie waited for a reaction. She continued when there was still no response. "He's going to be so happy to see you. And I know you're going to be over the moon about having him back. Won't it be great not to feel sad anymore?"

Fate blinked and Finn thought he glimpsed the warmth of her cinnamon-brown eyes melt through that glaring white gaze. "Keep talking, Jessie."

"Do you remember what we said we'd do when Eustace wakes up?" Jessie didn't wait for an answer. "We're going to do one of our famous movie marathons with your dad, just like we used to. We'll have every kind of flavored popcorn ever invented and top it off with fresh baked brownies. We'll eat all day until we're so full we're miserable. Eustace will complain about his heartburn and swallow back a bottle of antacids, while swearing he'll never make that mistake again."

Jessie shot Finn a nervous glance. "I'm not reaching her," she said under her breath.

"No, I think you are." He stole close to Jessie, while keeping his voice to a low whisper. "Maybe she needs to hear something urgently important to pull her all the way out."

"Um, sure." His suggestion made Jessie all the more anxious as he watched her grapple for an idea off the top of her head. She finally looked at Fate, fearful, hesitant. "Fate, there's something you need to know. I, uh... I checked on the case holding Eustace and found a tiny crack in the glass. The multidimensional magic keeping him... *fresh* has been leaking out. If we don't get him back to the Keep right away and refill the tank, rapid decay will set in before we can do the resurrection spell."

"Yup, that's right, we have to get back, *ASAP*," Darcy added, from the far end of the ship. "The spell takes time to set up. The thistle seed won't be fully distilled for another few days yet. And I still need to prepare the marshwort and alicorn." She quickly receded into the shadows beneath Fate's forbidding gaze.

Fate folded her massive wings and they vanished from sight altogether.

Suddenly, the ship tilted, like a giant hand tipped it upside down. But it wasn't the ship. It was Finn's head spinning from a severe bout of vertigo. A nauseating force tugged at his solar plexus. He bent at the waist, gripping his gut as his surroundings blurred into a dizzying array of motion.

Finn was close to vomiting when whatever held him in its grip let go with the same violent swiftness. Swallowing back bile, he lifted his aching head and glanced around.

They were all inside the Keep sanctuary!

Sithias slapped his hands over his mouth, retching as he fought to hold onto the contents of his stomach. Looking ghostlier than ever, if that was even possible, Darcy grabbed the edge of the main table to keep from falling over. Jessie stood with legs astride, wobbling in place with hands cupped over each temple. Azrael lay on the floor, curled in on himself. No doubt in the throes of the same physical misery as the rest of them.

Hearing a soft groan from behind, Finn turned expecting to see Fate but it was Tove. She was on her knees and holding her stomach.

"Tove!" He kneeled next to her, his relief equal to his shock.

"How did I get here?" Her voice was faint, weak.

"Fate. She moved us all here. None of us were expecting it." He reached out to her, but she shrank from his touch. That's when he noticed the beautiful coral gown she was wearing, a rich shimmering fabric with silver thread woven into swirling designs by the talented hands of the Elrinye. Her raven hair was loosely braided and fastened at the ends with fine golden cords. Accustomed to her usual hunter's wardrobe, Finn was more than a little taken aback by such feminine attire.

Her green eyes filled with tears. "Why?"

Finn stared back, wordless, confused.

"Why didn't she leave me there?" She broke into a quiet sob. "I was happy there."

"Tove, I had no idea. I feared you were in danger this whole time."

Tove looked at him, enraged even as tears streamed down her face. "I can't be here in these walls of steel. Make her send me back! I need to be in the forest with..."

"Prince Ethlan?" Finn asked, remembering the name of Queen Nueleth's son.

She nodded.

"The queen told me he'd taken a liking to you and that you returned his feelings." He shook his head. "I didn't trust her enough to believe what she was saying."

"She spoke the truth. I am in love with Ethlan. We were to be married on Lithamas. I was to become a member of the Elrinye." Her face darkened with the same unforgivable rage she'd shown him when she first lost Grysla and Leif. "You spurned my love. You destroyed my family. And now you rip me from the peace and joy I thought would never be mine again. Why do you seek to ruin me at every turn?"

Guilt gnawed a hole into Finn's chest. "I'm sorry, Tove. I never meant to hurt you. Not ever!"

"If you mean that, you will find Fate and make her send me back to Feldoril."

"I'll go find her. Stay here with the others."

Finn raced to the hatch, hoping to find Fate on the ship, if it was even there. He thumped the button, impatient as the metal iris spiraled open. He squinted into the desert glare, washed in crimson by the early morning sunrise–a sudden, sharp contrast from the nighttime sky they'd left behind mere moments ago.

The ship was docked next to the hatch but there was no sign of Fate on deck. Was she down inside the hull where they'd been keeping the case holding Eustace's body? Finn flew over to the ship, hurriedly descending into the lower cabin.

The glass case was gone. Fate must have moved it, but where? The only place Finn could think of was the room Brune had originally stored it in. Finn grabbed the bottom rung of the ladder, when a sudden blow to the ship knocked him back. The boat heaved upward with the screech of splitting wood. Finn slammed against the opposite wall.

The other side of the hull was demolished. Vaporous mist poured through the broken floorboards and out the hole. Finn rose, hovering inside the ship's cabin, unsure if he should leave through the newly made exit. His answer came in the form of an enormous, scaly hide flying past the gaping hole.

Finn darted to the ladder, rising swiftly toward the upper deck, when blistering heat raked his backside. Tensing every muscle, Finn shot through the opening, speeding straight into the sky until he felt safe enough to look down. Black smoke billowed from raging flames as a dragon breathed fire into the belly of Azrael's ship.

Finn shot to the topmost arch of the nearest ring of the Keep and landed, stunned as he watched the dragon. Oily shades of violet-blue shimmered over its ebony scales as its great leathery wings flapped to hold its position. Distant roars echoed out over the dunes, drawing Finn's attention to the horizon, where three more dragons claimed the skies.

They were Serpen dragons. He had no doubt of that after seeing one of them in action during the war against Kaliena. But why were there more all of a sudden? The Serpens in lock-up must have somehow summoned them.

With hands shaking, he retrieved his spyglass, focusing in on the dragon burning Azrael's ships to cinders. He drew in a sharp breath when he saw a Serpen knight sitting astride the beast's back. Easy to miss from a distance because of the way his dark armor and saddle blended in with the dragon's black hide. He lifted the spyglass to the three dragons sweeping the skyline. Each had a dragon rider, which could mean only one thing. A Serpen army had arrived.

Lying down on his front, Finn slid his arms over the edge, using the spyglass to scan the ground far below. He stopped on the first sign of an encampment. Slowly, he focused in on countless tents and Serpen knights moving amongst them. They were everywhere, a dark sprawling stain upon pristine white sands.

Fire grazed the metal surface, hitting Finn with a wave of scorching heat. Rolling onto his back, he jumped into the air; narrowly escaping a jet stream of flames blasting the space he'd occupied a split second before. A fourth dragon blocked the sun, casting a massive shadow over Finn as it swooped past him. The rider twisted in his saddle, holding Finn in his sights as the dragon swept back around to take another run at him.

Finn leaped off the top of the ring, weaving between gouts of fire as the dragon gave chase. Fixing his gaze on the hatch, he hit his target with as much speed as he could muster. Flames clawed at his heels, with heat so intense, Finn was certain the soles of his boots were melting.

He shot through the hatch, slammed onto the floor and slid across the room as a blast of fire streamed into the sanctuary. Racing back to the opening, Finn punched the button to close the hatch. A furious roar resounded from the other side.

"Close, damn it," Finn growled under his breath as the spiraling metal moved all too slowly. Flames shot through the shrinking closure, cut off abruptly into tendrils of smoke when the hatch finally snapped shut.

"Tell me there aren't fire breathing dragons out there." Sithias stared at the hatch in horror.

"Would if I could." Finn leaned against the wall, catching his breath.

Sithias's expression turned to one of worry. "Did you see Fate out there? She's not here. I don't know where she is."

"I checked the ship before the dragon burned it to ash. She wasn't on it. Eustace was gone too."

"Oh, thank goodness!"

A terrible screech of dragon's talons reverberated through the exterior wall. Finn leaped into the middle of the sanctuary, half expecting it to break through at any second.

"Can it get in?" Sithias squeaked.

Jessie rushed to the hatch and swept her palm across the control panel, activating it with the guardian seal. "It'll hold," she assured them as a glimmering light washed over the sanctuary walls. The worn bronze surface turned translucent, revealing the enormous dark shape of the dragon outside the hatch, doing its best to rip through the metal. The wards protecting the exterior blazed golden with each clawed strike.

Sithias fanned his face. "To sssay I'm relieved would be an understatement!"

Jessie stared at the dragon as it flew off. "Where's Brune? She needs to know about this."

Finn headed for the door. "I'd say she already does. There's an entire Serpen army camped out down there, and by my count, they brought four more dragons with them." He opened the door to leave but stopped when he heard Azrael's pained groan. "Sithias, you'd best see to Azrael while I look for Fate."

Jessie caught up to him. "I'm going too."

"Can't Darcy do it?" Sithias asked. "I'd rather go with you."

Finn glanced at Darcy. The faintest pink had returned to her normally bloodless cheeks. "Can you tend to Azrael?" he asked her.

"Sithias should play nurse so I can start setting up the spell."

"Stay for Azrael's sake," Finn whispered to Sithias.

"Fine." Sithias sagged. "But I want to know the minute you find Fate."

"Me too," Darcy added. "I need the marshwort and alicorn." She smiled secretively. "Just so you know, I lied to Fate about needing time to prepare. I already have more than enough oil from the thistle seeds to get the job done."

"How was that a lie?" Jessie asked with obvious suspicion. "You've been telling us the spell would take weeks after we gathered all the ingredients."

"That's what I originally thought. As it turns out, I miscalculated." Darcy scowled. "Don't give me that look. You lied about the case leaking."

Jessie looked offended enough to punch her. "Finn told me to give Fate something urgent to care about and that was the first thing that came to mind!"

"Which is exactly why I added to your fake emergency with a few more harmless white lies." Darcy smiled smugly. "Working together here, people."

Finn had lost all patience. "The spell's not important right now! All I care about is figuring out whether or not Ananke's taken Fate over completely. And I want to know more about the Eldritch Gloom and any possible effects it may have on Fate."

Darcy folded her arms with a frown. "That's a steep order."

"I'll dig into the books as soon as I'm done here." Sithias lugged the big wooden rescue kit over to Azrael, nearly dropping it as he knelt down with the heavy box in his arms.

"I suppose I could switch gears and help with the research," Darcy offered begrudgingly. "But first I want it on record that getting Fate straightened out by bringing Eustace back to life is still our best bet."

"Darcy's right on this one." Jessie sounded apologetic for agreeing.

"Fine, we'll do the spell," Finn conceded. "Jessie, you can help me find Fate."

They ran down the hallway, turned the corner and came to a swift halt when they saw the press of Beldereth knights, Eldunough warriors and hawk riders filling the narrow space. They were ready for war, dressed in full armor and packing weapons.

Finn caught the attention of one of the Beldereth knights. "I saw the dragons and Serpen army outside." She turned sharply before recognition eased her fierce expression. "How long have they been here?" he asked.

"Three days. They arrived at the same time the Serpen prisoners broke free and seized King Rudwor."

Adrenaline singed Finn's already fried nerves to a crisp. "Is he still alive?"

Doubt moved in her eyes. "We can't be sure," she admitted.

Her answer hit like a cannon ball to the chest.

"The strike happened all at once." She shook her head with a pained frown. "An entire legion of Serpens attacked from the outside, using eight dragons to break in."

Finn stared back in horror. "*Eight*? I thought five was bad."

She nodded. "They ripped into the exterior walls of the main section of residential suites. We never saw it coming. Our only recourse was to barricade this section with wards. It won't last though. The dragons have been weakening the barriers with fire, teeth and talons."

"But the Serpens were locked up and under heavy guard," Jessie said. "How the heck did they call for reinforcements?"

"We can't say for sure," the knight replied. "But it's looking like they planned the invasion well before the Great War. The attack was simply too well orchestrated to be otherwise."

Unwanted memories returned of the dragon empress and her nearly two decades long plan to bring the kingdom of Asgar to absolute ruin. "Aye," Finn agreed, "the Serpens are nothing if not the most patient of planners. I should've known better than to invite them into the alliance."

"They proved useful against the enemy at the time." The knight glanced over her shoulder, nodding at someone further down the corridor. "Excuse me, I'm needed."

"Where's Brune in all this?" Jessie asked Finn, searching the press of soldiers.

"Good question. Let's split up. I'll look for Fate while you track down Brune."

"No, I'll go after Fate," Jessie insisted. "I'm the only one who's been able to talk her down lately."

"Aye, no argument there." Finn sighed wearily. "Check the room where Eustace was being kept before we moved him onto the ship."

Jessie sprinted off, quickly disappearing amidst the soldiers crowding the halls.

Finn weaved his way through the throng. The tension building in the soldiers was palpable. His mind reeled with the news of Rudwor and the weight of war upon an already shaky alliance. The timing of it all couldn't be worse, what with Fate's slaughter of the black unicorn and Ananke's emergence. He felt pulled in a million different directions, wanting desperately to help but not knowing which problem to attend to first.

He knocked on the door of Brune's suite, his fist beating the metal surface with more urgency than intended. She opened the door in a disheveled mess. Her uncombed blonde hair hung loosely around her flushed face and her half buttoned shirt was untucked. Finn couldn't remember a time when Brune wasn't fully dressed in her Keep Guardian uniform with hair pulled back in a neat bun.

"Finn? When did you get back?" Frowning, she finished buttoning her shirt and tucked it in, though sloppily.

"Less than thirty minutes ago."

Brune swept her hair back, tying it into a loose ponytail. "How did you manage to get past the dragons in the ship?"

"Fate transported us to the sanctuary." Movement at the back of Brune's bedchamber distracted Finn. When he saw it was Meara, one of the Beldereth knights he'd come to know during his time in the kingdom, he gave her a friendly wave.

"Hello, Finn." The beautiful blonde tied off her robe and walked across the room.

"We've all had to double up on beds since the invasion." A bright shade of pink flooded Brune's fair cheeks.

Meara winked at Finn.

"Uh, Finn and I have much to discuss," Brune told her. "Meet me in the sanctuary with the latest report from your troops in one hour."

Surprised by this new development, Finn smiled and turned around to allow them some privacy. A few seconds later, Brune marched swiftly past him. "Don't say a word," she warned him.

"What?" He fell in step beside her. "Meara's a lovely lass. I'm happy for you both."

Brune's sidelong glance was filled with bewilderment. "You don't find it strange?"

"Why would I?"

Brune set her shoulders straight and frowned. "No reason. I suppose I've grown so used to being alone that sharing my personal space with someone is alien. And full of confusing emotions."

"I think most people feel that way, no matter how wildly in love they are."

The rigidity in Brune's posture eased momentarily and then she snapped back into being all business. "Fill me in on your trip, namely why you're back much sooner than expected."

Finn barely knew where to begin. Once he started recounting events, they came in a sudden flood, with each new detail increasing the horror in Brune's eyes. She directed him into a dead-end hallway absent of foot traffic, where they could speak without the interruption of being jostled. "Is that everything?" she asked.

"No, I haven't told you the worst of it. Ananke's close to making a permanent appearance, if not already."

"How did this happen? The whole point of the trip was to make Fate strong against Ananke." She huffed in frustration. "If you have all the ingredients from Feldoril Forest, why didn't you perform the resurrection spell immediately?"

"There wasn't time. Fate showed up after killing the unicorn. It was obvious she was losing to Ananke, so Jessie gave her a reason to be concerned about losing Eustace by saying the glass case was cracked and had a leak."

Brune considered the solution. "That was good thinking on Jessie's part."

Finn nodded grimly. "Aye, it was, as long as the reason Fate returned was to plug Eustace's case back into the Keep's supply of multidimensional magic. That's where Jessie went. She's been the only one able to get through to Fate lately."

"Let's go see if she found her." Brune brushed past him.

Finn followed her hurried pace with a drag in his step. Part of him didn't want to find Fate. Not if it meant he'd lost her to Ananke.

36
THE SHADOW IN THE SPELL

"I HEAR VOICES." Brune pressed her ear to the door with a puzzled frown. "And laughing."

Relief washed through Finn, banishing the dread weighing him down. "Jessie found her. Open the door."

Hesitating, Brune cracked the door and peeked in. Fate's voice filtered out into the hall. She sounded normal, even happy. Finn followed Brune inside. As soon as he saw the brilliant light rimming Fate's form, his heart plummeted. She turned around to look at them, her eyes still lit with fire. At least he could still see the color of her eyes and he was thankful the vacant stare was gone.

Finn noticed the case holding Eustace at the back of the room. Jessie was leaning against it, one leg crossed over the other in an attempt to appear casual. She was nervous. Finn could tell by the way she was chewing at a hangnail on her thumb. "How is Eustace?" he asked.

"Safe." Fate's lips curved into a peaceful smile as she returned her disturbing gaze to Eustace.

Brune eyed the alicorn sheathed over Fate's shoulder. "You made the unicorn's horn into a sword?"

Jessie laughed with a nervous pitch close to hysteria. "Yeah, isn't that cool?" She nodded at Brune with an exaggerated smile that held a warning.

"I knew the alicorn was mine the moment I held it in my hand. It was always supposed to belong to me."

The casual air in Fate's voice set Finn on edge. "Will you still be using it in the resurrection spell?"

"Yes," Fate replied without taking her eyes off Eustace's face. "I have everything I need now. It's time to perform the spell. I've waited long enough."

Jessie pushed away from the case with a disturbing eagerness. "I'll go get Darcy."

"No need." Fate waved a hand, tracing a shimmer into the air.

Darcy appeared from within the folds of wavering space. She grabbed her stomach and dry-heaved. Still bent with her hands resting on her knees, she raised her head, glancing around to see where she was. "What the hell?" Her gaze fixed on Fate. "Oh, of course. Fate beckons. You could've just used the intercom and waited the extra ten minutes."

"No more waiting." The light in Fate's eyes consumed the warm brown of her irises. "Perform the resurrection spell."

"I need my stuff."

Fate gestured to the floor, surprising everyone with the contents of the spell spread out at their feet. A royal blue silk cloth with symbols stitched in gold thread lay perfectly smooth on the floor with a few dozen candles placed around the edges. A stack of spell books, a large silver bowl, a slimy pile of marshwort and several bottles of thistle seed oil sat neatly lined outside the candles.

Darcy shook her head, more out of fear than obstinance. "I can't work under this kind of–"

"I'll help," Jessie jumped in. "We don't want to upset anyone, right?" She let out another nervous laugh.

Darcy glanced at Fate fearfully and kneeled beside the cloth. She sifted through the books with trembling hands. Noticeable relief smoothed her brow when she found the book she was looking for at the bottom of the pile. She opened it to a page marked with a frayed black satin ribbon and silently read the instructions. "Put the bowl in the center," she said in her usual bossy tone, an indication she'd recovered rather swiftly from her fear of Fate.

Jessie did as she was told. "Next?"

Darcy nudged her chin at the wall. "Sit over there. In fact, all of you sit over there. I need space to work."

Fate was the only one who didn't move.

"Or not," Darcy grumbled. She raised her arm and snapped her fingers without looking at Fate. "I'll be needing the alicorn now."

When Fate didn't respond, Darcy tilted her head to look at her. "It's up to you, but I can't do the spell without it."

Several long seconds passed before Fate reluctantly pulled the alicorn from its sheath and placed her prized new weapon in Darcy's hands. When Fate released the hilt, Darcy nearly dropped the horn. "Whoa, this thing's way heavier than you made it look."

Darcy set the alicorn down in front of her knees, referring to the pages of the book again. "Okay, here we go." Taking a deep breath, Darcy spoke a command, lighting the candles all at once.

Taking the marshwort, she held it over the bowl, whispering the first verse of the spell as she stripped the heart-shaped leaves from the stems and let them fall into the bowl. Upon speaking the second verse, she poured the thistle seed oil over the leaves.

Violet misty tendrils snaked from the mixture, thickening as she recited the mysterious, whispered words of magic. The mist rose, gathering into a bright purple cloud that hovered several feet above the bowl.

Lifting the alicorn with some effort, Darcy leaned forward and spoke the third verse with full volume. Her arms shook with the strain of holding the sharp point of the alicorn poised over the bowl. On the last word, she stabbed the horn into the mixture.

Black ribbons of smoke exploded from the bowl, threading through the purple mist, a sentient shadowy form that chilled Finn. He rose to his feet as the ominous shape swarmed over the case holding Eustace. In an instant, the shadow seeped through the glass, absorbing the glittering gold dust preserving Eustace's body.

Unable to see the body beneath the thickening darkness, Finn glanced at Fate, wondering if she too had sensed the same disturbing emanations that now filled him with a sense of doom. Fate stood still, her stance tense as she waited for her deepest desire to come true.

He didn't have to probe with his senses to know she was frightened of what the shadow was doing to her father. Finn yearned to take her into his arms. To hold her close in case her hopes were brutally dashed within the next few seconds.

The sound of glass cracking pulled his attention back to the case. Cracks were fast spidering up the sides and over the top. Glass shattered in a sudden explosion of glittering shards. Finn turned from the shower, wincing from cuts drilling into his back.

All was quiet as he slowly turned back to the case. Eustace lay still on the platform, his body completely unscathed.

Jessie had taken the same hit to her backside as Finn. Darcy stood from where she'd been sitting, one arm embedded with chips of glass and bleeding. She'd managed to protect her face, save for the top of her forehead, which dripped red from a long shard sticking into bone. One side of Brune's body, mainly her arm and shoulder bore the same multiple injuries as the rest of them.

Fate, on the other hand, hadn't been touched by a single splinter. The unearthly armor she wore had protected her. Even her face, which should have received at least one knick. She strode over to the case. Broken glass ground beneath her boots as she absently toppled the brass bowl, spilling its charred ingredients over the silk cloth.

Reaching for Eustace's hand, she stared at his face, and then placed her palm over his chest. "He's breathing." Her voice was shaky, childlike. Gone was the detached tone she'd displayed minutes earlier.

Finn rushed to her side, startled when Eustace opened his eyes. Jessie, Darcy and Brune rushed in around the other side, each silent and no doubt wondering what exactly the spell had awakened.

Eustace stared at the ceiling, blinking sleepily.

"Dad?" Fate leaned over him, drawing his gaze to her face.

"Doodles." His voice was a dry croak.

Tears filled Fate's eyes. "I'm here."

"Was I asleep?" he rasped.

"You could say that," she said through a faint sob.

Eustace gave her a stiff pat on the head as she buried his face in his shirt and cried. "What's wrong?" He looked at Finn and then at the others. "Why are you all standing around in my..." His confusion deepened. "This isn't my room. Where am I?"

Nobody seemed to want to answer him and Fate was too emotional to do the explaining.

"You're probably thirsty." Finn had no idea where to begin. "Can we get you some water?"

Fate straightened and wiped her eyes. "Yes, somebody grab some water."

"I'll get it." Jessie ran out of the room.

Eustace struggled to rise. Finn took an elbow, startled by how cold his skin was. Brune moved in on the other side and helped. The moment she touched Eustace's arm she locked eyes with Finn, visibly disturbed and repulsed.

Jessie rushed back in with the water sloshing over the lip of a tall glass.

Eustace took a sip and handed it back. "Thank you."

Fate shuddered with another flood of tears.

"Why are you crying?" Eustace asked.

Finn noticed a hint of irritation in his flat tone, but chalked it up to disorientation.

Fate opened her mouth to speak, but all she could do was cry and shake her head.

Eustace frowned sternly. "Would someone tell me why my daughter is so upset?"

"What was your last memory, sir?" Finn asked, hoping to figure out a safe starting point. The last thing he wanted to do was shock Eustace by beginning with how he'd been dead for months.

Eustace stared blankly into space. "I remember a cake and candles."

He looked at Fate. "It was for your birthday. Not the actual day, but I wanted to–"

"I can't do this!" Fate backed away then turned and ran from the room.

Her abrupt departure did nothing to change Eustace's wooden expression.

"I should go after her," Finn offered.

"Yes, go," Jessie encouraged him. "We'll explain everything." She looked at Eustace with reluctance.

Grateful to be relieved of the difficult task, Finn chased after Fate. She wasn't outside the door so he raced into the crowded halls, grunting apologies as he bumped into warriors preparing for war in a hurried but orderly manner. He was once again reminded of Rudwor's plight and the urgent desire to rescue his friend.

"One problem at a time, boyo," he muttered to himself.

Tracking Fate down had to be his first priority. Resurrecting Eustace was supposed to have given her much needed solace and balance. Finn understood the strong emotional reaction, but he hadn't expected Fate to flee from her feelings after all she'd done to bring Eustace back.

Had Fate sensed the shadow in the spell before it entered Eustace's body? Finn clenched his fists as he marched through the cramped corridor, no longer seeing the warriors he passed. Distrust burned at the forefront of his mind. He couldn't shake the feeling he'd participated in necromancy, the darkest of arts, which went against the natural order of the universe.

Finn shook his head, wanting desperately to clear an avalanche of doubts. The deed was done. He had to trust the resurrection spell was not of a sinister ilk.

He stormed past Fate's suite and had to stop and turn back. Rapping on the door, he waited impatiently, each second ticking by all too slowly. At last Fate's grandmotherly chamber bot cracked the door open. "Is she here?" he asked.

"She wishes not to be disturbed," the bot replied with a perpetually kind smile.

"Fate!" he shouted. "I'm coming in." He stepped forward but the chamber bot placed a hand on his chest, a blockade that did not budge no matter how much strength he put behind it.

"Let him in," Fate mumbled from somewhere within the dim interior of her suite.

"Welcome. You may enter," the bot said cheerfully and stepped aside.

Finn walked in to find Fate curled on her bed hugging a pillow. Ananke's gleaming armor was nowhere to be seen and Fate was dressed in a simple cotton shift, looking ready for a night's sleep despite the early morning hour. She glanced at him with red, puffy eyes. He couldn't remember the last time he'd seen her girlish, vulnerable side.

All of Finn's defenses fell away as he sat on the edge of the bed. "I've been worried about you, love."

She stared back, tired and worn, but there was something else in her eyes that unsettled him. Something sharp, pointed.

"Talk to me. I'm here to listen," he told her.

"I don't feel like talking." Her voice was muffled behind the pillow but he caught the resentment in her tone.

"Beg to differ with you on that. I'm sensing you have much to say, and to me in particular."

Fate sat up suddenly, her auburn hair falling down over her face in long wavy strands, framing angry eyes. "Not everything is about you. I have other things on my mind, such as watching my dad come back from the dead."

Finn nodded. "That's why I came. I know you're overwhelmed and I didn't want you to be alone."

"I'm *not* alone."

Finn made a cursory glance around the room. "I don't see anyone else here besides the chamber bot. Do you want me to get Jessie?"

"No. I don't need anyone else."

"What about Eustace? I know you need him."

Tears brimmed in her eyes. "I do." Her voice was small again, devoid of anger.

Finn gently brushed back a stray lock shadowing her face. She was beautiful, even in all her messiness. "What are you afraid of, love?"

"That he's not the same Eustace I used to know." Her chin quivered. "Is it me or does he seem different?"

"Aye, he's not himself right now," Finn agreed ruefully. "But you have to remember what he's been through. It could be awhile before he's back to normal."

Fate nodded frantically. "Time, he just needs time to heal." She crumpled into tears again.

"Fate, what is it you're not saying? I won't judge. You can tell me."

"What if the spell doesn't last? I can't go through losing him all over again. I just can't. I think it's better if I stay away until we know for sure."

That was the last thing Finn had expected to hear, but he didn't want to press her. Not while she was in a state of distress. Instead, he drew her into his arms.

There was no resistance this time. Fate collapsed against him, trembling, sobbing into his shoulder. Finn held her close, kissing the top of her head, stroking her back. Time ceased as he whispered soothing words of love into her ear. He had no idea how long he held her, only that he could hold her forever without ever tiring.

Fate finally settled in his arms and met his gaze with a longing he hadn't seen since before they'd traveled to Feldoril Forest. Her eyes dropped to his mouth. Licking her full lips, she lifted her face, waiting for his kiss. Craving the sweet taste of her mouth, Finn leaned in.

Their lips met, gently at first, then deepened into something ravenous, needful. Fate's hunger matched his own. Pressing her body against his, she slid her arms around his waist, raking her fingers over his back. Pain knifed across his backside. Finn drew in a sharp breath, unable to stop himself from jerking free of her embrace.

"What's wrong?" Fate's breath came in short bursts as she stared wide-eyed at a stain of red on her hands. "Are you bleeding?"

"I'm fine. I have a few wee cuts, is all."

Fate jumped from the bed to have a look at his back and gasped.

"I'm sure it looks worse than it is."

"Finn, there's glass sticking out of your back and your shirt's drenched in blood." She gestured to the chamber bot. "Bring warm water, clothes and bandages. Oh, and scissors and tweezers. Lay down on your stomach," she instructed.

Finn did as he was told. The chamber bot trundled over with a tray and set it on the bedside table. Fate carefully peeled his shirt away from his skin. Finn bit down on the pain as she used the scissors to cut the shirt off his body. The bot delivered a bowl of steaming water and carried the bloody shirt away.

Fate dipped one of the cloths into the hot water before wringing it over his back. The warm water spilled over his skin, stinging the raw cuts. Finn clenched his jaw as she slowly rinsed his back.

"Here comes the worst part," she warned.

"You mean besides leaving that kiss unfinished?"

"Tweezing these glass shards, silly. Do you want something to bite down on?"

"I can handle it. Ouch!"

"You were saying?"

Finn tensed through the next string of painful extractions.

"How'd this happen?" she asked as she dropped another piece of glass on the tray.

Finn frowned. "When Eustace's glass case exploded."

Fate didn't say anything.

"Don't you remember?"

"Sure... there was a lot going on." Her voice wavered and he knew she was lying.

He thought about mentioning she was the only one in the room who hadn't been touched by the explosion but decided against it. She was closer to being herself more than ever. It wouldn't do to upset her with concerns of Ananke's emergence.

"That's the last one," Fate said. The small piece of glass clinked on the tray as she set the tweezers down and reached for a jar. Finn relaxed as she dabbed ointment on the cuts.

She rose from the bed, lightly nudging him to sit so she could wrap a wide roll of bandages around his torso. He breathed in the flowery scent of her hair each time she had to move close to reach around his waist. When she finished, she stood back to view her work. "Hmm, not bad for someone who has no idea what she's doing. How does it feel to be almost mummified?"

"Better than you'd expect." Finn reached for her waist and pulled her onto his lap.

She smiled. "Are you trying to tell me something?"

"Aye, love, I am." Finn swept her down onto the bed, allowing every nagging thought to fall away as he let go of all his concerns and surrendered to this rare and precious moment in time.

37
GODLIKE POWERS ASIDE

"WAKE, MY DAUGHTER. *There is work to do.*"

Ananke's voice startled Fate from a deep, peaceful slumber. Blinking away the sleep, she stretched and wriggled, holding still when her hip grazed Finn's leg. She smiled, remembering the past few blissful hours they'd enjoyed before falling asleep together. Rolling onto her side, Fate propped her chin on her hand to stare at his face. Serene as an angel and oh so irresistible. She leaned in to kiss him but stopped when Ananke spoke again.

"*Do not disturb him. Slip away before he wakes.*"

Fate refused to move. All she wanted was to stay nestled next to Finn, where she didn't have to face the world and its troublesome complexities.

"*Beautiful boys are pleasurable diversions, but you must beware of human desires. They are beneath you. Remember his lies and how he left you in the swamp.*"

The resentment Fate had decided to leave unexpressed reasserted itself. Talking about it was best. Finn must have had good reason for what he'd done. She just needed to hear it from him.

"*He will only lie to you again.*"

Sorrow and anger swelled in Fate's chest. She didn't want to believe Ananke, but her mother spoke the truth. Finn had lied about Eustace, the most hurtful lie anyone could tell. She thought she'd forgiven him, but her heart still ached from the bruises of those lies. It didn't matter that Eustace was alive again. Life was too fragile to trust anymore. Better to remain distant from the human attachments that made her weak.

Fate let out a heavy sigh and slid out from beneath the sheets. Taking care not to make a sound, she dressed, tiptoed across the room and shut the door softly behind her.

Warriors of Beldereth and Eldunough stopped to tip their heads in respect as she passed by. Mildly puzzled by this, Fate acknowledged them by doing the same as she headed for the warded barrier. It wasn't until she glanced down and saw the white-gold armor that she knew why. Hippolyta's girdle gleamed at her waist, lighting the sculpted metal with an ethereal radiance that commanded attention. The alicorn sword was back in place, sheathed over her shoulder. An impressive weapon the warriors admired with open envy.

The sentinels posted to defend the barrier stepped aside for Fate. She stopped in front of the massive wall of mangled metal and debris, magically fused together to keep the enemy out. Tilting her head, Fate listened, hearing the far away rhythmic beat of sledgehammers on the other side of the solid barrier.

"Fate, what are you doing here? You should be with Eustace. He's been asking about you." Brune waved a hand in front of Fate's face. "Hello?"

Fate shifted her gaze to Brune, fully suited in her Keep Guardian uniform and wearing a look of concern, bordering on fear.

"How is he?" Fate asked.

"In shock," Brune replied. "A perfectly natural reaction to being told he's been dead for the last several months."

Fate's throat tightened with lingering grief. "I do want to see him," she confessed, caught off guard by a moment of weakness. Ananke pushed to the forefront. "Later though. After I deal with the Serpens."

Brune's gaze swept over Fate's armor. "All on your own and without a word of warning to those of us who've been strategizing counter attacks?"

Fate hesitated, unsure of how to answer that. Ananke spoke for her, through her. "Do you doubt what I can do?"

Brune folded her arms. "I know full well what you're capable of, but defending the Keep is my job."

"And mine."

"Not anymore." Small beads of sweat glistened on Brune's upper lip. Fate focused in on Brune's heartbeat. Her pulse was hammering.

"Do you deny you need my help?"

"I've been handling it."

A Beldereth warrior, who stood a few feet behind Brune, stepped forward. It was Meara. Fate had made friends with many Beldereth warriors during her time there, but all she remembered of Meara was how closely she'd danced with Finn at the coronation ball. "Brune, we can use whatever help we can get," Meara pressed.

Brune stiffened. "We need allies, not rogue soldiers."

Meara slid a hand over Brune's shoulder and spoke softly in her ear, an intimate gesture Fate noted with curious surprise. "Better to work together than separately. The generals are gathering in the sanctuary. Fate should join us."

"Fine," Brune conceded. She turned on her heel. "Let's go."

"*STAY.*"

When Brune noticed Fate didn't follow, she turned back. "Well?"

"Go ahead. I'm right behind you. I just need a moment." Fate gestured with a casual wave of her hand.

Suspicious, Brune stared at Fate without moving. Meara tugged on her arm. "Come on Brune, what trouble can she get into before the meeting?"

"Plenty," Brune argued as Meara pulled her down the hall.

Fate waited for them to disappear from sight before turning back to the barrier. Fixing a hard stare on the wall, she cast her senses outward, scanning the other side. Robed men stood in a half circle, facing the barrier, reciting sinister incantations. Dark utterings of corrupt energy issued past rotten teeth and black tongues. Smoke snaked from their ugly mouths, smothering the metal, decaying the structure, and making it easier for the Serpen knights to pulverize the brittle metal into dust.

Ananke's hatred for sorcerers filled Fate's mouth with acidic bile. She swallowed it down, making the hatred her own.

Fate rearranged the atoms of the barrier and opened a tunnel swirling with loose particles of glinting matter. She strode into the twisted jungle of solid metal as easily as moving through a thick flurry of snowflakes. When she reached the other side, she unsheathed the alicorn sword, shearing through the veil of black magic, its touch shredding the corrosive spell-rich smoke into harmless specs.

The sorcerers retreated into the corridor's deepest shadows, making room for the Serpen knights to charge at Fate. Time shifted around her. She streaked through space, while their movements slowed to the point of looking like they trudged underwater as they sought to strike her with their broadswords.

Rage ignited in her belly. Her core flared bright crimson as the bloodlust of Ares and Ananke's fury pulsed hot in her veins. Fate weaved between the Serpens faster than they could detect, piercing the alicorn through torsos, plunging deep until ribs and spines scraped against the horn. Blood sprayed from the holes as she yanked the spike from their bodies and speared the next knight and the next.

They stumbled backward in pain, bewildered by the blackened holes fast growing larger. Within seconds of the alicorn's rotting touch, the men transformed into desiccated husks that disintegrated into a burst of ashen flakes. Clouds of dark specks scattered as their armored skeletons collapsed to the floor in broken heaps.

Ananke's power expanded, directing Fate's attention back to the Serpen sorcerers. They'd come out of the shadows and were pressing forward, flinging black magic curses that slithered around her like wraiths of death.

Fate sliced the alicorn through the swarming specters, chilled by their icy touch. Malignant faces with black pits for eyes shrieked at her, surrounding her in a wall of concentrated evil, filling her head with terror. Flailing with her sword, Fate tried to beat them back but they were unaffected. Flesh and blood. That she knew how to destroy, but these things were made of smoke and malice.

"*Fear not, my daughter. Force is useless on this level. You must use power. My power.*"

Fate opened to what Ananke offered, allowing the power to flow through her, a cleansing flood that dissolved her fears and cleared her mind. Finally able to think, she looked past the malicious wraiths and fixed her sights on the sorcerers.

"*What would you have me do to them, my daughter?*"

"Remove their black tongues so I can get close to them."

The words were no sooner spoken, when all at once the row of sorcerers went rigid, their wizened mouths gaping in horror. Fate closed the space between them faster than it took her to intend the movement. The sorcerers squirmed, shrinking from her as they mouthed unintelligible sounds, no longer able to speak their foul magic into the air.

Repulsed by their presence, Fate struck them down with the alicorn, as effortless as toppling a row of bowling pins. Their wizened faces shriveled inward as they swiftly crumbled in on themselves, leaving behind piles of black robes amidst a flurry of ashen flecks.

"*Time to get what we came for.*"

Fate flung her awareness over the Serpen occupied residential suites, probing every long, winding hall, every bedchamber all the way to the sparring arena. Other than where she stood, there wasn't an inch of space that a Serpen knight was not present. They'd used their dragons to fly as many knights as they could up into the Keep's ring.

She closed her eyes and cast her senses wider, enraged to discover they'd been raiding the Keep surface. Several hundred vaults had been forced opened. There was no telling what sort of objects of magic they'd stolen. Her bloodlust surged, triggering a desire to rampage.

"*Patience. Destinies are decided in right time. Focus.*"

Fate withdrew her awareness from the Keep surface, questing for what she had come for. At last, she found him on the opposite end. Locked in the dark, chained, hungry and furious. Thousands of Serpen knights stood between them but this was of no matter.

Picturing the shackles on his wrists and ankles, Fate imagined them gone, catching the smell of iron in the same instance. She opened her eyes to darkness.

A startled shuffle in the room did nothing to break her concentration. "Who's there?"

Fate ignored the question and brought the sanctuary to mind–the large, rectangular table with its heavy wooden top and the curved bronze walls lined with bookcases. Brune stood at the head of the table, facing Beldereth and Eldunough's highest-ranking officers.

"We need more defenses in the air before we can strike," Brune said. "There are too many dragons. Does anyone know if the hawk rider we sent with a message for help from the Eldunough Islands has returned yet?"

An Eldunough officer shook his head. "We should have heard by now. I fear the messenger may not have made it past the–" He stiffened when he saw Fate appear behind Brune.

Brune turned around to see what he and all the others were staring at. "Fate? Where'd you come–" Her gaze moved to Rudwor, who was pale with nausea and gripping his barreled chest like someone suffering a heart attack.

His officers hurried to his side to help him sit down. Rudwor looked around the sanctuary, bedraggled and disoriented. "How...?"

Finn stormed through the door, tense and upset. "Has anyone seen–" He fell silent when he saw his friend. "Rudwor, you escaped!" He rushed over to the king, looking him over with concern. "How do you feel?"

Rudwor smoothed a palm greasy with grime over his bald spot. "Like a bog troll dunked me in swamp water after it danced on my spine."

Finn smiled wryly. "Aye, you look it. And smell it." He patted Rudwor on the shoulder. "Good to see you all the same."

Rudwor rubbed the chafed skin of his wrists and winced.

"How bad was it?" Finn asked.

"Remember the Bane?"

"A tough lot, thanks to that savage chieftain of theirs." Finn winked, remembering the beating he'd suffered when the Bane had taken him to beg for Rudwor's mercy.

Rudwor grinned. "Aye, well the Serpens make the Bane seem like cuddly kittens."

Finn nodded solemnly. "How'd you make it out?"

"No idea." Rudwor looked truly puzzled. "One minute I was there in the dark and the next I was here."

"It was Fate," Brune said.

Finn scanned the room. His confused gaze skipped over Fate before flicking back with a startled expression. He'd obviously assumed she was one of the other officers dressed in full armor. When she stepped out from behind them, he took in her glimmering armor and his green eyes filled with alarm.

"So that's where you went off to." He didn't bother to hide his disappointment.

Rudwor eyed her warily. "So it's you I have to thank for getting me out of that fix." His face softened with appreciation as he tilted his head in her direction. "Thank you, lass."

"You're welcome," Fate replied coolly as she glanced at Finn.

Rudwor stood and arched his back with a pained grimace. "I hate to be rescued and run, but you'll have to excuse me. I'm told I require a hot bath. Something my aching back will welcome."

"Aye, I'll check in on you later," Finn told him.

Rudwor trudged across the room with two of his officers ready to catch him in case he tipped over. "Much later, laddie. I'll be busy soaking up the sympathies of some female companionship for the next few days." He threw Finn a mischievous grin as he glanced at the two beautiful women aiding him.

Finn's amused smile vanished when he looked at Fate. "We need to talk. In private."

Ananke staunched the irresistible tug Fate felt to go to him. "*Refuse. We have more important matters to attend to.*"

Fate shook her head. "It'll have to wait." The hurt in Finn's eyes knifed her in the chest. "I'm here to discuss plans for defending the Keep."

"I'll stay and help then." Finn clenched his jaw as he stepped up to the table. "Anyone care to fill me in?"

"We need reinforcements in the sky," Fate stated. "To distract the dragons when we make our first strike, both here inside the Keep and on the ground."

Brune gave her a sharp look, but didn't press the issue of who was in charge.

"I can help with that," Finn offered. "If you pull the dragons away from here, I'll summon a sandstorm that'll hold them long enough to give troops a good running start."

Brune nodded. "I like it, but we'd have to dangle enough tantalizing bait to get all eight dragons to abandon their positions."

"If you're thinking of hawk riders to do that, there are not enough left," an Eldunough officer countered. "To do that, we'd need the entire legion from across all the islands of Eldunough. Even if we could get word to Prince

Kelare, he would never allow the islands to be left completely unprotected to defend a foreign land."

"Maybe you should ask Prince Kelare before you speak for him." Fate stared at the man, mildly taken aback as Ananke continued to speak for her. "His answer might surprise you if he saw the Keep and its countless treasures of powerful magic for himself. Would he really want all that power to end up in the hands of the Serpen race?"

The officer frowned. "I can promise you, he would not. The Serpens are an age-old enemy of Eldunough."

Ananke's satisfaction flowed through Fate. "Hawk riders combined with all the desert fleets of airships surrounding the Keep will be more than enough to attract the dragons."

Brune let out a frustrated, derisive laugh. "Biraktar will *never* answer our call after the massive loss they took in the war."

Ananke presented Fate with a flash of Biraktar and the impressive number of new fleets they'd built over the last several months. "Biraktar will answer the call."

Brune crossed her arms and glared at Fate. "All conjecture without the heads of each empire present."

"Easily remedied." Ananke's power swelled within Fate, propelling her awareness into the ether, rushing swiftly across the sprawling dunes, splitting off in two parts. One to rush across the seas until the air grew moist over dense jungles. The other arched skyward, sheering through clear skies until she dove into the misty clouds of ranemist surrounding Biraktar and phased through the pearlescent walls of the royal white palace.

The alluring face of a flaxen-haired prince came into view. He was sparring with his mentor, his gray eyes stormy as he moved with lethal grace. His youthful features were mesmerizing in their beauty, reminding Fate of someone else she'd seen before. She remembered Princess Kaura, realizing this was her brother in the same moment Ananke ripped him from his home, stretching his very essence through space and time.

Simultaneously, Fate caught the dark-eyed gaze of Azrael's father and the look of bewilderment on his face as Ananke snatched him from Biraktar.

Both appeared within the sanctuary, upsetting the room of already on-edge officers. They backed away from her as the king of Biraktar and the prince of Eldunough struggled to regain their equilibrium and orient themselves.

The king's face was ashen as he glanced around. He was the first to express his outrage when he saw Fate. He shouted in his native language with no one present to understand him other than Fate. She knew the meaning of the words, not with the aid of a transmodulator to interpret his words, but because Ananke understood all languages.

"What is the meaning of this?" he shouted at Fate. "I will have you executed for this!"

"Calm yourself," she replied in his native tongue.

He was visibly struck by her shocking brand new ability to speak his language, though this did not silence him. "Where is Azrael? What have you done with my son?"

Ananke's power reached through the walls and pulled Azrael forward, all while maintaining her full attention on the king. When Azrael appeared in front of them, he stood and wavered in place, his face still gray from the poisoning he'd been slowly recovering from. The king hurried over to Azrael, catching him as he slumped weakly at the waist.

Ananke noticed Fate's fierce concern for his health. *Do you wish him healed?*

Yes.

So be it.

Ananke amplified the affection in Fate's heart, using the force of her emotion to stream healing into Azrael's body.

He lifted his head, his blue eyes filled with wonder as he stared back at Fate. He straightened and stood tall with renewed strength while his father barraged him with questions. "Do not worry, father. I am well."

"Do you know what this woman did?" his father shouted.

"Her name is Fate," Azrael corrected him. "Please refer to her with respect."

"She belongs to *him*!" The king jabbed a finger in Finn's direction. "You lower yourself by remaining in the presence of the woman who shamed you and our family."

"Father!" Azrael's voice held a razor's edge that stopped the king's rants. He looked at Fate. "Why have you brought my father here? Please tell me this is not about revenge."

Strangely, Fate held no animosity toward the king who'd diminished her to a prize object to be won in the trials. "We're in need of Biraktar to rejoin the alliance." She glanced at Prince Kelare. "As well as Eldunough. We require all the hawk riders you can spare."

Azrael translated this to his father, while she watched the prince's reaction. Prince Kelare's composed expression proved unreadable as he stared back at her. One of his officers moved to his side to whisper the reasons for the request. Alarm registered on his face ever so slightly, before swiftly returning to that of cool detachment.

"I will see this Serpen invasion for myself before agreeing to any further alliance." Prince Kelare gestured for his officers to lead the way.

The door closed behind them and Azrael's father launched into another tirade. "Biraktar will *never* be your ally!" His features pinched together into tight, implacable lines. "My people have not yet recovered from the loss we took in the last war you brought down upon us. Yet now you expect to take more from them? How dare you!"

Fate opened her mouth to counter with what Ananke had shown her, but Azrael held up a hand to stop her. "I will speak to him," he assured her. "Come with me, father."

The sanctuary fell quiet with the prompt removal of Azrael's irate father.

Brune sighed wearily. "Well, I think we can call this meeting adjourned for now. We'll resume once we have their decisions."

The officers cleared the sanctuary. Meara glanced at Brune expectantly. "Are you coming?"

Brune started to smile, but her expression turned serious and she shook her head. "Not yet. I have a few things to go over with Fate."

"As do I," Finn added.

Fate tensed, knowing she was about to be ganged up on.

Brune looked from Finn to Fate and narrowed her eyes. "All right, I'm just going to say it. Who are we talking to? Fate or Ananke?"

Finn nodded uneasily in agreement.

"It's me, guys." Fate smiled uneasily.

"Then what's with the glowing armor?" Brune swept her arms at Fate's impressive gear. "And the godlike powers you're throwing around like it's as normal as sneezing?"

Fate had no answers that would satisfy them. Instead, she focused inward and reassembled the armor into a regular Keep uniform, with the exception of the alicorn sword holstered to her back. "There. No more glow-in-the-dark armor. Feel better now?"

Brune stared back grimly. "The very fact that you shifted pure matter into something else in under two seconds is equally worrisome. What's worse is you think it's okay."

"Aye, this isn't normal, Fate." Finn took a step closer but maintained a certain distance.

Seeing him hold back hurt more than she wanted to admit. "I am very much the person you know and love," she said to Finn. "And hate, in your case, Brune."

"I don't hate you," Brune admitted. "You terrify me."

Brune's harsh declaration bit hard. Fate searched Finn's eyes. "Do you feel the same way?"

Finn glanced away and swallowed. When he finally met her gaze again, she dreaded what he would say. "I'll always love you. That will never change, but you're not the same person I fell in love with. Godlike powers aside, the lass I knew would never stay away from her father upon his miraculous return. Not after grieving his loss the way you did. I know how torn up you've been. Honestly, Fate. What are you doing here, throwing your weight around when you should be with your father right now?"

Tears swam across Fate's vision, distorting everything around her. Finn wasn't wrong. She'd lost all sight of what was most important to her. Eustace was alive. It was all she'd wanted and now that he was back, she'd done nothing but avoid him.

"*There's a time and a place for everything, my daughter. Now is the time for war. Your father will understand this once we've shown the world the hammer of justice.*"

"No! You're wrong!" Fate cried out, not knowing whom she was arguing with. Was it Finn or Ananke? Desperate to escape the confusion, she closed her eyes and surrendered to the vast nothingness of the ether and left the sanctuary far behind.

38
DEAD MAN'S ASHES

FATE'S ABRUPT VANISHING ACT left Finn gutted. How could she switch from the passionate lover she'd been the night before, to this cold, distant stranger focused only on war? The astounding powers she'd demonstrated with such ease was simply too sudden. How could Fate not see that Ananke was behind all this?

The answer caved in on him, heavy and painful. Fate couldn't see it because her soul was being absorbed into Ananke, slowly but surely. The awful truth squeezed out the hope in his heart.

"We need to do something about her. And fast." Brune echoed his thoughts as she leaned her back against the table and stared at the ceiling. "It's time to go after Dantalion's Key."

"I don't know about that anymore. We have no idea how long it'll take to find the key in the hell dimension. Given how quickly Fate's changing, I can't help wondering if there'll be anything left of her to save by the time we return. If we return."

Brune's frown was filled with concern. "Are you giving up on her? Because if *you're* giving up, then all is lost for sure."

Finn's throat tightened with enough sorrow to finish him.

Brune's face smoothed with compassion. "I get it. We all hit a breaking point. But will you be the glass that shatters, or will you be the sword that's forged into steel?"

As bad as he felt, he knew this wasn't the time to give into defeat. "I'll talk to the others." He strode to the door, turning back as he opened it. "Thanks."

Brune's encouraging words lingered as Finn headed for the library. Fate needed him, whether she realized it or not. The promise he'd made her before they'd left for Feldoril Forest rushed to the forefront.

I'll be by your side for as long as there's life in me.

How could he live with himself if he didn't hold true to his word? Giving up wasn't an option.

Finn pushed through the library door and stopped in his tracks, startled by an unexpected sense of déjà vu. Gathered around one of the many large tables placed in the middle of the enormous library was the entire gang. Sithias and Gerdie were arguing and pointing vehemently at the pages of an open book. Darcy was off to one side of the table sitting behind stacks of large tomes and scrolls. Jessie sat resting her chin on her hand, outwardly bored with whatever book she'd been assigned to read, watching the many-armed librarian bots spidering to higher levels in search of whatever titles they'd been sent to retrieve.

And then there was Eustace, bent over a thick scroll, flattened out with the corners held down by books. He was so deeply engrossed in what he was studying he was the only one who didn't turn to see who'd entered, something Finn had grown used to from earlier times.

It was as if Eustace had never been gone. Finn could almost fool himself into thinking nothing had changed. But so much had changed. Starting with Fate.

Finn strode across the marble floor, wondering how to broach the subject without alarming Eustace about Fate's urgent condition. Jessie jumped from her seat, all too eagerly, and met Finn before he reached the table.

She steered him off to one side, glancing nervously over her shoulder at the others. "Where have you been?" Finn started to answer, but she was too impatient to let him speak. "We can't let Fate anywhere near Eustace."

"Wait. What?" Finn thought he was hearing things.

"There's something not right with him," Jessie whispered.

Finn glanced at Eustace, startled when he looked up from the scroll he'd been so completely absorbed in. Had he heard Jessie's whisper? Finn dismissed the thought as ridiculous. They were standing too far away for that to be possible.

Sithias and Gerdie brought a halt to their heated debate, each watching curiously. Darcy yawned and went back to reading.

Concerned about raising any suspicions, Finn waved and walked over to the table. "How are you feeling, sir?" Finn studied Eustace, noting his trademark tidy attire and neatly combed hair with some relief. His complexion was slightly chalky and there was a hint of shadow around his eyes, but Finn figured that was to be expected after being dead for months.

"I'd feel better if everyone would stop asking me that." Eustace's smile was restrained. "Did you find Fate? I thought you might've convinced her to come see me by now."

"Oh... I caught up with her but she has her hands full with the Serpen invasion. Not to worry though. She assured me she wants to come see you as soon as she's free." Finn held Eustace's gaze directly, hoping the man wouldn't sense the loose string of half-truths he'd been forced to spin.

"It's probably best." Eustace turned back to studying the scroll.

Finn couldn't have been more surprised. "Uh, why's that?" He waited for a response that never came.

Jessie scooted past Finn and sat down. "See what I mean?"

Sithias waved Finn over to the end of the table. "Eustace has picked up where he left off." He nudged his head meaningfully in Eustace's direction.

"Uh huh, we've been diggin' into all the old grimoires to get the whole scoop on the Great Duke of Hell before we go bargin' into his kingdom." Gerdie pointed a stubborn scowl at Sithias. "Only problem is we're missin' one of the books. But someone here keeps insistin' the grimoire is already on the list and to refer to the notes."

Sithias stooped low and pointed a frown back at her. "Copious notes that I took. Myself. Personally."

Gerdie shrugged. "As I keep sayin', I'd rather read through the grimoires–*myself, personally*–in case you missed somethin' important."

Sithias straightened, blinking with outrage. "Is that an insult? Because I feel insulted."

"It wasn't meant to be, I'm just bein' thorough like always."

"Fine then. I'll accept that as an apology."

Gerdie rolled her eyes.

Sithias took a deep breath, smiling politely upon restoring his dignity. "Back to the missing grimoire. I keep telling you, the one you want is part of a triptych, so it can't be missing. If anything, I'd say it's misplaced and all we have to do is locate it."

"It's not in the library," Gerdie insisted.

"It has to be."

"Can this wait?" Finn asked. More concerned with the worn, yellowed scroll filled with ancient text laid out before Eustace. "Is that the *Papyri Graecae Magicae* you told me about?" he asked Sithias.

"Why yesss, it's the recounting of Ananke's eons-old plan to create a vessel strong enough to hold her immense power."

"Good. It's a relief to know you're finalizing plans to retrieve Dantalion's Key."

"Has something more happened?" Jessie asked.

Finn glanced at Eustace and nodded. "It's best we move fast on this."

Jessie, Sithias and Gerdie all nodded back knowingly. Though Finn could see the questions they wanted to ask but weren't voicing.

Darcy rose from behind the towers of books stacked around her work area. "You can drop the cloak and dagger routine. I've already filled Eustace in on the latest about Fate, which is why he's decided to take the lead on the expedition into the hell dimension."

Jessie stood after a few seconds of shocked silence, which Finn shared. "That's news to me. When did this happen exactly? I've been with Eustace pretty much solid since yesterday."

"Does it really matter?" Darcy's flippant demeanor was more troublesome than usual, but Finn couldn't pinpoint why.

Eustace pulled his attention from the scroll. "As you know, speed is of the essence if we're going to succeed in freeing Fate of Hippolyta's girdle before Ananke's handhold becomes permanent. Darcy has found a way into the hell dimension and mapped out a direct path to Hadean's kingdom."

"Are you sure it's wise for you to go, sir?" Finn asked. "Shouldn't you wait to fully recover?"

Defiance transformed the calm surface of Eustace's expression into a mask of harsh lines. "My days of staying behind while others battle evil are over. I will be the one to put an end to this."

Unsettled by Eustace's uncharacteristic outburst, Finn decided not to argue. Clearly there would be no changing his mind. "Understood. When do we leave?"

"Immediately, but you won't be going," Eustace told him. "Darcy and I will handle this."

"No offense, sir, but I can't let you go without protection. You're going to need all the muscle you can get in there."

"He has protection," Darcy said. "Me."

"He needs more than a noob witch to protect him against a dimension rotten with demons," Finn argued.

"Who do you think controls demons?" Darcy pointed a thumb back at herself. "Witches. Demons have been the minions of witches since the dawn of time. Surely you're familiar with the concept."

"I agree with Finn," Sithias jumped in. "He should go. If anything were to happen to you again, Eustace, it will ruin Fate irretrievably."

Eustace looked from Sithias to Darcy. She gave him a nod before he continued. "I suppose it can't hurt to have Finn along."

"And me." Jessie moved in to stand next to Finn.

"No," Finn said, in unison with Eustace and Darcy.

Jessie frowned at Finn. "I get why they'd say no, but I can't believe you'd agree."

"I need you to stay close to Fate while we're away."

"You do know that's like trying to stay close to lightning, right?"

Finn stared back beseechingly.

"All right. I'll stay with her," she muttered.

"Thank you."

Gerdie waved her little arm back and forth from the other end of the table. "Um, I'd like to point out that I haven't finished my research. Wouldn't it be prudent to wait until it's complete?"

"It's complete, because *I've* done all the research." Darcy shoved her book of towers aside, lifted a canvas backpack from under the table and set it in front of her. She winked at Gerdie. "I was just giving you something to do."

"Something pointless to do? Do I look like a kid that needs to be given crayons to be kept busy?"

"Well, yeah, you do actually." Darcy snickered as she chose a few books from the stacks and stuffed them into the pack.

An unhappy expression settled on Gerdie's impish features. "Did you know about this?" she asked Sithias.

"No. Apparently, I was given crayons too."

Darcy waved them off. "Oh stop looking like I insulted your mothers."

Finn was stunned by how fast Darcy and Eustace were moving everything forward. "I know better than anyone the need for urgency, but this feels way too rushed. We haven't told Fate and Brune what we're planning."

"The whole point of going now is because Fate won't be expecting us to make the move this soon. You can't tell her, Finn," Darcy insisted. "Ananke knows everything Fate knows. The last thing Ananke wants is for us to take her carefully cultivated human vessel away from her."

Eustace stood calmly by, unaffected by the talk of Ananke's use of his daughter's body and mind. Finn knew Eustace to be a deeply caring father whose only priority in life had been to ensure Fate's safety and happiness. Eustace had never hidden his turmoil over Fate whenever she'd left to face danger in the past. So far all Finn noted from Eustace was an extreme swing between disturbing detachment and volatile anger. Neither of which characterized the man he'd come to know.

"What about Brune?" Finn asked. "She should know what we're planning to do."

"Nope." Darcy heaved the backpack off the table, slung the straps over her shoulders and walked in the direction of one of the library's many galleries, forcing the rest of them to follow.

"Why not?" Finn was growing increasingly unsure of Darcy's spur-of-the-moment plan of action.

"You just told us Fate–aka, Ananke–is more concerned about warring with the Serpens. It's the perfect distraction actually." Darcy smiled. "Except that means she'll be working closely with Brune, which is why we have to leave Brune out of the loop on this. Ananke can't catch a whiff of what's coming her way."

Darcy turned a corner into the spacious corridor. They passed by a myriad of galleries filled with beautiful paintings and statues, before arriving at a large archway closed off by two sliding doors at the very end.

The doors were plain and painted black, as though they'd been added hastily, if only to close off that particular section. A large circular lock inscribed with wards had been placed over the center where the two panels came together. Finn stared at the lock with trepidation, sensing immediately the lock was more of a seal to prevent the contents from escaping.

"What's inside?" he asked, his nerves on edge.

"A way station of sorts. Hold this." Darcy handed him her backpack.

Finn frowned as she dug through one of the front pockets. She drew out a bottle filled with dark, swirling mist and two silk pouches. "Hold out your hand," she instructed.

Finn reluctantly allowed her to pour a fine gray powder into his palm.

"Wipe that on your face," she told him, while doing the same.

Finn hesitated, then followed her instructions.

She tightened the string on the pouch and handed it to him. "Keep this on you in case what's on your face comes off."

He took the pouch and held the backpack out for Darcy to take.

"Too heavy for me. Be a gentleman and carry it for me." She smiled coyly, obviously forgetting the unattractive smears of gray powder on her face.

Finn sighed as he stuck his arms through the straps, adjusting the lengths when they dug tightly into his shoulders. "Care to let me in on what's in the pouch?" he grumbled as he shoved it into his pocket.

"Dead man's ashes."

"Ew!" Sithias made a face.

Gerdie looked at him like he was being a complete sissy. "What's so gross about that? It's not like she handed him a bag of blood to smear all over his face."

"Is there anything that bothers you?" Sithias stared back in horror.

"You tend to grow a thick skin after runnin' your whole life from a witch who wants to eat you for dinner and use your hide to make her clothes." Gerdie shook her head at him.

"Oh yesss, I forgot," Sithias mumbled.

"Why dead man's ashes?" Finn asked.

"Because only dead people can enter hell. Wearing the ashes is our ticket in. Plus it masks the scent of the living and should keep us hidden from demons." Darcy turned to face the doors, her hands poised to uncork the bottle of mist.

"Hold on a second." Finn moved in front of the doors. "You didn't give Eustace a pouch."

Darcy's gaze shifted to Eustace before settling back on Finn. "Do I really need to state the obvious?"

"Aye, you do. In fact, I demand to know exactly what you have planned. You're daft if you think I'll blindly follow you into a hell dimension without a clue about what to expect." He started removing the backpack.

Darcy put a hand on his arm to stop him. "Eustace doesn't need dead man's ashes. Not after being brought back from death."

"Well, that makes sense," Finn conceded. "But I still need to know the plan."

"I can't tell you that." Darcy's customary bravado dropped away. "This is uncharted territory for me too. All I can say is, I've accounted for every contingency I can think of, which are all stored in that backpack. So guard it with your life."

That wasn't the answer he'd hoped for. "And you're completely comfortable with this?" Finn asked Eustace.

"Let me put it this way," Eustace replied. "I'd feel entirely *uncomfortable* if I didn't do everything within my power to save my daughter from being annihilated."

"Aye, I feel the same." Finn heaved a sigh and stepped aside. "Lead the way."

Darcy moved in front of the seal, pulled the cork from the bottle and spoke. Finn picked out a few words of Latin, but most of the incantation was a crude, guttural language he didn't recognize. Each time she uttered one of those primitive-sounding words, he felt a chill against his skin that only increased his dread.

Dark mist snaked from the bottle and flowed over the seal. The engraved wards lit bright red as the large iron disc turned counter clockwise and cracked down the middle in a sharp, jagged line.

Prompted by a glance from Darcy, Eustace pried the doors open, revealing a gallery of paintings, each of gateways into horrifying worlds. Everything inside Finn screamed to turn and run the other way.

Sithias put a hand on Finn's shoulder. "Sir, please don't do thisss. My scales are quivering."

Finn mustered a brave grin. "That's tweed you're wearing, Sithias. Not scales."

"You know what I mean," Sithias fretted.

"I'm with Sithias," Jessie agreed. "My goose bumps have goose bumps."

Gerdie leaned to one side to see past Finn into the gallery with its frightful paintings. "I take it back, Sithias. My skin's not as thick as I thought it was." She hugged her arms and rubbed them. "Don't go in there, Finn."

"You know I have to," he told them. "I should've known to do this before we ever set foot in Feldoril Forest. Everything changed the second Fate killed the black unicorn. She's become an even more powerful vessel for Ananke now that she has the alicorn. It's only a matter of time before there's nothing left of her."

Jessie nodded solemnly. "Get in and get out. Hear me?"

"Aye, that's the plan."

Sithias patted Gerdie's head. "We'll be waiting right here for you."

Gerdie swatted his hand away. "Good luck. You're gonna need it."

"Thanks." Finn turned and followed Darcy and Eustace inside. The second he passed the threshold, an ill breeze raked past, icy and filled with rancor. Chills slithered along his spine like cold, clammy fingers. The stench of sulfur and decay hung on the air, twisting his insides into knots of terror. He turned to reconsider, but Eustace had already closed the doors.

39
DAEMONIUM CONJURATIO

SITHIAS WATCHED EUSTACE as he pulled the doors shut, more disturbed than ever by the emptiness in his expression. There was no mistaking Eustace had come back changed. He may have spoken the words of a loving father determined to protect his daughter, but they'd fallen flat and emotionless, with the exception of that angry outburst. The mean, vengeful look in Eustace's eyes was equally unsettling, if not more so.

Something was wrong with Eustace and Sithias was determined to find out what that was. Sooner, rather than later.

"Are you really gonna stand there until they get back?" Gerdie yelled from the other end of the corridor.

Startled from his thoughts, Sithias hurried to catch up with her and Jessie.

Jessie branched off toward the main entrance. "I'll check on Fate and do my best to steer her off course if she starts heading in your direction."

"Good luck with that," Sithias replied, distractedly.

"Yeah, she's gonna need it," Gerdie muttered. "How come you're so quiet?"

"I'm troubled about this whole thing. Eustace is... different. Darcy is... She's too..."

"Shifty?"

"Yesss, for lack of a better word. Did you know I offered to use the Words of Making to retrieve Dantalion's Key from the hell dimension and Darcy turned me down?"

"That doesn't make a lick of sense."

"That's what I thought! Until she started on about how badly the Words of Making could backfire."

"Like how?"

"Oh my, Darcy had a lengthy list of worst-case scenarios. The scariest was the possibility of a horde of demons descending upon us in search of the key. There was much talk of hellfire and utter destruction of everything we've come to know." Sithias fanned his face. "You know how imaginative I am. Her descriptions were chilling! That was quite enough for me to retract the offer."

Gerdie screwed up her face. "Who in their right mind would want to go into a hell dimension if they don't have to? She should've jumped at the offer. So why didn't she?"

"I'm flummoxed. I can't fathom a single reason why."

"I think it has something to do with that missing grimoire. Darcy got real slippery when I asked her where it was."

Gerdie signaled a Keep librarian. One of the tall, spindly bots turned around and climbed headfirst down from the top terrace to the main floor, ready for the next request. "Name the missing volume of the *Infernal Triptych*," she said.

The lights and copper coils behind the librarian's porcelain face blinked and zapped. "*Daemonium Conjuratio*, a compendium of demons and how to summon them."

"Where can I find the *Daemonium Conjuratio*?"

"The volume was borrowed and removed by..." The librarian's blinking lights and electrical zaps increased. After a few seconds of this, the bot tilted its head. "I have no record of a name."

Gerdie looked at Sithias. "What do you wanna bet it was Darcy who erased her name?"

"Do you think she has the grimoire in the backpack Finn's carrying?"

"Maybe, but I think we should do some snooping around in her room for clues."

"Really? Wouldn't that be–"

"Sensible? Come on, Sithias." Gerdie crossed her arms impatiently. "Do your thing and put us in her room. We need answers now!"

Sithias reached for a pencil, scribbled down a few quick words and spoke them aloud. "*Gerdie and I are now standing in Darcy's suite.*"

The bright surroundings of the library melted away into the dingy confines of Darcy's bedchamber. An abundance of black netting was draped around an unmade bed of garish, dark pink silk bedding. A chandelier hung over the center of the bed, its light dim and casting a ghostly glow through the sheer drapes. Black furry throw pillows littered the floor, along with dirty laundry thrown aside in wrinkled heaps. Dishes crusty with weeks-old food were strewn around the bed's perimeter. The odious smell of stale leftovers permeated the air.

"Oh!" Sithias plugged his nose. "I think we found our clues. Darcy is a slob of the worst kind."

"Is her chamber bot broken?"

“A likely guess is the bot’s gears eroded after Darcy had it sewing all this atrocious, overdone décor. It’s probably buried somewhere underneath this mound of dross.” Sithias backed up toward the door.

Gerdie picked her way past the debris and turned the corner into the sitting room. “Jackpot! Get in here, Sithias. You need to see this.”

“Do I have to?”

“*Yes.*”

The urgency in Gerdie’s tone propelled Sithias forward with enough curiosity to make him wade through Darcy’s junk. He was just about there, when the toe of his shoe caught on something, causing him to fall onto a pile of throw pillows. The one next to his face was embroidered with ‘Bite Me’ under a pair of fangs. “Bite me, indeed,” he grumbled as he rose from the floor.

“Would you stop messin’ around and come see this already,” Gerdie scolded.

“I was hardly mess–” Sithias froze in shock when he walked into the sitting room.

The furniture was pushed against the walls to make room for a ceremonial summoning circle. A pentacle drawn with crushed onyx sat in the center. The ground ebony gemstones glittered darkly in the light of five burning candles, each placed on the five points of the star.

In the far corner of the room was an altar to a robed statue with the face of a skeleton. Candles in tall, slender votives flickered amidst grinning skulls and bouquets of once-red roses, now shrunken and browned like dried blood. A framed picture of Darcy’s deceased boyfriend, Mason, was nestled in amongst the crumbling roses. The memorial would have been touching, if not for the grim deity the shrine appeared to be dedicated to.

“Do you recognize the spooky statue?” Sithias asked.

“That’s the Lady of Shadows, Santa Muerte. Praying to her ensures the dead are safely delivered into the afterlife.” Gerdie kneeled next to a stack of books to read the spines.

Sithias was becoming more confused by the minute. “Hmm, I didn’t think Darcy was the superstitious type.”

“Must be a family thing. She did say she was a fifth generation bruja.”

“I specifically remember her saying witch.”

“Bruja is Spanish for witch.” Gerdie moved to the next stack of books.

“I didn’t know Darcy was Spanish. She doesn’t have an accent.”

“She’s not from Spain. Her grandparents moved from Mexico. Darcy was born in Seattle, the same place Fate is from.”

"How do you know so much?"

"Darcy used to brag about her witch heritage and how powerful her family's line of brujas was when it was just me in the room. She was real lonely after Mason died and mostly talked about how miserable she was. But other times, when she was really into the books, she'd get boastful about witch stuff. I suppose she figured I wouldn't remember what she'd said once my memory was restored." Gerdie smiled slyly. "But I do. I remember it all."

Sithias spun around, excited by the thought of exploring an entire world he'd only heard about. "Did Darcy ever talk about the Space Needle? I would love to go there someday."

"Believe me, it's no big deal." Gerdie stood with her hands on her hips, looking frustrated. "Why would you want to go to a world with no real magic in it?"

"There's magic. A different kind of magic, but magic all the same."

"Like what?"

"Literature for one. Some of the greatest stories I've ever had the pleasure of shedding tears over have come from that world."

Gerdie waved her hand dismissively. "The Keep library's full of great literature."

"Some of which came from that world."

"You're not gonna let this go are you?"

Sithias shook his head.

"Fine. There's magic in the Space Needle. Feel better?"

Sithias didn't, but before he could say so, Gerdie was investigating a large book propped open on one of the chairs. "This is it!" she announced excitedly. "*Daemonium Conjuratio*, the missing grimoire."

He rushed over to have a look at the page the book was open to. When he read the title, his blood ran cold. "*How to Summon a Persian Shedreakai Demon.*"

Gerdie teetered in her fright, almost dropping the heavy tome onto one of the candles sitting next to her foot. Sithias caught hold of the book before it could fall and tip the candle over. There was no telling what catastrophes might befall them if they interrupted the spell before fully understanding what stage it was in.

"I can't believe this." Gerdie stared into space. "Darcy summoned Farouk. Why? I don't understand."

"Maybe it was a different Shedreakai demon she summoned."

Gerdie pointed at something in the middle of the pentagram. "Isn't that Farouk's hairbrush?"

Sithias gulped, remembering the many times he'd seen the small, mostly harmless fox-faced Farouk sitting in his cage grooming himself with that very brush. "She summoned Farouk." He trembled as he scanned the shadowy corners of the room. "Do you think he's in here?"

"Let me see the spell." Gerdie took the grimoire from his shaking hands and sat down on the floor with it. She ran her finger over the inked words, mouthing them silently until she reached the last line of the incantation. She lifted her gaze from the page, more puzzled than ever. "Huh. I thought there'd be a way to control Farouk in this spell, but there isn't. Workin' with demons is dangerous enough, but doin' it without using a leash and muzzle is suicidal."

"Do you think Darcy has a death wish?" Sithias glanced at Mason's picture. "I know she's been terribly grief stricken over Mason's death. She must have plummeted into abject despair. That would explain these deplorable living conditions."

"Maybe. Except if that was her wish, she'd be dead."

Sithias started to nod in agreement, when he was suddenly struck with a terrifying thought. "What if Darcy isn't Darcy? What if we've been working with Farouk this entire time?"

Equally frightened, Gerdie drew her knees close to her chest and hugged her legs. "Why'd you have to go and put that in my head?"

"We have to find a way to warn Finn and Eustace!" Reaching into the breast pocket of his tweed blazer, he pulled out his notepad and pencil.

Gerdie jumped to her feet. "What do you think you're doin' with that?"

"I have to go after them! Tell them Darcy is Farouk!"

Gerdie snatched the pencil from his hand. "Hold on. We don't know that for sure."

"We don't know she's *not* Farouk either." Sithias reached for his pencil but Gerdie held it out of reach. "Give me that!"

She raced around to the other side of the pentagram. "No, I need to think about this before you go makin' a mess of things."

Sithias stomped his foot. "I'm trying to fix things, thank you very much."

Gerdie chewed on the eraser, deep in thought as she stared at the hairbrush sitting in the middle of the pentagram.

"Stop mangling my pencil!"

Gerdie pointed the chewed end of the pencil at the center of the pentagram. "What's that under the brush?"

Sithias leaned in, squinting for a better look. "A piece of paper maybe? Wait, no it's a folded handkerchief." He cocked his head to one side. "With the letters EF embroidered in the corner."

"As in Eustace Floyd?"

Sithias straightened. "Yesss, Eustace is the only EF I know. *And* the only other one gentlemanly enough to always carry a handkerchief on his person." He cleared his throat as he proudly tugged on the crisp point of the starched handkerchief sticking from the pocket of his blazer.

"I had this all wrong!" Gerdie ran over to the nearest stack of books, tossing each aside before running to the next stack. Her cheeks were shiny and flushed bright pink, giving her a feverish look as she rummaged through the books. "Found it."

Sithias moved in behind her as she rifled through the pages. "What are you looking for?"

"A resurrection spell."

"You mean the spell used to resurrect Eustace?"

"Nope. I can't believe I missed this." Gerdie shook her head ruefully. "I figured Darcy had all these books on necromancy because she was bein' thorough with her research on resurrection spells." She was mumbling to herself.

Sithias huffed. "Well, I'm lost."

Gerdie stopped on a page and rapped his mutilated pencil over the ancient ink, now faded to a dull brown. "Here it is."

Bending to read over her shoulder, Sithias wobbled to a kneeling position. Goose bumps raced over his skin at the horrifying realization of what Darcy had done. "Tell me she didn't do thisss!" he rasped.

Gerdie nodded solemnly. "She did."

"But that would mean Eustace isn't... alive. He's..."

"A revenant. A dead man brought back to life long enough to carry out a mission of vengeance." Gerdie nudged her chin toward the hairbrush. "Darcy made Farouk the target. I gotta give her credit for bein' creative. Choosin' a revenant to go after Farouk might just work. Revenants are hard to kill and they won't stop until their mission is complete."

"What happens once the mission is complete?" Sithias asked, thinking of Fate.

The expression on Gerdie's face wasn't hopeful. "The vengeance spirit leaves the body."

Sithias felt sick. "Meaning Eustace dies all over again."

Gerdie's mouth angled downward into sad lines. "That's not Eustace. Not really. The Eustace we knew died months ago. His body's being animated by somethin' Darcy conjured *and* controls." She stood and helped

Sithias rise when his limbs proved stiff with defeat.

He rubbed away the ache in his knees. "Fate will be devastated. What are we to do about all this?"

"We let it play out and hope Eustace–I mean the revenant–kills Farouk."

"Oh dear. I don't like the sound of that. What of Finn? He's smack in the middle of this without a clue of what Darcy's scheming to do. We have to get news to him."

Gerdie looked doubtful. "How do we do that without tipping Darcy off that we know what she's done."

Sithias glanced around the room, searching for an answer that wouldn't come. He pulled out his pocket watch, noting the time. "I don't know, but we have to do something. The longer we wait, the worse it will get for Finn." He snapped the lid shut and dropped it back in his pocket.

"This is too big for us to handle by ourselves. We gotta bring Brune in on this." Gerdie handed him his pencil. "Do your thing."

Sithias frowned at the chewed eraser and teeth marks she'd left in the wood. "It's wet."

"Get over yourself. It's just a little spit."

"You are–" Pressing his lips together in frustration, he scratched out a quick message and spoke it aloud. "*Brune is now standing beside us.*"

Brune appeared in the room, alarmed and confused, until she noticed Sithias and Gerdie next to her. Her confusion transformed to instantaneous anger. "How dare you yank me out of delicate negotiations with the king of Biraktar and the Eldunough prince like I'm a servant you rang for!"

Sithias raised his hands in surrender then pointed at Gerdie. "It was her idea."

Brune turned her heated gaze on her little sister. "This better be important."

"It's an emergency." Gerdie directed Brune to look at the pentagram.

Brune's anger only increased as she studied the items impatiently. But when she saw Farouk's hairbrush, fear leached the color from her face. Gerdie quickly explained before Brune launched into a long list of questions.

As Sithias listened to the recounting of Darcy's plan to retrieve Dantalion's Key and the troubling revelation of Eustace's true condition, he strode around the pentagram, nagged by a question that hadn't yet fully formed in his mind. The shock had been too great to think clearly, but now that he was listening to it all again, he realized with sudden clarity what had been bothering him.

"Darcy isn't going after Dantalion's Key!"

Gerdie and Brune watched as he scampered around to the grimoire, lugging the heavy book up into his arms with a groan. "Persian Shedreakai Demons come from..." He ran his finger down through the detailed description of the demon in question. "Ah! The Reaverneth realm. The Hadean kingdom is in the Ghodroh realm. Two very distinctly different locations!"

Gerdie nodded. "Darcy's taking her revenant straight to Farouk."

"I see the logic, but something's still off," Brune added. "Darcy could just as easily have summoned Farouk here and trapped him in the pentagram to let her revenant kill him. Why enter the hell dimension and risk your own life if you could get the job done in the safety of your room?"

Sithias felt like he should know the answer, but try as he might, he couldn't think of one. He shrugged with a flap of his arms. "Sorry, I appear to be out of revelations. I've come up empty."

Brune exchanged a knowing glance with her little sister.

"Yup, that has to be it," Gerdie replied, grinning with satisfaction.

"Care to let me in on your telepathic conversation?" Sithias asked in frustration.

"Darcy must be working both ends to the middle," Brune explained. "It's the only thing that makes sense. She must've figured out a way to banish Farouk to his home dimension. That would explain why he hasn't made any appearances, as well as the need to summon him here into the circle."

Brune walked around the pentagram slowly. "After she sent him back, Darcy layered the revenant curse over the traces of energy he left behind inside the pentagram, effectively bonding her revenant to Farouk. She would know Farouk has no powers in his own dimension, making it the best place to play out her double cross."

"I didn't know demons have no powers where they come from," Sithias said, even more mystified by this new piece of information.

"Seriously?" Gerdie screwed up her face. "With all the research you've done, you never read about how demons are as ordinary as us humans in their own dimensions?"

Sithias wagged his head. "No, I didn't."

"The whole reason this world is plagued with demons is because they can shift in and out of this dimension and manipulate reality. That's how they mess with us." Gerdie's look of exasperation was offensive. "You really need to scrub up on your demonology."

"I will now," Sithias grumbled. "Do you really think Darcy's as diabolical as you're making her out to be?"

"You'd be surprised what grief and the desire for vengeance will do to a person." Brune sighed as she strode toward the bedchamber. "Time to rip this place apart. We're looking for something that will show us what kind of deal Darcy made with Farouk."

Sithias followed, wrinkling his nose as he bent down to retrieve a rumpled shirt with a piece of salami stuck to it. Tweezing a tiny piece of the material between his thumb and forefinger, he held the revolting shirt out at arm's length. "*Please*, let us find one quickly."

40

THE GOOD, THE BAD AND THE HIDEOUS

A BLANKET OF STARS TWINKLED behind clouds of swirling color as Fate sailed slowly through them. Dazzling hues of violet, azure and crimson shifted into cotton candy pinks, sunset golds and forest greens. Fate had no idea where she was. Only that she was at peace in this faraway place, away from the unbearable turmoil that had caused her to bolt from the sanctuary.

Here, there was a sense of unlimited possibility and new beginnings.

"*Welcome to the womb of creation, dear daughter. This is where you will find the renewal you seek. Stay, while I take on the burdens of earthly matters for you.*"

The weight on Fate's soul lifted at the mere thought of escaping her troubles. She'd grown utterly weary of being torn in half, forced to choose sides, pushed and pulled in every direction by everyone and every circumstance in her life. The temptation to accept Ananke's offer was overwhelming.

She had to wonder though. Would saying yes truly solve her problems?

"*Better to flow with the current than swim against it.*"

Fate relaxed into the idea, longing for a return to the joy and ease she'd once known as a child. Images of her enchanting childhood bedroom immediately flooded in. Suddenly she was inside her old bedroom lying on top of her big double bed, draped in generous layers of sparkling pink tulle. Her white butterfly comforter was strewn with crayons, glitter pens and sketchpads.

Oz, her orange-striped kitten, was curled up next to her. Jessie was there too, holding up a drawing of two smiling, stick figure girls–one with orange hair, the other with black hair–holding hands amidst a background of gold glitter starbursts.

Eustace entered wearing his baking apron smeared with floury handprints. He set a plate of chocolate chip cookies and two big glasses of chocolate milk on the bed stand for them. His doting smile filled her vision and she yearned to touch his face the way she had when she was little. Had she noticed the limitless love in his eyes then? She wasn't sure. If anything, she'd taken her father's unconditional love for granted. It had never occurred to her there was no such thing as limitless.

There was an inescapable end to everything and everyone.

Having her heart carved out by the crudest of knives would have been less painful than losing her father. The safe magical fortress Eustace had carefully crafted around her had washed away too easily, as fragile and temporary as a sandcastle destroyed by the inevitable rise of the tides. Her grief may not have killed her, but a huge part of her died with him. She'd become a ghost of herself, haunting an old life that no longer existed.

Fate's soul cried out, reminding her: *Eustace is alive!*

She'd been granted a second chance. There was no way to know how long he would be in her life, but it was time to stop running from her fears of losing him again.

"*You will lose him again,*" Ananke promised.

The sharp, painful point of those cruel words sliced deep. "Why would you say that?"

"*I wish only to protect you, my daughter.*"

"How can you know Eustace's future?"

"*I rule the destinies of all mortals and can see the beginning and end of each life.*"

Panic fired through Fate's veins. "If you care about me, you'll ensure my father has a long life."

"*Destinies are intertwined. Loosening the threads of one destiny means unraveling the threads of others, on into infinity. There are cosmic rules even I must abide by. This is why I created you to unite with. The blood of my first daughters, the Furies, runs through you. The Furies were given the power to change destinies as they saw fit. The universal laws I am forced to adhere to did not bind my daughters. If you wish to change your father's destiny, we must do this together.*"

"First you say you rule all destinies, and then you say you can't change them?"

"*The matter is complex. You will come to understand in time. For now, clear your mind and heal your soul. This is why you must remain here.*"

"No." Fate sensed Ananke's surprise. "I want to see my father."

"*I command you to take this time to renew.*" Ananke's will bore down on Fate with the weight of a planet.

Fate pushed back. "Get out of my way!"

Rage surged through her, awakening an indomitable force fueled by her love for Eustace. Wild bolts of energy crackled over Fate's body, expanding her awareness in every direction as she sought her target.

The second her dark sight locked onto the Keep, Fate was there, passing through walls, questing for her best friend. The one person Fate knew would help her return to the girl her father knew as his daughter.

Fate found Jessie pacing the length of her suite, tense and deep in thought. When she turned on her heel and saw Fate standing in the room, she screamed.

"Sorry, didn't mean to scare you like that."

Jessie clutched at her heart. "You really have to stop doing that. It's freaking everyone out. Me included."

Fate flopped down in a chair and slung her leg over the arm. "Yeah, I know."

Jessie warily took the seat opposite her. "Where've you been? I've been looking all over the place for you."

"I went out for a bit. Needed to clear my head." Fate omitted the part about being at the center of the universe struggling with the temptation of taking an indefinite hiatus from life.

"Looks like it did you some good," Jessie admitted, her expression relaxing somewhat. "You don't have that radioactive glow about you anymore."

"I never expected to explode into an emotional mess when I saw Eustace open his eyes. But I've worked through a whole bunch of stuff and I want to get back to who I used to be."

Jessie nodded. "I get it. Seeing him come back to life was... *is* intense."

"I'm ready to see him now." Fate planted both feet on the floor and leaned forward. "Will you go with me? I don't want to do it alone."

"Oh, I would but..."

Fear crashed back in. "Did something happen? Am I too late? Please tell me he's still alive."

"It's nothing like that. Eustace is still up and around." Jessie squirmed in her seat. Something she only did when she was trying not to lie.

"What happened, Jess? Tell me the truth. I'll find out regardless, and I'd much rather hear it from you." Fate could see her searching for the right words. "Tell me. I can handle it."

"Can you?"

The fear in Jessie's eyes saddened Fate. "Look, I know I haven't been myself lately."

"Uh... that's an understatement. If anything, I'd say you've been Ananke lately."

This time it was Fate who squirmed. "I know it probably looks that way, but I've been here the whole time."

"I'm not sure I believe you."

"Ouch."

"Sorry, but it's truth time. I'll tell you everything about Eustace after you share what's been going on with you." Jessie gave her a warning look. "No holding back. I want to hear it all. The good, the bad and the hideous."

"*I forbid you to speak my secrets.*"

Fate's resolve to follow her heart blazed hotter than ever. Honesty with her trusted best friend was what would free her of this ceaseless turmoil. "Something changed for me when I killed the black unicorn. The forces inside the alicorn unlocked something inside. I think that's when my powers merged with–"

Ananke squeezed down on Fate's throat, cutting off her voice. Fate touched her neck, struggling to speak.

"What's wrong?" Jessie asked in alarm.

This was a fight she couldn't win. Fate surrendered to Ananke. The tightness around her vocal cords released. "Nothing. Must've inhaled a bug." She cleared her throat. "Where was I?"

Jessie narrowed her eyes on Fate. "There aren't any bugs in here."

"Hmm, I don't know what it was." Fate shrugged, forcing a casual air. "Anyway, back to my powers. They've really kicked in for reasons even I don't fully understand. And I know I scared everyone with it but there just hasn't been time to ease you all into it. Not with the Serpens breathing down our necks. I only ever wanted to help."

Jessie didn't look convinced. "By going rogue? We're a team here. That means talking to us about what the next step should be. Brune's been working overtime to undo the damage you did to our potential alliance with Eldunough and Biraktar after you yanked the prince and king from their homes and brought them here. Thankfully, Azrael was here to smooth things over with his father."

Fate stared sheepishly at the floor.

"Brune said you healed Azrael just by looking at him."

"I couldn't stand seeing him weak and sickly."

"How are able to do all these things?"

"Like I said, I don't understand how it works. Only that I can do more than ever now." Fate bit down on her frustration. Ananke was forcing her to leave out so much.

Jessie gestured toward the alicorn sword holstered over Fate's shoulder. "So that's the source of these scary new powers?"

"Not the source. I'd say more of a catalyst."

"Is it because you had to kill to get it?"

"What are you trying to say, Jess? That I should feel guilty for what I did to bring Eustace back to us?"

Jessie stared back. "Do you?"

"No, I don't. FYI, that unicorn came out of nowhere and gored me. If I didn't have the regenerative powers of Hippolyta's girdle, I would've been playing a harp next to Eustace."

"Oh, I didn't know."

"Are you done grilling me? Because I have one burning question I need answered, and now. Where's my dad?"

Jessie let out a heavy sigh. "There's no easy way to say this, so I'll just go for the full blurt. Eustace went with Darcy and Finn into the hell dimension to find Dantalion's Key."

The news came out of nowhere and knifed into Fate, every bit as shocking and painful as her encounter with the black unicorn. Her head spun with questions, tangling into a ball of confusion and betrayal. Finn and Eustace were working together to dismantle her powers? Why would they still want that after she'd rescued Rudwor and demonstrated how vital her powers were to defeating the Serpens?

"Because they fear you more than they fear the Serpens. Do you see why I want to carry this burden for you, sweet daughter?"

"Hey, did you hear me?" Jessie asked.

Fate nodded. "I heard you."

"Are you upset? I can't tell with you anymore."

"Yeah I'm upset," Fate admitted. "A lot."

"But we all talked about getting Dantalion's Key as soon as we brought Eustace back."

"Exactly. We talked about it, but I wasn't expecting Finn and my father to sneak off as soon as my back was turned. I don't know whether to be furious or frantic. Eustace has *never* been outside the safety of the library and now he's walking into a hell dimension like he's a seasoned warrior?"

"You might say dying had an effect on Eustace." Jessie screwed up her face. "He came back more on the hard-edged side."

"Are you saying Eustace came back wrong?"

"Not wrong. Different," Jessie replied hastily. Nervously. "His first priority has always been to be a good father. Only this time, he's a father out to protect his daughter at any cost. If I had to guess, that calls for a tough side we've never seen in Eustace before."

Fate's racing pulse steadied. "That makes sense."

"Just so you know, Finn tried to talk him out of going, but Eustace wasn't about to be stopped."

Fate stood. "I have to go after them."

Jessie eyed her suspiciously. "To stop them from finding Dantalion's Key, or to help them find it?"

"To help them. Jeez, how can you ask me that?"

"Still not used to the new you."

Fate let that slide. "When did they leave?"

"About an hour ago."

"I should be with them."

"Sure," Jessie agreed. "But you shouldn't go in with zero knowledge, which means talking to Sithias and Gerdie to see what's what. That's what a team player would do."

"Fine." Fate closed her eyes, scanning the Keep quarters for Sithias and Gerdie. "That's weird. They're in Darcy's suite making a real mess of the place. Brune's there too." She opened her eyes and looked at Jessie, ready to pull her friend through space with her.

"Oh no you don't!" Jessie yelled. "Darcy's room is three doors down from here. We're walking." She marched to the door.

"I'm just trying to save time."

"Phasing from one place to another might be a snap for you. For the rest of us mere mortals it's as bad as riding the Gravitron. I yacked the last time you moved us."

"Oh come on," Fate chided. "The Tilt-A-Whirl used to make you blow chunks."

Unamused, Jessie slammed the door behind them, stormed down the busy hall and stopped in front of Darcy's suite. She tried the door handle and knocked when she found it locked.

When no one answered, Fate pushed her awareness inside to see Sithias, Gerdie and Brune looking like thieves caught red-handed. Fate stepped through the thick metal door, frightening all three of them with her sudden appearance.

"What's going on in here?" Fate asked as she unlocked the door for Jessie.

Sithias visibly shook as he stared back at her. Gerdie didn't move a muscle from where she crouched behind a pile of discarded throw pillows like a mouse hoping to avoid detection. Brune recovered from her fright and did what she always did–countered with a question of her own. "What are *you* doing in here?"

"Looking for Sithias and Gerdie, because I plan to go after Finn and Eustace before they do something stupid. Like get themselves killed."

Brune walked through the detritus covering the floor with a scrutinizing gaze. "Sounds more like you want to stop them before they can get what they went in for."

"Not this again." Fate flung her arms up and looked at her best friend. "Tell them all I want is to help find Dantalion's Key and get them out safely."

Jessie nodded. "I believe her."

Brune's suspicious expression remained, thanks to Jessie's lackluster endorsement. "I think it best you let us handle this."

Gerdie rose from behind the pile of pillows, her movements timid yet determined. "Yup, we're handling this."

Sithias bobbed his head excessively. "That's right, misss."

Fate wasn't buying it. "All I see is the three of you rifling through Darcy's room."

No one said a word. The only noise was Sithias's loud, nervous gulp. Fate stared back at each of them, allowing the silence to fill the room, knowing it would eventually become unbearable for at least one of them.

Sithias was the first to cave. "Oh, I can't do this anymore!"

Brune shot him a warning look.

"No, we're past the point of no return. I'm telling Fate everything," Sithias argued.

Fate listened as patiently as she could while he recounted the discoveries of the missing grimoire and hording of books on necromancy spells they'd found in Darcy's suite. Her trust in Darcy had always been tenuous at best, so it didn't come as a shock that she hadn't been entirely honest. But Fate wasn't forming a complete picture from the pieces of information he was giving her. Sithias seemed to be leaving out major details.

"Hold on." Fate interrupted as he stammered clumsily along. "What aren't you telling me?"

Sithias glanced at Gerdie. "I take it back. I can't be the one to say it..." His voice trailed off in a whimper.

Gerdie started to speak, but Brune cut her off. "If you're going to hear this from anyone, it should be from me since I'm the one who instigated this from the start." The regret in Brune's face indicated she was about to confess something horrible.

Dread gripped Fate in its cold clutch. "What did you do, Brune?"

"I asked Darcy to research resurrection spells for me. I didn't do it myself, as I might have led you to believe. Darcy found out about the black unicorn and she compiled the books I gave you." The straight line of her shoulders sagged. "With all the dissension going on in the Keep, I never checked her research and just assumed what she performed on Eustace was a resurrection spell. As it turns out, she cast a revenant making spell."

"I don't understand. What's a revenant?" Fate's stomach coiled with dread.

"The spirit of a murder victim returned, whose sole purpose for being resurrected is to exact revenge on the killer."

Pain stabbed Fate's temples as bile burned the back of her throat. She was going to be sick.

41
A WITCH IS A WITCH

FATE'S LEGS BUCKLED. Crashing to her knees, she vomited. Jessie ran to hold her hair back as she retched until her stomach was empty. The nausea passed, but the sickening ache of grief remained.

The only thing that had seen her through the pain of losing Eustace was her mission to bring him back to life. Her gentle, loving father was now an unnatural, sinister thing. Knowing she'd played a part in making him into that was more than she could bear.

Jessie helped her stand and guided her to a chair. "I'll get you some water."

"*Let me take this pain from you, daughter.*"

The desire to surrender welled up in Fate. The temptation to recede back into the peaceful sanctuary Ananke had shown her was stronger than ever. Beads of sweat dripped from Fate's forehead onto her lap as she wrestled with the decision.

The smell of vomit mixed with the moldering odor in the room brought on another bout of nausea. A bitter reminder of how ugly this world could be. Hugging her waist, Fate swallowed down the rising bile, grateful for the glass of water Jessie offered her. She gulped it down, rinsing the acidic taste from her mouth. A simple act, but so very cleansing.

What if there was something as simple as this glass of water that would fix Eustace? She had to find out if any such thing existed. How could she live with herself if she didn't try?

Fate set the glass down with a loud thud that made everyone jump. "There has to be a way to undo this revenant curse. One that'll make Eustace alive for real. Right?" She searched their faces for assurance.

All she saw was horrid doubt.

Fate refused to take no for an answer. She stood. Too fast, because Jessie had to catch her before she tipped over from dizziness. "Don't look at me like that!" she yelled as she found her footing. "I want all of you in the library and on this while I go after them."

"You're still going in?" Jessie's concern only deepened Fate's despair.

"Why wouldn't I?"

"Because you're not... well enough," Jessie insisted.

"I'm fine," Fate snapped, instantly regretting her sharp tone when Jessie flinched. She softened her voice. "I really am fine. That was a violent reaction to terrible news. But I won't be brought down by it, not as long as there's hope."

"We don't know if there's a way to undo what's been done to Eustace," Brune said.

"Have any of you dug into it?" Fate looked at Sithias and Gerdie as well. "That's what I thought. Until you've searched every nook and cranny of that library and tell me there's nothing that can be done, then Eustace has a chance. Unless of course you think I should use the Words of Making to undo the revenant curse."

"No, no," Sithias replied hastily. "We'll look into it immediately."

"Yup," Gerdie agreed.

"Well, what are you waiting for?" Fate asked when they didn't move. "Get to it."

"Right, misss, we'll gather up all the books Darcy stole from the library." Sithias disappeared around the corner with Gerdie fast on his heels. He reappeared with as many books as he could carry, while Gerdie followed, lugging a huge tome out into the ransacked bedchamber.

Fate opened the door for them. "I'll meet you back in the library in less than an hour." The monstrous ache in her heart subsided, if only slightly. They might be up against a lost cause, but doing something–*anything*–was better than giving up.

She closed the door and nudged her chin toward the other room, where the walls flickered with the soft glow of candlelight. "What's back there?"

"Darcy's spell casting room." Brune led Fate and Jessie around the corner.

Fate tensed when she saw the lit pentagram.

"*A demon was here.*" Ananke's sheer revulsion and contempt made Fate shiver. She spied Farouk's hairbrush and Eustace's handkerchief underneath. In that instant, she knew what Ananke knew. The spell was active and it was designed to connect Eustace to Farouk.

Rage exploded in Fate's belly, a wildfire of hatred that hammered through her veins. Heat poured off her in waves. "*Darcy summoned Farouk.*" Her voice boomed and shook the walls.

Brune stood rigid.

Jessie's face filled with fright. Inching forward, she touched Fate's arm and winced from the heat. "Hey," she whispered, "are you still with us?"

Fate's breath came in short bursts as she focused on her friend's feather-light touch. Human contact. Jessie knew exactly how to keep her grounded.

"Look at me." Jessie smiled uneasily. "Stay calm."

The fiery blaze in Fate's core died down as she listened to Jessie's soothing voice. Her focus returned the more she relaxed and let go. "Thanks, Jess. I'm good now."

Jessie blew on the tips of her fingers. "Whew! I thought we lost you there for a minute."

Brune let out a sigh of relief and nodded in agreement.

There was no way to explain that Ananke's hatred of demons had magnified her own loathing of Farouk. Ananke would only block her if she tried. "When I saw what Darcy had done, I saw red. I'll do my best not to lose it again."

"How did you know Darcy summoned Farouk?" Brune asked. "You're not exactly well versed in spell magic."

"Obvious clues." Fate gestured at the brush and handkerchief.

Fury burned anew but she was quick to quell it this time. How had she let herself fall for Darcy's deceptions? A witch is a witch by any other name. She only had herself to blame for trusting Darcy.

Brune circled the pentagram. "We know Darcy summoned Farouk to make some sort of deal with him." She sighed heavily. "If we knew what that deal was exactly, we'd know our next step."

"I take it that's why you tore her room apart," Fate said.

"It was like this when we got here." Brune frowned in disgust. "It turns out Darcy's likes to live like swine."

Jessie made a face. "That explains the many varied and vague funky smells in here."

Fate walked over to the altar in the corner. A memorial lovingly devoted to the unbearable amount of grief Darcy had been in ever since Mason's death. The creepy statue and skulls, she didn't understand, but Fate knew what it was to lose someone who had been her whole world. And Farouk was at the center of all of this.

Fate stared at Mason's picture, remembering how Farouk had assumed his form. How many times since then had she wondered if Farouk was lurking behind another trusted friend's face? Countless times. An icy chill raced over her skin. What must Darcy have felt when she realized the horror of knowing she'd welcomed into her bed a demon wearing the skin of her lover? The thought was too horrifying to imagine.

The desire for vengeance would be all consuming and a witch would know exactly how to exact her revenge. For the briefest second, Fate understood why Darcy would choose to raise Eustace as her avenging angel.

He was Farouk's murder victim. All the pieces had been in place to carry out a perfect plan of retribution.

But this was personal now. Darcy had used Fate's grief and blind need to save her father to obtain the alicorn for a revenant-making spell. This, she could never forgive.

Darcy had made herself an enemy for life. Molten rage erupted inside Fate's core. She focused on breathing deeply again. *Inhale. Exhale. Inhale. Exhale.*

"Everything all right over there?" Jessie asked.

Fate turned away from the altar. "For now. Though I can't promise to hold back the next time I see Darcy."

"I'd be careful what you do to her," Brune warned. "She left this spell open, which may mean it can be undone. But only by the witch who cast the spell."

"Lovely," Fate muttered.

"Are we done here?" Jessie kicked a pile of clothes aside. "I've had quiet enough of the zombiance in here. It's not only grody, but depressing."

"We're finished here." Fate was just as anxious to leave. "Too bad we can't watch the replay on what happened with Farouk."

Jessie's eyes widened. "Are you completely sure we can't?"

Fate laughed bitterly. "I wish! Only problem is I don't see a cosmic video player lying around. Do you?"

"Maybe it's buried under all of Darcy's crap."

"Let's go girls." Brune's voice was sharp with impatience as she picked her way to the door.

"No, wait," Jessie called out. "I was serious about the replay thing."

Brune stopped and looked at her. "Make it quick. I have a war to get back to."

Jessie nodded. "Fate, if you can walk through walls and phase from one place to another just by thinking it, who's to say you can't step back through time to when Darcy summoned Farouk?"

"Um... I can try." Fate stared hard at the pentagram, willing the events that had taken place inside the circle to rewind to the beginning. When nothing happened, she strained her muscles and held her breath until her lungs burned. She sucked air in with a shake of her head.

"*Forcing will get you nowhere, daughter. To unfold time, you must combine imagination with our power and channel both through clear intent.*"

Fate relaxed her limbs and softened her gaze on the pentagram. Ananke's power quickly swelled to bursting, ready to do her bidding. Searching for a picture of time she could wrap her mind around, she visualized a book filled with pages penned with detailed events of the spell.

Starting at the end of the book, Fate turned one page after the other toward the beginning. At first there were no noticeable changes, but then she realized the candles placed around the pentagram, which had burned low, were growing taller, reaching their original height.

Then Darcy appeared in the center of the pentagram. She was kneeling next to Farouk's brush. She picked up the brush and pulled Eustace's handkerchief out. It wasn't until she stood and walked backwards out of the circle that Fate fully understood she was watching the spell rewinding from end to start in front of her very eyes.

Darcy stood outside the pentagram. There was a spell book beside her feet, which had been set down, except in reverse, because it only looked like she was picking it up. When she spoke the incantation, Darcy's words came out backwards, sounding distorted and eerie.

Dark tendrils of smoke hovered above the brush. Darcy set aside the spell book as the smoke expanded, a writhing mass that solidified into a hulking, beastly form. Real fear set in as Fate watched Farouk fully materialize until he stood over the brush. At twelve-feet-tall, he was a goliath within the confines of the bedchamber, forced to crook his head low beneath the limits of the ceiling.

Fate slowed the turning of each page, momentarily sidetracked by the awful sight of him, then increased the speed, wanting more than ever to play the scene from the beginning to know the meaning of the backwards conversation.

Brune moved in beside Jessie to watch the disturbing scene play out.

Fate stopped on the page where Farouk began dissolving into smoke again. "Listen carefully," she told Brune and Jessie. "I only want to have to do this once." They each nodded silently as she turned the page, this time in the proper direction.

Wreaths of black smoke dissipated around Farouk's large wolfish head. He fixed his red burning gaze on Darcy and snarled. It was a vicious, feral sound that was without language, reminding Fate that he invaded minds to communicate. They would only be able to hear Darcy's side of the conversation. Hopefully that would be enough.

Darcy stared back unflinchingly at Farouk's baleful gaze. "Everything is in place and happening as you planned. I have to say, it was almost too easy. They all fell in line like the useful idiots you said they'd be."

Fate's mind numbed with shock. This wasn't Darcy's first meeting with

Farouk. How long had she been working with the demon?

"Fate has no idea killing the black unicorn corrupted the purity of Hippolyta's girdle." Darcy smirked. "Can you believe she kept the alicorn? She's made it her personal sword."

Fate broke out in a cold sweat. Was she changing into something horrible? Aradif's nightmarish vision returned to haunt her, filling her head with images of the dark winged knight she feared she might become–an abomination of her former self destined to rule in a hellish world with Farouk.

A low, rumbling growl issued from Farouk's throat.

Tension replaced Darcy's arrogant smile. "You're wrong. It only *looks* like Fate's more powerful than ever. Ananke's power must be slowing the rate of corruption on the girdle. But trust me, it'll happen once Ananke succumbs to merging with the Eldritch Gloom. It shouldn't be long before you have Fate right where you want her."

The second Fate questioned what this Eldritch Gloom was, Ananke answered. "*Lies. All lies to make you doubt the true might of the powers we wield together. Do not listen to the witch.*"

Fate wanted to believe, but the icy knot growing in the pit of her stomach filled her with doubt. Before she could press for more answers, Farouk lunged at Darcy. Blue flames shot up around the circle's edge, holding him inside the pentagram. Infuriated, he lashed out with silvered claws, streaking the barrier with crackling light, gnashing his fangs.

Darcy took a step back even though Farouk was clearly bound to the pentagram. She waited for him to settle down before speaking again. "Now that I've come through with everything you asked of me, it's my turn to name what I want."

She reached for a long sheet of paper filled with a surprising amount of handwritten text and set it inside the circle "A list of my demands."

Farouk snarled.

"Nope, we're doing this by the book. If you want me to go any further with this, you're going to have to open a vein and stamp the contract in blood."

Crouching, Farouk poked a claw into the corner of the page, pulled the contract across the floor and hunched over it. After a few minutes of reading, he looked at Darcy, his snout curled back as he shook his great head with a firm no.

Darcy crossed her arms. "Those are my terms. I bring you Finn, you use the Orb of Aeternitis to remove the Rod from him and hand them both over to me."

Fate's skin crawled with unbridled terror, remembering how Kaliena had used the Orb to dismantle Finn with the intention of reassembling the Rod for herself. She knew Darcy was cold, but she never thought her to be completely heartless. How could someone pretend to be on the same team, while at the same time planning the cruel demise of those she'd worked with so closely?

Farouk slowly stood with a menacing growl that built to a blood-curdling roar.

Darcy covered her ears, waiting for an end to his tantrum. "Are you finished?"

Farouk's chest heaved and shook with rage as he glared at the witch holding him captive.

"I know what you're thinking," Darcy continued. "You want to use the Orb and Rod of Aeternitis to build your big scary kingdom in *this* world, where you'll be all powerful. Am I right?"

Farouk glowered threateningly.

"All beastie brawn and no brain." Darcy smiled and shook her head at him like he was being silly. "Allow me to remind you that you won't need them, because you'll have Fate to make all that happen for you. Her powers will be yours to command as you please once she's fully corrupted."

Fate shook with undiluted disgust. She'd never been so close to murderous rage than in that moment. Fate crossed her arms and brought them down with a sharp swipe, ripping the scene from the folds of time. Darcy and Farouk shattered into blurred scraps before vanishing from sight altogether.

Brune stared at Fate in disbelief. "Why did you end it? There might've been more! Why do you always let your emotions override good common sense?"

"I couldn't stomach hearing another word of that twisted conversation." Fate focused on her breathing to cool the heat scorching at her insides.

"Same here," Jessie agreed. "We heard enough to know what Darcy's planning."

Exhaling slowly, Fate nodded. "Eustace isn't the only one who needs saving. Finn's in just as much trouble."

42
OPEN SESAME

AZRAEL WAS IN THE LIBRARY talking to Sithias and Gerdie when Fate arrived with Jessie and Brune. Fate's pulse raced at the sight of him, a reaction she was still unable to tame. His presence had always captivated her attention in a way that was both infuriating and thrilling, and she hated herself for it. Particularly after the heavenly night she'd spent with Finn.

How was it that every time she thought she'd solidly chosen Finn as her one and only, Azrael showed up to rattle her resolve? What was it going to take to get Azrael out of her system once and for all?

He stood, watching her approach, his desire raw and plainly displayed for all to see. Fate felt herself drowning in the clear blue depths of his eyes. She wanted to run her fingers through his silky long hair, feel his beautiful mouth against hers.

She tore her gaze from Azrael. "I'm despicable," she muttered.

"What?" Jessie asked.

"Nothing." Guilt mixed with the heat flushing Fate's cheeks. "Have you found anything to undo the revenant curse yet?" she asked Sithias and Gerdie. Best to get down to business before she lost all control of her emotions.

"We found an alchemical formula that looks quite promising," Sithias replied, his smile forced.

"Emphasis on *looks*." Gerdie glanced at Sithias reproachfully. "Don't go gettin' her hopes up before we know for sure."

"That's fine," Fate assured them. "I'll take promising over a flat no any day of the week. You two keep up the good work, while I get Eustace and Finn out ASAP."

"Darcy too?" Sithias asked.

"Darcy can rot in hell!" Fury churned in Fate's core. When she saw Sithias recoil from her, she forced the searing heat down, intent on saving it for when she caught up with the witch. "Jess, tell them about her heinous deal with Farouk."

Fate walked away from the table, counting backwards from one hundred to avoid listening to Jessie's retelling of Darcy's treachery.

Sithias gasped in horror. "I can't believe thisss!"

"Just when you think things can't get any worse, they always do," Gerdie grumbled.

"Why would Darcy betray us like that?" Sithias began to tear up.

"Revenge. And something else..." When Brune trailed off, Fate rejoined them.

"What sort of something else?" Fate asked.

Brune's expression hardened. "Aside from the unforgivable deception and betrayal we already know of, there's the matter of the Orb and Rod of Aeternitis. Darcy's taken extreme measures to ensure she ends up with them both. Which begs the question: What does she plan to do with them?"

"Rule the universe," Fate said. "Isn't that every arch-villain's main agenda?"

"Usually," Brune agreed. "But in Darcy's case, I think this is about love. She knows Finn was created with the Orb. She also knows his existence was shaky without the balancing forces of the Rod to stabilize the Orb's creative energy. That is, until O'Deldar integrated the Rod into his essence."

Fate slapped her forehead. "Duh, Darcy plans to recreate Mason! That's why she wants Farouk to rip Finn apart. Why didn't I see it before?"

"Because you're not diabolical." Brune smiled wearily. "You're impulsive, rash and bullheaded, but not diabolical." She retrieved a ping-pong sized octagonal object from her utility belt and handed it to Fate.

"Isn't this the expandable cage thingy you used on Mahelia when we thought she was Farouk?" Fate asked.

"The very same."

"I don't want it. This is a search and destroy mission. Not a capture and revert wolfzilla back into Puss in Boots." Fate tried to hand it back, but Brune wouldn't take it.

"Farouk probably won't revert back to what he used to be. I think it's too late for that now. Use the cage to trap him. It'll make killing him easier."

"I like easier." Fate stuck it into one of the pockets on her utility belt and snapped the flap shut.

"*Aperta Captionem Reverti.*"

"What?"

"That's the incantation to activate the trap."

"I doubt I'll need it, but thanks." Fate frowned. She felt like she was going to detonate if she didn't take action within the next few seconds. "Where exactly did Darcy take Finn and Eustace?" she asked Sithias.

"The Reaverneth realm, the demon dimension Farouk is bound to by birth. Darcy, of course, led us to believe she was taking Finn and Eustace to the Hadean kingdom in the Ghodroh realm, where she said they'd find Dantalion's Key." He stared back anxiously. "Unless that was a lie too. Dantalion's Key could be anywhere. Here in the Keep, for all we know."

"You might want to look into that," Fate suggested.

"If it's here, I'll find out where it is," Gerdie offered. "You show Fate the gallery with the portal Darcy used."

Sithias nodded fretfully. "Follow me, misss."

"Be careful in there, Fate," Brune warned. "Demons have no real powers in their own dimensions, but that doesn't mean they can't hurt you."

Fate was stunned. "Are you saying Farouk will be normal? As in, he can't shape shift or vanish into a puff of rank smoke while I'm trying to stab him?"

"More or less," Brune replied with a frown of concern. "Just remember he was born with claws and fangs, and most importantly, a devious mind."

Fate's spirits lifted in light of this revelatory news. "Lead the way, Sithias."

Before she could go, Jessie stopped her by tugging her aside. "I'm afraid for you." Tears filled her eyes and her voice dropped to a hoarse whisper. "I know you have to go, but I'm scared I'll never see you again."

A painful lump formed in Fate's throat. "Don't worry. I can take care of myself."

Jessie nodded. "I know. But what if you're too late to stop Darcy and Farouk? I won't be there to help talk you down off the edge if the worst happens. I should go with you."

"No, I'm already anxious enough about Finn and Eustace. If I add you to the list, I'll lose my mind with worry."

Azrael stepped forward. "I will go."

Fate's heart hammered against her breastbone as she considered his offer. How wrong was that?

"Excuse me, Azrael," Brune interjected, "but I need you here to help me negotiate with your father."

"There was much arguing, but he surprised me by agreeing to the alliance." Azrael kept his gaze fixed on Fate. "That was what I came to see you about. My father would appreciate being returned to Biraktar, where he can make arrangements to send more fleets."

"Are you sure you don't want to go home with him?" Fate asked. Her pulse skipped a beat as she waited for his answer.

"I made my choice. I wish to go with you. Who better to accompany you in the demon realm than the one who faced the Hinn with you in the desert?" His lips curved into a secretive smile that made Fate's heart thud even harder.

"Need I remind you I was raised on demon lore? Such as the night time stories of Sarayna and the demon king you enjoyed and requested of me more than once."

Fate's face warmed as she stared into his eyes, entranced beyond reason.

Jessie nudged her, breaking the spell. "Say yes. I'd feel much better knowing you're not alone."

"I suppose it can't hurt to have a demon historian along." Fate tried her best to sound hesitant, but her voice trembled with eagerness. She glanced away from Azrael's pleased smile before her blush deepened. "Let's go then."

Azrael didn't move. "First my father."

"Oh, right." Fate closed her eyes, reaching her awareness outward until she located the king. For the briefest second, she focused all her attention on the gleaming pearlescent palace that was the king's home and visualized him standing in the royal family's quarters. She opened her eyes. "Done."

"One king down, one prince to go." Brune started to leave, then turned back to Fate. "Do your best to not die in there. I'm sure Prince Kelare would appreciate being returned to his islands as soon as he's made his final decision."

"Sure, Brune. I'll try not to screw up the negotiations by getting inconveniently killed."

"Stop that!" Jessie yelled. "I can't stand around listening to my best friend talk about dying like it's no big deal." Color rushed to her face, feverish and panicked. "Why do you have to go after Eustace and Finn and put your life in danger when you could locate them with your mind and pull them out with a thought? How is that any different than what you just did with the king?"

"I guess I thought I should do this by the book and start working with the team instead of going rogue," Fate said.

Jessie's bottom lip quivered. "That's why you're risking your life and doing this the hard way? Because I called you rogue?"

"I called her that too," Brune admitted. "And just to be clear, I don't take it back. But I do agree with Fate that she needs our help on this one. It's dangerous to go poking around in the hell dimension on an etheric level. That's an open invitation for demons on the other side to hitch a ride back and wreak havoc here on our side."

"Oh." The disappointment in Jessie's voice was heartbreaking.

"Glad we cleared that up. I'll be in the sanctuary if you need me." Brune marched for the door.

"Everything will be fine, Jess," Fate assured her.

"I really hate this," Jessie grumbled.

"Hey, come on, I've been in worse situations." Fate gave her playful smile. "Like you said, I won't be alone."

Azrael took Fate's hand and bowed his head ever so slightly. "Thank you for allowing me to join you."

Fate nodded, guiltily pulling her hand from his light grasp.

Jessie moved in for a tearful hug. "Wow," she whispered. "He's so into you it's almost too painful to watch."

"*Shhh*, he'll hear you!" Fate squeezed her friend and let go with a wink. "No more worrying. I'll be back in a jif."

Sniffing, Jessie waved goodbye as Fate turned with Azrael to follow Sithias into the gallery. Fate didn't look back, lest she tear up as bad as Jessie.

Sithias stopped at the very end of the hall in front of two black doors with a cracked metal disc engraved with symbols. He handed each of them pouches. "This is dead man's ash. You must smear the ash on your face to gain entrance into the hell dimension and stay hidden from demons."

Fate held the bag at arm's length. "Ew, gross!"

"My sentiments exactly." Sithias made a face. "Thankfully, the library reliquary has it in ample supply and I was spared from having to describe it with the Words of Making."

Azrael opened the bag and poured a small amount of ash on his palm. "Allow me."

Fate closed her eyes as he gently dusted her cheeks, nose and forehead with the gritty ash. Azrael did the same for himself, tightened the string and tucked the pouch inside the sash at his waist.

Sithias slid one of the doors back and moved aside to allow them to see inside the dim interior. Fate took an immediate dislike to the frightening imagery within the paintings hanging on the walls.

"You're on your own once you step inside," Sithias informed them. "Eustace closed the doors before Darcy activated the portal. It would appear each painting holds a gateway, but as to which one she chose to go through, I have no idea."

"There are ways to detect which gateway was opened," Azrael assured him.

"That's encouraging," Sithias said, though he looked dubious. "I wish there was more I could do to help. Here's the incantation to open the gateway." Fate took the folded piece of paper he offered and stuck it in her pocket.

Sithias looked at Fate with round watery eyes. "I'm with Jessie. I too am thankful you're not going in alone, misss." He turned to Azrael. "Take care of her for us."

"I will protect her with my life, should the situation demand," Azrael promised.

His declaration was moving, but it hurt to think of him dying for her. "Hello," she chided, "seasoned warrior with kickass powers standing right here. I can take care of myself, thank you very much."

"How can you know for sure?" Sithias asked. "The powers you've been drawing on might be neutralized in the demon dimension."

"Just because demons are powerless in their dimension doesn't mean I will be." Fate bit her bottom lip, suddenly less confident.

"Are you so sure of that?" Sithias stared back regretfully. "I don't mean to shake your confidence, but your powers come from the gods. Have you forgotten demons are their one weakness?"

Fate pulled on the silver chain of her protective pendant, placing it outside her uniform for Sithias to see. "Recognize this?"

"Certainly, the symbol of Aradif, the great serpent in the sky. My exact likeness, of which I portrayed to perfection, I might add." Sithias lifted his chin proudly.

"This protects my powers from weakening when I'm in the presence of demons. Boom." Fate smiled when she saw Sithias's surprise. "In fact, I'd go so far as to say this nifty piece of jewelry might just be a demon repellent. It would explain why Farouk hasn't paid me any visits."

"Actually, Brune thinks we haven't seen Farouk because Darcy found a way to banish him to the Reaverneth realm." Sithias smiled apologetically.

"Oh." Fate felt momentarily deflated. "Well, the necklace will help. Right, Azrael?"

"Yes, I have my mother's word on the pendant's protective qualities." Azrael hesitated a moment, his eyes clouding with doubt before continuing. "Though, I must agree there may be some validity to Sithias's concerns in regards to your powers."

"No, don't say that!" Fate huffed. "It doesn't matter. Powers or not, I'm going in. Are you coming?"

"Of course." Without waiting for her, Azrael entered the gallery. His back went rigid when he passed the threshold, like something had touched him. When he turned around, his jaw was clenched with tension.

Sithias looked like he might leap at Fate with a goodbye hug. Instead, he turned suddenly very serious. "I refuse to say goodbye. Instead, let's say we'll see each other very soon."

Fate saluted him. "I'll be back so fast you'll hardly know I'm gone."

Sithias nodded, his lips trembling. Before a tear could escape, he turned on his heel and trotted back toward the library.

Swallowing down her own trepidation, Fate marched into the gallery. She stopped in her tracks when a dank, graveyard stench assaulted her nose. A deathly chill seeped through her uniform all the way to her bones. Shivering and queasy, she hugged her arms. "Why is it freezing in here?"

Azrael shook his head in disgust. "I suspect the paintings are the source."

Fate shuddered as she glanced at the framed art covering the tall gallery walls from top to bottom. Every single one of the oil paintings depicted an entrance of some kind, be it an archway, a mirror, a door, even a crack in a mountain or staircase into the clouds. The scenery around each entrance was bright and lush with life, but the landscape the gateways opened onto were dark, dreadful places filled with bleak wastelands, fiery lakes or pits of writhing, monstrous shapes.

"I have no idea which portal Darcy opened, but if we don't find it quick, I'm going to heave." Fate covered her nose and gulped.

"Remove the pendant."

Fate frowned. "Uh, remember that conversation about protection we had back there?"

"Trust me, this is the only way."

"Fine, but you'll have to take it off for me. My hand stays on my nose."

Azrael moved in behind her and unclasped the chain.

Fate stared at her protective pendant, surprised by how vulnerable she felt without it. "Now what?"

"Walk the edges of the room, close to each wall. Tell me if you feel anything."

Still holding her nose, Fate moved to the corner of the farthest wall and strolled the length of it. She stopped to frown at Azrael. "Nothing. Are you sure you know what you're doing?"

"Please continue."

Fate walked along the next wall. "Nope."

Azrael encouraged her to keep going with a patient wave of his hand.

Fate was beginning to doubt his methods but did as she was asked. Halfway down the third wall her vision blurred and all the strength left her limbs. She staggered dizzily, reaching for something to hold herself up but her legs gave out and she fell.

Azrael hurried to help her rise. Leaning heavy against him, she wrapped her arms around his waist, frightened by the sheer weakness that had overtaken her. "What's happening?" she panted.

"You are feeling the harmful emanations left behind from the portal they opened."

Fate let go of him with one arm and pressed on her throbbing temple. "This feels exactly like when I was around Farouk. If I didn't know better, I'd swear he was in the room."

Holding her close, Azrael nudged his chin toward the painting next to them. "It must be this one."

Fate studied the painting, struck by the benign setting of a stone staircase covered in dry autumn leaves. At the top of the steps was an aged, pointed arch and the wooden door had been left open. The entrance itself was not attached to a building. It stood alone against a gray, cloudy sky. The door opened onto a cracked desert floor. Layers of dark mist in the distance obscured unrecognizable shapes she hoped were old ruins and not monsters waiting to eat them.

Azrael shifted around to face Fate, balancing her against his chest as he slipped the necklace back on and fastened the clasp. "How do you feel now?"

The unexpected flood of energy was a welcome relief. Fate tested her strength by letting go of Azrael and took a step back. The dizziness was gone and her legs felt strong again. "Much better."

"Shall I say the incantation?" Azrael asked.

"I can do it." Fate dug for the paper in her pocket. She smiled at Azrael. "Want to bet it says *Open Sesame?*"

He raised a brow. "Why would it say that?"

"You know, *A Thousand and One Nights*, from the old Persian fairy tales. Not ringing any bells?"

Azrael shook his head.

"You're definitely going to want to read those stories when we get back."

He smiled. "I will. If you promise to let me read them to you."

Tempted by his invitation, Fate blushed and quickly dropped her gaze to Sithias's neat lettering. "Hmm, I couldn't have been more wrong about the incantation. It's the usual boring Latin. Ready?"

"Only if you are."

Fate turned to the painting and read the words. "*Aperiam inter mundos.*"

A hot, sulfurous wind blew from the painting. The strong gust came from the picture's arch, scattering the crisp autumn leaves into such a flurry some of them whirled out of the painting into the gallery. Fate watched them flutter to the marble floor and land next to several others.

Azrael noticed the leaves at the same time and glanced at her with regret.

"I know, don't say it." She held up a hand to stop him from apologizing for putting her through the misery of taking off the protective pendant, when they should've been looking for visible clues instead.

More leaves whisked past her as Fate stepped inside the painting and climbed the stone steps to the arch. The arid wind grew hotter as she stopped at the threshold and peered through the opening. A bleak wasteland blanketed with black smoke stretched out before her as far as the eye could see.

Azrael stood still behind her. "Shall I go first?"

"No, I will." But Fate reached for his hand before she took her first step into darkness.

43
NECROMANTIC TREACHERY

"WE'VE BEEN WALKING THIS GRUESOME ROAD for hours." Finn downed the last sip of water in his canteen. Squinting into the murky smoke-filled distance, he wiped his brow before another deluge of sweat stung his eyes. The oppressive heat and scorching wind beating against them was taking its toll and now he was out of water. "Are you positive we're not lost? Seems to me we should've found Hadean's kingdom by now."

"How many times do I have to say it?" Darcy snapped. "This is the only road and it leads *one* way." She was crankier than usual, dragging her feet over the crude road made entirely of crushed human bones. Her foot caught on a protruding bone and she tripped. Again. Eustace, the only one who wasn't sweating buckets of precious salt, caught her by the arm before she fell.

Finn scowled at the grisly road, his nerves on edge from the ever-present stink of sulfur and general malaise of low spirits. "It's disrespectful trampling over people's bones this way."

"They're dead. They don't care anymore."

"I still don't see why we can't walk off to the side on the clay bed, where it's smoother. Wouldn't you prefer to stop tripping over bits of femur and ribs?"

Darcy shot him a venomous look, made all the darker by the mascara smeared beneath her eyes. "Who's the one who did all the research on this place? *Me*. And the book said to stay on the road after paying the toll."

Finn had to wonder about that. The payment had been one of Mason's old t-shirts, of all things. Darcy had muttered something about surrendering an object of tremendous value. Except that there hadn't even been a toll keeper in attendance to take the payment. She'd simply wadded the shirt into a ball and placed it under a big rock etched with a weathered symbol.

"Who's going to know if we step off?" Finn pressed. "The absentee toll keeper?"

Darcy stopped to glare at him. "How about we don't test the rules by stepping off a road in the hell dimension. Can you handle that?" She turned and trudged forward.

Finn looked at Eustace. "Any thoughts from you, sir? After all, you were the first to do the research on all this."

Eustace stood as straight as an oak, unbending in the brutal wind. He shook his head without saying a word and turned to follow Darcy.

Finn lagged behind, more troubled than ever by Eustace's persistent silence and the way he shadowed Darcy's every move. It was creepy, like he was in a trance. Finn had noticed hints of subservient behavior from him before they'd entered the portal but had chalked it up to focused cooperation. After spending more time around the two of them together, this was clearly a master pulling the strings of her puppet.

"There it is!"

The excitement in Darcy's voice had Finn scanning the horizon. The relentless smoke-filled windstorm had revealed only sharp, windblown rocks knifing up from the endless clay bed since the start. Suddenly he caught a glimpse of a different and far larger shape up ahead. The bone highway appeared to lead straight there.

Finn raised his arm to shield his face. "Is that the kingdom up ahead?"

"Yeah, sure."

Darcy walked faster now, her head bent into the wind, stronger than ever as if to challenge their intent to continue. Sand and sharp bits of bone whipped through the air, scratching at Finn's skin. "How about I fly ahead and scout things out?" he suggested, impatient to put an end to this wretched trek.

"No way!" Darcy shouted. "I didn't come all this way to have you screw things up just before the finish line." She gestured for Eustace to walk in front of her to block the pelting sand.

"What an asinine mistake this was," Finn grumbled.

Turning his back to the wind, he tore a few narrow strips off the bottom of his shirt and tied one over his nose and mouth to avoid sucking any more sand into his lungs. He slit two holes in the other and cinched the cloth in place over his watering eyes. It wasn't as good as goggles, but at least it cut back on the barrage of grit.

He only had himself to blame for being so ill equipped by allowing Darcy to rush him into leaving without thorough preparation. Everything about this mission was horribly off. Eustace wasn't himself and Darcy was controlling him. That much was clear, but Finn sensed there was more to it. She was hiding something.

He'd been a fool to think she'd been completely honest with him.

The colossal structure came into full view as they approached the end of the road. Up close it looked like giant brambles had grown together into a dome of twisted thorns, long since petrified over eons of time. The last part of the road ended in bone so pulverized it might as well have been sand. A tall, roughhewn entrance large enough for giants to pass through loomed in front of them. Embedded within the edges of the archway were countless human skulls. Two stone doors stood closed at the entrance, depicting carvings of twin, giant hooded figures standing on top of a writhing mass of snarling, wolfish demons. One of the doors was broken away in the bottom corner, a crack plenty large enough to allow them entry.

Goose bumps shivered over Finn's skin despite the stifling heat. This was the most desolate, empty place he'd ever had the pure misery of being in. Where had all the poor souls come from that had been slaughtered to build that abhorrent massive arch and bone highway?

Another more disturbing question pushed its way to the forefront of his mind. One he'd been asking since they'd stepped through the portal. Where were all the demons that were supposed to inhabit this realm? And why smear dead man's ash on their faces if there were no demons around to stay hidden from?

Something was very, very wrong here.

They left the torturous wind behind as soon as they walked through the crack in the door. Finn pulled the cloth strips off his face, letting them hang around his neck in case he needed them later. Darcy's black hair was stiff and gray with dust, as was Eustace's. Creases of skin showed through the ashen film covering their faces. Finn didn't need a mirror to know he was every bit as grimy as they were. Not that he gave a damn, but he could do without the parched, dusty taste in his mouth.

Shifting the straps of the backpack off his shoulders, he set it down and unzipped the top compartment in search of more water.

"What are you doing?" Darcy's shrill voice rang with panic.

"Getting some water."

"Have mine." Eustace shoved his canteen in front of Finn. Darcy grabbed the backpack out from under Finn's grasp at the same time.

Finn stood and took the full canteen. Eustace hadn't taken a single drink from it. While this was unsettling, he was more concerned with Darcy's secretiveness. "What's the problem, Darcy? Is there something in there you don't want me to see?"

"No." She glowered at him. "I don't want you drinking from the wrong bottle. I have tinctures and potions in there."

Finn wasn't convinced but refrained from pressing her. He took a swig of water, swished it around his mouth and spit it out. "What is this place? It doesn't look like the kingdom of a duke of Hell. If anything, it seems more like a cage."

He studied the huge curving pillars of rock overhead. "See all the deep scratches in the rock? This was most definitely built to keep things in. And from the looks of it, they clawed their way up and broke out through the top." He pointed at a large jagged opening near the center of the domed ceiling. "The question is, what was being caged here?"

A deep, guttural voice invaded Finn's mind–one he recognized immediately. "*Curious creatures. Isn't that how you referred to me once? I believe your exact words were: There's a reason curious creatures in cages aren't allowed to roam free.*"

Finn withdrew his flute from his pocket, anxiously searching for Farouk. All he saw was Darcy and Eustace. They both turned toward a huge pile of rubble in the center of the dome.

Farouk's massive lupine head appeared off to one side, his shoulder blades sliding beneath bristling fur as he skulked on all fours around to the front. The fiery, incandescent gleam of the demon's eyes filled Finn with terror as he stood to his full height. Farouk was twice the size Finn remembered from their last encounter.

Farouk tilted his head to stare at Finn. Silvered flames flared from his claws as his deadly, barb-tipped tail snaked hypnotically behind him. "*No words were ever more true. My kind has always been caged.*" His black lips curled back. Smoke swirled past his fangs as a menacing growl rolled from his throat. "*As you can well see, no one could keep us caged.*"

Finn transformed his flute into a wind sword by blowing two sharp rune notes. "Maybe not, but from what I can tell, your kind lost the war a long time ago and you're the only one of them left. But don't fret, I'm happy to make it so you don't have to live out an eternity alone."

Farouk's ears flattened to his head. "*I'll gut you so you bleed out slowly. I want you alive long enough to watch Fate die before your eyes.*"

"Farouk, your business is with me!" Darcy shouted. "It's time to meet your end of the bargain or I'll make sure you stay trapped in this snorendous dimension forever. You know I can do it. Or do I need to remind you I'm the one who banished you here?"

Farouk bared his fangs at Darcy, like the leashed dog wanting to rip into its master.

"You made a bargain with this demon?" Shock spread through Finn cold as frost. "We never were after Dantalion's Key. What's this really about and where in the hell are we, Darcy?" When she didn't answer him, he looked at Eustace. "Did you know about this?"

Eustace ignored him. He stood rigid and still as stone, staring at Farouk. He looked wrong. His eyes were yellowed and there was a mean, hateful look in them Finn didn't think Eustace could ever be capable of.

"Eustace!" Finn yelled to get his attention. "Did you know?"

Farouk's burning gaze slid to Eustace. "*I killed this one. How is he alive?*" He sniffed the air, growling low when he caught the scent. He turned back to Darcy. "*You brought a revenant?*"

Darcy looked as surprised as Finn was confused.

"*Did you really think I wouldn't smell the vengeance you spelled into his dead flesh? What necromantic treachery is this?*"

"Call it insurance." Darcy's voice quavered, betraying her fear.

Farouk drew within inches of her face. The smoke sifting past his slavering fangs curled around her head. "*I call this a breach of contract.*"

Darcy shrank from him, coughing on the noxious smoke. "There's no breach. The revenant won't attack as long as I choose to hold him back. All you have to do is follow through with your end of the deal and I'll destroy the revenant."

Another wave of shock slammed into Finn. He studied Eustace through a whole new lens, one that brought the man into crystal clear focus. The immutable set of his expression from the second he'd been brought to life, the inhuman resistance to the harsh beating wind and robotic responses to Darcy all made sense now.

Finn knew very little about what a revenant was. Only that it explained the repulsion he'd felt during the resurrection spell: The shadow that had risen from mixing the spell's three ingredients. The sinister incantation. All of it had been exactly what he'd feared it was.

Darcy had used necromancy, the blackest of the dark arts.

Eustace's body had been taken over by a vengeful spirit conjured to leech precious memories from his brain matter in order to pass as the man he once was. Even when the revenant had failed to pull off a convincing performance, Finn had willingly overlooked the falsity standing right in front of him. Hope had blinded him. He'd wanted Fate to have her father back.

Finn finally understood why she hadn't been able to face Eustace upon his return. She must have sensed the abomination pretending to be her father. Admitting it would have meant accepting Eustace was truly gone.

Finn kicked himself. He should've trusted his instincts. He should've stopped the abomination–

A violent tugging at Finn's center had him doubling over in excruciating pain. He gulped for air as the atoms of his body unraveled like a loosely woven sweater. Raising his head, he glanced around for help. Farouk swung the Orb of Aeternitis, growling out a ruinous incantation as Darcy stood by, watching with a mixture of horror and fascination.

Finn's wind sword dropped and he watched in silent horror as the skin on his arm flaked away into glinting grains of gold dust and floated away.

44
THE BLINDERS ARE OFF

FATE FLEW HIGH ABOVE the dreadful road of bones, tossed by rough currents on the howling wind, where she was at least clear of the pelting sand. Azrael, on the other hand, was forced to walk the road with the sandstorm raging against him. Fortunately, his traditional desert garb provided ample material for wrapping his head and face for proper protection. Though she had trouble spotting him since the fabric of his robe reflected his surroundings, making him nearly invisible.

She landed in front of him with her back to the wind. "The road's coming to an end. There's a weird looking dome up ahead."

Azrael peered from the folds of his wrappings to study the smoke-filled horizon. "Yes, I see it."

"I saw light coming from inside. I'll fly ahead and make sure it's safe to enter."

Nodding, he bent his head back into the wind and pushed on.

Hoping to find Finn and Eustace in the dome, Fate strained her muscles for acceleration. Her superhuman powers of strength and speed were greatly diminished but she was happy enough to have retained her ability to fly.

Sithias had been right to be concerned. The demon dimension had weakened all powers derived from the old gods, even the oldest of them. Ever since they'd crossed through the portal, her motherly guide had been uncharacteristically silent. Fate was beginning to think Ananke had been forced back into dormancy.

She touched the protective pendant Azrael had given her; grateful she didn't have to suffer the sickening and disorienting effect the demon dimension would otherwise have on her.

When she reached the strangely domed rock formation, she followed the golden light shooting between the cracks of the tangled structure's ceiling. The beautiful light didn't belong in this desolate place of smoke and bone. That much Fate knew for sure.

Spotting a craggy opening at the very top, she descended and leaned over the jagged edge, searching for the light's source.

The breath went out of her, like a cruel fist squeezed her lungs, hard and painful. Finn's entire body was lit from the inside out. His eyes were all but white blazing orbs burning within his skull. His veins and bones blazed bright beneath muscle rapidly scorching away into brilliant sparks of gold dust.

Her blood chilled all the more when she saw Farouk. The monstrous titan was hunched over the delicate gold chain holding the Orb of Aeternitis hooked over one claw. Darcy stood by with a maniacal look in her eyes. Eustace was stone-faced as he watched Finn's painful unraveling.

The last time Fate had seen this destructive light was when Kaliena had used the Orb to separate the Rod from Finn. Farouk was doing the very same to him.

Chaotic panic collided with sheer disbelief, clouding her mind with a jumble of questions she didn't have time to separate. The awfulness of it all was enough to paralyze her with fear, but she forced herself to move, to reach for the alicorn and leap through the hole.

Fate flew at Farouk, ready to plunge the length of the alicorn deep into his spine. The fur on his thick neck bristled in response. Turning his wolfish head, he snapped his massive jaw at her. Fate pulled back from the clack of his fangs and circled back around. Calling upon all the strength and speed she could gather, she aimed the sharp tip of the sword at Farouk's chest and catapulted through the air.

Farouk roared, a terrifying shriek that rumbled through the dome as he lashed out with one arm. Claws as long as swords raked across her field of vision, the deadly tips missing her by a few inches.

Fate shot upward, but not fast enough. Searing pain drilled down the length of her backside from a brutal strike from behind. Tumbling through the air, she smashed into the rock wall and fell to the ground.

Blood flooded her mouth, coating her tongue with a nauseating, metallic tang. She reached around to feel the damage, wincing when she touched ragged flesh. Farouk had sliced through her leather armor like it was threadbare cotton. She drew in a shaky breath, knowing her regenerative powers were weak and possibly nonexistent.

Grabbing the alicorn sword, Fate struggled to rise. Her bones ached to the marrow and every muscle hurt. Blood ran down her legs from the open wound. Every move she made caused excruciating pain as she lifted off the ground and turned to face Farouk.

The demon fixed his blood red gaze on her. "*Together again at last. I was beginning to think you might never arrive.*"

With Farouk's attention averted, Finn remained in a state of partial destruction. It killed her to think what physical agony he must be in, but prolonging the distraction was the only thing she could do. She had to buy him the time she needed to rip the Orb from Farouk's grasp.

Hopefully, Azrael would arrive at any minute. An added distraction would give her the opening she was looking for.

"Farouk, finish what you started!" Darcy screeched. "End him now. I want Fate to see every single second of this!"

Farouk's gaze shifted to Finn as he restarted the Orb's deadly oscillation. Fate rushed at him. In her weakness, she swung the sword too soon, clumsily clubbing him but hard enough to throw him off balance.

The tiny chain slipped off his claw and dropped into a crack in the ground. Snarling, he crouched low, warily watching Fate as he scratched around searching for the Orb.

Fate plunged again but Farouk reared back, knocking the alicorn from her grip. She turned in a panic, searching for where it had landed.

"Why are you doing this?" Fate screamed at Darcy as she raced to find her weapon. "What did Finn ever do to you to deserve this?"

Darcy laughed. "Typical, obtuse, Fate. You've never been able to see what's staring you in the face! Take the goggles off and look around."

Infuriated by Darcy's babble, Fate continued her search and finally spotted her sword. Hurrying to retrieve it, she glanced back at Farouk, who was still digging around in search of the Orb. She grabbed the alicorn and raced back to finish Farouk.

When he saw her coming, he abandoned his search, facing her with fangs bared. She wasn't going to get anywhere being this weak. The best she could do was keep Farouk busy until Azrael arrived.

Fate slowed and hovered above Farouk threateningly.

"The blinders are off, Darcy. And you know what I see? Someone so filled with hatred she's willing to sacrifice two perfectly innocent people. How could you do this to Finn? He never did anything to you! And Eustace too? You worked side by side with him in the library every day." She choked out the last few words as she glanced at Eustace, a hollow thing that only looked like her father.

The manic grin on Darcy's face vanished. "Just so you know, I liked Eustace. He actually took the time to talk to me. He understood my pain. You have no idea how lucky you were to have a dad like that. But you were mean to him. Always pushing him away and throwing tantrums just for being a concerned parent. Not everyone gets to be born a spoiled brat. I didn't get the princess treatment from my dad like you did, Fate. So I can honestly say you took Eustace for granted."

Fate tried not to let Darcy's sadistic barrage affect her, but it hurt.

Darcy looked at Eustace with genuine sorrow. "I didn't think I'd ever stop crying the day Eustace died. He was the only person left who cared how I was feeling."

"If that's how you felt about Eustace, why would you bring him back as this... empty shell?" Fate fought back a flood of tears.

"Because you wanted him back. So I gave you exactly what you wished for."

Fate quaked with fury. "And Finn?"

"Still wearing the blinders. Think hard, Fate. Why would I want to take your boyfriend away from you?"

"Because it's always been hate at first sight for you!"

"Not true. You've obviously forgotten how we met." The bitterness in Darcy's expression softened as she stared into the past for the briefest second before a hateful scowl returned. "I *admired* you back then. But that ended when my friends started dropping like flies. Including my boyfriend. Meeting you was the worst thing that ever happened to me."

"I never asked you to follow me into the Keep!" Fate shouted. "You did that all on your own."

"Don't you get it? We were your fans!" Darcy shrieked. "We were willing to follow you anywhere!"

The guilt Fate felt over the loss of Lincoln and Mason weighed heavier than ever. Maybe Darcy was right. Fate might not have been fully prepared for the troubles they'd encountered upon first reaching the Keep, but she'd certainly experienced enough perils during her time trapped inside the *Book of Fables* to know that Darcy and the others were out of their depth. She should've insisted they all be sent home, in spite of Brune and Farouk's arguments against it. That included Jessie and Eustace.

Fate sighed, ready to accept full responsibility and say so. She wasn't given the chance because Darcy continued her tirade.

"As for Finn, he's useful to me in so many wondrous ways." Darcy fixed her gaze on his anguished expression. There wasn't a drop of compassion in her eyes for the unceasing loop of fiery torment Finn was in. "He carries the Rod of Aeternitis and I *want* it."

Tears glittered in Darcy's hard stare. "Justice is sweet, because ironically enough, Finn has to be ripped apart to get the Rod." She let out a harsh laugh. "You'll finally feel the same gut wrenching agony I go through every night when I close my eyes and see Mason bursting into flames... his skin burning, charring black and crumbling away. Nothing will ever erase the sickening sound of his bones cracking as his body broke and stretched into that monstrous thing!" She pointed at Farouk, jabbing her finger vehemently.

Darcy's eyes glazed over with icy hatred. "Do you have any idea how revolted I was to find out I'd been fooled into thinking that hideous demon was *my* Mason?"

Farouk growled out a deep chortle. *"I'm hurt. I have only the fondest memories of our tender moments together."*

"Shut up!" Darcy shrieked.

For the first time Fate understood the depth of Darcy's pain at falling victim to that level of insidiousness. But why would Darcy ever bargain with the very monster that had violated her?

Fate glanced at Farouk. The black lips of his snout were stretched back in a ghoulish grin. He appeared to be taking great pleasure from Darcy's emotional outburst.

"I'm sorry for everything you've been through, Darcy." Slipping her hand discreetly into one of the pockets of her utility belt, Fate flew a little lower. "If there was some way I could undo it all I would."

The hatred in Darcy's expression deepened. "You know what? I think you disgust me even more than this hairy creep show. You've had the power to undo every awful thing that's ever happened to us. But do you? Oh no, you're too busy sniveling over how afraid you are to use the Words of Making." She shook her head. "You may have the powers of a god, but you're just a weak sauce snot-bubble."

"And you're incapable of accepting an apology." Fate's fingers touched the expandable cage Brune had given her.

"You think an apology can make up for all I've lost?" Darcy laughed again, this time with a hysterical pitch in her voice. "That's rich!"

Fate's patience had reached its limit. Finn was suffering. He didn't deserve to pay for her mistakes. Not again. "Please, don't hurt Finn anymore. You don't need the Rod. I'll use the Words of Making to recreate Mason for you. Right here and now. Just call off your hellhound."

Farouk snarled.

Darcy shook with rage. "I don't want a remade version of Mason. I want the original."

"Done. Give me a thorough description and I'll make it happen." Fate curled her fingers around the cage. Darcy grew quiet a moment and Fate thought she might be tempted to accept the offer.

"It's too late for that. I want more than Mason now and I can only have it all with the Orb and Rod."

"Sorry, but I can't let that happen." In the same breath, Fate tightened her grip on the cage and threw it at Farouk. The movement caused nearly unbearable pain, making her gasp with agony.

Farouk saw it coming and flattened himself to the ground. The cage missed, landed several yards away and rolled to a stop. Taking the opening, Fate descended, intent on staking the monster to the ground with her alicorn sword.

The light radiating from Finn glinted on the Orb. Farouk saw the Orb at the same time Fate did. He scrabbled toward it, digging his claws into the earth as he struggled to make ground, instead, kicking up a cloud of dust around him. Fate dove for the Orb, but she was slow from all the blood loss.

Farouk reached it first, hooking a claw through the chain. Fate screamed and shot past him, grabbed the cage and hurled it at Farouk's back as he struggled to rise from the ground.

"*Aperta Captionem Reverti!*" Fate yelled.

The instant the cage slammed against his coarse fur, the closed bars opened in a flash and elongated like spider's legs, stretching around Farouk's immense height and girth. Within a few short seconds he was fully enclosed within a network of crisscrossed bars engraved with binding sigils activated and glowing bright.

Farouk thrashed against the slim, unbending bars, which Fate guessed must be razor sharp, because they sliced into his hide, opening bloody gashes down his backside and arms. Howling in pain, Farouk turned in circles, his jaws snapping like he was biting at something behind him. He seemed to be chasing his tail.

Relishing his misery, Fate strolled closer, wondering if Farouk might revert to his former, diminutive self. But he didn't. Brune had guessed correctly. It was too late for that. Farouk would remain the hulking monster Fate had come to hate with with every fibre of her being.

She was glad for that. It would make killing him that much more satisfying.

Fate stopped in her tracks, sucking pure terror into her lungs when the hood of Azrael's camouflage robe slipped off his head.

Farouk hadn't been biting at nothing. He'd been fending off Azrael's attack!

Why hadn't she seen what was right in front of her? She'd known she was off her game, but this proved she wasn't thinking straight. It should've been obvious Azrael was Farouk's invisible assailant. But instead, she'd trapped Azrael inside a cage with a demon whose soul desire was to increase her suffering.

45
CONSENT

FAROUK TIGHTENED HIS GRIP on Azrael, who was entirely unable to lift his bloodied saber to kill the monster whose jaw opened wide to bite down on his neck.

"Stop!" Fate begged. "Please don't hurt him."

Darcy laughed maniacally. "Wow, a two for one deal. This vendetta keeps getting better and better."

Farouk's burning gaze slid to Fate, making a show of swinging the Orb to show her he held the power of life and death over two lives. His ugly voice snaked into her brain. "*Which one?*"

"What do you mean?" Fate pressed her palm against the knifing pain in her chest.

"*One will die. One will live. Choose.*"

"No... I can't."

Azrael struggled to breathe beneath Farouk's tight hold. The demon loosened his grip and Azrael coughed, drawing in precious air as Farouk pressed his face between the bars. "*Look at him. Tell him who you choose.*"

"Don't do this!" Fate pleaded. "I'll do anything else you ask of me, but I won't choose between them."

Farouk leaned forward, his shoulders shaking with silent laughter. "*And how has that been working for you?*"

"Fate," Azrael rasped, "push the devil dog from your mind. Do not barter with it. Have no fear for me. Destroy the Hinn and take back the–"

Farouk bashed Azrael's forehead against the cage to silence him. "*Tell me what you would give to save yourself from having to choose.*"

Fate looked away from the blood streaming down over Azrael's blue eyes and hardened her gaze on Farouk. "I'll use the Words of Making to build your kingdom. But only if you free Azrael and make Finn whole again."

"No!" Azrael blindly thrust his saber behind him, stabbing the hulking demon in his hind leg.

Farouk grabbed hold of Azrael with a furious snarl and slammed him sideways into the cage wall. Azrael's head bounced forward. His body went limp and his saber slipped from his hand. Farouk kicked the offending weapon through the bars.

"Hurt him again and the deal's off," Fate warned, her heart hammering with concern.

"*He's dazed. Nothing more. Continue with your offer.*"

"Excuse me." Darcy marched over to the cage. "There will be no deals made here. I'm the one in charge." She held out an upturned hand. "Farouk, give me the Orb."

Farouk looked at her. "*Your jurisdiction over me ends on the other side of this cage.*"

"How do you figure?" Darcy waved Eustace over.

His quiet, immediate response pained Fate beyond all reasoning. She aimed the sharp tip of the alicorn at Darcy. "Leave my father out of this."

"That's not your father anymore. Accept it already." Darcy rolled her eyes.

Eustace kicked Fate's arm, stunning her so completely she let go of her sword. He caught it by the hilt before the point touched the ground and backed away. The murderous look in his yellowing eyes immobilized her, a malicious presence that wasn't Eustace. The hackles on her neck rose, triggering the instinct to destroy the wicked thing inside the husk that was once her father.

Love forced the urge down. There was still hope. Sithias was waiting with an alchemical formula to restore Eustace if she could deliver her father's walking corpse back to the Keep undamaged. Which meant no violence.

"Looks like you're finally getting it." Darcy's voice never sounded smugger.

Fate staggered forward, her fist curled to punch the smirk off Darcy's crusty, dust-covered face. She swiped and missed when Darcy stepped out of the way. Dizzy and weak, Fate put her hands on her knees to keep from falling over. Breathing hard, she glanced down at the blood pooling around the rubber soles of her boots.

"Enough out of you." Fate's breathing came in shallow pants, but she said it with enough rage to momentarily silence Darcy.

Fate straightened and looked at Farouk. "I'll give you everything you want and more." Her throat tightened, making each word a painful effort. "I have to see a show of good faith first. Make Finn whole. And I mean right now, or the deal's off."

Farouk raised his arm, swinging the Orb by its chain in small circles. The faster it moved, the wider the circles. He growled out a spell-rich word, igniting a soft, luminescent glow from within the tiny, all-powerful object. Tracers of golden light sparkled with each gentle oscillation and drifted downward. The glittering haze pooled, flowed over the ground and met with Finn's feet.

The destructive light crackling throughout Finn's body calmed, transformed to a warm shimmer. His tortured features smoothed to a peaceful expression as the liquid-gold light of creation transformed to the color of flesh, fast spreading over his perfectly sculpted form. Thankfully, the ruination had not been complete enough to destroy the darkly inked Elder race runes running down the length of his muscular arms.

At last the restorative energies reached the smooth sheen of his head, which fluidly molded into long bronzed-gold wisps of hair that fell in waves around the seductive curve of his lips, the ends grazing the strong line of his jaw.

Fate's heart leapt when Finn opened his eyes, greener than a spring meadow and far more inviting. He glanced around, momentarily confused until he locked eyes with her. He started to smile, until he saw the blood pooling around her feet.

He rushed over and caught hold of her as she swayed dizzily. Fate drew in a sharp breath when he touched her open wound. "You're hurt," he said, frowning at the blood on his hand. "And you're not healing as usual."

Darcy clapped. "Well, well, isn't this touching. Everybody here gets what they want." She dropped her arms. "Except me."

Azrael groaned as he came to.

"I take it back," Darcy added. "Azrael's not getting what he wants either."

"*It would appear not.*" Farouk yanked Azrael off his feet, raised his neck to his mouth and sank his fangs deep into the soft vulnerable flesh.

Fate screamed as Azrael's blue eyes opened wide and his mouth stretched back in agony. His life's blood flooded around Farouk's snout as he shook his massive head back and forth–shaking until Azrael's arms and legs flopped like a rag doll. Unhinging his jaw, Farouk let Azrael fall at his feet in a crumpled heap.

It was over that quick.

A precious life ended in a matter of seconds. Azrael was dead and Fate was heartsick enough to want to die. "Why?" she cried out at last.

"I told you to choose and you did." Farouk's bloodstained muzzle wrinkled into a gruesome grin.

"No, I didn't. I wouldn't... I couldn't." Fate collapsed against Finn, drained of tears, energy and hope.

Had she chosen? Her answer came when the soul ring she'd placed on Azrael's ankle rolled outside the cage. The jingling sound of the beads inside worsened her remorse. The brass anklet had no break or hinge, making it impossible to remove. The only thing that would ever unlock the soul ring was a heartfelt decision to sever the bond.

When forced, her heart had chosen Finn. Poor Azrael had died knowing the deepest truth of her soul. She'd hurt him in the worst possible way.

"I'm getting you out of here," Finn whispered in her ear. "You're hurt. You've lost too much blood."

"No." She wiped at her eyes roughly and looked at Azrael's lifeless body. Facing what she'd done was the least she could do. "We can't leave him here in this awful place. I won't do it. And Eustace. I have to get him back to the Keep too. Sithias found a way to fix him."

"We'll come back for them once you're strong again." Finn moved to lift her in his arms.

Fate pushed him away. "We had a deal, Farouk, but you broke it. You can kiss your kingdom goodbye. I'll never give you what you want now. *Never!*"

"*Wait and see. You'll give me my kingdom and it will be of your own free will.*"

Farouk's snarling laugh filled Fate with venomous rage. If only his words didn't riddle her with doubt. She would never believe him if not for Aradif's vision of an unbelievable alliance with the demon. How could Farouk have seen the same possible future? He must know something she didn't.

"Explain to me how that could *ever* happen." Desperation forced her to ask a question she had no expectation of him answering.

Farouk scratched his silvered claws along the bars of his cage, sparking miniature streams of lightning. "*Do you want to tell her, or should I?*" he asked Darcy.

Darcy strolled casually over to his cage. "She'll never hear it from these lips." She leaned close enough to have an eye gouged out, should Farouk choose to jab a claw through the small opening. "Or you, for that matter."

Wisps of black smoke curled past Farouk's fangs as he growled threateningly. But that low savage growl ended abruptly, cut off by a gurgling in his throat. He dropped the Orb and gripped the bars of his prison, roaring in pain as the sharp tip of the alicorn burst through the lower half of his ribcage.

Black rot spread from the wound at an unbelievable rate, peeling his hide away. Clouds of fur billowed into the air. Farouk locked eyes with Fate, quaking and shuddering as the fire behind his incandescent gaze dimmed like the batteries running low in a flashlight.

He laughed again. Only this time it was more of a bleating, rasping noise that was almost piteous. "*Listen carefully, Fate. No one... not even Ananke is immune to the Eldritch Gloom. I can already see it eating away at–*"

A grotesque implosion of his skull put an end to his power to trespass and impose his thoughts into the minds of everyone there. His fanged snout collapsed into crumbling cinder. Seconds later, all that was left was a moldering skeleton. These last decaying remnants teetered, then crashed against the cage and disintegrated, covering Azrael in a thick blanket of fine black ash.

Eustace stood on the other side of the cage gripping the alicorn. He stood stone still, staring at the swirling embers drifting between the bars. His purpose for being resurrected was complete. He'd exacted revenge on his killer.

Fate stayed where she was, terrified of what she knew would come next.

Eustace dropped to the ground in the same moment her strength deserted her. Finn was there to catch her before she hit the dirt. She slumped against him, numb to the grievous wound on her back. The agony of untold sorrow was all she could feel as she stared into her father's dead eyes.

Finn turned her around and she buried her face against his chest. His grip was fierce, his breathing strained as he shook with anger. "Darcy, you're going to pay for all the misery you've caused."

"Careful how you talk to me," Darcy warned in a singsong voice. "Look who has the Orb."

Adrenaline fired through Fate as she turned to see Darcy dangling the Orb with a malicious smile. She pushed away from Finn and staggered toward Darcy, too weak to fight, hoping for mercy. "Darcy, I give up," she sobbed. "You win. Please, leave Finn out of this."

Darcy wagged a finger at her. "You know I can't do that. He has something I want."

"Are you really this cold-hearted? Haven't I lost enough to make you happy?"

"We're this close to making me happy." Darcy held her thumb and finger close together. "Finn's the one that'll break you completely. And then I'll be... ecstatic, actually."

"He's innocent in this."

"Boohoo." Darcy wiggled her fists in front of her eyes with the overdramatic movements of a street mime. Flopping her arms to her sides, she shrugged. "Phff. Come on, Fate. He's not even a real boy. Not like Mason was."

"Enough!"

The sharp edge in Finn's voice startled Darcy. Taking a step back, she swung the Orb. Before she could utter a word of her destructive incantation, he spoke in the Elder race language. His voice boomed with such volume and power, Fate had to cover her ears.

The ground shook as huge slabs of earth shifted violently beneath them, knocking Fate off her feet. Darcy stumbled, losing all momentum with the Orb's swing. She looked frightened but stubbornly determined. Regaining her balance, she swung the Orb in full circles while shouting out the incantation.

Bright jagged light exploded from the Orb. Finn went rigid, paralyzed as the veins in his arms and face lit into blazing networks of fiery light and the earthquake he'd invoked ended as suddenly as it began. Fate watched helplessly as he shook in agony, trapped within the painful cycle of uncreation once more.

Fate crawled toward the alicorn. She tugged on the pointed end to free the hilt from Eustace's tight grip. It wouldn't come loose. Inching forward, she touched his cold, dead hand to pry his fingers loose but jerked her arm back. She tried again, stopped by a sudden onset of nausea that had her vomiting.

When the convulsions ended, she was too weak to move. Hopelessness crashed in, threatening to drop her into a bottomless pit of despair.

"*Now do you see what it is to be without my power and wisdom?*"

Fate thought she must be delirious. Blood loss and grief had her hearing things, because surely Ananke would never have abandoned her this long.

Would she?

"*I had to teach you a lesson, my precious daughter. You needed to see that without me you are nothing.*"

Fate shook her head, confused, hurt. What mother would do this?

"*This is no time for denial. Not if you wish to save him in time.*"

"I do. I want to save him."

"*Very good.*" Ananke's power trickled in, a small infusion to let Fate know she was truly present. "*First, you must accept me fully. Do you consent to merge with me, my daughter?*"

Fate didn't understand.

"*We will finally become one. Say yes and you will never have to experience the weaknesses of human frailties and the endless pain that comes with it.*"

Fate's bleary gaze drifted to Eustace. His eyes were already glazed over with a milky film. Now that the magic was gone, inevitable decay had set in, graying his skin, shriveling it into papery cracks.

She turned away with a dry sob as unbearable sorrow clawed at the bruised, frail remnants of her heart. Her gaze fell on Azrael, driving the anguish deeper as surely as a blade buried in her chest. His face was hidden beneath the folds of his cloak and she was thankful for that. But when she looked at Finn–burning away from the inside out–her torment intensified and she begged for death to take her too.

"*You cannot give up.*" Ananke pressed down on Fate with the full weight of the leviathan she truly was. Fate had never felt this tiny and insignificant before. "*You were bred to withstand every challenge and hardship I've laid in your path. I've waited eons for a descendant worthy enough to house my power. You, above all others, have proven yourself worthy. Accept me now.*"

"No, I'm tired of fighting," Fate rasped. "I can't do it anymore. I have nothing left to fight for." She curled into a ball, tucking her face beneath her arms, wanting only to hide. But there was no hiding from Ananke's inescapable presence.

"*What of Finn? It's not too late for him. Would you give up now and let him perish?*"

Ananke had never used Finn's name before. Hearing his name stirred Fate enough to lift her head.

"*Say yes and I will restore Finn with every power he has ever possessed and more. He will be born anew, blessed with his own life force. The Orb will be powerless over him because it will no longer be the source of his creation.*"

All Fate had ever wanted for Finn was that he be his own sovereign being. She'd wanted it every bit as much as he did. Nothing else was as important as that.

Fate surrendered with every fiber of her being and screamed *YES!*

46
THE ELDRITCH GLOOM

RED-HOT AGONY SEARED along Finn's nerves. His eyes were on fire, his vision blinded by a shower of radiant gold sparks. He was stuck, unable to connect with his body. There seemed to be nothing of substance to move. All that remained was excruciating pain, scorching through every pathway of his nervous system. He tried crying out, to make the smallest sound. His voice was gone, as if his throat and vocal cords had shattered into a million tiny particles.

He was dying. That much he knew. But what was this killing light? He reached for a memory. Something to tell him what was happening and why.

There was nothing. His mind was empty. Blank.

Brilliant white light overtook the fiery, golden flare filling his vision. Warmth poured through the last vestiges of his body, repairing the damage, soothing the raging pain.

The healing light flowed into his eyes, dousing the unbearable fire. Like honeyed syrup, the light flooded through his brain, down his throat, filling phantom limbs with precious, life giving energy, substance and form. The weight of his arms and legs returned. His lungs expanded with air.

Finn ran his hands over his arms, grateful to be touching skin, muscle and bone. Overwhelming relief curved his mouth into a smile as he opened his eyes.

Everything that had happened crashed in all at once. Farouk had murdered Azrael. Eustace had killed the demon and had died as a consequence. Finn remembered trying to stop Darcy from using the Orb on him. Loathing returned when he remembered the torture she'd inflicted upon him.

Darcy was still swinging the Orb, lit with the same terrible fire that had blinded him when his eyes were burning out of his skull. For whatever reason, the killing fire had no power over him. Darcy lost all concentration as she came to the same realization. The Orb swung to a dangling stop. "Why isn't this working?" She looked at the Orb, then back at Finn.

She nervously turned in the opposite direction. "Where's Fate?"

Finn's anger evaporated with the memory of Fate's wound. She'd been weak and unable to heal. He didn't see her anywhere.

"Dios mio!" Darcy's voice was a frightened gasp.

Finn followed her gaze and his mouth went as dry as the clay beneath his feet.

Fate hovered high above them. Only it wasn't Fate. This was Ananke, an enormous giantess, wearing the armor of a black knight. Hot air rose from the red blazing core of her illumined waist, blowing her long hair skyward in glistening waves. She stared down at them with a fiery gaze. Inky smoke flecked with smoldering embers trailed off the flaming tips of massive wings as dark as night. Blistering heat raked over him with each mighty sweep of those fearsome wings, whipping clouds of dust into the air that rose to obscure his view.

Where was Ananke's silvered armor? Why was she so huge? And where were her wings of white-gold light? Was this Ananke's true form?

This dark visage struck more dread in his heart than anything he'd witnessed thus far.

Finn's spirits withered, dropping him to his knees. His greatest fear had come to pass. Fate had lost the battle against Ananke. Losing Eustace in the most horrendous way possible had finished her. Everything he'd done–all the lies he'd told to protect her– had been for naught.

Yet Finn could not bring himself to believe she was lost. Fate was still inside that winged nightmare. She had to be!

Darcy shrieked and ran in the opposite direction as Ananke landed near them.

Seeing this might be his only chance to connect, Finn placed his hand on the hard clay and thrust his awareness down through the earth, touching the soles of Ananke's feet, searching for Fate's spirit.

Darkness flooded over his senses, tossing him on violent currents he feared would drown him. He fought to pull out but the undertow was too great. Something horrible was hiding in the dark tide, dragging him down, down, down.

Ananke was suddenly upon him, peeling back his mind, splaying his soul open. Nothing could have prepared him for the sheer enormity of her presence as she raked through his most sacred, private thoughts and memories. The anguish this caused was torturous. He forced himself to endure the violation in the hope of finding Fate and looked inside. The floodgates opened, pouring eon's worth of knowledge about Ananke into Finn within the span of a second's glance.

The deluge was overwhelming, more than he could consciously assimilate.

This was once a nameless entity of such incomprehensible immensity, it coiled around the universe, creating worlds, controlling the heavens, ruling destinies through the alignment of planets and stars. The ancient history dwelling within her essence reached back into a void without end. There seemed to be no time when Ananke had not existed.

The connection broke without warning, ended abruptly by Ananke. Finn rose shakily to his feet, certain he'd be struck down for his trespass. To his relief, she appeared to be finished with him, discarding him like a scrap of rubbish. Or maybe Fate had interceded. He could only hope.

"You!" Ananke's thunderous voice shook the dome, startling Finn as she pointed the alicorn at Darcy. "Step forward."

Darcy drew backward, muttering incantations under her breath. A defense Finn assumed would be useless against a deity of such magnitude, but his assumption proved surprisingly wrong.

Ananke moved in a swift blur, arching the alicorn down on the witch. The air warped around Darcy as Ananke pushed against a well-conjured force field. Finn might have expected Darcy's usual smug bravado, but she was clearly terrified as she chanted the warded shield over and over again. Black strands of hair clung to her wet brow as she concentrated with her palm facing the giantess, her arm shaking under the strain.

With one powerful thrust of her enormous wings, Ananke rose directly above Darcy, this time driving the alicorn straight down. When the point hit Darcy's shield, the sheer impact jarred the hilt from Ananke's grip. She turned and swept after the alicorn as it plummeted across the dome's large expanse.

Darcy swung the Orb in hard, fast circles, speaking two words again and again. It sounded Arabic, but Finn couldn't be sure. Violet tracers formed in the air, darkening into a deep purple vapor. Glinting with stardust, the vaporous mist coiled to the ground and swirled in front of her. Shaking with fright, Darcy glanced up long enough to see Ananke catch the sword and turn back.

Darcy stared at the ground, yelling the strange words repeatedly until the ground cracked and crumbled away into a gaping hole. She was using the Orb to make her escape. If only he understood the language she spoke, he might know exactly where the Orb would transport her.

Darcy looked at Finn and laughed. "Sucks to be you."

Finn glanced at Ananke's swift, impending return. "Beg to differ with you, lass."

Darcy leaned over the hole, ready to jump. "You really have no idea what's coming, do you?" Utter confidence had replaced the fear in her eyes and that disturbed him. Darcy knew something he didn't.

"Do the decent thing for once. Tell me what you know."

"Can't, no time."

"I could end you right here," he threatened; ready to call down a storm that would obliterate the witch.

"You won't though. You're the decent one here."

"You've obviously never seen my bad side!" Finn invoked Air, summoning the winds into his hands.

"Ooh, black eyes. Scary." Darcy winked. "Catch me if you can." With that, she dropped into the dark glittering hole.

The voice of giants spoke through Finn as he shouted his command and unleashed the cutting winds. The deafening sound collided with Ananke's furious roar as she raced to stop Darcy's escape. The reverberations shook the dome, cracking the stone. Dust and rubble showered down from the ceiling.

The ground sealed over Darcy's glinting portal in the same moment Ananke's fist met the earth, rupturing a hole of her own. Finn ducked as chunks of clay flew in every direction, made worse by the windstorm he'd conjured.

Rising to her full, imposing height, Ananke stared at the shallow hole she'd punched into the ground. The wrathful furrow in her brow smoothed as she closed her eyes and vanished.

"*Fate!*" Finn yelled.

Gutted, he hung his head and weakly commanded the winds to leave. The air settled and the dust thinned, but the sound of the constant winds outside the dome remained to mirror his despair with their desolate shrieks.

Fate was gone. Consumed by an all-powerful being he couldn't begin to understand, let alone expect to defeat. Ananke moved through space and time like he moved through air. She possessed the ultimate power to order the stars to rule destinies. Ananke had planned everything that had led to this single point in time eons ago.

The realization slammed in that his destiny was never his to steer. Fate's destiny was surely never hers. They'd never stood a chance.

How was he supposed to fight that?

Maybe he wasn't. He hated himself for even thinking it. But what else could he think? He'd been powerless to save Fate.

Finn glanced at the wreckage. His gaze fell reluctantly on Eustace and Azrael. He couldn't leave their bodies in this dreadful place. Of course he had no idea how he was going to make that happen. He sighed heavily, resolved to carry each body back to the gateway one at a time if it came to that.

This would at least honor Fate's last wish.

Miserable about the task before him, Finn walked over to the bodies. He closed Eustace's lids, unable look upon his glazed-over eyes. He leaned down to lift him, further forcing down his revulsion as the bones in his stiff arm cracked. Finn positioned Eustace onto his right shoulder with a grimace. His body was lighter than he would have expected for a man of Eustace's height. He was little more than a dried out husk.

Finn staggered, slammed by a sudden bout of dizziness. He stood with a wide stance to keep from falling, figuring he was more sickened than he realized. The last thing he wanted was to drop Eustace and hear the crunch of bones when his brittle corpse hit the ground.

He waited for his head to stop spinning, a sensation that only worsened. His surroundings blurred and whirled around him like a tornado. Everything turned black, ending the incessant shriek of the wild winds beating at the outside walls of the dome. For one terrifying moment, he thought Ananke had yanked him through space to finish what she'd started. Then to his relief, the lights came on, revealing the library.

Gerdie clapped gleefully from the top end of the library table. "You did it Sithias! See? All that worry over usin' the Words of Makin' was wasted time. You got them... out." Her smile vanished when she saw Finn with Eustace slung over his shoulder and Azrael on the floor.

Sithias shrieked at the top of his lungs. "My words murdered them!" Teetering, his eyes rolled to the back of his head and he toppled backward onto the floor as stiff as a wooden board. The sheet of paper he was holding caught air and flitted down onto his chest.

Finn lowered Eustace's corpse gently next to Azrael, then hurried over to Sithias. Gerdie folded the piece of paper and used it to fan Sithias's face.

Sithias's eyes fluttered open. Disoriented and shaken, he stared at the ceiling before his roving gaze locked onto Finn. "What happened to Fate?" he asked tremulously. "Did I..." He closed his eyes and cried.

"You had nothing to do with this, except to deliver us here," Finn assured him.

"Then where is she?" Sithias sat up, turning his head to the bodies lying on the floor. His shoulders shook with more sobs.

Finn choked back his own grief. "Ananke has fully possessed Fate. It happened after Eustace killed Farouk and died."

"How did Azrael..." Gerdie trailed off.

"Farouk killed Azrael. It was all too much for Fate. She had nothing left to fight Ananke." Barely able to voice the last few words, Finn helped Sithias to his feet.

Finn turned his thoughts to Darcy, drawing upon rage to override being further weakened by grief. "Darcy was working with Farouk the entire time," he seethed. "We never went to the Hadean kingdom. I have no idea where we were, except that Darcy led me into a trap so Farouk could use the Orb to rip me apart to get the Rod. The whole time there Eustace was acting strangely and then I come to find out why. Darcy resurrected him as a revenant! Eustace was never actually brought back to life. That's why he looks like he's been dead for days already, poor sot." He sighed.

Sithias drew out his handkerchief. "We know."

"You know?" Finn lowered his voice when Sithias cringed. "When did you find out?"

"Shortly after you left." Sithias blew his nose. "We found a trail of clues behind in Darcy's deplorable suite. That's why Fate and Azrael went in after you."

"And look what happened!" Finn scolded. "You never should've let them go."

Gerdie stepped in front of Sithias to stop Finn from closing in. "You say that like we could've stopped Fate."

"Sorry," Finn muttered. "I shouldn't be blaming you." He punched his fist into the palm of his hand. "I'm lost. I don't know what to do."

Gerdie took his hand in hers and squeezed. "We'll figure somethin' out. But first we need to show some respect to our fallen friends."

Finn nodded as she trotted over to the intercom, calling for several med bots. They arrived within minutes with two hover stretchers. Finn turned his back as they gathered up the bodies and Gerdie instructed them to make them ready for burial.

The doors of the library banged open loudly. It was Jessie. "Hey guys, it's been over four hours. Are they back yet?" She raced across the marble floor then skidded to a stop when she saw Eustace being carried out.

"No!" Tears welled in her eyes as she stopped the med bots to stare at his gray, chalky face. She turned away stiffly. Her complexion blanched when she saw the other stretcher covered with a sheet. Her hand shook as she drew it back to see who it was. Gasping with a mixture of horror and relief, she let go of the cloth and stepped aside to let the med bots take the bodies away. "Poor Azrael. I thought for sure it was Fate. Where is she?"

"Ananke took over," Finn replied. "I'm fairly sure she went after Darcy."

Jessie wiped the tears from her eyes. "Wait. Why would Ananke chase after Darcy? That sounds like something Fate would do."

"Aye," Finn agreed, feeling the tiniest glimmer of hope. "Come to think of it, I'm fairly certain Ananke stopped Darcy from using the Orb to destroy me."

Jessie nodded. "There you go. That's a sure sign Fate's still on board."

Finn stared past her as doubt moved in to banish hope.

"What?" Jessie frowned at him. "Don't tell me you don't think so all of a sudden."

"I want that to be true more than anything. But something happened when I connected with Ananke to see if I could reach Fate. There was so much darkness inside Ananke and I sensed a presence hiding inside it before she severed the connection."

"Did you sense Fate?" Sithias asked.

Finn shook his head. "No."

"Ananke must've kicked you out before you could get anywhere near her." Jessie's voice pitched with desperation. She wasn't going to let this go.

"That's possible," Finn admitted.

"Damn right, it's possible," Jessie insisted. "Ananke has every reason to isolate Fate, from you especially. She can control her better that way. Keep her from busting out."

Encouraged, Finn nodded.

Gerdie climbed onto the tabletop, letting her legs dangle over the edge. "Tell us more about this dark presence."

Jessie huffed impatiently. "We don't have time for this. It was obviously Ananke and you got close enough to see the evil she's really made of."

"No," Finn was quick to say. "I saw and felt what Ananke's made of. Believe me when I say we're up against a force beyond reckoning, but she's not evil in the true sense of the word. Ananke considers herself the great mother of all and she's furious with her children. She's become disgusted with their apathy and mediocrity, even when the stars are aligned to favor them. Most of all, she abhors their weakness to perpetrating evil."

Finn leaned against the table's edge next to Gerdie. "Ananke wants to be directly involved in deciding destinies through punishment by pouring all her fire into Fate. The same fire she once spread amongst her three daughters, the Furies. With Fate as her carefully cultivated vessel, Ananke will possess the sum total of that power here on the physical plane."

"What about the dark presence you sensed?" Sithias asked

"That was something else entirely and I believe it's the Eldritch Gloom. Farouk said not even Ananke is immune to it. He went so far as to say he could see it eating away at her, but Darcy shut him up before he could finish."

"That's right!" Jessie interjected. "When Fate did a rewind on time and played back Darcy's last meeting with Farouk, Darcy said it was only a matter of time before Ananke succumbs to the Eldritch Gloom."

"Fate rewound time?" Flabbergasted, Finn waved a hand when Jessie started to explain. "Never mind. What you're saying lines up with what I sensed. I had the distinct feeling the darkness was allowing Ananke to use its power, while slowly infecting her."

Sithias looked horrified. "How dreadful! What do you propose we do?"

Finn marched around to the other side of the table and pressed his fists into the hard surface. "We go back to our original plan. Get Dantalion's Key and unlock Hippolyta's girdle. By making it impossible for Fate to be the vessel, Ananke will be banished and the darkness with her."

Sithias raised his hand like a timid first-grader afraid of his teacher.

"What is it, Sithias?"

"We can banish Ananke, but Fate will still have the alicorn. She'll become infected and who's to say she would survive once she's a normal human."

Jessie pointed at Sithias. "Yup, that's something to consider."

"Then we get the alicorn from Ananke *before* we use the key."

"Takin' the alicorn first is best, but it's possible Fate might already be infected." Gerdie sat across from him, deep in thought while wiggling a loose tooth. "Without knowing more about the Eldritch Gloom, it's tough to say if the spread of the infection would be slow or fast. Fast means it could kill her."

Finn stared at her, incredulous. "Are you saying we shouldn't unlock the girdle?" he growled.

"Not sure." Gerdie crawled across the tabletop to a stack of books as tall she was when sitting beside them. When she noticed Finn frowning, she stopped reading the spines with her head tilted to one side. "What? I need to know more about the Eldritch Gloom before I can answer that."

"Aye, we'll leave it to you then." Finn turned to Sithias. "I know you don't like to use the Words of Making for complicated matters such as this, but I'm begging you to use them to get me in and out of Hadean's Kingdom so I can find that confounded key."

Sithias straightened, his eyes brightening. "Oh, there's no need for that, sir." He scampered over to a narrow wooden box, spun around with a dramatic sweep of his arm and held up a long slender rod, wrought in delicate gold filigree encrusted with jewels. "I have it right here!"

Finn was stunned and bewildered. "That doesn't look like any key I've ever seen before. If anything, I'd say it's a wand."

"Actually, that's exactly what it is." Sithias waved the wand with all the daintiness of a cartoon tooth fairy. All that was missing were the sparkles. "It's only called a key because its sole purpose for being made was to unlock Hippolyta's girdle merely by aiming it. Just make sure you point the end with the ruby."

Finn could hardly believe this incredible stroke of good luck. "But..." He was suddenly angry. "Wait a minute. All this talk of the key and you had it the entire–"

Sithias tapped him on the nose with the tip of the wand. "We found it a few hours ago, right here in the library! Once we discovered Darcy had no plans of taking you to Hadean's kingdom, we figured she must have found the key and hid it away along with all her other lies. The credit really goes to Gerdie. She's the one who figured out Darcy's notes and the new name she gave the key in order to keep it logged in the records and stored in the library reliquary without us ever suspecting a thing."

Jessie stepped in beside Sithias to have a closer look at the wand. "It's about time things started going our way."

An alarm clamored, a sharp ringing that echoed throughout the library, making everyone jump.

"Why'd you have to go and say that?" Gerdie huffed. "You jinxed us."

Finn sighed. "Come on, Jessie. Let's see what the emergency is this time."

"What about me?" Sithias asked.

"Stay and help Gerdie. Dig up everything you can on the Eldritch Gloom and be quick about it. There's no telling when, or even *if* I'll get the chance to use the key." Finn plucked the wand from Sithias's fingers and stuck it into the longest pocket of his army pants. "I won't wait if the chance comes. Fate's already gone and if I can use this key to try to get her back then I have to. Otherwise, we might as well say our goodbyes to Fate forever."

47
THE FIGHT BETWEEN HORNS AND HALOS

THE SANCTUARY WAS PACKED with heavily armed Beldereth knights. They had aeronaut packs strapped on and were waiting in line to jump through the open hatch. Vicious roars of Serpen dragons and the boom of cannons resounded beyond the thick bronze walls. Brune, Rudwor and his officers were gathered around the meeting table, absorbed in watching a holographic projection of what was happening outside.

The Serpens had launched a full on attack.

"How bad is it?" Finn asked as he stepped up to the table with Jessie at his side.

"Which do you want first? The good news or the bad?" Rudwor grumbled.

"Give me the good."

Rudwor wiped a meaty hand down over his nose and beard in frustration. "There is none, lad. That's the bad news."

Finn glanced at the projection of dragons wheeling through the sky, spewing rivers of fire at Eldunough hawk riders and Biraktar airships. The front line of Biraktar's fleet listed downward in flames, having taken a heavy hit so the second line could blast the dragons with cannon fire. Two dragons plummeted down and slammed into the dunes below.

"At least we have the help of Biraktar. That's something," Finn said.

Brune shook her head, her gaze fixed on the horrors unfolding before them. "Look again."

Archers lining the decks of Biraktar sprayed the sky dark with arrows, not at the dragons, but at Beldereth knights and Eldunough hawk riders. Knights who weren't killed instantly, spun out of control, spiraling from tremendous heights to their death. The Biraktar archers targeted the majestic giant hawks with hundreds of arrows to take the raptors down, at the same time running their riders through with just as many arrows.

Finn swore under his breath and looked away.

"What the heck?" Jessie exclaimed. "Why are they attacking us? Brune, you were there in the library too. Tell me I'm not losing my mind. You heard Azrael say his father agreed to the alliance. Right?"

"There's no way the fleet could've made it here so quickly," Brune asserted, furious as she watched the battle. "This was planned, even before Fate brought the king here. Azrael obviously lied to get his father back to safety."

"Azrael's dead," Jessie informed her. "Farouk killed him. And in case you haven't noticed, Finn's the only one who made it out."

Tearing her gaze from the terrible slaughter, Brune looked at Finn. Slow realization replaced the bitter rage on her face. "What happened?" she asked him.

"I'll tell you, but first I want to clear the air about Azrael." Finn could hardly believe he was about to defend the guy who'd caused him so much turmoil. "He never would have lied to Fate about his father's true intentions. He loved her too much for that."

Brune's expression didn't change. "That's touching. Not that it matters much now. What I want to know is what happened with Farouk."

"Eustace killed Farouk. Darcy got away with the Orb. Ananke took over and vanished." Finn forced back the pain, always there, just below the surface.

"I'm sorry, laddie." Rudwor patted Finn on the shoulder, jostling him off balance before grabbing hold to steady him back on his feet. "You must be miserable."

"Aye, I can only hope Fate finds her way back to us."

Brune banged the table with her fist. "Enough about Fate. She made her bed and it's time we let her lie in it. We have more urgent matters to attend to. People are dying out there."

Finn bit down on the urge to defend Fate. As calloused as Brune was being, she wasn't wrong about their desperate state of affairs. He could see Jessie warring with the same desire to come to Fate's defense. She followed his lead and remained silent.

"I'll suit up." Finn walked over to the arsenal of armor and weapons piled at the back end of the sanctuary. He wasn't about to stand by and watch others die. Fighting the good fight was better than sitting around being eaten alive by the angst of not knowing if he would ever see Fate again.

Jessie followed. "I'm fighting too." She sorted through the armor, settling on a leather coat embedded with cybernetic enhancements.

"No you're not." Finn swiped the coat from her. "Fate will never forgive me if I let anything happen to you."

"Fate's not here and we don't know if she's ever coming back." Tears filled Jessie's eyes and she blinked hard to stop the flood. "I can't just stand by and wring my hands. I have to do something. I'm a good fighter and I know how to defend myself."

"I remember, but that was when you were a suped up killing machine."

"Thanks for the painful reminder." Jessie stared back hurt and Finn felt terrible for his thoughtless remark.

"I suppose it's not my place to tell you what you can and can't do." He turned back to looking for a helmet but there was none left. Grabbing a pair of goggles, he pulled the strap over his head and let it hang from his neck. He held out a pair of goggles to Jessie as a peace offering. "Take this, you'll need it during the sandstorm."

They dressed silently and returned to the table, where Brune and Rudwor's generals spoke in hushed tones. "What's the plan?" Finn asked.

Brune straightened. The dark rings circling her eyes seemed deeper, more pronounced. "The few remaining hawks and riders have retreated. I assume somewhere outside the visual perimeter, because we can't see them anymore. Two dragons went after them. That leaves six dragons in the vicinity and they're keeping busy with the Biraktar fleet." She glanced at Rudwor with a pained expression. "By the last count, Beldereth has lost half its numbers. We've ordered them to retreat and we won't be sending out any more until we have a solid plan. Which, to answer your question, we don't have."

"I don't have a plan exactly, but I can summon a sandstorm that'll destroy those airships, which will rid us of their archers," Finn offered. "With them gone, the hawks will have a better chance against the dragons."

Rudwor grinned proudly. "That's my First Knight talking." He slapped Finn on the back, knocking the air from his lungs.

His officers nodded approvingly. "If you can do that," one of the women said, "we'll be able to deploy forces to attack the Serpen troops on the ground as well."

Finn glanced at the projection and the alarming sprawl of Serpen legions covering miles of sand in and around the Keep's colossal rings. "You don't have the numbers for that."

"Beldereth doesn't, but the Asgar army does."

Finn frowned. "I thought they weren't to be trusted after they joined the Serpens in the takeover attempt."

"You're forgetting the Serpens betrayed them and the bloodbath they suffered as a result," Brune said. "Believe me, the Asgar army is highly motivated to obliterate the Serpens."

"How will you get the entire Asgar army down there without the Serpens seeing them coming?" Finn asked.

"Sithias will use the Words of Making and place them strategically."

Brune glanced around the room. "Speaking of, where is the snake?"

"In the library doing some research for me." Finn decided to omit the subject of the research.

She narrowed her eyes. "What more is there to research?"

Finn launched into an outright lie. "I'm having Sithias and Gerdie confirm whether Dantalion's Key is in Hadean's kingdom. Since Darcy lied about pretty much everything else, we thought it best to ensure this wasn't another one." He glanced at Jessie then back at Brune.

"Good idea," Brune agreed. "How fast can you call up that sandstorm?"

"In no time at all."

"Excellent. Have at it then." Brune gestured to one of the officers. "Send for Sithias."

Finn pardoned himself as he pushed through the dense crowd of knights blocking his way to the hatch. He jumped out of the way as several wounded knights flew in through the opening, barely able to stand when they landed. The warriors waiting inside the sanctuary rushed in to carry their bloodied comrades away to medical.

At last the platform cleared and Finn stepped to the very edge of the hatch. Holding on with one hand, he leaned out for a look. Patches of blue sky showed through a thickening haze of smoke veiling the shadowy forms of Biraktar airships circling the Keep. Cannon fire blasted from the huge hulls of the warships. Some moved within the gigantic rings, while most of the fleet was positioned further out along the skyline.

Dragons, as large as the ships, dodged the cannons with an intelligence that was disturbing. From where Finn stood, it looked like a few of the winged serpents were purposely acting as bait, giving the other dragons the opportunity to attack from a higher angle. They rammed into the ships and grappled on, breathing fire over the deck and sails. The far off screams of burning soldiers was horrible.

Finn leaped into the air, sped toward to the closest ring and landed on the highest crest. From there he could see the full extent of Biraktar's fleets and sister alliances flying under the colors of many different banners. Brune had surmised correctly, this had been planned. Probably from the moment the last war ended. Only this battle was not to save an entire world from utter destruction when they'd fought together against Kaliena, but to conquer others who would take the Keep and claim it for their own nation.

Jessie landed next to Finn, giving him a start. "What are you doing here?"

"Watching your back while you do your thing." She turned off the aeronaut pack and glanced around. "Whoa, everything looks way worse from up here than it did in the sanctuary. That projection's so much smaller. Kind of deceiving, and not in a good way."

"You think?" Finn hit the ignition on the aeronaut pack, triggering the metal dragonfly-shaped wings into a shiny blur of motion. "I changed my mind. You need to go back."

Jessie frowned at him as she was lifted off her feet involuntarily. "You're being a jerk!"

"You said it yourself, it's worse out here than it looks from the safety of the sanctuary." Finn turned to the battle below and fixed his gaze on the horizon. Taking in a deep breath, he invoked Earth and Air. The rune powers exploded from inside with heat, streaming from his mouth in hot waves of fiery sparks.

The distant dunes swelled like tidal waves, rising to incredible heights so high they blocked the sun. The winds rushed to meet the rising wall of sand, a collision of elements that turned the massive wave into a titanic, billowing cloud that crashed into the Biraktar fleets and swallowed them whole.

Dust-filled winds slammed into Finn. Turning his back to it, he pulled the goggles on and rocketed upward in a race to escape the storm's full onslaught. A panicked scream stalled his climb. He slowed, scanning the churning sands before he spotted Jessie tumbling out of control.

Finn dove, catching her by the waist, narrowly saving her from smashing into the side of the ring and lifted her with him. Shrieking wind and sand pelted into them, cutting into exposed skin as he strained hard to rise above the fierce currents.

He would have commanded the elements to stop if other lives weren't at stake. But clearing the skies of Biraktar ships would give their side a much-needed advantage.

At last Finn broke through the top of the sandstorm into clear, calm skies. Jessie was hanging on so tightly with her arm around his neck she was nearly strangling him. "Jessie, ease up." he croaked.

She loosened her grip. "Oops, didn't mean to be the scorpion on your back."

"Huh?"

"You know, the scorpion and the frog story, where the frog offers a ride–"

"Jessie." Finn started to scold her for coming after him, then pressed his lips together.

"You're mad."

"You might say that." Seeing that the aeronaut wings were working and undamaged, he let go, allowing her to hover in front of him.

Jessie tested the gears, moving up, down and sideways. "Whew! Looks like I'm good to go." She glanced at the swirling mass beneath them. "As soon as the storm's over. It's still kind of churny down there at the moment. I'll just wait here, if you don't mind."

Finn nodded grimly.

"That's some uber-crazy power you've got there with those Alder runes, or whatever you call them."

"Elder race runes."

"Right. I knew I had that wrong." Jessie smiled ruefully. "You know, since I have you here and all, I've always wondered if powers come with built-in knowledge of how to use them or if someone has to teach you."

"Tove taught me the basics, the rest came on instinct."

Jessie nodded, clearly dissatisfied with his clipped reply. "Tove's a real kickass fighter."

"Aye, that she is."

"I saw her in the halls all suited up. Looked to me like she's joining the battle."

Finn frowned. "When was this?"

"A half hour ago, when we came from the library. She was looking straight at you. I thought you saw her too."

"Damn it," he muttered guiltily. Tove had asked him to have Fate send her back to Feldoril Forest. He'd forgotten her tearful request entirely, what with the troubles that ensued upon their return. A terrible excuse really. If he was being truly honest, Tove hadn't crossed his mind until this very moment.

"What's wrong?" Jessie asked.

"This isn't Tove's fight. She hates being in the Keep. Tove wanted to stay in Feldoril Forest and I was supposed to make that happen. I should've asked Sithias to do it, but I was distracted and eventually forgot. Who am I kidding? I was too involved with my own concerns."

"Nah, I think you have it all wrong. If Tove *really* wanted to leave, she would've asked Sithias herself."

Finn stared back in surprise.

Jessie rolled her eyes with an amused chuckle. "Wow, why is it guys never see the obvious?" When Finn had nothing to offer, she continued. "Fate told me all about Tove and how she feels about you. The girl's still madly in love with you and that's why she stayed. She wants to be here to pick up the pieces when it doesn't work out between you and Fate."

"No, no, no," Finn argued. "Tove's in love with Prince Ethlan."

Jessie shook her head, annoying Finn to no end.

"She hates me for breaking her heart and the loss of her family in the war," Finn added. "Can't say I disagree with any of the above. I'd hate me too."

"The line between love and hate is fine and razor-sharp, but I can say with absolute confidence, Tove still loves you. It was all over her face when she saw you walk by."

Knots of guilt twisted in Finn's stomach. He cared deeply for Tove and the last thing he wanted to do was cause her any more pain than he already had. And he certainly didn't want her putting her life in danger over something that could never be. "Maybe you're right, but it doesn't change anything," he confessed. "We both know who my heart belongs to."

"We do," Jessie agreed.

"I suppose it's time to clear the air." They both knew he was referring to Tove. Ironically, ending the raging sandstorm was the only thing he could address at the moment.

Finn whispered his gratitude to the elements and withdrew his command, releasing them from his will. The vicious winds dissipated suddenly, then stilled altogether. Sand showered to the ground in thick, white sheaths, until all that was left were drifts of fine dust.

He and Jessie descended slowly as the dust clouds thinned, allowing them a clearer view. Jessie's sharp gasp matched Finn's own horror at the devastation wreaked upon the airships. He'd known the damage would be tremendous, but he never failed to be awestruck by how thorough the destructive elemental forces could be.

Only a small number of ships had escaped the storm, some of them were sinking, losing too much ranemist to make it home. Most of Biraktar's armada and allied forces had been torn to pieces. The dunes were littered with death and debris as far as the eye could see–shattered hulls broken in half, sails shredded and bodies everywhere. Serpen ground troops were scattered in a state of complete disorder amongst the wreckage, having been battered by the storm and then bombarded with huge warships falling from the sky.

"I'm thoroughly impressed with you," Jessie commented. "And a touch terrified. Who needs weapons of mass destruction when we have you?"

"I don't see any sign of the dragons," Finn said, ignoring her grim praise. He scanned the horizon, his search interrupted by the sudden sounds of battle below.

Jessie drifted lower. "Here we go. The fight between horns and halos is on."

True to her word, Brune had directed Sithias to parcel their forces into hundreds of small troops and place them wherever the Serpens were spread thinnest. Essentially blocking any attempts at unifying into their usual battle formations, which would have otherwise turned the tide back in their favor.

Beldereth warriors swept in between randomly dispersed clumps of disoriented Serpens, their blue capes easy to spot amongst the black armor worn by the enemy. Using the element of surprise, they launched their arrows with deadly precision. The crimson shields of Asgar soldiers poured over the Serpens, a swift and brutal slaughter that left lakes of blood in their wake.

Finn's pulse pounded with the need to join the fray, battle side by side with his allies. Taking his flute, he blew the notes, transforming it into his wind sword.

Jessie unsheathed her sword. "So we're doing this?" She waited for him to say the word with a feverish look in her eyes that dampened the fight in him.

"You won't stand a chance down there." He cringed inwardly at the hurt displayed on her face.

"I can fight. You've seen what I can do."

"Aye, you were formidable, for sure. But that was when you were a juiced up super soldier. Be real, Jessie. That's not you anymore."

Jessie hung her head. "I know. I'm useless."

"Look, I've been where you are now and I understand what you're feeling. To possess that kind of power and then have it taken from you is crippling. But that power was and never has been about your worth. You have everything to offer the world just for being you. It's that simple."

Jessie lifted her gaze, sad at first but suddenly frightened. "Watch out!" she screamed.

Finn turned in time to see the widening jaws of a dragon.

48
DANTALION'S KEY

VICIOUS FANGS FRAMED A THROAT of blazing fire. Finn grabbed Jessie's arm and shot straight up. Scorching heat enveloped them. Flames burned the soles of his boots as he strained to rise above the fiery jet stream.

After he reached a great enough height the dragon seemingly gave up and they watched as the gargantuan reptile passed beneath them. The sun's glare lit the texture of its membranous wings, shimmering over its oily black scales to the very end of its snaking tail. The dragon roared, circling back around and climbing higher, its underbelly glowing scarlet as it generated another inferno.

Gripping his wind sword, Finn pushed Jessie aside. "Go! Get out of here, Jess!"

Jessie cranked on the gears and zipped off to one side. Tensing every muscle, Finn prepared to meet the beast head on, but the reptile's yellow eyes followed Jessie, its slitted pupils dilating with excitement.

"Faster, Jessie, fly as fast as you can!" Finn shouted, knowing full well the aeronaut pack was at maximum acceleration. There was no way she was going to outrun the dragon.

Tightening his body as straight as a board, Finn hurtled after the dragon. He reached the spiked tail when it was nearly upon her. The dragon's jaw unhinged, belching volcanic fire that would incinerate Jessie to a cinderblock.

Finn arched the wind blade down, slicing off the tip of the dragon's tail. The dragon jerked its horned head around to look back at him with a pained growl. Flames spewed past its fangs before its jaws snapped shut. No longer interested in Jessie, the dragon changed direction, its leathery wings twitching with rage, thrusting downward, catapulting its great weight through the air with terrifying speed.

Hovering in place, Finn waited, measuring the distance, watching for the telltale glow of molten fire traveling from within the dragon's belly up along the length of its long serpentine neck. Ridges of fiery light shot through the cracks of the dragon's closed mouth. Finn's every instinct screamed at him to run but he held his position.

The dragon's jaws parted and stretched wide. An explosion of fire, so hot it was white in the center, surged into a spray of red flames laced in gold and orange.

Finn rocketed upward, racing from the blast of melting heat. The dragon lifted its head, wasting the fire pouring from its gullet in a useless effort to engulf him. Fortunately for Finn, the behemoth was unable to course correct as quickly as him, or stop him from sweeping over the top of its head to stay hidden behind the dragon's blind spot.

Having exhausted its store of fire, the dragon inhaled, fanning the flames of its internal furnace. Its head twisted this way and that, looking for Finn. He stayed hidden, flying just above the dragon's head, where he could best target the blade of his wind sword.

Choosing the hollow between its horns, Finn drove the blade deep into the dragon's skull. The dragon bucked, howling and hissing in pain, flinging Finn from side to side. He held onto the base of his flute, determined to keep the blade buried in its brain until the dragon was dead.

He wasn't given that chance.

Another dragon swooped in from above, raining fire down over him. Pulling the sword free, Finn leaped off, barely escaping a wall of searing flames. The fire hit the dragon he was trying to kill, glancing harmlessly off its thick scales as both monsters circled back around and came at him from both sides.

Five giant Eldunough hawks appeared as if out of nowhere, tearing at the dragons with sharp talons and beaks from all directions. They were riderless. A few dug their claws in and wouldn't let go. No amount of writhing and thrashing could shake them off.

Six more hawks appeared with riders. The soldiers flew beneath the dragons, shooting one arrow after the other into their vulnerable underbellies. The dragons bellowed as blood sprayed from too many fatal wounds. The hawks crowded in around them, dragging them downward until the dragons went limp and plunged from the sky.

"Whew, that was a close call."

Startled and still very much on edge, Finn turned as Jessie flew in beside him. "I thought I told you to get out of here."

"You saw me. I totally scrammed while you were duking it out with the dragons." She pointed down in an attempt to distract him. "Hey, it looks like we might just win this thing."

Annoyed, Finn glanced at the battlefield. The Beldereth and Asgar armies had driven the straggling remains of the Serpen ground troops into the center, where they had them surrounded and outnumbered. There was very little recourse for them but to surrender.

Finn smiled for the first time in a long while. "Aye, you may be right about that."

A deafening sound stole the smile from his face, chilling him with its familiarity. The noise was like that of countless discordant trumpets blaring from the heavens, combined with the steel screech of a giant locomotive rumbling over the earth. The terrible din seemed to be coming from everywhere, making it impossible to pinpoint the source.

The haze drifting over the blue sky warped and rippled suddenly, an inexplicable disturbance that unnerved Finn for reasons he didn't recognize. The buckling air swirled inward, funneling into one central point, an unnatural sight he knew did not bode well.

Fire and smoke burst from the center of the vortex, radiating outward into thick, black tendrils swiftly forming into wings. A giant figure as brilliant as the sun formed between the dark writhing wings and Finn had to shield his eyes.

The unearthly clamor ceased, as did the glaring light. The figure solidified into a knight with black armor, save for the illumined glow of Hippolyta's girdle shining crimson through the breastplate.

Jessie clapped her hand over her mouth. "No, it can't be!"

Finn didn't speak. The tightening in his chest clamped down on his lungs as Fate's features came into full view. Her long hair flowed skyward, blown into wild disarray from the heat pouring off her body.

Ananke turned her cold, hard gaze to the battlefield.

"Do we try to talk to her, see if we can reach Fate?" Jessie asked. "Maybe we can keep her distracted long enough for Sithias to bring any info Gerdie might've dug up about the Eldritch Gloom infection."

Finn glanced around in a panic. "I don't think that info's coming our way."

"I guess Brune kept Sithias too busy with getting our forces down on the ground." Jessie looked at Ananke and gulped. "Back to Plan A. I'll try talking to her."

"No, it's too dangerous. We'll wait until we can't wait any–"

Ananke descended upon the armies below, gouging the daggered point of the alicorn into the bloodied sands, cutting a deep trench into the earth that sliced through soldiers trying to escape. The attack was indiscriminate, slashing Beldereth warriors and Serpens alike.

The same dark smoky substance as Ananke's wings rose from the trench, splitting off before quickly assuming the shape of black knights. Fire burned like coal at their core as they advanced on the living. Their size was human, yet they were anything but. The swords they wielded disintegrated flesh into ash and ember, leaving only charred skeletons dressed in armor to litter the ground.

Ananke's army grew into a monstrous horde that flooded over the battlefield. Terrorized cries rang from the desert floor as enemy and ally alike tried desperately to escape. But there was nowhere to run and the air filled with the ashen clouds of their demise.

Jessie pushed Finn, rousing him from a stunned stupor. "Use the key before she kills them all!"

He yanked the key from his pocket. When he hesitated, Jessie thumped him in the arm, nearly knocking it from his grasp.

"What are you waiting for?" she yelled.

"That's the Eldritch Gloom at work down there. It's worse than we thought. I'd venture to say Ananke might not even exist anymore. If Ananke's not powerful enough to stop it from consuming her completely, Fate's surely lost."

"We don't know that!" Jessie argued as tears rushed in. "All we know is that we have one shot at *maybe* turning this around."

Finn returned his gaze to Ananke, where she'd risen back into the sky to watch her dark legion from above and set his sights on the gleaming light of Hippolyta's girdle. Focusing all his attention at the very center, he pointed the ruby end of the wand.

Dantalion's Key vibrated in his hand and emitted a high-pitched musical note at the same time. Ananke ripped her gaze from the ground and zeroed in on Finn with terrifying ferocity.

The ruby exploded with light, shooting a solid beam straight across the skyline. Ananke thrust her wings, catapulting upward to avoid the beam. The ruby red light curved in the same direction, like a heat seeking missile, chasing her relentlessly before closing the space in a burst of crimson sparks.

Ananke shrieked, grappling at her waist, clutching Hippolyta's girdle in place. But the ancient weapon of the old gods lost its luminous gleam. Ananke's fiery wings of smoke thinned away and she tumbled, her giant body shrinking to normal size. The black armor dissolved into ragged wisps of smoke, until all that was left was Fate.

Naked, unconscious and about to fall to her death.

Adrenaline coursed through Finn's body as he raced to catch her. But she was falling fast and he was too far away. Tensing every muscle until he hurt all over, Finn drove himself, hitting his absolute limit, then pushed beyond even that to close the gap in time.

His heart plunged with Fate, knowing he couldn't save her. A roar of pure terror tore from his chest, scorching his throat as he invoked Earth, commanding the sands to rise, if only to break her fall. The dunes obeyed and rose in a great, mountainous plume.

Fate vanished within the sands. Zipping the long collar of his jacket up over his nose and mouth, Finn dove into the plume, his speed slowed by the upward rush of sand beating hard against him. Thankful for the goggles, he searched for Fate, but it was impossible to see anything beyond the length of his arm. It pained him beyond no end to know the sand was blasting over her unprotected skin.

Something huge swept past Finn, knocking him aside. He couldn't imagine anything other than a dragon would fly into the thick of this maelstrom unless it was purposely after Fate. Finn chased after the beast with everything he had, bursting free of the sand within seconds of changing direction.

One of the giant Eldunough hawks flew ahead of him with Fate clutched in its talons. Finn didn't know whether to be relieved or worried when he saw the hawk heading away from the Keep, far from the battlefield. It was riderless and didn't look like most of the other hawks. It lacked the rich russet coloring. This one was a light tawny brown along the wings with an ivory colored head and body.

"Stop!" Finn shouted as he raced to catch up.

The hawk slowly descended, flapping more vigorously as it gently set Fate down on the highest crest of a smooth untouched dune. Hopping off to one side, the raptor turned to look at Finn and he recognized the amber eyes of his friend. "Sorry I'm late, sir. Brune kept me quite busy."

Finn breathed a deep sigh of relief as he landed. "Your timing couldn't be more perfect, Sithias."

Ripping his goggles off, he ran over to Fate. She was lying on her side, eyes closed, curled in a ball. Her skin was red, burned by blasting sand, but she was breathing evenly. Finn quickly removed his jacket to cover her up. Her auburn hair–lit almost red by the sun–spilled over the sand. She'd never looked more beautiful.

"How is she?" Sithias asked.

Finn wished he knew the answer. Fate was safe and alive, but unconscious and that worried him. "I'd like to think she's having a good nap after what she's been through, but we can't be sure until we get her looked at." He wrapped her fully in his coat and lifted her into his arms.

"She does look rather peaceful," Sithias agreed.

"Aye, that she does." Finn kissed the top of her head and glanced back from where they'd come, looking for dragons or any other form of danger. The pluming sand was all that disturbed the horizon and was dwindling from lack of attention. He released the elements fully and the sands collapsed into stillness.

His thoughts returned to the horrible battle he'd witnessed. With Fate delivered into his arms, his concerns inevitably turned to Tove and the devastating losses they were about to return to. He could only hope she was not amongst the dead. "Jessie told me Tove was suited up to fight. I'd like you to see Fate safely back to the sanctuary so I can search for her. I owe her that much."

"Oh, no need, sir. I returned Tove to the Twisted Bone Forest."

Finn couldn't have been more surprised. "Did she ask you to do that?"

"No, in fact, she was quite adamant about going into battle. But I couldn't bring myself to do it. Not in good conscience anyway. The dear girl was plainly hoping for an end to her torment. She's simply not over you, sir. Or the loss of her family. It's been tearing her apart."

Finn didn't know whether to be relieved or troubled. "Hmm, I'm not sure she'll be happy with that. Tove told me she wanted to marry Prince Ethlan and live in Feldoril."

"I think we both know the fae are fickle creatures and not to be trusted. If Tove truly belongs with them, she won't be able to stay away from the Falinorin. At least this way, she'll have time to think and return to her roots."

Finn nodded. "Sithias, you don't have them often, but when you do have that rare moment of wisdom, I'm always gobsmacked."

Sithias was immediately offended. "Excuse me? I'm wise more often than not."

"Do I need to remind you about the trouble Mr. Romance got you into? And most recently, the remembering spell of too many Elsinas? If that's not enough, how about helping Fate find Hippolyta's Gird–"

"Say no more!"

Finn chuckled as his flustered friend attempted to regain his composure.

"Let's get back, Sithias." He started to lift off, hesitating when a whirlwind appeared in the distance. It skimmed across the dunes toward them, purposely enough to make him stay where he was.

Sithias tilted his head. "That mini cyclone looks curiously familiar."

"Doesn't it," Finn agreed.

Dust drifted over them as the whirlwind came to a halt. When the sands stilled in mid swirl and floated around a man in white robes, Finn knew exactly who he was.

"We meet again." Aradif's smile was sphinx-like, reminding Finn of his last words to him. *The next time we meet will be under less agreeable circumstances.*

49
TAINTED

SITHIAS TRADED HIS HAWK FORM for his usual human appearance, though he chose the wardrobe of a Safari hunter with the traditional straw helmet to protect his delicately pale complexion. "What brings you here, Aradif?" he asked with a tremulous quaver in his voice.

Aradif directed his answer to Finn. "You have fulfilled the Oracle's prophecy. It is now time to leave the Marajaran Desert. You and your kind are no longer welcome here."

Sithias gulped audibly.

Finn frowned. "And what prophecy would that be? The one where you told me I was the destroyer of destroyers and would fight Kaliena to the death? Your Oracle was way off. I didn't destroy Kaliena. It was the other way around actually. She destroyed me. And Sithias was the one who came up with how to send her back to where she came from."

Aradif's calm expression remained unchanged. "I said there would be a great war and that you would fight Kaliena to the death here in the Marajaran Desert. I did not say whose death that would be."

"Well, I suppose when you put it that way," Finn muttered. "But you were wrong about me being the destroyer of destroyers."

"Did you not destroy, Ananke, the mother of all gods, a few mere moments ago?"

"I wouldn't go so far as to say she was destroyed," Finn argued. "I made it impossible for her to use Fate as her vessel any longer. And that was accomplished with the wave of a wand. Literally. I'd hardly say I deserve any grand titles for what it took to accomplish that small feat."

"You forget the journey you took to arrive at that accomplishment. Or would you say it was a smooth, easy journey that anyone other than a champion could endure?"

"Ooh, he has a point, sir," Sithias chimed in. "You are a true champion and should be proud of this triumph."

Finn turned his frown on Sithias. "I don't feel triumphant. I'm weary to the bone and concerned about my–" He was about to say wife, but he didn't know if Fate felt the same way. "I'm concerned about Fate. There's something wrong. She should've woken by now."

"I will have my healers attend to her if you wish," Aradif offered.

Finn stared back in surprise. "Aye, I would appreciate that very much."

Aradif walked off to one side, drawing both hands together before parting them like he was drawing back the flaps of a tent. And indeed, he was, because the backdrop of sand against the blue horizon rippled like curtains, opening onto the interior of a huge tent filled with rich, lavish carpets, silken pillows and softly glowing lanterns. A feast of sumptuous food was laid out in the center of the tent. The delicious scent of spices wafting in the air was enticing.

Holding the flaps aside, Aradif waved them inside and directed Finn to lay Fate down on a bedroom partitioned off by generous layers of silk. He gently set her down and stepped back as several veiled women in robes of white gathered around her. One of them ushered him out and closed the curtains.

"Come, let us break bread together while we wait for news of Fate's health." Aradif took a seat and poured three cups from a carafe of wine.

Finn sagged down onto a cushion and took a sip of the dark purple wine. As soon as the sweet, refreshing liquid hit the back of his parched throat, he drank the whole cup in two more gulps. The wine went straight to his head, making him dizzily relaxed despite the underlying tension. When he couldn't remember the last time he'd eaten, he tore off a piece of flat bread and scooped up a bite from the rice dish one of the servants handed him. "Thank you," he said through a mouthful of food.

Sithias was making appreciative noises as he ate with eyes closed, chewing and smiling all at once. He pointed at his dish. "Thisss is scrumptious!"

Aradif smiled. "I am pleased you find the food enjoyable."

Finn glanced over at the curtains, anxious to know what the healers were doing with Fate.

Aradif noticed. "Ease your mind. My healers will know how to help her." He filled Finn's cup with more wine. "Drink while we discuss the matter of your people's exodus from my desert."

Sithias froze with mouth open, unable to take another bite of his meal.

"I was wondering when you'd circle back around to that." Finn set his cup down. "We can't leave the Keep to fall into the wrong hands. It's ours to protect. In case you haven't noticed, we've been doing a fine job of that so far."

"I've noticed." Aradif sipped on his wine. "Let me ask you. Are you prepared for a lifetime of war?"

"Of course not, and I don't see why you would ask that."

"Power hungry forces will always be drawn to seize the Keep. This war you won today is the first of many more to come. This will be a place of war as long as the Keep is here, and I cannot allow that."

Finn laughed, a tired laugh that ended in a heavy sigh. "I'm sorry, but it's not like we can toss it back where it came from. Or maybe we can. Sithias, you could use the Words of Making to send it there. Right?"

Sithias set his food down with a disappointed slump of his wiry shoulders. "I suppose I could, but I'm not so sure–"

"The Keep should not exist." Stern lines sharpened Aradif's formerly placid expression. "The power it holds is a magnet for war and strife, regardless of where it resides. You are aware of its history, are you not?"

Reluctant to agree, Finn nodded, all too aware of the thousand-year war fought over the right to occupy the Keep. "Say we leave. What will you do with the Keep? Move in and take its treasures for yourself?"

"I have no need of treasures or the power they hold. I already have those things." Serenity returned to smooth Aradif's features once again. "The desert will take the Keep."

Finn leaned forward, doubtful but intrigued. "Does that mean you'll cloak the Keep, same as this tent?"

Aradif laughed softly. "This is not hidden by illusion. What you see around you exists elsewhere. I merely parted the dimensional folds to allow you entrance into my home."

Sithias sat straight with excitement. "Fascinating!"

"As for the Keep, it will be buried deep beneath the desert sands, never to be seen again."

Finn couldn't fathom the depths that hole would have to be to fully cover the Keep and its gargantuan rings. "If we agree, we'll have your word on that?" He narrowed his gaze on Aradif. "If this is some kind of trick to take the Keep for yourself, things will go badly between us."

"If I wanted to take the Keep it would already be mine and you would not be sitting here partaking of my generosity."

Finn believed him. "We'll need at least seven days to vacate, maybe more."

"You have until dawn."

"That's impossible," Finn argued. "We have dead to bury and wounded to attend to before they can be moved any great distance. And we need to deal with whatever amount of Serpens are left. Then there's the little matter of how we're going to travel." He glanced at Sithias again, deciding the Words of Making were the only way to meet Aradif's outrageous demand.

"No, no, don't look at me!" Sithias protested. "That's too many names to take down and list off to ensure every single person is sent to wherever it is you want to go. It was a nightmare when Brune made me position all those separate troops to the ground. It took forever! That's why I was so late."

"You weren't late. You showed up in the nick of time." Finn sighed, exhausted by the idea of solving yet another problem.

"I will see that you have all the airships required to carry your numbers," Aradif offered.

"You're going to steal ships from Biraktar's fleet?" Sithias scrunched his face with disapproval. "They may be our enemy now, but those people are your devoted worshipers. Your name is spoken with the utmost reverence in Biraktar. They make effigies of you, well, you as a snake with wings. A fine choice, I might add."

"I am well aware of the religious beliefs built around my name," Aradif confirmed. "Unfortunately, humans have never understood the Djinn. They think us immortal gods, because unlike them, we live out of time and can change shape, amongst many other seemingly miraculous abilities."

Sithias seemed disappointed. "You're *not* their Guiding Star?"

"I might have helped a traveler long ago who later built a myth around a winged serpent that saved him from perishing in the desert. I do this from time to time if I deem the human worthy of the effort. As to how I appear depends upon my mood in that particular century."

"Oh, I take it this is the century of a smelly, rude-mannered camel." Sithias crossed his arms, looking more disillusioned by the minute. "I can't believe an entire religion was formed around a capricious appearance you chose at random."

"You of all people should understand capricious appearances," Finn jested.

Sithias was not amused.

One of the healers slipped through the curtains, capturing Finn's immediate attention. She padded quietly over to Aradif and leaned to whisper in his ear.

"What did she say?" Finn tensed, ready to rise and yank the curtains back if he didn't like the answer.

"Fate is dressing and will be out in a moment."

"How is she? Did they find anything wrong?"

"Her health is fine..." The way Aradif trailed off suggested there was more.

"I sense a but in that sentence." Finn clenched his jaw.

"Me too," Sithias agreed.

The curtains parted and Finn stood, anxious as the healers filed out and left through a flap at the far end of the large tent. His fast-beating heart leaped into his throat when Fate stepped out of the dim shadows into the light.

She was a vision in silvery white. The pale gown they'd dressed her in would be otherwise plain had it not been for the translucent silk layered over top. Airy, curling vines–stitched together by countless tiny silver beads–flowed over the skirt and wound their way upward, where they clustered into a solid, glittering bodice.

Her hair had been brushed, left to fall down her back in smooth, lustrous waves. They'd washed her skin free of desert grit and her cheeks shone with the softest blush of pink. She stood shyly before them, her hands clasped behind her.

Finn rushed over to her when he saw her brown eyes glistening with sadness. He stopped in front of her, coaxing her to meet his gaze with a gentle nudge of her chin. "Hey, love. Talk to me."

She pressed her lips together and looked away.

"What's wrong?"

Fate's shoulders shuddered as she brought her hands to her face and sobbed softly. Clasping her by the wrists, Finn drew her arms down. Fear sliced into his heart when he noticed the fingertips of her sword hand, stained black all the way to the first knuckles. A squeak of alarm came from Sithias when Finn held Fate's hand out for them to see. "Aradif, do you know what this is?"

Fate jerked her hand from his grasp, holding her arm behind her back. Shame filled her eyes as she backed away from Finn.

Aradif stood. "She is tainted by what was inside the black unicorn."

The Eldritch Gloom.

"Can your healers cure her?"

"I wish I could say otherwise, but I cannot."

"There must be someone who knows how to heal this," Finn insisted.

"Possibly. But only if you can find that someone before the taint reaches her heart."

Icy terror gripped hold of Finn. "What happens if... we run out of time?"

Aradif shook his head. "I do not know."

Finn looked at Sithias. "You can write up a cure for her. Do it now."

Sithias's worried gaze darted to Aradif, then to Fate and back to Finn. "I wouldn't know what to write exactly. Oh, what am I thinking? Yesss, of course I'll do it!" He fumbled around in his pocket and pulled a small notebook and pen.

"No."

They all looked at Fate in surprise.

"Aradif showed me no good can come from using the Words of Making when they're written out of fear." She wiped at her tears with the back of her normal hand and stared at Finn defiantly.

"When did this happen? He's been with us the entire time you were in there with the healers." Finn frowned in confusion when Fate remained silent. He looked at Aradif. "What is she talking about? You haven't spoken to Fate about anything. *Ever.*"

Aradif noted Finn's surprise but chose to ignore it. "As I said, you humans do not understand the Djinn. I was here, while I was also in there with Fate. You now know everything."

"We have to do something," Finn seethed. He started toward her but she held the stained hand up to stop him from coming any closer.

"Beldereth warriors–women I knew–are lying dead on the sands along with practically every soldier who fought beside them. I'm responsible for that." She thrust her shoulders back, not proudly, but with sorrowful resolve. "I won't put anymore lives in danger to save myself. You have to let me go."

"Let you go?" Finn was stunned. "I can't. No! We'll fight this together the way we always have."

"This is my choice, Finn. Ananke robbed me of that by forcing her will upon me. I have to exercise my own will power. It's all I have left. If you can't honor my right to choose, I'll disappear and you'll never see me again."

The full weight of her words crushed Finn. A rock giant might as well have stepped on his chest. He could hardly breathe, let alone rally a response.

Pain moved behind Fate's eyes as she tore her gaze from him to look at Aradif. "Before we go, there's one last thing I would ask of you."

"Very well," Aradif replied.

"Please return Azrael's body to his mother in Biraktar. I may not like the woman but she was close to her son. She should be the one to bury him." A tear trickled down one cheek.

"As you wish." Aradif closed his eyes for the briefest moment. "It is done."

"Thank you," Fate whispered.

"Can you do the same for all our fallen soldiers?" Sithias asked.

"You test my generosity. Azrael is of Djinn blood. Our kind do not clean up after humans. That is for you to do, unless you choose to let the desert bury your dead with the Keep."

Sithias squirmed under Aradif's aloof gaze. "I understand. I suppose we'll be going now. We have much to do before the next sunrise."

Aradif waved his arm, a gesture that washed away the tent's luxurious surroundings, leaving the dunes stretching out before them. The air wavered around him as he faded from sight, gone within seconds without a word of farewell.

The sun was low, sinking toward a sunset only hours away. Fate stood with her back to Finn, staring at the horizon. A gentle breeze caught the hem of her gown, tossing the filmy fabric around her legs. The last rays of sun glittered over the silver beads, rimming her silhouette in sparkles.

She was all of a sudden ethereal, too perfect for this cruel, brutal world and all Finn wanted to do was hold her in his arms. Protect her. Shelter her from harm. But then his gaze strayed to her stained fingertips and he trembled, because this time, he was helpless to save her.

50
GOING HOME

FATE STARED AT THE SMALL GLASS BOTTLE filled with ash, corked and sealed with black wax. A round silver plate the size of a quarter was embedded into one side of the waxed neck. Engraved on its shiny surface was *Eustace Floyd*, in all caps, and the date of his first death in Roman numerals. His reading glasses sat beside the bottle.

This was the sum total of what remained of her father. There'd been nothing left of him to bury. His body had crumbled into a cup of fine dust a few hours after his avenging spirit abandoned the corpse.

Fate prayed he was at peace and with her mother somewhere behind that mysterious veil called Death. Imagining them happy and together again might have been comforting if she could feel anything other than abject despair.

Her fight to change her world into exactly what she'd needed it to be had been futile. None of it had saved her from having to face the pain of untold heartache.

Where had all the struggle gotten her? Nowhere. At least nowhere she wanted to be.

She'd been powerless to mold her reality back into the perfect ideal, where everyone she loved and cared about was alive, happy and safe. How foolish she'd been to think she could bend the universe to her will.

All of Ananke's talk of ruling destinies was one big joke. Even she had failed to shape her own destiny in the end. Proof that destiny was really just a random course of events left to chance.

Fate laughed bitterly at her former hubris, a sound heard only by the chamber bot packing her belongings. The bot paused and turned its porcelain grandmotherly face and unceasing smile in her direction. "Would you care for a tasty treat before you leave?"

"No thanks." The thought of eating nauseated her.

The lights in the room suddenly dwindled to a feeble gleam and the bot's movements slowed to a complete standstill. Puzzled by the unexpected dysfunction, Fate wrapped the bottle of her father's ashes and glasses in a cloth and tucked the bundle into one of her bags.

A soft knock on the door startled her and she hurried to open it. Finn greeted her with a look of concern, intently gauging her mood with a sweep of his green eyes.

"What's with the lights?" she asked. "And my chamber bot just conked out."

"Brune programmed the Keep settings to power down. She had concerns about the gravity defiers around the Keep making it impossible for the desert to bury it."

"Wow, she's taking this way better than I thought she would."

"Brune's been full of surprises lately." Finn was quiet a moment, almost as if he was waiting for Fate to say something.

"Are you packed and ready?" he asked when she remained quiet. "The ships are loaded with everyone we could gather from the ground, what with the limited time and resources. Rudwor already sent the first ship on its way. He's waiting for us to board. Jessie and the others are there too. We'll all be making the trip together."

"To Beldereth."

"That's the plan."

Finn followed her inside as she pulled on her jacket. Putting her back to him, she slipped on a pair of lightweight gloves to hide the stain of her sins on her right hand. She lifted her packed bags and turned to face him. "I'm not going to Beldereth," she announced flatly.

The muscles of his jaw tensed as he swallowed hard. "You can't stay here."

"I plan to take the portal back to Fables Bookstore."

"Why? Without Eustace, there's nothing left in that life for you. We can make a good life in Beldereth. I can take you to Almsdeep. I'm certain the monks will know how to heal the... your hand."

Fate shook her head. "Aradif told me I have to go where there's no magic. If I do, the spread will slow down. Possibly even long enough for me to die of old age."

Finn winced. "Don't talk like that."

"I'm fine with it, Finn. I'm actually craving normal. I don't want to be around magic anymore. Magic is... it's too tempting. As long as I know there's the smallest possibility I can get my dad back and undo every bad thing that's ever happened I'll end up abusing my powers all over again."

Tears burned behind her eyes. "Going home is the only way I'll ever be able to accept that Eustace is gone forever."

"You don't have any powers left to abuse."

"I still have the Words of Making."

Finn opened his mouth to argue but she silenced him by putting her finger to his lips. "Please stop trying to change my mind. I have to do this. I *need* to do this."

His resistance fell away and he nodded. "Then I'll go with you."

Fate's heart skipped a beat. She'd been prepared to go alone and only now realized how terribly afraid she'd been that he wouldn't want to join her. "Are you sure?"

"I'm your husband. Where else would I go if not with you?" Fear pulled at the edges of his eyes. "That is if you still want to be married to me."

"I do."

Finn pulled her into his arms and held her close. "You don't know how long I've waited to hear you say that without hesitation."

Fate winced at how badly she'd hurt him with her mixed emotions over Azrael. "I've been awful–"

"Shhh." Finn leaned back to look at her. His eyes lit with a brilliant emerald as his mouth curled into a smile. "No regrets. We're together now and that's all that counts."

He reached into his pocket and pulled out two hand fasting bracelets. They matched the originals with the treasured white silk ribbon he'd given her so very long ago, braided together with a strip of grey tartan from the kilt of his First Knight's uniform. Dangling from the braids were the Tree of Life and Celtic Love Knot silver charms.

Finn slipped the bracelet onto her wrist and pulled the string for a perfect fit. Fate took his bracelet and placed it on his.

"Tied together, always." The love in his shining eyes swelled to overflowing.

"*Always*," she replied breathlessly. Joy collided with the sorrow that had taken up residence in her heart.

Finn drew her into his strong embrace, steadying her internal quaking like nothing else could. If only they could trap the moment in amber.

Time was a luxury they didn't have. The relentless countdown toward sunrise ticked by mercilessly. "We should go," she whispered.

"Aye," he agreed. "Best to leave now before I sweep you into that bed and lose all track of time." The look of longing in his eyes mirrored her own.

Finn grabbed her bags. When Fate reached the door she cast a last glance back at her room and the chamber bot. Her bedchamber had been the closest thing to home since leaving the bookstore. A small part of her would miss it, if only for the happiest memories that had taken place in her own private refuge. The rest of her was ready to move on and return home.

Fate closed the door and they hurried through the dark, empty corridors to the sanctuary. Their friends were waiting there, all turning at once when the door banged against the wall as Finn kicked it ajar with more strength than necessary.

Rudwor looked them over with a wry grin. "Pushing it a might close, aren't we? You do know there are beds on the ship, hey, laddie?"

"We were *talking*." Finn set Fate's bags next to the portal. "And we've decided we're not going with you."

"What?" Sithias squawked. "Where will you go?"

Finn began the lengthy explanation. The weariness Fate had been feeling earlier caved in again as everyone listened, each casting troubled glances her way, while he skirted around her unsettling condition.

Jessie made her way over to Fate. She was angry. "You were planning on going home without me?"

"Actually, I was hoping you'd come with us. As long you want to."

"I'm peeved you'd think I wouldn't." Jessie's frown turned playful. "I was looking forward to visiting Beldereth, but home sounds better. Of course, the first thing we're going to do is rip the unicorn posters off your bedroom walls."

Fate smiled halfheartedly. "I know what you mean. I can't promise to hold back from rear ending any cars with '*I brake for unicorns*' bumper stickers."

"That's the spirit." Jessie moved her bags over to the portal.

"Count me in on your trek home." Sithias hurried over, his back arched as he balanced a cumbersome stack of books in his arms. "You'll be happy to know I've gathered everything together with any mention of the Eldritch Gloom. I'm determined to find a solution to your affliction."

"You're a good friend, Sithias, but this is a one-way trip. Plus, I don't see how you'd be able to shape shift. Unfortunately, showing up as a huge winged snake could get you shot."

"On the contrary, misss. I have my just-in-case-of-emergency glamour." Sithias waved a coral necklace at her. It was the siren's glamour he'd used to change form before Fate had given him the power to shape shift. "Not that I expect to have to use it though. There was enough magic in the bookstore for me to change shape the last time I was there."

"That's true," Finn agreed. "The magic came from the *Book of Fables*."

"I can't be sure, but that may not be the case now." Brune set her ring of Keep Guardian keys down on the table with a loud clank. "The key that unlocks the *Book of Fables* and the Keep Lock is missing. I only noticed when I was packing my things. I suspect Darcy stole it."

"Why would Darcy want *that* key?" Fate asked.

"This appears to be a conversation that's about to outlast my arms." Sithias squatted, teetered under the weight of the books and dropped them on the floor.

"Use this," Gerdie dragged over a large canvas bag for his books and helped him fill it.

Brune picked up the key ring. "I've considered a number of reasons and none of them are good. Darcy might be looking to travel through the *Book of Fables* as a reader, which means she'll be creating terrible endings for each story."

"Hold on!" Rudwor bellowed. "That would spell doom for Beldereth all over again! We can't let that happen. Not after all we've lost in the wars."

"We'll look into it as soon as we return to the bookstore," Finn assured his friend. "What other reasons were you thinking Darcy might steal the key?" he asked Brune.

"She may simply want to steal it from our family as a final act of revenge." Brune clenched the keys. "I keep thinking back to all the time Darcy spent with Wodrid in the library back when we still only knew him as Steve. I'd bet every treasure stored in the Keep he passed on a trick or two. She mastered magic a little too quickly for someone her age and experience."

"Aye, I remember Wodrid spouting off about cursing the *Book of Fables*." Finn's expression tightened with concern. "He's the one who created the rules for using the Words of Making."

Fate gulped. "If Darcy goes into the *Book of Fables* as the next reader she'll have the power of the Words of Making."

"Combine that with the Orb," Brune added, "and you have–"

"Mayhem and monsters like Old Mother Grim," Gerdie interjected.

"I told you why I did that." Regret filled Brune's eyes. "Are you still carrying that grudge?"

"No," Gerdie grumbled. "I forgive you."

"You'd best fire up the portal so we can investigate," Finn told Brune.

Nodding grimly, she walked over to the round iron door edged with engraved symbols and pulled the lever. The iris spiraled open, revealing a circular tunnel of inner rings, each rotating in opposite directions. Waves of neon-blue light spun into a cyclonic flux path that would deliver them back to the bookstore.

Brune glanced at her watch. "You have about fifteen minutes before there's no power to run the portal," she warned.

Rudwor pulled Finn into a crushing bear hug. "Godspeed, laddie. May we reunite one day down the road and may it be soon. On that day we'll celebrate ourselves into oblivion." He let go of Finn, his light brown eyes misty with emotion.

"Aye, I look forward it." Doubt moved in Finn's eyes.

Rubbing his nose, Rudwor sniffed back his unmanly tears and glanced at Fate. "Promise me you'll take care of each other."

"I promise."

He looked as though he was about to suffocate her in one of his meaty hugs. Instead, he turned abruptly and strode across the gangplank to the airship waiting outside the sanctuary hatch.

"Will you be going back to the bookstore with us?" Fate asked Brune. "You know you're welcome to. I plan to get the bookstore going again and I'd love the help." She was surprised by how much she hoped Brune would accept her invitation. All they'd ever done was butt heads with each other, but she'd also come to understand and respect Brune. She'd never been the kindly great-aunt Fate would've preferred, but Brune was family.

A sudden pang of realization struck Fate. Brune and Gerdie were the only family she had left.

Brune's ever-stern expression softened. "I have no life back in that world. I've always belonged here in the Keep." Looking torn, she glanced over her shoulder in the direction of the airship. "As hard as it'll be letting go of being Keep Guardian, I think there might be a new life waiting for me."

"Oh." Fate hid her disappointment by changing the subject. "How did you manage to break the Keep Guardian oath? I'll never forget how painfully binding it was."

"Actually, I didn't break it." Brune raised her hand to show the guardian seal stamped under the skin of her palm was a pale glimmer and barely active. "I'm not bound anymore and I can't tell you why."

Fate pulled the glove back and checked her palm. The glimmering guardian seal she'd been stamped with on the day of her initiation as Keep Guardian, was all but a faint flicker as well.

"Mine's almost out too," Jessie chimed in.

"By all appearances, I'd say our family line is free of the Keep. You won't have to worry about any children you decide to have being summoned to duty." Brune smiled, a rarity that was always startling.

Fate was stunned. "That's amazing. I'd sure like to know how this happened though. Is this Darcy's doing?"

"That's a mystery we may never solve," Brune admitted. "I'm just grateful I'm not bound to the Keep anymore. The idea of being buried with it isn't exactly appealing."

“Too bad Darcy isn’t bound to the Keep.” A wicked delight tugged at the corners of Fate’s mouth. “Her being buried alive in here would be a satisfying karmic reward.”

Brune’s smile vanished. “Darcy buried with access to all the power stored here? Perish the thought.” She looked at the time and grew tense again. She gestured to Gerdie with a tap on the watch face. “Let’s go, the clock’s ticking.”

“You’re going with Brune?” Fate asked Gerdie. The unspoken invitation to return to the bookstore with her hung heavy between them.

Gerdie gave her that lopsided grin Fate had grown so fond of. “Yeah, I’m gonna go with Brune. I liked Beldereth. The library there is decent, plus I wouldn’t mind picking back up with the herbal treatments I was mixin’ for Rudwor’s niece. I always felt bad for leavin’ Valesca’s recovery unfinished. Besides that, you don’t need a six-year-old centenarian around to slow you down.”

“Don’t be silly,” Fate scolded. “I’d love to have you there with me and I think you’d love being back home. We can go over all the old pictures of you and Gran. And Brune and Oma and all the other relatives I never met. Oh, and I can take you to see all the places you used to go. A lot has changed, but there’s lots that hasn’t changed, like the old soda shop and the bakery.”

“Sweet Dreams Bakery,” Brune added. “It’s exactly the same. I made enough donut runs for Farouk to know that.”

“I did like Sweet Dreams.” Gerdie’s wistful smile saddened. “That all sounds real nice, but I’d only be a fish out of water there. I can’t imagine bein’ treated like a kid for as long as it’ll take me to start lookin’ old enough to be given the respect of an adult.”

Fate swallowed back the painful lump in her throat and gave her tiny great-aunt a hug. “I’ll miss you terribly.”

“Me too.” Gerdie’s brown eyes glittered with tears as she reached into her skirt pocket and drew out the miniature clockwork cat Eustace had given Fate as an unbirthday gift. “You should have Poz back.”

“Are you sure?” Fate smiled as the little cat stretched and peered up at her with sparkling green eyes. She’d named it Poz, short for pocket Oz, after her real cat. She would be so happy to see him again.

“Positive.” Gerdie placed the purring cat into Fate’s hand. She looked at Finn. “Take care of her.”

“Aye, you know I will.”

Gerdie pointed at Sithias. “And you! Do your homework and fix this girl.”

Sithias's face pinched with disapproval. "I object to that. I always do my homework."

Fate patted Sithias's arm. "I'm in good hands," she assured Gerdie.

Brune stepped forward with her hand extended. "You'll come through this just fine. You're too stubborn not to."

Fate shook Brune's hand with a sad chuckle. "Thanks, I think."

Brune cleared her throat, blinking back what might have been the first sign of a tear. Nodding, she turned and left with Gerdie scampering after her.

Fate tucked the little clockwork cat into her bag for safekeeping. Finn stepped in behind her, pulling her to his chest. She closed her eyes as he whispered into her ear. "Don't fret, love. We'll make a good life together. I promise." He spoke with such certainty she could almost let herself believe him.

Jessie stood next to the hatch, watching as they withdrew the gangplank onto the ship and pulled away. The first glimmerings of sunrise pierced the darkness of the desert, rimming the horizon with a dim outline of the distant dunes. She banged the button with the side of her fist, triggering the hatch to close.

Brune had left the hologram running of the Keep's exterior. They all gathered around it, anxiously curious to see if Aradif would hold true to his promise to bury the Keep.

Sunlight splashed across the dunes, glaring off the shiny surface of the colossal rings and towering iron titans, which cast long slender shadows over the countless, ancient vaults landscaping the Keep's surface.

A sudden quake had Fate gripping the edge of the table.

"And so it begins," Finn said grimly as they glanced at each other.

The floor shook beneath their feet and the walls rattled. Paintings banged against the bronze walls of the sanctuary until gilded frames cracked and canvases fell away. Marble statues crashed and broke into jagged chunks. Books flew off the shelves of heavy wooden bookcases as they wobbled and toppled over.

While the shaking was proof enough, the evidence was clear as Fate watched the hologram. The gargantuan rings hadn't moved since they'd first crash-landed in the desert. They were now lining up, one next to the other, like bracelets stacked together and laid flat on the sand. Whatever mysterious magnetic forces the rings had been generating to hold the massive round construct of the Keep suspended in the air, ceased altogether and it smashed into the dunes.

Innumerable architectural wonders broke and shattered into pieces–

the treasures of those crushed vaults either destroyed or flung into sands that had suddenly come alive. The dunes swirled around the Keep and the rings, widening into a massive churning hole to encompass the mountainous structure.

A hungry desert, as Azrael had once said of the Dunbala Desert. She'd assumed he was referring to the monstrous creatures dwelling beneath the dunes, but maybe he'd meant the desert itself. How many ruins had she glimpsed beneath Dunbala's ever-shifting, oceanic sands from the airship when they'd sailed across that bleak expanse together? More than she would care to admit.

By all accounts, the Mirajaran Desert was every bit as ravenous when a being such as Aradif commanded it to be.

"Time to leave before we lose the portal." Sithias glanced nervously at the debris clattering and bouncing over the quaking floor.

"I second that," Jessie agreed.

Sithias lugged the canvas bag, heavy with books, to the portal and tossed it in the tunnel. Bolts of electricity crackled around it, before the bag vanished in a blink. He turned to them with a grimace. "It's still working. Though the unpleasantness of being stretched like a rubber band through space and time has suddenly returned to mind." He flapped his long skinny arms. "What was I thinking agreeing to do this?"

"It's not too late to join Rudwor and the others," Fate said, hating the thought of another heart-wrenching goodbye. "You can write yourself onto the ship right here and now."

"And miss the chance of discovering a whole new world and the wonderful adventures it has to offer?" Sithias raised a fist in the air. "I will not let fear stop me."

"If you insist." Jessie grabbed his raised arm and yanked him into the portal. "See you on the other side!" she shouted over Sithias's panicked shriek. Which lasted a split second before they disappeared within the crackling vortex.

Finn threw their bags into the portal and turned to Fate. "Ready, love?"

Fate glanced at the hologram one last time. There was no sign of the gigantic rings. A whirling mass of sand swarmed over the last vestiges of the Keep, sucking the round structure deep down inside the dark belly of the desert. Any doubts she might have had that Aradif meant to possess the Keep for himself were erased.

It boggled her mind to know they were buried under tons of earth. The Keep had become a tomb and they didn't belong there anymore. The lights sputtered and every broken item cluttering the floor suddenly rolled sideways. The huge table in the center of the sanctuary slid, slowly at first, then picked up speed and crashed against the far wall.

At the same time, the floor tilted and Fate lost her balance, falling toward the furthest wall. Before she could think to take flight, Finn jumped into the air, catching her by the hand. He scooped her into his arms in one swift move and she felt the hammer of his heart beneath his muscular chest.

"Our fifteen minutes is up," he told her. "Everything's shutting down, including the oscillator holding the sanctuary level within the ring."

Finn flew toward the portal, slowing before entering. The blue swirling light reflected and merged with the luminous green of his eyes as he leaned in to kiss her. The touch of his lips took hold of Fate's senses, chasing away every troubling thought, soothing the deepest wounds of her soul like nothing else could, in this world, or the next.

Deepening the kiss, Finn carried Fate through the threshold and they hurtled through space together, melding into one beating heart.

Books by T. Rae Mitchell

~ Her Dark Destiny Series ~

Fate's Fables - Book 1
Fate's Keep - Book 2
Fate's War - Book 3
Fate's Fury - Book 4

~ Stand Alone ~

Magic Brew

Read more by T. Rae Mitchell for FREE!

An urban fantasy retelling from the previously published bestselling anthology, *Once Upon a Happy Ending*. This gorgeously written novelette weaves together the echo of the classic fairy tale with deadly magic, a dark heroine, and a romance sure to sweep you away.

Visit www.traemitchell.com/signup

Acknowledgements

Each one of the books I've written for this series has come with its own unique set of challenges, but this fourth installment was especially trying. In part because my main character hit the crescendo of emotional storms in Fate's Fury, which was often heart wrenching to write. Also, because finishing the manuscript for publication in the year 2020 had a sideways affect with my pace faltering here and there along the way.

Fortunately, I am blessed with the support and encouragement of family, friends and readers, who I simply could not make this crazy writing journey without.

Thank you to my husband, Tony, and my son, Tyler, for your daily injections of joy and laughter. And for being my trusted first round readers, who I can always count on to help ensure the latest volume of Her Dark Destiny is filled with magic and adventure, and even that mushy romance you could both do with less of.

A huge thank you goes to my good friend and eagle-eyed editor, Nora Mader, whose steadfastness and flexibility in the varied ways we go about meeting those looming publish dates–with this book in particular–continues to amaze me.

Every once in awhile someone special steps forward to stoke, what was this year, my low-burning creative embers, into a roaring fire. That person, (dare I say angel?) is Taylor Beach, and she has since become a dear, sweet friend. Thank you Taylor for the love you've shown for my work, for shouting out about it to everyone you know and for introducing me to the most beautiful community of book lovers I've ever met.

Special thanks to Rose Gray, who won the fun naming contest I ran during the writing of this book by inventing the magical name 'Mornavar', used for the hidden valley in Feldoril Forest. And also to Kelly Jean Taylor, for submitting the enchanting name 'Falinorin', used to call the fierce elven race of the forest.

Last, but definitely not least, I thank each and every reader who's been with me since my first book's publication, as well as those new to reading my books. You are who I keep writing for!

Bestselling author T. Rae Mitchell is an incurable fantasy junkie who spent much of her youth dreaming up worlds and bringing characters to life. While most kids outgrow such things, T. Rae didn't and sometimes took playing make-believe a bit far. Like the time a wizard hid a bottle of dragon beans in the back yard and left her son convinced he could grow his own dragons. Needless to say, the beans failed to produce and disappointments were had. That's when T. Rae decided to funnel her crazy imagination into writing young and new adult fantasy.

Sign-up for T. Rae Mitchell's
Exclusive VIP List
for upcoming notifications:
www.traemitchell.com/sign-up

You can also find T. Rae Mitchell on...

Instagram: www.instagram.com/t.raemitchell

Facebook: www.facebook.com/mitchelltrae

Bookbub: www.bookbub.com/authors/t-rae-mitchell

Goodreads: www.goodreads.com/author/show/6926344.T_Rae_Mitchell

Twitter: www.twitter.com/TRaeMitchell

Pinterest: www.pinterest.com/TRaeMitchell

www.ingramcontent.com/pod-product-compliance
Lightning Source LLC
Chambersburg PA
CBHW010446310726
48979CB00018B/2837/J

* 9 7 8 1 7 7 7 1 4 7 2 4 2 *